629
25

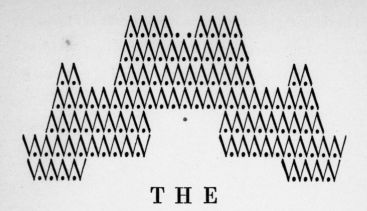

THE
FAR-AWAY BRIDE

by STELLA BENSON

with a Foreword by CLIFTON FADIMAN

THE PRESS OF THE READERS CLUB NEW YORK

PRINTED IN THE UNITED STATES OF AMERICA

FOREWORD

In 1930, a black year for books and bonds, stories and stocks, *The Far-Away Bride* was timidly published, breathed its little breath, and seemingly expired, to be followed, with tragic despatch, by its creator. On December 7, 1933, far from her Shropshire birthplace, in the town of Hongai, Tongking, French Indo-China, at the age of forty-one, Stella Benson died of pneumonia. She had led an adventurous and not over-tranquil life; she wrote delicately and truly; she does not deserve to be forgotten.

The Far-Away Bride is her best book and one of the tenderest and funniest books of its decade. But if it were only of its decade The Readers Club would not be called upon to re-publish it. It has certain qualities of wit and insight that preserve it, and, though on the surface it deals with two families of White Russian refugees in Manchuria and Korea during the 1920's, in reality it is dateless.

The Selecting Committee, who have forced themselves to reread hundreds of books, know only too well the drear sensation, a kind of sinking of the mind, that comes over you when, after a lapse of time, you take up a book you once intensely enjoyed but which now seems pale, depress-

IV

ing, the embers of what once must have been a fire. They know too, but more rarely, that lift of the mind when you re-experience the old enthusiasm.

The Far-Away Bride has never during the last ten years faded completely from my memory. In my household when something particularly savory is served we still comment gravely, "Very fine biting," a phrase, I believe, uttered by Mr. Wilfrid Chew, one of the characters you will encounter with a shout of joy in *The Far-Away Bride*. "All this bib-bing and tuckering," — a golden comment from the lips of Mrs. Malinin — is an observation I have used more than once in connection with fussy dressers. The Malinins and the Ostapenkos I kept on remembering, vaguely but with pleasure: Mr. Chew I remembered acutely: this precious London-trained Chinese barrister, with his deliciously comic Wesleyan conscience, his irresistible spate of elegant words, his pathetic mania for being "in" on all conversations, whether comprehensible to him or not. The recollection of the great scene in which Mr. Chew gets drunk and draws up, in a kind of mechanical stupor, the marriage contract that unites the Malinins and the Ostapenkos, had never faded from my mind; but I did not realize how magnificent the scene was until I reread it just recently.

Old Ostapenko, a Gogolesque figure with his fine, mellow lies, his old-Russian generosity, his engaging freedom from scruples, is almost as delicious as Mr. Chew. Tatiana Osta-penko, the shy sleeping beauty who is thawed to life by the animal simplicity of young Seryozha, is a delightful, if fanci-ful character. Old Malinin, whose hobby is death and whose art self-pity, might have stepped out of Chekhov: indeed the whole book, in its delicate but precise balance of humor, sadness, tenderness, and gentle skepticism, might have been written by Chekhov.

And, while speaking of these droll and poignant charac-ters, I must not forget Seryozha's dog, who accompanies his

V

master on his journey to Korea, and who is so clear-edged a personality that it is with a small shock of surprise we realize he is never named.

I must warn the prospective reader (of whom, frankly, I am deeply envious) to pay no attention whatsoever to that annoying bee in Stella Benson's bonnet which prompted her to call the English edition of this book *Tobit Transplanted* and to reprint in the back of it the Tobit story from the Apocrypha. It is perfectly true that her story of White Russians in China follows the outline of the Tobit legend. It is perfectly true and, though the author did not think so, perfectly unimportant. The Book of Tobit is one of the dullest books in the Bible; *The Far-Away Bride* is one of the most delightful novels of its period. The parallels that you may trace, if you wish to waste your time, cannot make the Tobit story less dull, or *The Far-Away Bride* more enchanting. Hence, pay no attention whatsoever to Stella Benson's earnest admonition (for once the springs of her humor failed her) to "read the Appendix of this book before beginning the story."

There is little else to say. *The Far-Away Bride* speaks for itself, in several different dialects, as you will find. As a love-story it is original; as a study of character it is unique; and as the vivid repository of the most delicate fun and humor it deserves and will have a long life. Sniffy-nosed critics will say of *The Far-Away Bride* that its savor is too fragile for appreciation by any but "the elect." As one who does not believe in the theory of the elect, and as one who feels that the obscurity into which the book has fallen is a matter of accident only, I prevailed upon my colleagues to join me in re-issuing, with joy and affection, this small masterpiece in which the sweet and the acid are so perfectly blended.

CLIFTON FADIMAN

AUTHOR'S NOTE

A REREADING of the Apocrypha, while I was living in Kanto, Manchuria, some years ago, seemed to me to show a curiously exact parallel between the position of the exiled Jews of Tobit's day and that of the exiled White Russians in ours. Even most of the details of Tobit's story, it seemed to me, might be read as referring, without irrelevance or even improbability, to the adventures of a White Russian refugee family. I am therefore very anxious that any reader of this book should keep, as it were, one eye on the Apocrypha, and, for this reason, I have included a complete copy of Tobit at the end of my book. I have not added Judith, since she makes but a shadowy and vicarious appearance in my story.

It is difficult for me now to read the Book of Tobit with an impartial eye. Perhaps over-frequent rereadings have thrown the book rather out of focus in my view, and perhaps I have identified too elaborately my Russians with the

VIII

ancient Jews. Certainly the rather complacent narrative of old Tobit leaves me with the impression that he wrote down the experiences of his family as he would have liked them to happen, rather than as they did happen. Tobit's partly tacit insistence on the I-told-you-so and father-always-knows-best motifs, suggests a wistfully self-compensating diary, rather than an impersonal record of facts, and his conception of his son's exclusively filial orientation makes a modern reader sceptical as to whether a few thousand years could make so much difference to youthful human nature as all that. The Book of Tobit seems to me to give, in fact, purely Tobit's side of what must have been a many-sided story. Old Tobit was the center of his picture, as Old Sergei in my book would have liked to be the center of his. My narrative discounts this patriarchal bias.

With regard to the setting of my story, my friend, the late Sir Valentine Chirol, and my husband, J. C. O'G. Anderson, have kindly supplied me with facts from their superior knowledge, to supplement and explain my own ignorant observations of the bewildering confusion of tongues and nationalities in the midst of which I have set my scene. This confusion is a commonplace of life in Manchuria, but may seem fantastic to readers unfamiliar with that part of the world.

Kanto, the part of Manchuria in which my Malinins live, is the Japanese name for a territory about the size of Wales, in the most southerly corner of the east side of Manchuria.

To the south of it is Korea, to the east—shutting it off from the sea—is the Maritime Province of Russian Siberia and Vladivostok. To the north and to the west is the rest of Manchuria.

Kanto, though a part of Chinese Manchuria, is chiefly populated by Koreans. The next most important element numerically is the Chinese; then come Japanese, and finally a sprinkling of Russians. I do not here include the few European and American missionaries, who are not permanent residents.

In the days when Korea was a tribute-paying dependency of China, the exact frontier between Korea and Chinese Manchuria was not a matter of great importance, and was probably never very clearly defined. In 1909, however, with the Japanese annexation of Korea—of 1910—in sight, China and Japan signed the Chientao (or Kanto) Agreement, determining what would shortly be the frontier between the two countries. This agreement awarded Kanto to China, although Koreans constituted an enormous majority of the population. The reason for this seemingly illogical award was doubtless that the T'umen River, to the north of which Kanto lies, offered an excellent natural boundary line from the military and geographical points of view, ethnological claims not having in those days the weight which they have since acquired. The decisions of governments did not affect—and have not affected to this day—the development of the soil of Kanto by Koreans.

The fertility of this soil, and the prosperity of the original Korean residents of this region, have attracted, and continue to attract, large numbers of immigrants from the south bank of the river—i.e., from Korea proper.

The fact of Chinese sovereignty sufficiently accounts for the presence of Chinese in Kanto. But here, as nowhere else in Manchuria, they are in a minority of the resident population. What Chinese there are in Kanto have not settled to any considerable extent on the land; most of them live there as territorial officials, merchants, and middlemen, or travel there as agents and peddlers, and are content to leave the bulk of the actual development of the soil to the Koreans. The million and more of Chinese immigrants who pour into other parts of Manchuria every year, mainly from the Shantung and Hopeh provinces, have not as yet penetrated in any great numbers to this remote corner, Kanto, and are still being absorbed by the vast fertile tracts of undeveloped land to the west and north, which are, to them, nearer home. It is to be noted, too, that much the most direct approach to Kanto from China proper is by rail through Korea—which is now a foreign country to Chinese. The only other approaches are from the north, and consist of very rough cart roads through unsettled and desolate country.

The absence, or apparent absence, of Manchus in what would seem to be their native land, Manchuria, is explained by the fact that, although they were at one time conquerors of China, China's superior civilization has conquered her conquerors; the Manchus adopted in a great measure China's language and customs, and have become — except in a few remote regions — almost indistinguishable from Chinese. In their own land, Manchuria, they have been swamped by the flood of immigrants from China proper. In this note and in the story, then, the word Chinese includes Manchus.

The Japanese, being now the overlords of Korea, are near neighbors of Kanto. Hence Japanese consulates, hospitals, and schools, with their appropriate staffs, are to be found in the towns of Kanto, and there are also Japanese mining and railway concessionaires, and considerable numbers of Japanese traders. The fact of Japanese police functioning in this district is more difficult to explain, but the following points may be noted as having a bearing on this anomaly. Japan has fought two life-and-death wars in Manchuria, and expended enormous sums of money on railway and other development there; in addition to the extra-territorial rights which her nationals — in common with the British, French, Americans, etc., — still enjoy in China, she claims special privileges in Manchuria and Kanto (which are in some cases contested by the Chinese), arising partly out of her succession to the privileged position which the Russians held in Manchuria before the Russo-Japanese war, and partly out of subsequent Sino-Japanese conventions and agreements; Korean "independence" movements have originated in

Kanto in the past, and it is known that the communistic doctrines which the Japanese view with such suspicion have made some headway among Kanto Koreans. Finally, the nationality — Chinese or Japanese — of Korean residents in Kanto is not infrequently in dispute.

There have always been a certain number of Russians in Manchuria. Imperialist Russia long cherished designs on this rich and handy country, and even after these hopes were overthrown by the Russian defeat at the hands of the Japanese, Russian official establishments were maintained in many centers in Manchuria and Kanto. The Russian revolution of 1917 cut off all officials of the Imperial regime from their sources of authority, and these families, for lack of anywhere else to go to, continued to live in Manchuria, as in other parts of China, living as best they might on their savings. These exiles were joined, little by little, by the more timid or foreseeing among White Russians already in Siberia. Among such early refugees I assume my Malinins and Ostapenkos to be numbered. These isolated exiles were presently swamped by a flood of White Russian fugitives — the remnants of a defeated army accompanied by thousands of non-military refugees — which poured into Kanto after the collapse of the short-lived Far Eastern White Republic in Siberia. The greater part of these latest refugees eventually passed on to other parts of China, but some settled in Kanto and other districts of Manchuria, establishing small businesses, investing what remained of their savings, taking humble employment or living from hand to mouth. The lives of Russian refugees in China — men and women frequently of a class not brought up to manual work — are often terribly hard, and their stories heart-rending. Suitable work is very difficult to find. Wages which will keep a Chinese or Korean working-man in what seems to him comfort, will not support the large frame or supply the more varied and aspiring wants of a Russian. The disorganization of life caused by the period of revolution, rootlessness, anarchy, bloodshed, and despair through which all these exiles have lived, has of course affected them psychologically — especially the younger generation. Many Russian young men, therefore, at the time of this story, were following the line of least resistance by joining the Chinese army and taking part in Chinese civil wars — often, poor souls, to lose their lives recklessly in causes that meant nothing to them.

The part of Kanto in which my Malinins settled is very inaccessible, now that the U. S. S. R. have closed the Siberian border, though in actual distance not far from Vladivostok. The nearest railway is near the Korean border, several days' walk south over trails often infested by brigands — and even when the railway is reached, it does not — or did not, at the time of this story — run direct into southern Korea, or connect with the South Manchurian Railway. A traveler in possession of money and a passport would travel for two days by train across the northwestern corner of

Korea to the Korean port of Seishin; whence he would take ship to another Korean port—Gensan—and from thence travel by train to Seoul. My Russian traveler would elect to walk all the way, partly because he could afford no better, and partly because in this way he could better escape the notice of the Japanese police, who, though present all along the border and in every considerable town of Kanto, concentrate particularly on the railways and harbors and are, perhaps naturally, very suspicious of Russians. It should be remembered that White Russians are everywhere on sufferance only. They have no political standing, no official representation, and no appeal in times of difficulty. Their Russian passports are symbols of a dead power, and the papers issued to them by Chinese local officials carry no great weight outside the neighborhoods where they are personally known.

A point in my story which perhaps needs elucidation is the confusion of tongues between one Chinese and another. This will surprise no one who has lived in China. The spoken language differs so considerably from one province—and even from one district—to another, that it is not at all unusual for a European to be found acting as interpreter between, say, an English-speaking Chinese from Canton and a Mandarin-speaking Chinese settled in North China. Supposing the European to have lived a few years in Manchuria, he would almost certainly be able to make himself understood by the local Chinese population, whereas

XV

the Chinese newcomer from Canton might well be unable to make himself understood at all. Failing such an interpreter, however, and supposing the northerner and the Cantonese both to have some knowledge of the Chinese script (a certain degree of literacy is fairly widespread in China), they could communicate readily enough by means of writing, Chinese script being ideographic, not alphabetical, and universal throughout China.

Kanto is a small region, and perhaps I should therefore add that the picture of the village of Chi-tao-kou is a composite picture having no exact counterpart in fact, and any references to individuals or local affairs — Russian, Chinese, Japanese, Korean, or missionary — are purely imaginary.

S. B.

Author's Request to Reader

PLEASE READ THE APPENDIX OF THIS BOOK BEFORE BE-
GINNING THE STORY. IT IS INTENDED THAT THE PARALLEL
BETWEEN THE STORY OF THE FAR-AWAY BRIDE AND
THE STORY GIVEN IN THE APPENDIX BE BORNE IN MIND
THROUGHOUT THE READING OF THIS BOOK.

S. B.

THE FAR-AWAY BRIDE

CHAPTER ONE

OLD SERGEI walked in front. All the conversation Seryozha had, for the space of fifteen miles, was the expression of his father's neck. The back of Old Sergei's neck was a little like a tortoise's neck, but more speaking. The neck spoke of duty about to be done—rapturously unpleasant duty. It was a nagging, over-articulate neck, but of course Seryozha was so well used to it that he did not think of it as anything except just Father's Neck. He knew, however, without knowing that he knew, that his father was satisfied to be followed on an unpleasant duty by an unwilling son.

The road returned and returned again to the river, crossing and recrossing it. The road and the river could not part because of the narrowness of the gorge; they could not even find room to run peacefully parallel, but got in each other's way. It was like the mutual irritation of marriage. But it was beautiful. The sunny side of the gorge was lacquered with flowers; the shadowed side was dark and stormy with color. The grass had an electric sheen on it, in memory of rain. Even Seryozha's dog had picked a flower by mistake; it was caught in the clasp of its collar, a blue two-winged butterfly of a flower.

Every time Seryozha waded across a ford he sang with excitement. The streaked blue-and-yellow water piled up against his thighs, his strong striding legs were like blunt scissors tearing silk. The great patched cliffs, the hills, the fiery flowers, were all very far away, very still and very alien, as though seen through glass, and Seryozha, singing hoarsely, was isolated in a dizzy world — a tall indomitable young rock in a storm, a little god inclosed in a roaring private universe.

"I am wet," said Old Sergei, standing bent double on a bank, unrolling his wet trousers. "I am just as wet if I roll up my trousers as if I leave them as they are."

"Then leave them as they are," said Seryozha, turning himself round to enjoy the feeling of the warm wind on hot legs through wet trousers.

"Then they will shrink."

"What of it? You are shrinking yourself," said his son.

Old Sergei flirted his trousers a little petulantly. It was certainly true that he was shrinking. But he thought rather highly of his trousers; it was so long since he had moved among real trousered men that he thought his looked like real trousers. They were made by Anna, his wife; his hair was cut by Anna, his shoes were adapted by Anna from Chinese cloth shoes. He was a home-made old man.

Seryozha watched, without anxiety, his dog valiantly following him across the stream. The dog rushed with high bounds into the swift water, and, after a little wallowing, lost its footing. The water spun it about, noosed it, and dragged it under, but the dog kept its head while losing its dignity and was able to shape some kind of wild course. It ran around, tail first and upside down, on a mudbank, and rose and shook itself complacently as though the crossing had happened exactly as it had intended. It had, however, lost the little flower out of its collar.

"There are some soldiers," said Seryozha.

"What of it?" said Old Sergei, with a slight nervous twitch in his voice. "They must be Li's men, certainly." But he looked with an anxious short-sighted squint across the river at the soldiers. (Anna, his wife, did not know how to make spectacles.)

The Chinese soldiers, sitting on a hooded Manchurian cart, swung, creaked, and clanked round the opposite bend into the river. The jolt, as the cart flopped from the bank into the stream, threw all the soldiers backward, so that their thin shabby shanks waved in the air. This contretemps spoiled their accuracy in hitting off the ford, and hardly had they regained their seating when the current swept their cart off its wheels. The horses, pulling at a right angle, were its only anchor. The five horses strained and clawed at the submerged boulders; some of them stumbled, but their senior horse — the only one pulling in shafts — its strong shoulders heaving under the high arched Russian yoke, saved the situation. That was what it was paid for. The soldiers all laughed as the bank was reached, but the horses hung their heads, blew their noses, and sighed.

Old Sergei, Seryozha, and the soldiers looked at one another. All the soldiers were dressed in gray cotton uniforms made for bigger men. Why is this, I wonder? The Chinese Army Clothing Department must possess a tailor's dummy of ideal size. I imagine them sitting at the feet of their utopian wax illusion, busy with their sewing-machines, never looking out-of-doors to see their poor actual champions, stunted and bent and lame, trudging like little skeletons across the mud of China's devastated fields. A little like the Lady of Shalott — but not, on second thoughts, very.

"Have you a cigarette?" said one soldier. Seryozha had one behind his ear. It had already been partly smoked and there was little left of it except the long cardboard mouthpiece, but the soldiers handed it round eagerly from one to another; they were used to makeshifts.

"Are you English?" asked the corporal, after spitting noisily as if to show that whatever they were they weren't worth much.

"No, we are White Russians. . . . We have a letter," stammered Old Sergei. "We are friends of your general, Li Lien-ching . . ."

He was much pleased that his sensitive trousers should have been mistaken for English trousers.

All the soldiers summarized his remark one to another, in the Chinese manner. "They are friends of Li Lien-ching. Hao-hao. . . . They are White Big-noses known to the general. . . . General Li knows them; they are Big-noses. . . . They have letters. . . . It is an old Big-nose and his son who say they are friends of Li Lien-ching. . . ." In a few minutes they all found that they had mastered these facts, and the corporal held out his hand for General Li's letter. The reading of the letter took a very long time. It had a pretty red and black border and was additionally beautified by a few bold characters expressing General Li's trust in Old Sergei's integrity. The soldiers looked upon it as an education in itself, and several of them committed to memory those characters which were new to them, writing invisible examples in the palms of their hands for one another's benefit.

"How much did you pay for the buckle of your belt?" the corporal asked Seryozha magisterially.

"One small frog," replied Seryozha, who spoke Chinese much better than his father, having lived two-thirds of his eighteen years of life in a Chinese village. "I gave another Russian boy one small tame green frog with a red stomach for this buckle."

"One small frog — he bought his buckle for one frog. . . . A frog for a buckle. . . . A buckle for a frog. . . . The frog was exchanged for a buckle. . . ." The simple fellows, telling one another the joke, appreciated it more and more. "Ha-ha! . . . Hao-hao! . . . A buckle for a frog! . . . A frog for a buckle. . . . Ha-ha! . . . Hao-hao! . . ."

"Where are you going?" the corporal persisted, hoping against hope that this might elicit another joke — perhaps about frogs again.

"We are going to see if we can help our friends," said Old Sergei, looking at the soldiers a little doubtfully. "Some White Russian soldiers in the army of your General Li were attacked somewhere near here by Chen's men, and some were killed and some wounded, we hear. We only heard about it in Chi-tao-kou this morning. We are going to bury our dead."

"To bury their dead," said the soldiers one to another, still laughing, since death is among the things that raise a smile in China. "They are going to bury their dead. . . . Big-noses want to bury Big-noses. . . . Ha-ha! . . . Hao-hao! . . ."

"It is forty *li* from Chi-tao-kou," said a soldier. "You must have walked fast. Big-noses have long legs. You can sit on our cart. We are going your way."

"Is Chen's army still in the neighborhood?"

"No, there was no army — it was only a small party of Chen's men that found the Big-noses off their guard. They must be two hundred *li* away by now."

Old Sergei and Seryozha sat on the cart, their wet legs dangling over the wheels in a row with the soldiers' weather-beaten ankles. The cart staggered along to the tune of a titter of bells and a ripping of whips and a snarling of drivers. The road lost itself among boulders. It became merged for miles with the cascading river bed. The cart never had four wheels on the ground at once. Soldiers' heads were knocked together; somebody's shoulder came in violent contact with Old Sergei's front gums. Seryozha, after won-

6

dering for a few minutes whether to be footsore was really worse than to be seatsore, jumped off the cart and stumbled down the heaped, gashed trail.

He walked more quickly than the laboring cart and at the turn of the gorge waited for it. Great ghostly clouds had been bowling up like smoke out of the peaks of the hills. Raindrops fell on Seryozha's nose — chin — hand — neck — then a wave of rain leapt over the near hill. He stood just inside a deserted and ruined Korean hut, waiting for the cart, watching the rain. The flowery slopes waved under the flying clouds. Far ahead there was a dwindling horizontal strip of calm blue sky strung like a taut cord over the stormy valley.

The mud floor of the hut was strewn with old sacks, straw, rags, broken crocks, and a crumpled brazier. It must be a very poor thing that is discarded as useless by a Korean. Part of one wall had fallen in and the thatch sagged and dripped. A gawky sunflower hung its silly head in the doorway. There was a smell of dirty humanity mixed with the smell of horse and wet grass.

Seryozha stood in the doorway and looked up a windy slope spotted with scrub-oaks and magenta azaleas. Against the outer wall of the shack, near the door, was a Korean oven, balancing a crooked jointed chimney on its shoulder as a juggler might balance a pile of top-hats. The oven's gaping lips were smeared with cold damp ashes. From behind the oven, across a puddle in the red mud, protruded a dead hand, palm upward.

Seryozha stared at the hand, his mind making no comment, only registering the fact — a dead man — a dead man — a dead man. . . . In two strides he stood beside the dead man. He looked down at the heavy, fair, unshaven face of a Russian soldier. Raindrops stood on the cheeks like tears; the eyes watched the sky intently and anxiously. The dead man had no boots on and no gun. His tunic was open at the neck to show a broken string. How curious to be robbed and not mind, thought Seryozha, and at once this seemed to him the most startling thing about death — the loss of the delight in possession. He thought of the property he himself loved so anxiously — his silk handkerchief, his spangled gilt picture of the crowned Christ, his English sweater that the missionaries had given him, his marvellously complete sloughed snakeskin (even the skin of the eyeballs unbroken) that lived in an abalone shell in a biscuit-box, the ribbon that Sonia gave him, his chisel with the black handle. . . . It was quite unimaginable that these things might be taken away before his open, indifferent eyes. This was death. The snakeskin would suddenly become no marvel but a thing good only for the rubbish heap; (oh, he would rise from the dead to prevent his mother from using the black-handled chisel as a screwdriver!). This dead man had probably known every wrinkle in his dear boots — poverty means such intimacy between a man and his possessions. Yet now his feet, muddy and swollen and ringed with callouses, bore nakedness without protest. And his boots, shorn of that familiarity which is the sacred soul of *things* — incased a thief's irreverent shins.

With a jingle and a splintering screech the cart arrived at the door of the hut. Old Sergei, followed by the soldiers, came round the corner of the ruin. One of the soldiers trod on the dead Russian's hand before he saw it, but after seeing it he trod on it again, as if to see if the man would mind.

"It is a dead Big-nose," all the soldiers told one another.

Old Sergei seemed to come alive when he saw the dead man. Death was Old Sergei's hobby. "How surprised he looks!" he said. "The surprise was soon over, though. Only just lasted long enough to raise his eyebrows. Or one might say it lasted forever — his eyebrows were never lowered

8

again." Old Sergei sighed. "One forgets," he said, "that bodies are so soft in a dangerous world — softer than cheese is to the knife. Why do we trust one another so, living in such soft bodies? Of course we *must* trust one another; we dare not remember the hardness of steel or of men's hearts — being so soft. If we had steel skins, we should dare to know everything."

Seryozha listened to his father with some interest, clutching the bosom of his blouse, pinching his chest to feel how soft his skin was. But he put on the mulish, deliberately prosaic expression sons generally wear when their fathers express themselves in a way that seems to the young unelderly.

"His boots have been stolen," said Seryozha.

"Oh, it is so very interesting," said Old Sergei, leaning eagerly over the dead man, "to think that this experience cannot escape us. We shall all, some day, know what it is to be dead."

"It escaped him," said Seryozha. "The experience must have been over almost before it began."

"How do you know?"

But Seryozha's interest flagged. He did not really believe he would ever die. This was why he so often killed things — birds — beetles — fishes . . . because he could not imagine death.

"There are probably more of them," he said, and looked up the hill. The soldiers were quicker-sighted than he was. So was his dog. The soldiers pointed out his dog, shoulder deep in brush, halfway up the hill. The dog, with its ears strained back, its nose waving, pointed doubtfully at a couple of gray mounds among the scrub-oaks.

As soon as Old Sergei and his son left the shelter of the sagging eaves, the rain hammered sharply on their faces and shoulders. Seryozha's dog, with a skin of wet mud, looking half its natural size, came down the hill to meet him and ask about this disquieting marvel of two dead gods. The dog had not known before that gods could die, but, like all dogs, it was perfectly open-minded about marvels, and, having learned its lesson of divine mortality, would not now have been surprised to see every god in sight fall down dead. Seryozha had carried two spades all the way, corded across his back. Halfway up the hill he unstrapped the spades. Old Sergei selected the site of the three graves.

It was hard work digging, though the northern earth, baked in summer and frozen in winter, was now, under rain, at its softest. The Chinese soldiers stood very close, watching each spadeful eagerly, as though it might disclose gold. They did not move till Seryozha actually came near to cutting the earth from under their feet. To a Chinese, any white man doing anything is an absorbing show.

"I'd rather be burying one of you," said Seryozha, rudely, to the smiling corporal. "You wouldn't need so big a hole." All the soldiers laughed affably.

Old Sergei worked rather weakly with his spade. As he dug he thought with deliberate pathos of the three dead men and presently made himself cry. "No doubt," he sniffed, "they had women they loved, and perhaps little children, too. Their last thoughts were perhaps of the sunshine filtering through the forests of happy Russia — dark Russian trees in whose shade they wooed their loves. Perhaps their last thought of all was a rapture — I have found my Russia again. . . ."

The dark trees of Russia meant nothing to Seryozha, who had had a hard-baked dusty north China childhood. He did not even think of it as exile. The word *exile* to him was just a whining plaint of parents. He grunted indifferently as he dug, the sweat dripping from his yellow forelock.

"You young things have no hearts," continued Old Sergei, turning over with his spade a few lumps of red earth and then holding his hand out to enjoy the pathos of its senile tremblings. "You have no tears to shed for the desecrated earth of Russia that bore you. You have never even worshiped God in a house of God in company with men and women of your own race. It is nothing to you that these men — no doubt men who feared God and loved His Son — should lie dead in these rough holes without a priest to bless them."

"Why don't you bless them yourself, then?" asked Seryozha, straightening his back. "You know so many prayers."

"How can I?" exclaimed Old Sergei, shocked. "It would be entirely improper for me to take a priest's words into my mouth."

In a silence broken only by the scraping of the spades and the sniffing of Old Sergei, they finished their digging. The Chinese watched them, as though in a trance. When, however, Seryozha took the shoulders of the first of the three dead men, and Old Sergei prepared to fumble with the feet, the Chinese corporal said, "Let's make sure there's no money on them. It is a pity to bury money."

"You wicked man," croaked Old Sergei passionately. "It is much more of a pity to rob the dead. We Russians hold our dead sacred. We shall bury these men with what few poor treasures they have."

But Seryozha laid the body down and looked at his father. "If we don't search them," he said in Russian, "these coolies will wait till we have gone and then come back and open the graves. Better to show them there is nothing."

"Oi! oi! Sacrilege!" cried Old Sergei. But, seeing Seryozha hesitate, he added on a firmer note, "Oi! Sacrilege! . . . but have it your own way. You young people always think you know best. You have no hearts. I shall certainly not be a party to your robbery of the dead." He walked away a few steps and, with his back to his son, bent down and fumbled with the boughs of a dark pink azalea. As he did so he recaptured his checked tearful mood by imagining the little weeping children of the dead men picking flowers in the darling forests of Russia.

The Chinese came and stood very close to Seryozha as he knelt down beside one dead man, then another, then the last. There was no money in their pockets; a cross or amulet had been torn from the neck of one. Their clothes were in rags, their fur caps were motheaten. "Ours are better," said the soldiers, laughing. The boots of all three Russians had already been taken by their assailants. In the pocket of one Seryozha found a bill for a bicycle; another wore a ring that might be gold of poor quality on his little finger. The ring was tightly fixed and for one moment Seryozha sweated cold as the Chinese corporal's hand went helpfully toward his dagger. But a cracking wrench drew the ring off the wet finger at last. They all looked at it. It was very light and was decorated with two little thin joined hearts. "It is the price of a ride in our cart," said the corporal, laughing winningly into Seryozha's face. He took it from Seryozha's palm as though to examine it, and slipped it into his wallet.

Seryozha stood a moment, thinking, and then called to his father, "The sacrilege is all over now."

"Oi! oi! Heartless, heartless!" cried Old Sergei, coming fussily back.

Between them, father and son lifted the first man into his grave, and Old Sergei, crying still, was going to shovel the earth into the trench when Seryozha seized his arm.

"Ah no, no, no!" cried Seryozha.

His father gaped at him. "What then? Are we not burying the poor fellow?"

Seryozha said, "But not earth on his face. . . ." Then, recollecting himself, the boy laughed sheepishly. "Oh, it was just an idea. . . ." He felt that their faces were their vanity, somehow, and the mud was so ugly. . . . "Let's put leaves on his face. . . . Let's put flowers on the poor fool. . . ."

There were plenty of flowers. They heaped heads of pink azaleas, purple scabeus, poppies, big blue daisies, scarlet lilies, leaves of scrub-oak, on the dead man's vanity. Seryozha was very much ashamed of his outburst. He giggled nervously several times, trying to think of something cynical and grown-up to say, to cover his childish mistake.

"Now I'll chant his blessing," he said, impudently. "I'm no priest, but what of it—he was no Christian, perhaps. Good-by, little brother, go and search the sky for a heaven. I can climb a tree without a ladder, so you can reach your sky without a prayer. I'll drink your health, little brother, in Japanese whisky, next time I can afford it. . . ." He said it in so solemn a tone that the Chinese were rather impressed. "That is a Big-nose prayer," said one soldier. But, watching the burial of the other two, they were rather disappointed. Over the second Seryozha chanted only, "To our next meeting, brother," and over the third, "Oi! to sleep with you," as he patted the last spadeful down.

"It is all sacrilege," said Old Sergei, who was rather afraid of his son in this boisterous mood. "Do go away for a little while, Seryozha, and take these Chinese pigs away, while I say a real fellow-Christian's prayer for their peace."

He bowed his head and Seryozha wandered away with his dog. Near the road was an ants'-nest and Seryozha scratched at it with his boot, and at once forgot everything else. Things in little always delighted him—the reflection in a convex mirror, a knight among his father's chessmen, a sprig of parsley stuck on his fish pie, like an oak tree on a crag—all such small perfect reminders of ordinary unwieldy things could hold his charmed attention. And he still secretly enjoyed playing with the missionary children because

13

he so much enjoyed building their wooden blocks into elaborate houses. Although he was eighteen years old, it was difficult for him not to lose his temper when an uncouth infant missionary kicked down a careful villa in which every staircase led to somewhere and there was a chimney to every room. So he liked to think of an ants'-nest as a nest of little tiny Seryozhas — a convex mirror set in the red earth.

When he first touched the nest a sort of shivering skin of swarming ants suddenly spread over it, but after a few seconds' panic, every ant remembered its duty, like a good sailor in a shipwreck, and went to its appointed place — to fetch an egg, to warn its queen, to guard the stores, to re-open a ruined doorway. . . . Supposing there was a dogs' nest, thought Seryozha, run on these lines, how stuffy and cheerful and inefficient! . . . Or a lions' nest, how slinky and undemocratic! . . . Or a man's nest, how restful and easy for poor men to be little bits of something ready-made, instead of worried creators — to owe allegiance to a cold queen instead of to a fussy old father and mother! . . .

The rain swept in windy waves down the valley. Seryozha's cap, which had been made by his mother from an old cloth dress of her own, became so wet that the pasteboard that ingeniously stiffened the peak lost its courage and sagged down over Seryozha's eyes. He was a mildly vain boy and, on removing the cap to try and make it more worthy of him, was disgusted to find that the color was running. He took his handkerchief from the cap to wipe a navy-blue tear from his brow, and as he did so a twenty-sen note fluttered from a secret place in the cap. The Chinese corporal, who had just come up, was teasing the ants into a new dazzle of frenzied movement. The corporal and Seryozha watched the little piece of paper money flutter down on to the ants'-nest. There for a moment it stirred and turned strangely, floating on the eddy of ants beneath it, and then the rain soaked, flattened, and weighed it down. Seryozha laughed and the corporal laughed. Seryozha picked up the note, folded it, and replaced it in the lining of his cap.

"Big-noses keep their money on the tops of their heads," said the corporal merrily to his subordinates.

And as Seryozha tossed back his wet yellow flap of hair to cover it with his cap, he met the corporal's eye and instantly knew that the Chinese was thinking, "*We never looked in the dead Russians' caps for money. . . .*"

Old Sergei came up, murmuring something about immortality. He had always loved strangers, and detached himself querulously from people with a claim on him. Now he had been imagining the lonely death and the lonely awakening of the three Russians; if they had sought his sympathy when alive, he would have withheld it. He was kinder to lost dogs than to his wife, and his own son had never seemed to him to come under that touching heading that so often brought tears to his eyes—"Helpless Little Child. . . ."

"We must be going home," he said. "I shall in any case have an attack of rheumatism after this, but every additional hour spent in this downpour will aggravate it."

"These soldiers mean to search the graves again for money," said Seryozha.

"Impossible—impossible!" cried Old Sergei tremulous once more. "They watched us bury them. They know our friends were poor like ourselves. . . ."

"They know something else now," said Seryozha. "Let's pretend to go away, and turn back at the pass to see if they have really gone." Now that the dead men were out of sight, Seryozha did not really very much care whether they were disturbed or not.

The father and son said a polite good-by to the soldiers and set their cramped faces against the rainy wind that swept down the pass. They reached the corner and, before

15

rounding it, stood a moment and looked back. The soldiers, wilting limply under the eaves of the shed, were looking after the retreating Russians, the distant white points of their faces boring like little gimlets through the intervening air.

"Certainly they seem to be waiting for us to go," said Old Sergei. "The swine! . . . Oi! I am so tired of wicked men."

"I am so tired of my wet skin," said Seryozha. "Let's pretend we never suspected the soldiers. Let's pretend they all went away in their cart and are safely out of sight. Let's go home."

Old Sergei cautiously considered this proposal. He began pretending to go home. The road home slowly diminished, slowly drew in its vistas inside his imagination. In infinitesimal jerks the new painted temple beside the home river cut sharply into his mind's sight. The ferry made its usual unlikely arrival, after apparently proceeding for ten minutes in the wrong direction; imaginary caravan ponies, cramped in the familiar rickety old barge of his vision, drooled down the necks of their human fellow-passengers; Korean women squatted in the bows in the middle of their semi-deflated balloon skirts; every one twittered in his dream ear; here was home. . . . Here was home—the low door, the window cut neatly but unnaturally like a surgical incision, the noise of Anna letting something metallic fall in the back yard. . . .

Seryozha's mind, as though following a secret groove, ran more quickly home—even more quickly than his dog, who was already several miles nearer supper than they were. Seryozha, who had arrived at the age when one is nothing but a brittle baby incased in a glass shell of cautious maturity, was already seeing himself walking nobly up the village street, being looked at with admiration by the Chinese boy neighbors—especially by little Hu-Lien—damn his eyes. . . .

"There goes the Young Big-nose," thought Seryozha on

their behalf, "who has been out on an adventure connected with a battle. . . ." Not that Chinese boys would ever admire a friend on such grounds, but poor Seryozha had no juniors of his own race to impress, so he had to make it all up. And once you begin to make things up, you might as well flatter as blame yourself.

"No," said Old Sergei. "We will, on second thoughts, not go home at once. We will not desert our friends. We will sit here for five minutes, hidden in the shelter of this rock, and then look back to see if the soldiers are safely gone."

They sat flattened like lizards against the rock, picking their teeth, though there was nothing much to pick, breakfast being six hours past.

"If I climb up that bank instead of back on to the road," said Seryozha. "I can look straight down the slope on to the graves."

"I will climb, too," said Old Sergei, who never liked to risk letting any one else see something first. News, however distressing, was far better to give than to receive.

They combed the wet scrub-oaks and the matted flowery grass with their legs as they climbed the short slope. Two hundred feet below them, the doubled up forms of six soldiers were knotted round one of the graves. The other grave was an inflamed scar of newly-turned mud.

"Yah!" screamed Old Sergei, and threw himself down the slope, his lank limp arms and legs flying. "You God-damned swine! You sacrilegious sons of tortoises! . . ."

Seryozha bounced after him, his stomach aching sharply with pleasurable excitement. His thoughts were joggled up and down like medicine in a bottle. Father and son were upon the soldiers as though in one windy stride. Seryozha's spade came in flat and glorious contact with fleeing Chinese buttocks. One soldier sprawled with his face in the mud; he twisted himself into a sitting position and fanned the air with futile arms, bellowing curses, his mouth a red hole in a mask of mud. Old Sergei, craning his long neck, stamping his silly old foot, stood over the opened grave like a flamingo defending its nest, creaking out curses in Russian and Chinese. The corporal, with a bloody nose, trying to feel safe and comparatively authoritative at a distance of about thirty feet, clung to the frail hut as though ready to whisk it before him as a shield should he be attacked again, and bawled to his men to come away. This they were only too anxious to do, poor things, only they dared not turn their backs for a second on the Russians.

"You shall hear of this again, dogs," shouted the corporal. "Have you forgotten that you are nothing but filthy Russians—homeless nobodies? . . . Our general shall teach you your place. . . ." His nose began to bleed afresh and he buried it in a bunch of sunflower leaves, shouting in a muffled voice to his men to retreat. This they did, assembling with anxious, crooked gait round their cart. How different were the voices that shocked the horses awake from the merry yodelings that gave the poor beasts license to graze an hour ago. A confused grumble and united hiccough of oaths accompanied the mounting of the cart. One soldier, crying shrilly and ostentatiously, lay on his face in the straw of the cart, rubbing his bruised behind.

"Ha-ha!" yelled Seryozha, brandishing his spade triumphantly in their direction as they drove away, but all the same, he felt a little pang when he remembered their peaceful, ingenuous jocosity of only a few short minutes before. He felt, somehow, as though he had taken a folly too seriously.

"Nothing is sacred to these swine—nothing," chattered Old Sergei. "Even Russian gentlemen . . . heroes, who have died in some paltry Chinese cause. . . ."

"Aw, shut up, father!" said Seryozha. "Nothing's so very sacred as all that to any of us, really . . . nothing except our vanity. . . ."

He met the quiet, anxious, opaque eyes of the disturbed dead Russian, leaning with shrugged shoulders out of his new grave. Seryozha caught his breath. "And when we're dead, our vanity's dead too, damn it all, so — what of it?"

CHAPTER TWO

Mrs. Butters's sinless smile was bracketed a little on one side, like a parenthesis. Even her nose was smiling kindly. Yet she was thinking: "These Russians are really not much use. That hemstitching doesn't look good." However the baby whom the hemstitching would adorn would not be her first. First babies need first-rate hemstitching. But Mrs. Butters had had four and the baby she expected in October was only having a new outfit made because its four predecessors had fairly worn the original set to rags.

Mrs. Butters looked over Anna's shoulder. "My dear Mrs. Malinin, how quick you work! It's just wonderful! . . ."

"Quick but not good," said Anna in a wistfully challenging voice.

"I think you're doing fine," said Mrs. Butters firmly, and then she faltered: "But — my dear — why have you drawn the threads out of this hem? That's the side hem. We don't want hemstitching up the side hem."

"Oi! oi!" cried Anna. "Is that the side hem? Oi! oi!"

"It doesn't matter," said Mrs. Butters, and then with gathering conviction: "It really *doesn't* matter, Mrs. Malinin. It will hardly show."

"It *will* show," said Anna. "It will show very bad indeed. Oi! what a stupid old woman I am! Can I not weave the threads in again, very watchfully?"

"No, really, Mrs. Malinin; that would look worse still. No, it will be all right. After all, why shouldn't the side hem be hemstitched? Quite original. Don't think of it again."

Anna went on sewing in silence for a moment, bending her fat abashed face over her work. Turning remorse in her tender heart like a sword in a wound, she imagined Mrs. Butters secretly broken with disappointment about the spoiled side hem. In her own affairs Anna was an optimist; disappointment never dwelt long with her. But she imagined the hopes of others as being much more susceptible to blight. She saw herself as an iron Anna living in a world of glass. "She will always see that stupid hem as she shows the baby to her missionary friends," thought Anna, violently. "She will be able to see nothing else. It will spoil the baby for her completely. I am not worth the money I take from these people. I will refuse today's two yen."

Mrs. Butters, seeing that Anna looked sad, hastened to tell a funny story. "Did I tell you what Betty, my quaint second girlie, said after her last Saturday-night bath, Mrs. Malinin? She said, 'Mummy, I'd like to say drace now — I'd like to say Thank Dod for a dood hot bath.'"

"Having done the stupidity now," said Anna. "Would it perhaps make it better to do another stupidity to match on the other side?" Then she noticed that she was once more disappointing Mrs. Butters, and added, "Ah — she said that? But she is funny — your little Betti!" She gave a boisterous if belated laugh.

"She is a very sensitive, queer child," said Mrs. Butters. "She cried when the goat died yesterday. And it wasn't because she liked the milk, either. She said to me, 'Mummy, I did love dat doatie.'"

"My husband also cries for such things," said Anna. "He

cried when the cat broke its neck. We all cried a little, but my husband most loudly. He is blind, you see, so he must value creatures that he can feel, now that he has lost the seeing of them. When he could see, he did not like creatures. So now we have an orphan kitten, Mrs. Butters, and you an orphan kid."

"An orphan kid! Haven't you a quaint way of saying things, Mrs. Malinin! But your English is wonderful, I'm sure. How did you learn such good English?"

"I was for many years a governess in England. I lived in a part of London called Kensington. The little girl I taught was also called Betti; her mother was called Honorable Mrs. Atkinson and wore always pink silk undervests of the most expensive kind. I taught Betti French and German, but I also learned a pretty good deal of English. How cheerfully I remember London! Climbing up the colored stairs on to the roofs of buses, I remember, and sitting on the right-hand corner seat, because in London all carriages drive on the left side, and therefore, sitting so, one may look down on the tops of all carriages going in — out — in — run — stop — in — out, like the ice in our rivers here in April. My little pupil, Betti, had a dog in London and always that dog catched buses before us, and climbed up skippingly to the roof, and sat on the right-hand corner seat. . . . Even if strangers were already there, that dog sat down on the strangers! Ha-ha-ha! A clever dog, called Paddy. Oh, the Kensington Gardens, Mrs. Butters! Crocuses — such things we never have in this damn country — purple some and white others — all in the green grass. Oh, pretty! . . . There is a lake in the Kensington Gardens, where Betti and I sailed a boat; sometimes many hours that boat went round foolishly in the middle of the lake, and we wait on the shore, saying, well, give her five more minutes . . . but sometimes — oh, the wind there! hairs, boats, skirts, dog's fur, all blowing one way, and sun — cloud — sun — cloud — running across that so rough pond.

. . . And once a duck bit our boat—she was called *Die Lustige Witwe.*"

"You Russians are such wonderful linguists," murmured Mrs. Butters. "And I suppose you married then and had a little boy of your own to teach."

"Yes I marry before Seryozha comes, because I think it is good for a child to have a father—even a father like my old husband. So I marry. We go back to Russia. I have taught Seryozha English as good as I can." Anna sighed gustily. A few hairpins dropped out as she sighed. "I thought English is the most useful business language in China—and now China is our country, since there is no Russia any more. But he will never be a business man, Seryozha. His father had no business gifts. Also Seryozha was born when I was too old. I was thirty-six. If a woman over thirty bears a child——"

Mrs. Butters was a little puzzled by parts of this sentence. Also she preferred the actual bearing of babies to talking about it.

"But Mr. Malinin must have some business gifts. That little shop flourished well, before his misfortune, didn't it?"

"It did not," said Anna, with a bursting laugh. "Nothing that my family does is ever flourishing. Somehow we always bought too much of what nobody wanted and none of what all customers would be asking for. We had much scent last year, and only two Japanese ladies ever bought—each one small bottle at reduced price. They smell of it always—it is never finished. They came in the shop stinking of our scent and asked for German camera films, which we have not. It is true my husband was—how do you say?—compradore? to the Tao-yin for some years, he has buyed for him his foreign goods—woolens, wines, jewels—but he has made very many mistakes, and after that Tao-yin has been dead, the new one wants not my blunderous old man's help. . . . Then this new Tao-yin is murdered (do you know people have said it is the two sons of his not-loved concubine have

murdered him?); then comes this modern chap who wants
no old men anywhere. He buys his foreign goods through
our nephew, Andrei Malinin. Our nephew is very trusted by
the now Tao-yin. It is Andryusha who has helped my old
husband in our trouble by entreating for him. But he cannot
entreat our business back. Pitying is kind, yes? but it is not
business. Well, it doesn't matter. My husband has never
been good business fellow; now it does not matter, for we
have no more business to blunder with."

"But surely," said Mrs. Butters, "with your nephew's help
you can get some compensation for the looting of your shop.
They had no right to do it."

"Every one has the right to do all things to Russians
now," said Anna. "Besides, my husband was certainly very
silly. He beat some Chinese soldiers, and so angered them."

Mrs. Butters tried for a moment, with confused missionary charity, to imagine Old Sergei beating anybody. "I suppose he did it in righteous anger," she said, hopefully.

"Oi! He did it in foolishness," said Anna. "There is no
need for so much defending of dead Russian heroes. Once
a man is dead he is dead and has not much honor to defend.
But my husband runs always after dead men; he beat these
Chinese for interrupting the peace of Russian dead soldiers
—so the Chinese interrupt the peace of his alive wife and
son. But alive ones don't matter to my husband. He is a man
full of folly."

"Very good of him, I'm sure," said Mrs. Butters vaguely,
though she did not really think Old Sergei good. He had
some inconvenient foreign religion which inspired him to
talk about God at missionary high-tea parties almost before
the canned clam chowder was on the table, but he never
came to church. "He *did* suffer for his championship of his
dead friends, didn't he, for I suppose in the tussle he got a
blow on the head which finally made him go blind. . . ."

"His head was not in the least blowed," said Anna in a

high, rather exasperated voice. "He came home very happy, smacking his chest for pride, saying, 'I have beaten these sacrilegious openers of heroes' graves — I have beaten them well' . . . and then some Russian man came and told us that the soldiers would come and beat *him* or perhaps put him in prison, for revenge. So my husband went away quickly, out of fear. Fortunately, it was good weather — in wet weather he becomes stiff and painful in his sitting down and must not go out, but this time the weather was dry and the poor silly old man went forty *li* to the house of a Korean cow-grower who is his friend. When he was gone the Chinese soldiers come to our house and ask where he is. My Seryozha knows Chinese people well — better than his father or I know them — and he can make Chinese laugh. So the soldiers laugh and go away. But in the night they come back, and they break the shutters and the door and took away all the tobacco and then the tins of vegetables and fruits, and the sweets and the cheap jewelry, but the bottles of hairwash and medicine and scent they broke after they had tasted. They took also eighty yen worth of cotton stuffs. The letter-paper they make dirty by treading on it, they spill the ink over the books, and the complexion oils they throw through the window. I would have beaten them myself. They were little soldiers and my hands are hard — I would rather use my hands to protect my properties than to protect dead men — but Seryozha would not let me. All the time he stood in the shop door and pretended to say different ideas what to do next, and pretended to remind them of goods they were forgetting — but really he tried, by talk, to pull their notice away from things more precious. He is a clever boy, Seryozha."

"But it was *very* wrong of the soldiers," said Mrs. Butters. "Somebody ought to do something about it. Surely you can get them punished and claim some redress."

"We are Russians," said Anna with an unintentionally loud snort. She had her limbs, her larynx, her stomach, her imagination under poor control, and often found herself doing things that she had not intended. "In the morning Seryozha and I went to the magistrate's yamen and complained, but we only saw an under man, and he said he will inquire of the colonel and ask to have the soldiers punished, and he would send our askings for the price of our goods to Kirin to be thought about. But there will be little thinking, I think, and no paying. Especially since the Tao-yin who knew my husband, is now dead. The new Tao-yin knows nothing about our complaints. My husband's nephew, Andrei Malinin, who is a friend of the new Tao-yin and builds bridges and trains horses and buys automobiles for him, said to us, 'Let Dyadya come back now to his home; no one will hurt him now. But let him ask no more for compensations.' So my husband came back."

"But I don't understand," said Mrs. Butters, who was saving up all this to tell her husband in the evening, entitled, "The Truth of the Malinin Story." "What made Mr. Malinin go blind so suddenly, if the soldiers did not hurt him?"

"God alone understands why he went blind," said Anna. "My husband, poor old man, thinks he understands too, but all he says is folly. That same day he came home he began again his follies. I had a good dinner for him that day — bortsch and a fine fat chicken — and when my husband saw, he said to Seryozha, 'Run now and fetch Alyosha; he loves good food and has no money.' But that was a very strange thing, Mrs. Butters, for my husband does not often love poor men — while they live. Seryozha went to the house of Alexei Vassileievitch, and there he was — the saddle-maker, you remember? — making bets with all his friends that he could drink more beer more fastly than they could drink. Perhaps you remember hearing — it was a very hot day, and Alexei Vassileievitch fell down dead——"

"I remember," said Mrs. Butters, shuddering. "Such a terrible judgment — a terrible death — with his sins upon him."

"Our sins are always upon us," said Anna. "They are more tight buttoned upon us than our clothes. Whenever we die — drinking at the first supper or the Last Supper — our sins are always upon us, Mrs. Butters. I did not like Alyosha the saddlemaker; he bought a floor mat from us and would not pay because it had a small smell. I am not sorrowing because of his death but only because of the more trouble it brought upon us. Seryozha was a long time away, watching the drinking game, and at home my old husband would not eat, though the soup became cold — waiting, waiting — for a poor man he never thinks of feeding in his life before. So Seryozha comes running to say, 'Alyosha is dead.' 'Sht boy,' I say, 'shsht — he will hear,' but my old husband has already heard. Oi, what folly begins at once. My husband runs to Alyosha's house and I runs after him — though the dinner would spoil and spoil — and there were Chinese policemen asking and examining in Alyosha's house and Alyosha himself lying on the floor with his tongue out all crookedly and a bluely red swollen face. My old Sergei pushed away the police, saying, this man is of my race, he is mine to bury. Oi! what a curse are these drunkard dead that they must be made so honorable. Two friends helped to carry Alexei Vassileievitch's body to our house; the Chinese police did not stop them, though they talked much, thinking perhaps Alyosha had been murdered, so they followed behind, talking angrily to my old fool, saying, 'Always you interfere with Chinese police officers doing their duties.' . . . My husband made Alyosha be carried in our house and all my nice dinner be swept off the table and the body be laid down on it, all red and dirty and dead, and no friend of ours, Mrs. Butters

—just a drunken saddlemaker, God forgive him. I tell you
he smelled of leather and horses, but he was on our table,
like a joint of meat that was no meat, so all day we ate our
meals on the bed, though the goodness of the dinner I had
prepared was all gone. And in the evening my husband
buried that poor damn man in the open green space behind
our house—after dark, that thieves might not know. Because he had it fixed in his thoughts that the Chinese would
again try to open the grave. So all night long he lay on a
blanket outside, against the wall of our yard. Three times—
four times—five times—I went out and said, 'Come in,
stupid man; you will have rheumatism again; tomorrow you
will not have power to bend,' but he is stubborn like a goat,
and early in the morning, as the sun rose up, I heard him
scream, high like a child—like this—'E-e-e-e! Oi! I am
blind!' . . . It was when he felt the sun on his cheek, then
he knew it was day and he was blind. He says it was the
sparrows' droppings from the top of the wall, but the Japanese doctor says no, it cannot be. The Japanese doctor says
it is a nervous—a hysteric. I do not know—but sparrows
I do not blame. So now my poor old fool he sits there all the
time sorrowing. There is no amusement or interest he can
do—only feel with his hands things that are alive, and that
makes him cry, but he always loves being made to cry. He
was in love with dead men when he could see—but now
that he must sit at home, the dead do not come to him. . . .
So now he cries over alive things that he can feel—it is all
the same really—he only seeks tears. He feels Seryozha's
ankle, and the cat, and puppies, and Seryozha found some
little small young birds in a nest—anything that moves he
must feel, that he may think the sad thoughts he wants to
think."

"It is all very sad," said Mrs. Butters. "It must make life
very difficult for you, Mrs. Malinin."

"Oh, not so difficult. Seryozha works—not every day, but

sometimes — on the new bridge. Our nephew, Andrei Malinin — that engineer who I told you is friend to the new
Tao-yin — he helps us a little. I think he arranged, too, so
that my old husband was not attacked by the Chinese policemen for taking Alyosha's body. And I come and sew —
oi! but how bad I sew — for you and the other mission
families."

"You certainly have known a great deal of trouble," said
Mrs. Butters, who had been punctuating the story with
clickings of her tongue and low abstracted moans. Then she
remembered the Christian duty of reassurance. "Oh, but I
think you sew very nicely."

"Hemstitching all down the baby's ribs — oh yes — very
nice," mourned Anna. The imperfection made a sore place
in her self-esteem. "How easy it would have been to think
before — not to pull those threads out. Never, never do I
think before. All my life is full of being sorry for not thinking before."

"Oh, *please* don't worry yourself," said Mrs. Butters, almost irritated by this extreme remorse.

One of the Butters children came in, talking in the ag-
grieved whine peculiar to the children of missionaries.

"Mah-mah!"

"It is so difficult for our finite minds to understand," said
Mrs. Butters, "the omnipotent wisdom which sometimes
sees fit——"

"Mah-mah."

"— to load so many grievous burdens on one——"

"Mah-mah."

"— shrinking sinner's shoulders. All we can do is——"

"Mah-mah."

"— to feel that behind it all shines——"

"Mah-mah."

"— a love that——"

"Mah-mah."

"Surely your child wishes to speak with you," said Anna, with difficulty restraining her hands from boxing the ears of both mother and child. A conflict of noises could always crack her temper as, it is said, some discords can crack a glass.

"Mah-mah's busy, lovey," said Mrs. Butters. "What does mah-mah's lovey want to ask mah-mah?"

"Mah-mah . . . it won't eat no ackles."

"Won't it, darling? . . . And it seems to me, Mrs. Malinin, that if——"

"But, mah-mah."

"——we could only learn to cast all our troub——"

"Mah-mah."

"——bles on that great heart that is so ready to bear them, we could turn and face the world with a perfect——"

"Mah-mah."

"Your child seems still to have some matter on its mind," said Anna between ground teeth.

"What is it, mah-mah's prettybird?"

"Mah-mah, it won't eat no ackles."

"No, darling, just fancy that! . . . And another thing, Mrs. Malinin——"

"But, mah-mah."

"For God's sake, child," said Anna, hoarsely, glaring at the child, "*what* will not eat *what?*"

Mrs. Butters put a protective arm round her child and directed a reproachful glance toward Anna. "These foreigners," she thought. "Even quite *nice* foreigners . . . so *different. . . .*"

"Betty is talking of the little kid," she said gently. "The mother goat—we call her Nannie—died yesterday—didn't she, loveybird? Mah-mah's loveybird's poor Nannie doatie went to heaven, and we are wondering if we can rear the kid. It is so difficult to make it take the bottle."

"And what has your child been giving it?"

"What has mah-mah's Bettybird been giving poor Nannie doatie's nitty tiddy to nyum-nyum?"

"Ackles, but it won't eat no ackles, mah-mah."

"Oh, she doesn't know any better, of course; she's been trying to make the poor little creature eat apples. Ackles, she calls them. . . ."

"Mah-mah, I opened the tiddie's moufie, and I pushed little bits of ackle down wiv my finger, and——"

"For God's sake!" shouted Anna, springing to her feet and knocking down her chair. "Is the child altogether without sense? Can it be possible——"

"Oh, Mrs. Malinin, she's just a wee thing—only six. How should she know?"

"Mrs. Butters, when I was five my mother and I used to bring up with our hands all the delicate lambs and calves. I could milk good long before that, and when I was seven I have helped my father's groom to accoucher my mare of a dead colt. All nature's ways were known by me as they should be by any child who lives in the country and is not blind or imbecile——"

"Mah-mah's own Bettylove must run away now," said Mrs. Butters. "And better not give nitty tiddy any more ackles just now, lovey."

Mrs. Butters, free of Betty's innocent presence, breathed several deep forgiving breaths through her nose before overcoming her indignation at Anna's vehemence and vulgarity. "I had no idea you were such a farmer, dear Mrs. Malinin," she said, folding up her sewing as a sign of mild dismissal. There was only just a trace of reproachful emphasis on the word *farmer*. "I believe I shall have to give you the little kid to rear. Evidently you know more about it than we do."

Anna was crossing the room at the moment to fetch a reel of cotton from a drawer. And, although she was fifty-four years old, when she heard that the kid might be hers she leaped into the air and smacked the top of her head. The floor shook. "Oh, *how* I should enjoy that! *How* I should enjoy it! And my poor old man to have a kid to stroke and a kid's heart to feel beating—most joyfully I accept, Mrs. Butters, most joyfully. . . ."

CHAPTER THREE

SERYOZHA SAW his mother coming home hugging a large bleating linen basket to her stomach.

Seryozha, born in an air too rarefied for most illusions, retained only one — the illusion of his own dignity. He did not mind what strange, boisterous, misunderstood activities the outer Seryozha took part in, as long as the inner Seryozha could explain to himself these seeming pranks by some formula of secret though freakish dignity. One has seen a weighted wooden tumbling toy, knocked down on a flat surface, preserving its integrity and fulfilling its purpose by finding, in the end, its own odd balance regardless of the mockery of the watchers — and only robbed of its birthright of eccentric equilibrium when the gods themselves fight against it and overset it on an unfairly tilted plane. So Seryozha, left to himself, could always account to himself for himself. But outside were parents, gods, insects, landscapes, animals, machines, and the elements — traitors to young individual dignity — all conspiring together unfairly to destroy the balance of valiant dignity.

To lack a camera or a wireless set, to be at home in a wooden Korean house with little squinting windows and a chronic smell, was bad enough, but to see a perspiring mother coming toward the home carrying a goat in a clothes-basket, in the sight of dozens of her less respectable Oriental neighbors, made Seryozha doubt whether he ever would attain to his rightful place in a world full of the rude laughter of inferiors. However, though he did not know it, Seryozha was very fond of his mother and, though she often shamed him, he very seldom punished her. He was much harsher to his father, and the same instinct in him that allowed his mother license to play the fool in her own whole-hearted hen-like way, resented the poverty of his father's vitality. He did not mind, for instance, the fact that his mother's large blousy bun of hair was always coming down, so much as he minded the way his father cautiously combed four or five streaks of hair from one ear to the other.

"I've got something new here, Seryozha," said Anna, putting down the basket to push a wisp of hair out of her eyes. She spilled the kid very gently out on to the living-room floor. For a moment the little creature did not remember that it knew how to stand. It crouched on the floor, its awkward pale legs crumpled under its body, its neck stretched, its pinched mouth open to utter an almost voiceless bleat.

Seryozha's grievance against his mother was overlaid for the moment by his pleasure in the color of the kid. Things that were pale below and colored above always looked dramatic and beautiful to his eye, as though he had some secret arctic memory of light growing from a low seed of moon. Japanese orchards of young fruit-trees with trunks painted white; great trees illuminated by a bonfire till they looked like cardboard trees towering over footlights; young horses with milky pale fur on legs and stomach darkening to shining russet along the upper ribs and back; young girls with light stockings and skirts and colored jackets — perhaps he felt a sort of kinship of pantomime youth with these footlight schemes of upslanting color.

He watched the kid and said nothing of his pleasure, however, and underneath his pleasure the feeling of soreness persisted. He knew obscurely that something in his mind was sore; he had forgotten what had wounded him; he did not know that the sore place was his vanity, bruised by his mother's lack of self-respect. Vanity is so reluctant to identify itself — yet it always is hurt vanity that gives that sense of live yet nameless tragedy.

Anna, having dipped a piece of clean rag in milk, was holding it to the kid's mouth.

"Ah-yah-yah!" sang Seryozha, loudly, feeling he was achieving something by thwarting his mother. The kid, startled, recoiled from the offered drop.

"Be quiet, child!" cried Anna, jolted into anger by the check in her breathless experiment. Her forehead sweated a little and her hand trembled as she stroked once more the kid's silly lips with the rag.

"Ah-yah-yah!" sang Seryozha, and shook the floor with a sudden bounce, to make sure.

Tears of anger came into Anna's eyes as she knelt, ungainly. She was so very whole-souled in all that she did. "Curse you, boy——" but she stopped, for the kid was nibbling with its lips upon the rag. Success was in sight.

"Ah-yah-yah!" yelled Seryozha, almost against his own inclination. He had got into a kind of groove of contradiction; for the moment it was entirely impossible for him to relent. Anna jumped to her feet, treading on her skirt and tearing it. She rushed at her son, swinging the linen basket by the handle, and dealt him a heavy blow which he caught partly on his defensive elbow and partly on the side of his nose. Through this tempest of bustle and anger he saw suddenly the rock-like fact that he was nearly nineteen years old and that this scene was inconsistent with his essential quiet manliness. His nose was scratched now, too.

"Oh, all right," he said, speaking, on purpose, in a foolish voice as though he had a potato in his mouth, since he was somehow ashamed to regain his amiability too abruptly. "Get the little brute fed, then, and get rid of it out of the house. It smells like the devil."

"What smells?" asked Old Sergei, feeling his way into the living-room from the yard.

The kid, swept aside and terrified by the bustle and noise, stood drooping on bent, trembling legs in a far corner, and gave a faint creaking bleat.

"A lamb?" cried Old Sergei. "Where did you get a lamb?"

"It is a kid," said Anna, crouching once more on the floor and taking the kid under her arm again with a gentle impatience. "Give me that cup of milk, Seryozha. Mrs. Butters gave me a kid today, as well as the two yen, for sewing her baby's dress quite wrongly."

"Why should she give you a kid for making sewing mistakes?" asked Old Sergei. "You can't sew; you never could sew."

Of course, everything he was wearing was sewn by Anna, but he felt that no stitch of it did either him or her credit. Almost all the seams either had, or would soon, burst. Anna never repaired things. She was far cleverer at contriving than at stitching, and mending was a work she never had time for until actual nakedness was in sight. She would always prefer to invent a new cut of trouser, or a new method of fastening a shoe, to patching existing trousers or replacing old laces. She would rather have a new kid or puppy every night to feed, than cook the supper for the same old everyday husband and son.

"You don't really earn a sen with your sewing," said Old Sergei, "much less a kid. The missionaries only pay you out of charity, because they know I am blind and cannot support my wife and child as I used to."

Seryozha made a rude noise.

"So why," persisted Old Sergei — "why should the missionaries be such fools as to give you a kid in addition to the two yen you don't earn? I don't believe they did give it to you."

"Why, here *is* the kid. Feel it," said Anna. "How do you suggest it got here? Did I steal it, do you think?"

"Heaven knows how it got here. Heaven knows what you will do next. How do I know you didn't steal it? We are sunk so low that nothing would surprise me. Or perhaps Mrs. Butters was joking and did not mean to give it to you at all and you made a mistake, as usual, and walked off with the creature. Why *should* she give us a smelly kid? We don't *want* a kid; we didn't ask for a kid; and it will make a mess in the house, too. What a place for a kid—in a gentleman's living-room! And, of course no supper prepared, I am sure, for me and Seryozha. . . . Oh no! the stolen kid must be fed before your husband and son——"

"Be silent, you horrid old man!" cried Anna, now full of anger and a diffident panic, because her sensitive conscience admitted the possibility that Mrs. Butters perhaps had *not* meant her offer of the kid to be accepted so literally and immediately. Anna heard, with her suddenly awakened mind's ear, her own boisterous voice crying, "Oh, Mrs. Butters, most cheerfully I accept. . . ." Too soon—too soon—and now too late remembered. To remember the sound of her own voice was almost always, for poor Anna, to hear a sort of bugle call calling to retreat—and retreat was always, alas, by then impossible. Every battle was always fought and lost by the time she heard that dreaded call.

"Take the creature," she said to Seryozha in a broken voice. "Let it die if you like, or take it back to the mission." She went out, loaded with sadness, to cook the supper.

Seryozha took the kid and the cup of milk out into the yard and sat crooning into its winking ear as he held it in his arms and dipped and redipped the rag. "Yoodle-doodle-doo . . . yoodle-doodle-dido," he sang in a small falsetto voice which the kid seemed to like. The breast of Seryozha's blouse was soon soaked in milk. The kid's yellow cynical eyes, slotted with vertical irises, were fixed on him as though it were trying to persuade itself that this was some eccentric relation of its late mother's.

Old Sergei sat alone in the living-room, his trembling veined old hands clasping and unclasping limply between his knees. Anna came to the door, mixing some egg and flour in a bowl, and said: "You horrid old man . . . you wearisome old man . . . running about honoring strangers and then coming home to break my heart. That kid was given to me — it was. . . ."

"God knows whether it was or not," said Old Sergei, but under his breath, thus satisfying his honor as a Husband with a Righteous Grievance without speaking loud enough to provoke the violence of his wife. Anna sighed petulantly and noisily and returned to the stove. Old Sergei sat drooping, opening and shutting his blind eyes to remind himself that he could not see. He laid his hand on his throbbing throat, for he craved to feel life always under his hand in order to titillate his fancy about death. He swallowed; his Adam's apple moved under his hand, and his vague thoughts floated round and round the strangeness of life and death.

He was old, he thought; he was not loved. He loved no one. He felt the breath climbing foolishly up and down the unsteady shaft that was his body, like an imprisoned bird never losing hope of escape. Some day the prisoner would find the loophole and fly from his lips. The sooner the better, thought Old Sergei — or rather he thought that he thought so; life was a curse without serenity. Who could be serene by Anna's side? He felt as home-sick for serenity as though he had once enjoyed it. He believed he had left it behind him in old lost Russia. He believed he would find it again in heaven, which was the only province of lost Russia left to him to visit now.

38

"To die — to die — to die . . ." whispered Old Sergei, enjoying the feeling of tears brimming over the quivering skin of his eye-sockets. He stroked and stroked his too living throat; in his sightless eyes he saw the sad picture of his lovelessness. Clasping his hands together, he laid this sad picture before his God, hoping to soften God's heart by a prostrate-spirited humility. "I have sinned, O God," he thought, for his vanity felt defiled by Anna's reproaches. "I have sinned, I am reproached, so let me die. I am cursed; I am found out . . . all life is too difficult for me, for I belong to a cursed race . . . wretched Russia — exiled and despoiled — a dying race — a reproach to all the nations of the earth among whom we are dispersed. . . . Here am I, a wretched sinner, a reproached sinner, member of a wretched and reproached race. O God, let me die. It's the only way to make people sorry for me instead of angry with me. . . ." He thought of oblivion as a revenge; death, not penitence, seemed to him the apposite answer to a justified reproach; he had no courage for penitence. He would refuse to be anything more responsible than a pitiful memory in Anna's mind, and in God's. "Let my spirit be taken from me . . . let me be dissolved and become earth. . . . Let me go into the everlasting place," he implored of his God, as a man faced by the irritation of shaving on a cold morning almost decides to go back to bed and sleep the day out.

He was interrupted in this limp ecstasy by hearing Seryozha's peaceful "Yoodle-doodle-doo," outside in the yard. He had heard it for some time, but it had not come to the forefront of his attention till now, suddenly, in a pause in Anna's kitchen clatter.

"Seryozha," called Old Sergei, "bring me that kid."

Seryozha, whistling very softly between his teeth, brought the kid, more than half asleep, huddled in a length of sacking, and put it on the floor between his father's feet. Old Sergei's hands — tense, as though they expected to find

something new—stroked the kid's hard little brow, the
thin ridge of its neck, the harsh hair on its narrow shoulders,
the heaving bulging ribs, the upturned hoofs tipping the
awkwardly kneeling legs. . . . Old Sergei's fingers ran up
and down the sleepy little animal's backbone, as though it
were an ecstatic instrument.

"Seryozha," said Old Sergei, turning his face down toward
the kid as though he could see it, "if I should die . . ."

Emotion checked his speech, and so long was the pause
that Seryozha, who was tapping with his foot the already flat
corpse of a cockroach in cold abstraction, as though it de-
served to die a hundred deaths, was obliged to say, "Oh, nonsense, papa! There's no reason why you should die. . . ."

"There is every reason," said Old Sergei, feeling a little
baffled as Seryozha began again whistling, almost in a whisper, through his teeth—an unsuitable obbligato to a talk on
death. "No one values my presence here—still less do I
value it myself. I am a weariness to those around me and to
myself. . . ."

"You don't really think that, papa," said Seryozha. His
father, with some surprise, took this as an affectionate filial
disclaimer of his proposition. Really Seryozha meant his remark quite literally. He knew that his father did not mean
his statement that the necessity for him to remain in the
world was now at an end. "Nobody believes that," thought
Seryozha, "however much they may say so. Papa's world
wouldn't be there if he weren't there. My world wouldn't
if I weren't. This cockroach's isn't, now it's dead. So none
of us really thinks our world can do without us. I'm sure
it had never before occurred to this cockroach that its world
could do without it—that anybody could wish it dead. Its
vanity was all comfortable inside itself—it felt valuable.
When it saw my foot coming, it thought—'an unnatural
accident is happening to a noble and unreplaceable cockroach—me!' That's what papa thinks." Seryozha scanned

his father's rather tiresome face, his leaking eyes, nose, mouth, dispassionately. "Poor old ass," thought Seryozha. "His vanity's a bit uncomfortable, inside him . . . hungry, perhaps. . . ."

"Just now I have been praying to die," said Old Sergei. ("Pretty safe," thought his son, arrogantly, "as experience must have shown him. Funny how old people don't learn by experience. Only we young people do that.")

"—and as I prayed I remembered how penniless and friendless you and your mother would be were I to leave you. The shop needs a business head, and if I were not here to talk things over with your cousin Andryusha, God knows what would happen. You and your mother do not realize the value of a business head quietly yet actively in the background—an asset quite as necessary to a family's prosperity, I assure you, as all this cadging of goats and hacking of logs. However, these things are not appreciated until one is dead, and, as I told you, I have been praying for death."

In order to prove to his wife and son the value of a business head, he had prayed to have it chopped off. Old Sergei had a different vanity every day. Sometimes he changed twice or thrice a day. When he got up in the morning, Anna and Seryozha usually gleaned—though too often in a rebellious spirit—what fancy aspect of his nature he was displaying for their admiration for the next few hours. Since four o'clock today he had been, as Seryozha saw, a Business Man, afflicted with blindness, to be sure, but quietly effective nevertheless.

"And as I prayed—since even in meditation and worship my business sense is awake—I remembered that two hundred rubles I left with Gavril Ilitch Isaev at Seoul, to invest in his hotel, many years ago, at a time when I feared for the safety of Chinese banks and decided that Seoul was safer. He banked the money in his own name, but I have the receipt. I wrote it and he signed it. I think it is in that volume of Pushkin's poems that props up the short leg of our bed. You see what it is, Seryozha, to have an orderly business mind. You would probably never have remembered that two hundred dollars."

"I couldn't have remembered it, since I never heard of it before," said Seryozha. "And I don't know now whether you mean dollars or rubles. You say both."

"I mean neither," said Old Sergei. "Really, Seryozha, you are not using your mind. What is the currency of Korea? Yen, of course. Should I be likely to have my savings put away in a bank in a currency not native to the country in which the bank does business? Yours is the kind of question which shows me how ill able to look after your mother you would be were I to leave you. You should certainly cultivate a business sense. Now my idea is that you should go on foot over the mountains to Seoul and fetch that money from Gavril Ilitch."

"Why don't you write and ask him to send it?"

"I did, of course, write to him, some time ago, in the summer of 1924, I think it was. Isaev did not answer. He is by no means a business man and I should say hardly knows how to put pen to paper except just to sign his name. He is a peasant — was my brother's gardener before the revolution, in Vladivostok. A devoted creature, but evidently deficient in business methods. Since I wrote to him my mind has been occupied with other matters and I only thought of the money just now, when praying to die. But, having once thought of it, I have no difficulty at all in recollecting every detail of the transaction, and in deciding on the best and most business-like solution of the problem — which is that you should walk to Seoul and——"

"Why in the world did you give your two hundred yen to a peasant who could neither read nor write? That wasn't very business-like, it seems to me."

"Seryozha, you are not using your mind. Surely you cannot expect me to explain all my business dealings to a raw lad like you, without financial experience of any kind. As a matter of fact, it was the best thing to do; I was in Seoul buying stock for the shop, and found that, since the goods I expected could not be delivered, I had two hundred yen too much — more than was safe to carry across the robber-infested Manchurian border. Isaev had had a good position as coachman to the Japanese bank-manager and was thinking of starting a hotel. His savings were banked in the Chosen Bank. Naturally I gave him my savings, too, to invest with his own until I should ask for them. I dare say the poor fellow is wondering every day why I do not return to claim my money."

"After ten years of wondering every day I should have thought he might have got a friend who could write to try and get in touch with you," said Seryozha, sulkily, but his mind was already, as it were, packing its wits for the journey; his toes were already throbbing with the starting fever. Every day in his unpromising life he woke up feeling "perhaps something great will happen today," and here was something great — a lonely, dignified journey, without any father and mother to be ashamed of at every turn.

Old Sergei straightened his back, and in doing so awoke the kid, which, after innocently making a little mess on the floor, tottered on unsteady legs toward Seryozha, who, it seemed to the kid, gave forth an inviting smell of milk and mother. Old Sergei did not notice the departure of his toy, he was so much interested in the deathbed advice he was determined to give his son before his fount of tears and high principles should be dried up by the arid discomforts of an actual deathbed.

"I have a feeling," he said, his words dipping under his shaking upper lip like chickens escaping under a rabbit-wire fence, "I have a feeling that this is the last talk we shall have together, Seryozha. . . . If, when you return, I should be already no more, I entreat you, my boy, to be good to your mother. Remember the dangers she went through for your sake in bearing you——"

"That wasn't for my sake, papa—she didn't know me then—it was for her pleasure and yours that she bore me," said Seryozha.

"Let her lie by my side in the grave," said Old Sergei, trying to ignore the possibility of an interval of healthy widowhood for poor Anna, "as she has lain so many nights by my side in the big bed."

"Oh, don't worry, papa," said Seryozha, "You'll both of you live till ninety, I'm sure." And he began to whistle softly through his teeth again.

Tears squeezed between Old Sergei's eyelids as he half-realized his impotence in imposing his posthumous pathos on the living. How could he force his wife and son to regret him all their lives? There was no way. There was no love or loyalty in the world.

"Supper is ready," said Anna, and stood in the doorway, suddenly thinking of something else, her eyes fixed on a fly on the wall. She was trying to think what had irritated and hurt her just before she began cooking the fish pie. Somehow she craved to identify that scar on her temper. But she could not trace any thought to its source because the tiresome wilderness of her old husband's presence kept on blossoming into silly words that distracted her attention. To stop him talking she said again, "Supper is ready." But Old Sergei went on talking. Anna went on thinking. Seryozha went on whistling. Anna caught words.

". . . and giving to those who are poorer than yourself. God remembers it even if the ungrateful forget it. He will repay. . . ."

"An investment only—not a gift," thought Anna, and stood in abstraction, scratching her head, till the next words intruded:

". . . sleeping with women, Seryozha. Remember your Russian blood is a pure sacred inheritance . . . an insult to the land of your fathers to mix your blood with . . ."

"For poor Seryozha," thought Anna, "Russia is unluckily becoming nothing but that—the land of his fathers—*father*—*Russia*—boring peevish words. And yet the high Russian fields . . ."

"Supper is ready," she said aloud. Seryozha, goaded by his empty stomach, got up so abruptly that he knocked his chair over. But still Old Sergei went on talking—commanding them to stay, with his weak, blind, upraised face.

". . . worth your while to earn, as I have earned, the reputation of a sound man—a man with a stake in the community—one who pays what he owes, no more, no less. . . ."

Anna's thought ran off to the little shop on the other side of the matchwood partition she leaned against—a place of business closed since the Chinese soldiers' raid, but still containing a tall pile of unwanted tins of Milkex, two dozen fancy diaries, four or five dozen celluloid hand mirrors in pastel shades, a case of comic can-openers in the form of bulldogs, a hundred or so silk-padded coat-hangers, and a few other temptations that could not even tempt thieves. These goods, Anna felt, shone in an idealized form in her old husband's imagination, and gave him the right, in his own eyes, to claim a stake in the community.

". . . and never was drunk in my life, Seryozha," she heard. It was true, she knew, the taste of alcohol had always made him feel sick. "Some young men think that manliness is found in drunkenness and coarseness and fornication, but there is a truer manliness——"

"For God's sake!" said Anna. "Supper is ready, I tell you." As Old Sergei's blind face turned to her, Anna remembered what it was that had offended her: he had suggested, by accident, what was probably true, that the offer of the kid had been accepted more precipitately than Mrs. Butters had intended. "Do you want to starve yourself as well as talk yourself hoarse, you silly old man?" she said, vehemently.

Old Sergei was conscious of an indecorous anticlimax to a Dying Man's Advice to His Son. "My son is going on a journey and I am giving him a few parting words of advice, since I am an old man and by the time he comes back I may have been called away on the long——"

"What journey do you mean?"

Old Sergei felt that her horrified question gave him an opportunity for tragic drama such as he seldom wrested from his family. "What journey? Why, death, Anna."

"No. I mean what journey is Seryozha taking, idiot?" said Anna, stamping irritably with both feet.

"I'm going to Seoul," said Seryozha, happily, "to fetch some money that papa forgot——"

"Forgot, Seryozha!" exclaimed his father. "It is you that forget——"

"But Seoul is four days' journey by train and road even when you get to the train," said Anna. "And on foot. . . . The police in Korea are most dangerous to poor Russians. . . . The bandits on the border——"

"Oh, that's all quite easy," said Seryozha. "Three weeks' walking will do it. And I'd like to see the Japanese policeman or the Chinese bandit that——"

"You will see neither," said Anna. "You will take no such journey. The idea! . . . Only a couple of imbeciles would have such an idea. Dancing off alone into nowhere. What a notion—and you a mere child still! Let us hear no more of it. Come, must I tell you for the hundredth time that supper is ready? For God's sake, old man, are you glued to your chair?"

CHAPTER FOUR

TATIANA PAVLOVNA OSTAPENKO and the servant, Katya, bent side by side over washtubs, looked like a sow and a hind feeding side by side from one trough. Both wore the same kind of headkerchief and faded blue cotton bodice and skirt. But Tatiana bent like some one finding flowers at her feet, and Katya bent like a bear offering a goblin a ride on its back.

A young man watched them from the shade of the wide tree that stood behind the village at the junction of three footpaths across the barley and bean fields. The young man, Piotr Gavrilovitch Isaev, almost wished that Tatiana would never turn round. He knew her face so well and was so much afraid of it. Yet he whistled — do-mi-do — his old call to her, and she turned. He knew she would make no gesture of enthusiasm. She looked at him across fifty yards of shimmering evening sunlight for a long moment and then flapped her hand toward him with an abashed, rather rigid, gesture. He watched her talk for a minute to Katya as she dried her hands on her apron. Then Katya went into the house and Tatiana walked along the raised footpath toward the young man under the tree. He could see her exquisite pale face,

her russet hair dragged tightly from her forehead under the
kerchief, her rather sunken light eyes, now twitching with
nervousness. Twice, as she approached, she smiled, as
though rehearsing a smile — just a little abrupt delicate grin
— a tautening and an instant slackening of her cheeks. It
was a smile that seemed to mean nothing but a good intention, and was obliterated like a duty done. As soon as she
reached him her expression changed like a changing light on
her face, and she said, "Forgive me, dear Piotr Gavrilovitch.
I have forgotten something; I must go back to the washing
for a minute." She turned away from him at once and began
walking back along the footpath, as a lady-bird hurrying
along a leaf, on being turned round, walks just as indus-
triously the other way.

Young Isaev, for a moment taken aback, caught up with
her in three strides. "What's the matter, Tatiana Pavlovna?
I want to tell you something. Won't you come and sit in
the shade of the tree for half an hour?"

"Yes, of course I will, presently, dear Petya. I must do
something I had forgotten, first."

She always called people *dear* in a cold voice. Like her
twitched-on, twitched-off smile, the *dear* was a sort of
concession, kind yet shy, to humanity. She walked back to
the washtubs and Piotr walked beside her.

"My aunt heard from my cousin Sasha Weber this
morning," said Piotr, after wondering for a moment what to
say.

"Did he find the world as wide as he expected?" asked
Tatiana.

"He hasn't been all over it yet, Tanya, so he can't tell.
He has only reached Pa-tao-kou."

"Oh," said Tatiana, with her apologetic smile. She
minded very much when her questions evoked dead answers. They often did. She tried to join in the talk in
the manner of other talkers, but so often the talk myste-

48

riously died of her gentle intervention. I think that a remark of hers, though dressed in the trappings of ordinary convenient comment, was often like a fairy coming into a room full of flesh-and-blood men and women. There was the fairy, in no tangible way different from themselves, dressed like themselves, walking, moving like themselves, yet somehow accompanied by cold airs, aloof, terrifying, humiliating. And one man finds that he has forgotten a letter he meant to write, another that he has a business appointment, another that he promised to take the dog for a walk . . . and so the poor fairy is left alone — not rudely but inexorably — left alone, looking itself up and down in the mirror, wondering what was wrong . . . wondering how they knew. . . .

Tatiana looked at Piotr with remorse, and saw uneasiness in his pink face. His face was ugly and anxious; his brassy hair and eyelashes looked lighter in tone than his face; his nose was sunburnt, prominent, and fat. Tatiana's ready, cold pity was aroused by the tight puckered skin that inclosed his hurt feelings. She thought of the skull inside that skin — sensitive to a blow; of the brain inside that skull — protesting, defensive, bewildered, also afraid of assault. She saw him as a besieged creature in a fortress, marshaling its defenses against her. She felt as if she were trespassing against her will on something almost unbearably sacred, by simply seeing his face. She was seeing too much. Poor Piotr! this is not the way young girls should see young men — yet so it was! Tatiana, however, though only eighteen, was wise enough not to put her compassion into words.

She could not think of anything else to put into words, either. She always boggled over words, and would not have recognized the properly girlish ones, even if they had occurred to her. Nor was she interested enough in spanning this giddy space between herself and Piotr to risk anything for the sake of building a bridge over it. She did not know how to approach him; she could not bear that he should approach her. Her body she did not know, but in her mind she was fanatically virgin. Every approach was a danger, she could not have explained why. And yet *she* must be allowed to trespass secretly upon her neighbors; she must have hostages in many camps; she must send herself often far away from home to be a protesting prisoner in other bodies. A little pang in every one's pain seemed hers, just as a lamb's leaping, an impudent flirt of a free bird's wing, so often seemed part of her vicarious youth — a word she herself had known but left unspoken, a satisfaction in itself, like a flattery. Perhaps she was an egoist — an egoist whose center had slipped — an egoist whose ego had spilled over, tainted too much. She was like a person who lived on a mountain instead of in her own house. That was poor Piotr's trouble, though he did not know it — Tatiana was never at home, waiting inside herself for visitors, as other young people are — waiting behind her own threshold — watching out of her own eyes. You might call — Tanya, Tanya — at her pretty ear, and her voice would reply, as it were, from a long way off. Her sight was unglazed by eyes and therefore too coldly clear — like frosty air as you come out too early in the dawn from your smoky house. Tanya, Tanya, you might call, posturing before her window, but she would be away, watching you quietly from the hill, seeing you, not as you, but as a little far part of herself, dancing in the distance.

She was both too far and too near. She loved her neighbor as herself because she found herself in her neighbor, but if you were her neighbor, you found that she loved you no better than herself — and therefore not at all.

What a detestable advantage it gave her, to be high on the hill, safe, away from home, yet near enough to hear, with her remote cold senses, your heart beating. How wrong that she should claim to have the key to your lock and yet, herself, present no lock, no door, no house, even, for your unlocking. And yet her face and body were so lovely that you must love them even more than you hated her passionless mind and heart—you could not help calling—Tanya, Tanya—before the empty windows of a deserted house at the foot of the hill, hoping always to lure her home, inside herself, to welcome you in at last.

She had a smile that pulled the corners of her lips up and the corners of her eyes down, but it was never meant for you, except secondarily; when you smiled in reply, hers vanished, was twitched away.

Tatiana did not know that she lived on a hill; she only knew that she had no neighbors; her neighbors all must harbor *her*, but *she* had no neighbors. To be approached was entirely unbearable; a desiring or acute glance was in itself an assault; see she must, but to be seen was somehow insult. She loathed touch and always avoided it; the lightest accidental touch rasped her like a cat's tongue. Love of her neighbor was a thing felt stilly, thinly diffused among pitied lovers—puppies—parents—flowers—insects—even things (she often felt guilty for disappointing *things*)—even *invented* things—blank pensioners of her compassionate fancy. She drew no ecstasy except through her eyes. And she felt a little giddy always because she saw so many things and had so little known self—or such a wide, unknown self—out of which to see them. She saw now, as she walked, a collapsing hour-glass of blue sky. She watched clouds crushing it in, and a sand of light spill out of it. Then, as she came to the washtub, her attention swooped suddenly to the reason of her return—a woolly-bear caterpillar, swimming in the suds. It had been swimming there for some time—not exactly swimming, for it was too light to break through the soapy skin of the water, and occasionally it found a sodden island of linen to walk across. Its fur was dry, but it looked exhausted. Tatiana, most of whose diversions of the mind were curiously cruel, had dared herself to let it nearly drown so that its relief at ultimate rescue might be the more glorious. Then Piotr's whistle had made her forget it—made her prolong the poor insect's ordeal more than she had intended. She put her finger under it now and caught it up to safety. She laid her finger against a blade of grass and, when the caterpillar had found its footing on its own world, she knelt down and watched it. She was imagining its incredulous delight. Piotr, puzzled, knelt down beside her. They looked as if they were about to pray together.

"But what did you come back for, Tanya?"

"For this."

"For what? This slug?"

"Well . . . I left it drowning. I forgot it for the moment. Then I remembered—so I had to come back."

"But—oh, Tanya—a caterpillar! When I told you I had something to tell you! Don't be so foolish, for God's sake, Tanya; don't be so cold. Listen to me—don't laugh at me."

He looked at her and could not pretend to himself that she was even paying him the compliment of laughing at him. Nor was he sure that she was listening. She was breathlessly following the caterpillar's course. It rippled earnestly along like a little machine running on concealed wheels well provided with shock-absorbers.

Piotr uttered a mild curse and then, seizing an empty glass jar that had contained washing soda, he placed it upside down over the caterpillar, involving that unlucky insect in yet another unmerited dilemma.

"Tanya, I believe I'm glad—I'm glad that you are so contrary and unkind. It makes it easier to say these things to you. Listen, I don't want to stay in Mi-san any more—I don't want to see your face any more. . . . I'm tired of your face. There's something wrong with it; though it is so pretty, there's no heart behind it. Listen, Tanya—don't look at

that damned bug—listen. I'm going away. There was no
reason why you should have treated me so—we were
betrothed. There is nothing to keep us apart now, except
your own hard heart. That and my feeling of being tired of
you, of course. You have lost something by your hard-
heartedness, I can tell you. Some day you will be sorry. You
are kinder to that caterpillar than to a man, Tanya. I can
tell you, some girls know a man's value better. Once lost,
I am lost forever. You will be sorry. . . . What do you expect? No man of flesh and blood can go on forever loving a
girl that only smiles at—caterpillars. What is the matter
with you, that you hold yourself so much above love? What
else is there for you? Do you want to live and die alone?"

"No—no—Petya," she said at once in tears. The word
alone had a terrible sound to her. Yet she had no defense
against it, because the *reality*, loneliness, was her right—her
unassailable pride. To live and die alone was like living and
dying on a throne; she took her queenship so much for
granted that she did not know of it. It was only the word
alone that had such a cruel, insulting sound—synonymous
with *undefended*. Her wordless diffused egoism demanded
defense against all that was implied by the word *alone*. A
queen has a right to be defended. Yet, of course, Tatiana
defended herself—she would have resented that intrusion,
actual defense. Perhaps she needed fairy counselors and was
only offered lovers. Perhaps she needed the comfort of
God and was only offered the love of men. At any rate, the
word *alone* made her cry. *Live and die alone.* It was uttered
like a threat and therefore it made her cry—just as the
words *be crowned a queen*, uttered portentously, might
make a queen-beginner cry. Words, heard by the ear, bring
tears from the eyes. But hearts are left firm on their thrones,
deep down, beyond the reach of threats and tears. *Alone*
—how ugly a word! *Alone*—how fierce a threat! *Alone*—
how sore and smarting must Piotr's poor vanity be, to utter

such a threat. She felt an unbearable compassion for him. She imagined she could hear his baffled vanity — rejected — driven home — going round and round in his breast, crying — why — why — why? Other girls, he said, knew his value better. That was his poor darling vanity that spoke; he was besieged inside himself — firing off the failing ammunition of his vanity from behind that pink serious face, those blinking blue eyes, that hard healthy nose, that deeply-breathing chest. Of course there was value in that bewildered body of his — of course other girls knew that value. Why not? She knew it herself. Yet suddenly, as she reviewed his deserts, the very thought of his touching her outraged her. She felt sick. She stopped crying.

"It's no use, dear Petya," she said in a quavering voice. "I'm not proud of this fear in me. I don't pretend it. I am what I am."

But, very deep down in her heart, she *was* proud of this birthmark of remoteness. It was not a fear — it was not a fleeing away, but a repelling. Somehow she knew without knowing it, that to be alone was to be judged by a strange calm standard — to be judged, in fact, by herself only — the ideal of pride. Loneliness was in itself a sort of license to live strangely — to live according to an outlaw's law.

There was a long silence during which Tatiana, her tears drying on her cheeks, watched the caterpillar under the jam-pot. She thought it was arguing to itself: "Now I must keep my head and think clearly. I got in here, so there must be a way out. That stands to reason." A perfectly good argument. But there was no way out.

Piotr, who had turned his face away, looked at her and saw where her attention was. Grunting with irritation, he knocked the jam-pot over, and the caterpillar, congratulating itself on this justification of its logic, rippled away.

"Come over to the tree, Tanya, and listen to what I have to say," said Piotr, hoping there would be no insect life or other distracting livestock there. But not hoping very firmly, for anything, he knew, could hold Tatiana's attention — anything, except a lover.

She was very docile. She walked by his side, back toward the tree. But, halfway, she stopped and said: "But Petya, is it any good talking? You know what happened — that day. It isn't words that can alter things like that."

Piotr remembered. The memory stabbed deeply and quickly through his tender body. He could feel still the generous heat of his accepted love — accepted, for she was docile, and had not refused her lips. Why should she refuse? They were betrothed. His memory still rang with her wild scream; his hands tingled still to recall the stiffening of her body as she had fainted. Thunderstruck, almost unbearably hurt, he had looked up — round — down — as he released her. Had she seen a tiger — heard a shot? No, nothing had happened except the natural gesture of a quite ordinary young man's quite ordinary love. . . . Words to alter this? He ground his teeth to think that such difficult unsimple things as words should be needed. For he knew no fresh words; he hoped for no inspiration of eloquence. All he had to say was, "But why — why — why?" His only argument was *being* what he was — a healthy decent young man in love with a beautiful healthy girl, whose parents sanctioned their betrothal. What was wrong with that? What was there left for words to explain in that? When he said, "Well then, I shall go away," he pictured himself obscurely in two halves; one half walking inexorably away over hill and dale, completely carefree, the other half gloating over the sight of the bereaved Tatiana's remorse, as she lay, cured of her folly, crying, Come back, come back. Petya my darling. . . .

"Well then, Tanya, I shall go away. You will not see me again."

Tatiana smiled at once. "Will you really, Piotr Gavrilovitch? Will you really be happy again? I shall think of you happy again, finding a new thing every minute—waving your stick—walking happily along. . . ."

"Happy? I am happy now," said Piotr, sullenly. "It isn't a woman that could make me unhappy."

She looked apologetic again. "Oi, Petya—I hurt you. . . . I wish I had never been born."

"You didn't hurt me. How could you hurt me? Certainly we would have been married; there was nothing to prevent it except some whim of yours, Tanya. But why should I care? I am the freer for your whim. This place is too small for a man like me. Perhaps I shall join the Chinese army as an officer. Danger doesn't frighten me. Almost certainly I shall never come back. There will be nobody ever again to bring you mushrooms."

"How frightful for him," thought Tatiana, "that he can't hurt me, though he is hurt by me. I wish I could seem hurt."
"Of course I shall be very sorry," she mumbled, awkwardly.

"Sorry! Sorry to miss the mushrooms," said Piotr, wildly. "You and your mushrooms!" The very mention of mushrooms suddenly filled his eyes with tears. Mushrooms, patterned on a morning field, seemed to spell Tanya to him for a moment. "Mushrooms, indeed!" he croaked. "You think of nothing but yourself."

"Myself—myself—myself," thought Tatiana. "Where is myself?" She sought through herself for some essential bone of personality to lay a finger on. "What is it that likes mushrooms? What is it that fears to be alone and yet must be alone? What is it that dies of horror when men come too near? Are my eyes, watching caterpillars and watching Petya's red face—are my eyes myself? What else? What else?" She tried even to imagine what her outer self looked like, sitting here on a tree-root one cautious yard away from Piotr. She could see the spreading tree, spangled with green light; she could see the red hills under that clear tense light that comes just before sunset, the gullies filling with long smoke-blue shadows. . . . She looked along the bent perspective of the gully that stretched below the village to a wide purple and gold valley. The crops, in all colors but all tinged with the same rich yellow late light, and in all shapes — uneven squares, stripes, oblongs, rhomboids — grew from a blood-red soil, so that the near barley seemed like pale green armies wading in blood. Here and there were intervals of naked red — acres that had been ploughed for a new sowing. The paths, angling about among the many-angled crops, were deepset, as though stitched firmly into the texture of patched quilted velvet. Villages, of the same dreamlike smoke-blue as the far mountains, were tucked into gullies and tributary gullies, and over each village a thin taut string of smoke — the smoke of evening cooking — was stretched flat on the windless air.

And in the middle of this jewel-like elaboration of shape and color — where was Tatiana? She could not see herself or put herself into words, but in her mind's eye a pillar of nothingness reared — a white mirror, passively accepting the image of hills and valleys, insects and lovers. . . .

"Well, have you nothing to say to me — before I say good-by?"

"I wish you happiness, dear Piotr Gavrilovitch."

"You really want me to go away and be happy somewhere else and leave you alone?"

"What else is there to do?"

"Do you realize what it is, you foolish girl, for a woman to live and die alone?"

"I realize very well."

"Well then. . . . Ah, Tanya, would you let me kiss your eyes — just once — before I go?"

Her heart froze. "Petya — would it make you go more happily?" There was a hissing in her ears, like something boiling over — louder and louder — higher and higher. "Ah,

but—*no*—*no*—*no*—*no!*" She burst into tears and
jumped giddily to her feet. She began running back toward
her father's house. She reached the washtubs and plunged
her arms in among the wet clothes, pounding, crying, gasping, trembling. A terrified glance back toward the tree
showed her that Piotr had gone. A puff of dust at the corner
of the temple was all that reminded her eyes of him. If her
eyes were her only self—he was gone from her sight now,
gone from her self. She felt suddenly safe—safe from seeing his poor face—safe from having to pity him—safe from
invasion. The blank page of herself was safe from inscrip-
tion now. She flapped a wet garment with wild joy in the air.

"Oi, what a splashing!" said the servant, Katya, coming
out, carrying two cans of hot water. "You have been crying
again, Tatiana Pavlovna."

"Only for a minute," said Tatiana. With the strength of
excitement she emptied out her washtub into the ditch and
wrung out the clothes. She poured the fresh hot water into
the tub from a foolish height, saying to herself, "The awed
traveler stood and watched the stupendous cataract from a
neighboring height." She imagined the awed traveler, about
half an inch high, standing on the opposite brim of the
washtub—but she drowned him at once, by mistake, for the
water, violently poured in, splashed violently over the brim.

"You are wasting half the hot water, you foolish girl!"
shouted Katya. "I have been nearly an hour heating that
water and now you throw it on the mud. Can't you be careful?"

"If I like," said Tatiana. She began swirling the water
round and round in the tub, saying below her breath, "The
horrors of the maelstrom," and pretending that a little ship,
the size of a peanut shell, full of despairing pinhead sailors,
was whirling round and round, nearer and nearer to the fatal
dark siren dint in the middle of the whirl.

"Tck tck!" said Katya, and, pushing Tatiana aside, she

plunged an armful of soapy linen into the water, instantly
calming the cyclone. "Now please, Tatiana Pavlovna, don't
waste time, but help me with the rinsing. It will be dark in
half an hour."

Tatiana began thoughtfully steeping the linen in the
water, pulling it, plunging it slowly, letting the white spines
of linen hems come to the surface here and there like slow
porpoises.

"Where is Piotr Gavrilovitch?" asked Katya.

"He is gone."

"Gone for good?"

"Going for good."

"Well, Tatiana Pavlovna, I hope you are properly proud
of yourself — emptying this village completely of its young
men. Piotr Isaev was the last. Now they are all gone. Seven
Russian boys came over in our party from Vladivostok when
we all settled here in Mi-san, and now they are all gone,
thanks to you. In my young days a pretty girl had all the
young men from miles around coming round her like wasps
round honey; she didn't drive them away as though she were
a bad smell."

"Some young woman somewhere's the better for each of
these goings-away of young men," said Tatiana in a high
voice. "Seven pots of honey somewhere have one bad smell
in Mi-san to thank for their seven wasps."

She had no defense against Katya's talk. Katya could not
help vomiting spiteful talk, thought Tatiana. One had to
forgive other people with weak stomachs, even if they disgusted one — so why not Katya's surfeit and indigestion of
crude words?

"It's no good pretending you don't care," went on Katya.
"No young girl wants to be an old maid. That's what you'll
be, Tatiana Pavlovna — a finicky old maid, whining over a
fat cat. Look at you now — left alone — not another young
man of your own race within a hundred miles. What do you

want to do about it — marry a smelly Korean or a Japanese shopkeeper who doesn't come up to your elbow and blows wind through his teeth? Do you like the idea? What's the matter with you that all the young men run away at the last minute? It's a disgrace to this house, I assure you. I've known you almost as long as your mother has, and I can tell you it keeps me awake of nights. The disgrace of it. It's not natural. Young men didn't run away from me, I can tell you, when I was a pretty girl. Of course, after I'd borne seven children and buried five and lost my figure, that was a different matter. Men always run away from a red nose and three hundred pounds of flesh — it's their nature. But from a pretty girl — that's not nature, Tatiana Pavlovna, there's something funny about that."

Tatiana did not speak. She tried to make a loud secret story inside her mind to drown Katya's voice. She pretended, as she wrung out the linen, that she was a hero, after a shipwreck, saving the drowning, applying artificial respiration. She did not know what artificial respiration was, but amused herself a little by pretending it was rather like this wringing process. Here, she thought, picking up one of her father's thick unbleached nightgowns — here was a fat old rich Jew all sodden and limp, and here she folded him up and twisted him round, wringing, jerking, laughing as she thought of his dignity all mixed up and intertwisted, his nose and his toes, his eyeglasses and his ankles, all in a little buckled salutary wet lump, being saved by her — and then, shake, flap — there he was, the old moneygrubber, flat, bloodless, and pale, but almost his own shape again, the light evening wind blowing him out as she ran him up on the clothes-line.

"What do you think women are for?" went on Katya, gasping and wheezing as she pounded and wrung. "What do you think men want of women? Pretty talk — poetry — sitting side by side and looking at stars? Why, my girl, I can tell you men wouldn't mind if women were dumb and imbecile, as long as the women could give them the one thing they want. I'll tell you what marriage is, Tatiana Pavlovna — it's just getting out of bed, cooking three meals, and getting back into bed again. Women can't run away from that — unless they're nuns. There's nothing makes a man so angry as a woman who plays the coward in bed — nothing else that a woman can do can hurt his feelings at all, except, perhaps, bad cooking. It makes a man mad for a woman not to know her duty; it's like stabbing him — it turns his love to bile. Love, indeed! . . . Why that's what love is — just the hope of going to bed together. But running away from fate is what you're doing, Tatiana Pavlovna, and I'm telling you for your good."

Tatiana had been pounding one pillow-case ever since she saved the scorned Jew. It was an old pillow-case and now she suddenly pounded a hole in it.

"Why, you ought to have been proud to be wanted by all those fine young men," persisted Katya, in a grinding voice. "A thin, white little thing like you — and all the good red-blooded Russian wenches that have to shrivel up as virgins, these days, or sleep with yellow men. God knows Piotr Isaev was no catch for your father's daughter, and he a common gardener's son; still, he was a man — the last man in Mi-san — and now he's turned his back on you. You ought to be ashamed, breaking your father's and mother's hearts by your whimsies."

"Real people like to be nagged at," thought Tatiana. "Nagged at by love and other things — asked and asked to give something. Only hills and rivers and flowers and animals are allowed to be free — not to ask for anything. The more you ask of people the more sure they feel that they are people. It's their *me* — to be nagged at. I don't ask for anything, so I'm not allowed to be alive. I'll be kind to them — I'll cry for them — I'll laugh for them — I'll pretend I'm them — but people don't want that; they want to claw my *me* and they want me to claw theirs. Not to nag is to insult them."

She saw little circles in outline, flying about on blankness, each circle trying to pursue, attack, overlap and obliterate another. Whenever one circle succeeded in overlapping another, the area of their intersection was suffused with black; the words *wicked black* formed in her mind. No circle seemed content to let its outline rest coolly on another's — to admit another's integrity. Black trespass was the inspiration of all.

"It's something not natural in you; it's like a devil in you," said Katya. "A devil sticking a knife into men's stomachs. It's like killing something — to scream and faint and kick up a fuss when a man offers to give you — all he has to give, poor beast. A man feels killed. It's as if you'd killed those seven lovers of yours, Tatiana Pavlovna."

"Yet they're not dead. They're offering it to some one else by now," thought Tatiana. "And I'm alive, too." Then that thought broke. "But *am* I? Am I? Is this a life — this seeing — this thinking for caterpillars and men? If in the morning I was hanging from a branch of that tree there, would there be one life less in the world — or only a pair of eyes shut for good? Where is Tanya — washing clothes — hanging from a tree? Tanya the nothing — who by her nothingness killed seven loves and broke the hearts of her father and mother. . . ."

And then, thinking of lovers, she saw the circles trespassing more and more within one another's outlines till some wholly covered others, each couple becoming one black circle. Her brain began to freeze. A high throbbing note began to sound in her ears. All the hills began rolling slowly on an upward slant behind the darkening window of her eyes.

"Katya! Katya!"

"Oh, little fool! Oh, my darling! Katya's coming!" cried the old woman, running towards her.

CHAPTER FIVE

SERYOZHA LAY in bed in his little room, which was just an oblong bite taken out of the kitchen. His bed was the original *kang* of this Korean house — a brick-and-plaster oven. On it — since it was summer — were spread all the winter quilts and blankets to intervene between Seryozha's heavy young bones and the hard *kang*. The colder it grew in autumn, the more quilts were taken from beneath his body to be placed above it. Seryozha always connected winter with heavy dreaming, since at that season he always had to sleep flat on his back to save his hip bones from contact with the almost unpadded heated *kang*. But now, in summer, there were three quilts beneath him, and Seryozha could lie comfortably on his side, bent into the shape of a query mark, glaring at the window. The window, carved by Anna long ago with a blunt saw out of the boards of the outer wall, was high up in the corner made by the flimsy kitchen partition and the ceiling. It was very crooked. Anna was, in all her contrivings, too ardent ever to measure things. "I work by eye only," she would boast, triumphantly daring you to make the obvious retort as she flaunted her results all askew.

Seryozha glared at the window till the foolish, crooked

block of sunny morning light printed itself on his retina, so that when his eye wandered, a black crooked window was stamped all over the room. He was so full of angry single-hearted determination that, as he clenched his teeth, he felt as if his burning self, pregnant with its passion to get its own way, was too big for his skin; he had to keep his aching jaws and the smarting muscles round his eyes locked against its rising, bursting growth. There seemed to be a kind of explosion impending of swelling, thwarted will.

"Kept at home like a little schoolboy," he thought, tears of irritation squeezing out of the corners of his eyes. Seoul, the city denied, rose like a palace before him. He thought of his mother in a distorted paroxysm of anger. Her ungainliness, her uncontrolled loud voice, her dusty abundant hair, her thick ankles, the hiccoughs that afflicted her when she was agitated — all made her a hateful effigy in his mind, into which he stuck pins of impotent protest.

He felt alternately rooted to this unloved little house — and far away, walking heroically along a resilient bright road — stopping where he liked — getting wet when he liked — never having to argue — kicking the behinds of rude little Chinese boys — buying sweets and cigarettes recklessly — banging his stick against trees with a various resonance — lighting little fires at the feet of fantastic rocks. Then suddenly — zip — his future telescoped, his traveling thoughts were snatched back to reality — back to prison, as the Reverend Mr. Butters's pincenez, when he let them go, were snatched back to concealment by a spring under his lapel.

Seryozha's dog, with a coarse, confident scratch born of long habit, threw open the latchless door from the kitchen and came in. Seeing Seryozha awake, the dog began to curtsy, to make a little falsetto humming noise through its nose, to wag about two-thirds of its spine — from shoulder-blades to tail tip — as it waltzed about the floor, never taking its eyes from Seryozha's face. Seryozha glared at the dog,

making no answer to its extravagant greeting. He was fond
of the dog, or rather, fundamentally accustomed to it; he
felt as if the dog were part of himself, so it never occurred
to him to be responsive or polite to it. Sometimes, to the
dog's rapturous delight, he swung it about by the teeth, or
threw it violently across the room in a frenzy of joviality.
But today he stared moodily through it, and the dog, though
experience had not given it much ground for hope, redoubled its efforts. It reared itself delicately up and planted
one tentative paw on the edge of the kang, swishing its tail
wildly from side to side. No protest, no encouragement. It
stretched its neck shyly forward and lightly licked the tip of
Seryozha's nose. As if this chaste kiss — like the prince's kiss
on the lips of the Sleeping Beauty — had called the dormant
energies of the prostrate god into action, Seryozha suddenly
sat up, and his bare leg, swinging out of bed with a scythe-
like action, cut down the erect figure of the dog as though it
had been a swathe of corn. Seryozha had heard through the
door left open by the dog's exuberant entrance sounds of
some one in the kitchen. He could begin worrying his
mother again. The impotent watches of the night were past.

The dog picked itself up, pleased. For it, too, the day had
begun. It began scratching its mastoid energetically.

Seryozha pulled on his trousers, wriggled his blouse over
his head, and, while still buckling his belt, was in the kitchen, glaring across the table at his mother.

Anna, dressed in a cotton underbodice that much ac-
centuated her stout flabby bust, a crocheted shawl, and a
thick crimson flounced petticoat, was sitting at the table,
playing patience. She looked up, a little abashed, as Seryozha
came in, and mumbled in tones that sank lower and lower,
"I was looking through the cupboard for that bar of wash-
ing-soap — I am sure I did not use it up; it is somewhere, I
know — and I came across the old pack of cards and I
thought I would try if I could remember that game that

Mrs. Atkinson . . ." Her voice faded away into a deep growling, "The four on the five and then the king goes up. . . ."

Her son's cold eye was fixed upon her in disgust. "Mamma, about the matter we were talking of last night," he cried, hoarsely. He had been rehearsing arguments during the small hours; they had seemed irresistible at the time, but now they eluded him.

"What were we talking of last night?" asked Anna, a mulish look coming over her face. She added, "And then the red nine on the black ten."

"Mamma, it isn't fair. . . . I'm a man now. . . . Mamma, remember I am in my nineteenth year. . . . You don't realize. . . . Look at the way I arranged things with the Chinese when papa was away . . . did I behave like a child then? And now, when it is simply a matter of a little business journey . . ."

"It is useless to go on talking like this, Seryozha. You and your father must have lost your wits, to have such an idea. Walking all alone to Seoul. What an idea! Why, you can't even walk from here to Erh-tao-kou without getting into a fight with Chinese coolies. . . . And it isn't age that makes any difference. Your father's as big a fool as you are, and God knows *he's* old enough to know better."

"But, mamma, I have admitted that *that* was a folly — it was papa's idea, and I protected him as far as I could. You said yourself at the time. . . . And look at those men we buried that day — soldiers — officers — and one of them looked younger than I am. *Their* mothers . . ." For a moment he thought enviously of the countless orphans of the revolution. Probably those dead soldiers had no mothers. "At any rate, that fight was, I admit, a stupid business — a whim of papa's. This Seoul idea is a real business matter."

"A pretty business matter," said Anna, sweeping her cards violently together, making a sort of splash of cards. "A very pretty business matter — taking a three weeks' holiday from your good regular work in order to wander off to ask an old rogue for some money your father lent him ten years ago. A likely thing, isn't it? . . . And even if you got the money, how long do you think you would keep such a sum? — thieves along every road and in every inn, and rogues and harlots always on the lookout for young fools like you. What about that five yen I gave you last Christmas to buy a boiler, and you spent it all on a present for that little brothel-grub, Sonia?"

"I was young then," said Seryozha, confused. "And in any case I give all the money I earn to you, so surely I have a right to spend five yen once in my life. However, I confess that I was mistaken in Sonia's character. It was a long time ago . . ."

Where were all the telling phrases that had filed so orderly through his mind in the dark clearness of the night?

"Mamma, another thing is . . ." He stopped distractedly. He had forgotten the other thing — all the other things.

"Well?"

Seryozha stamped his foot with an oath. He thought of the rather dashing, mocking, grown-up attitude he habitually maintained toward his father and mother, in his own eyes — and even, to some extent, in theirs. He remembered, in a rather glorified form, his conversation with his father about the two hundred yen. "My good papa, to leave two hundred yen in the hands of a probably dishonest and certainly incompetent peasant! Was that business-like?" . . . "Dear old man, do you mean rubles, dollars, or yen? I want to understand this matter thoroughly so that I can help you . . ." That was the proper tone — the usual tone. And now — "Oh, mamma — oh, please, mamma, let me go! . . . Really, mamma, do believe that I'm not a child any more. . . ." Poor Seryozha, he felt robbed of something that he violently resented losing — a king robbed of his

crown and suddenly made a beggar. He began to despair.
Never had the journey to Seoul seemed more necessary to
his happiness than at that moment. Then suddenly, with a
sort of artificial revulsion of feeling, he let it go. The only
thing left, then, was not to want to go — to want not to go.
Not only to cease pleading, but to be actually glad that he
was not going on a hot, dusty journey among silly, whining,
flapping Koreans. By ceasing to want to go he could get even
with his mother, he could save his self-esteem. Even if his
mother were to implore him to go now, he would refuse.
"Too much trouble, mamma," he rehearsed inwardly in a
languid, superior, secret voice. "And nothing to show for it
in the end. You and papa would waste the money on mud-
dles and follies, even if I were to get it for you."

He looked round with a cold, critical look, collecting evidence of his parents' inferiority, in order to comfort himself. Anna had upset a saucepan full of greasy water in the
corner near the stove, and, since the mud floor was slightly
concave, a long dark snake of water stretched slowly toward
the middle of the kitchen. There was no neatness anywhere.
The edge of the window — now hanging open on limp
home-made hinges — was tattered with the strips of paper
that in winter had been pasted round the edges of the panes
to keep out the cold. The wall was all mottled with damp
patches; a great marbled shape of damp had been there for
years, and, in Seryozha's unconsciously ingenious eyes, represented a woman in a flying cloak reaching for a great flying rose. She had three arms, to be sure, but you can't expect nature's artistic by-products to be so accurate as all
that. . . .

Poor Seryozha bit his lips and sucked them in as he turned
away to stare moodily down at his dog. The dog would have
enjoyed the walk to Seoul; they would have been like two
parts of the same Seryozha — one part walking proudly, the
other part leaping, blowing in the wind, barking at larks,

scratching at rat-holes, drinking puddles. . . . However, Seryozha thought, I wouldn't go now if I were asked. Certainly the dog would have had a good time. But a man can't take a three weeks' walk simply to please a dog.

The dog lay in a curve on the floor. Evidently some other dog—probably its last lady-love—was thinking of it, for its ear itched—the traditional symptom. It wriggled and wagged its ear repeatedly. Its eyes were open. It liked the sound of voices. That damn goat, too, was somewhere else. Everything seemed to the dog to be going nicely.

Anna squeezed her face into an upside-down isosceles triangle between her hands, her elbows pressed on the table among the cards. She looked at her son, restless with pity for him, as he stood staring down at the dog, raising his eyebrows in childish and studied indifference, shuffling his toe, pretending to tread on the dog's tail. She would make him some curd cakes this afternoon; he loved those. Perhaps she could afford that Brownie kodak in the Japanese shop, if she did without her new dress length. After all, he gave her almost all his earnings. It never occurred to her to relent on the Seoul question. All the dangers that lurked for him outside her sight accumulated round the very thought of the ridiculous journey—brigands, swindlers, earthquakes and other convulsions of nature, tigers, brothels, Japanese policemen, prisons, diseases, drownings in rivers. . . . Seryozha would have been a super-boy to have suffered even a third of them in three weeks. But Anna's imagination was always over-exuberant. She did not follow up her fears at all because —well, simply, he was not going to Seoul. Curd cakes and perhaps a kodak for him. Still, the sight of his tremulous eyebrows and pursed lips made her throat ache with pity.

Old Sergei felt his way in at the door. "No breakfast yet?" he exclaimed in an unusually high sweet voice. "Ah well, these glorious summer days tempt one to procrastinate. . . ." It was at once obvious that today he was The

Perfect Christian; serenity was the password of the moment.
Anna and Seryozha were to realize that they had an afflicted
saint in their midst. He had had slight qualms in the night,
thinking that, if he were really to die, Anna in her present
mood would be but a tearless widow and Seryozha an all too
resilient orphan.

The kid bleated outside in the shed. The dog mumbled a
growl of jealous irritation into its own tail as it lay sleepily
curved in a bar of sunlight.

"And the little goat?" asked Old Sergei with a sugared
playfulness. "The most important member of the household? Did it sleep well? Has it breakfasted?"

With a loud crude snort, Anna rose and began slamming
down bread, cups, knives, and spoons on the bare table
among the playing-cards. Old Sergei sat down at the foot of
the table. His thin, gaunt hands, like little wan giraffes striding, patted about among the cards. "Playing cards before
breakfast? Well, well, well! . . ." he said in a voice of resignation, but with an effort made no complaining comment.
"If we had money," he added, "we could allow ourselves,
perhaps, a little Korean girl as servant. But I dare say you
are right, Annitchka my dove, in thinking that we are best
as we are—without the money I left with Isaev in Seoul.
Of course the interest would have mounted up very considerably in ten years—but as you say, Annitchka, what is
money? Poverty is nothing, as long as we have love and
peace in our home. It was only for your sake and Seryozha's
that I thought of it. You are not so young as you were, and
I thought a little maidservant. . . . However, it is not
to be."

"It certainly is not," said Anna, who had never appreciated the effective weight of silence as an argument. "The
child is most certainly not going to Seoul by himself, so you
had better give up the idea."

An almost agonizing pang went through Seryozha as he

heard this, but he thought, "If they only knew — I wouldn't go now, even if they went down on their knees to me. Probably I shall run away altogether; they can expect nothing better, treating me as they do. But certainly I will not do their fetching and carrying, either to Seoul or anywhere else."

"Did you not hear me say, my dove, that I *had* given up the idea?" said Old Sergei, gently. "I am only explaining to you now, in retrospect, what my idea had been. I had not, of course, thought of sending the child unprotected. If you are a mother, dearest Annitchka, remember that I am a father, and Seryozha's safety is as much my preoccupation as yours. I had thought of looking for some trustworthy fellow — a superior coolie — who for a small wage——"

"If he found an angel from God to go with him," said Anna raucously, "I might let him go. Short of that . . ." Seryozha, who actually stood before her nearly six feet tall and with a slight shimmer of very young beard on his pink cheeks, was shrinking in her imagination with every word of the discussion. He had now almost got back to the weaning stage, and she saw a flashing picture of one of God's angels pushing her baby away from her in a pram.

"An angel from God, Seryozha," said Old Sergei, whimsically and plaintively. "You will have to look long to find an angel from God willing to protect a poor Russian. Poor Russians indeed! God has forgotten them — he sends no angels now. . . . But of course, my dear," he interrupted himself, cooing, as he turned to Anna, "I was not insisting on the boy's taking the journey. I had only referred to the fact that it had been for your sake I had entertained the idea. The money would have been useful to you rather than to me. A little maidservant . . . an oil stove instead of that mud oven. . . . Such things would have made life easier for you — given you leisure, perhaps, to play cards in the mornings instead of troubling about your husband's breakfast. Poverty and discomfort wear out even the most devoted. . . . For myself, why should I mind? I have not long to live in this world . . . an old blind man on the brink of the grave has no temptation to think of himself."

"Why don't you write for the money? If Isaev is really willing to repay it, he could send it."

"You do not understand the ins and outs of the affair, dear Annitchka. How should you — a trusting, sweet-hearted woman like yourself? It is for the head of the family to wrestle with such sordid problems — to protect those he loves from the miseries of ——"

"I don't want any breakfast," said Seryozha, suddenly. "And I shall not go to work today. My back aches. I am going out."

His dog, as ready for its call as a good fireman, reached the door as soon as he did. Their shadows merged in a muddle of wagging, striding black and white at the door. Seryozha and the dog stood together in the doorway, looking out at the bright day.

Anna looked at Seryozha and felt, on his behalf, an elaborate fanciful female version of the boy's impotent disappointment. She sat hacking violently at the bread, muttering and hiccoughing to herself, clapping her knees together under her absurd petticoat. She was always hurting some one, she thought, making some mistake or being obliged to correct some one else's mistake in a painful way. She so seldom managed to feel that she was giving satisfaction; wherever she went she imagined people thinking, "Why doesn't Anna . . . ? Why does Anna . . . ? If it weren't for Anna. . . ." She felt that she had been endowed with a superfluity of power to hurt and thwart people. Curd cakes and a kodak would be nothing but a bribe to her son —a bribe to persuade him to overlook her accursed genius for being an obstacle.

"I'm making some curd cakes for tea," she said in a

defiant cross voice toward her son's defiant cross back in the doorway.

"I don't like curd cakes. I was sick last time I ate your curd cakes," said Seryozha. Simply because he had loved curd cakes as a child, he thought, she retained her obsession that they were a poultice for all the austere wounds of his maturity.

He walked away into the wide, straggling, pitted street. His dog burst out of the yard like a torpedo and exploded in facetious barkings at the tail of the debased but nimble Korean dog that lived next door. The Korean dog had such short legs that they were little more than four bumps on its lower corners — nevertheless, it fled with the lowly agility of a lizard. Seryozha's dog walked with the stiffness of pride for a few minutes after that, and followed its master to the river.

The river was crossed by a wooden bridge with a sort of petticoat of dog-toothed wooden frill prudishly concealing the upper part of its piers. This decoration showed that it was a Russian-built bridge, and, in fact, Seryozha's own hands had sawed and planed some of its planks. One could not say, however, that it was well built. A Russian refugee, a military engineer, a heroic but untrustworthy creature, had contracted for and designed the work only the year before, and now the thing was, unfortunately, tumbling down. The Chinese local authorities did not mind very much; they were well used to things tumbling down immediately after they were finished. Obstinately proud, therefore, of their petticoated but frail bridge, they quite cheerfully paid for endless pinnings together, proppings up and general coddlings of their treasure. At present the river was in flood, and logs rushing down the swollen stream from far lumber camps were a constant menace to the knock-kneed piers of the bridge, so, clinging to the toe of every pier, a coolie sat, chivalrously pushing fierce logs away with a pole. Wher-

ever one person is found doing something definite in China,
there also are found a score of people watching him do it.
The sagging balustrade of the bridge was lined with shaven
heads bending over to watch the defense against the blun-
dering attack of the logs.

Seryozha thrust himself into this line of watchers, his
strong square shoulders and forearms wedged between two
skinny Chinese torsos. Seryozha's dog swaggered along the
line of human behinds and calves, sniffing lightly at each leg,
as if playing with the idea of biting a piece out of one —
though of course it had too sacred a respect for the integrity
of human skin actually to lift a tooth against it. Still, it
would be a damn good joke, thought the dog, opening and
shutting its nose jovially against one calf after another.

Next to Seryozha a young Chinese in European clothes
lolled superciliously over the balustrade. This young man
had a nose that sprang abruptly like a little eagle's beak
from a flatness between very bright black eyes. He lifted his
rather negroid upper lip often to show one sparkling gold
tooth in the middle of a row of ordinary yellow bone ones.
On the top of his very thick, coarse, carefully parted black
hair a too small Panama hat cocked a flaunting brim, and
round the crown of the hat a ribbon showed what may well
have been a medley of the colors of Eton, one of the more
refined cycling clubs, and the Salvation Army. The young
man had a very lively, acute expression, in spite of his deliberate attitude of scorn, and from the moment when
Seryozha settled his elbows on the adjoining yard of balustrade, the sparkling lidless eyes of the young Chinese never
left the Russian's face.

"You speak English?" said the stranger to Seryozha.

For a moment Seryozha, who was in a very bad temper,
considered ignoring the remark. He spoke fairly fluent English, taught by his Anglophil mother, and often used that
language with her to annoy his father by shutting him out

from jokes or secrets. He glowered at the stranger and then, struck in his tender heart by the look of polite confident expectancy on the face of the Chinese, he said, "I speak English—not much, but enough."

"I could see at once you were not English, of course," said the young man. "You are Russian. I could not, of course, make a mistake on a thing like that. Yet, since I speak no Russian and you, probably, no Cantonese dialect, I thought I was perhaps justified in addressing you in English. I was right. Allow me to introduce myself—Mr. Wilfred Chew—Chu Wei-fu."

He watched closely for Seryozha's bow, but Seryozha's large untutored body knew none of these graces. Seryozha simply looked at the Chinese with a cold rather stolid intensity, his mouth a little open, his fingers drumming rather impudently on the wooden rail in front of him. Mr. Chew himself bowed, therefore, once for Seryozha and once for himself. He was evidently a young man who never spared himself this kind of effort.

"I myself speak English quite perfectly," he said. "I have lived in England for many years—in London, to be exact, as a law student. I am now qualified to practice as a barrister. I could have made a fortune in London in the law, I dare say. But I am not the kind of man who deserts his country. I am Chinese. I am not ashamed of being Chinese. On the contrary. I therefore return to China to lay my services at her feet."

"Oi-oi!" said Seryozha. He had never heard the English tongue spoken so fast—or through a gold tooth. The combination of speed and sparkle he found intriguing but bewildering.

"Russians," went on Mr. Chew, "are a people of very striking intelligence, influence, and—in short, a people full of soul. Nevertheless, in Canton, my native city, I must confess that, from the point of view of an English trained professional man like myself, the Russian influence seems perhaps not altogether —— Excuse me, sir, what are your politics?"

"Politics?" squeaked Seryozha. "Oi! I am sorry, I am not a political person."

"No politics? Well, of course, my dear Mr. — er — I sympathise with your point of view. It shows intelligence. Living in a foreign land as your business evidently obliges you to do, you feel, very reasonably, that you cannot sufficiently keep in touch with the conflicting ideas that followed upon the Russian revolution — that the Bolshevik theory, interesting though it may be ——"

"Eh — *Bolshevik!*" said Seryozha. "I mistook. I thought you have said *politics*. Eh no, of course, my family is a very White Russian family — most White indeed."

"I thought so. I was right. Well, as I was saying, the Bolsheviks have made Canton, my native city, a quite impossible place for a man like myself to conduct a career in. They are called 'bloody Bolshies,' you know, sir, in London — and truly it is so. Shanghai is almost as bad, and — to make a long story short ——"

"You cannot," said Seryozha, who had been listening intently.

"Cannot what?"

"You cannot make a long story now short. It is too late. The story already is long. Though very interesting," he added politely, seeing the expression of poor Mr. Chew's face.

Wilfred Chew swallowed twice, with two little clicks, and his face looked suddenly childishly abashed and disappointed. One thin eyebrow puckered and rose high, as if that eye were trying to say, "Well, *I* at least don't care . . ."

"Ah," said Mr. Chew, and was silent, trying to be brave.

They leaned on the balustrade side by side, watching in silence the logs coming down in a disorderly scattered charge. Every approaching log was announced to the bridge's defenders by a roar of warning from the spectators. Logs that traveled meekly endways were allowed to pass under the bridge unmolested, with a ready pole held hoveringly over them at the crucial moment, or, if they steered too close to a pier, a light kick from a coolie's bare outstretched foot. But other logs, broadside on to their course, rolled clumsily down the muddy stream like rolling pins on yellow flour, and these, to the tune of howls of advice and applause, were deftly turned and steered under the bridge by the poles of the coolies. In the full central flow of the current, the logs rushed down like dragons to the attack. But near the banks of the river they traveled sleepily, even occasionally making long waltzing pauses in quiet eddies. These more dilatory attackers exerted a fascination for not too scrupulous citizens. Somehow, out of a group of logs that remained too long in harbor, one or two were likely never to put to sea again. All the cottages near by had the smoke of a good supply of firewood rising out of their chimneys, and one householder was frankly building a new bullock-shed of damp planks.

Seryozha's dog squeezed itself between Seryozha and Wilfred Chew and, putting both paws on a horizontal rail below the balustrade, leaned out intelligently to watch the doings on the river. It barked once or twice in rather an affected voice, and then, deciding that it had shown all the interest that it could be expected to show in an almost smell-less entertainment, went away to talk with a group of farm dogs outside an inn near by.

Seryozha was uncomfortable about this deathlike silence in his right ear. He disliked the feeling of snubbing or interrupting anything. He obscurely wanted things to go on happily by themselves — puppies to go on playing, suns to go on rising and setting, flowers to go on growing, babblers to go on babbling. . . . Of course, killing animals was different. Killing was part of the game of life that had a right to go on. Killing was allowed but snubbing was not.

"And London?" he said, in a grumbling, ungracious voice. "It is a good city?"

"London," said Mr. Chew instantly, as if a cork had been pulled out, "is not, conventionally speaking, perhaps, a beautiful city. There are fogs and a great many rains. Westminster Abbey, the Tower of London, Buckingham and Saint James's Palaces, Madame Tussaud's, the Nelson lions, Selfridge's, and the home of the late Charles Dickens — all these are sublime structures and, what is very odd, the dirtiness of the London air and light makes their color beautiful, streaky, and fitting with their surroundings. If, however, by the word good you perhaps mean to refer to morality, it is certainly a fact, Mr. — er —, that the London streets are full of moral dangers for a young man. Luckily for me, I was very carefully educated in the Christian principles at the Wesleyan Academy at Yueh-lai-chou, where I studied in my boyhood. The second master, namely Reverend Mr. Oswald Fawcett, has been the good influence on my life. He well prepared me for the temptations of life in a great city, and so I may say that I passed unscathed through the fire."

"Oi-oi!" said Seryozha, putting a careful note of enthusiasm into the ejaculation this time. "And I think there is very many motor-cars in London."

"How many are there in Chi-tao-kou?"

"I think five, not speaking about Mr. Chang's motor-bicycle."

"There are probably a thousand times as many in London. Motor-cars are undoubtedly among the dangers of the streets in London. But I was referring to moral dangers — wine, women, song——"

"We too have singing girls in Chi-tao-kou. Even one Russian one called Sonia Matvievna."

"I dare say you have. But singing girls mean nothing to me. I take morals and religion very seriously, you see, Mr. —er—. . . . *Ethics*, as we call them in London. Reverend Mr. Fawcett used always to say, 'One can have a good time—God likes us to have a good time—but it should be God's brand of good time.' I always think of those words when I am in a moral danger. 'Is this God's brand of good time?' I say to myself, silently. 'No, it is Satan's brand.' So I say, 'Get behind.'"

"Tck tck!" clicked Seryozha, shaking his head ambiguously as it sank lower and lower between his hunched shoulders.

"You are asking yourself," continued Mr. Chew, "what is this man Chew, a barrister from the Middle Temple, London, E. C. 4., and a Christian of devout morality, doing in a little halfpenny-farthing town like Chi-tao-kou? And you may well ask, Mr. —er——"

"Very well indeed," said Seryozha.

"The truth is that, under the present confused regime in China, aggravated by 'bloody Bolshies' (as Londoners say), it is extremely difficult for a highly educated member of the Middle Temple, called to the bar in London, and, until recently, the devil of Mr. W. I. Morgan, the renowned barrister, to get a living out of practising law in Shanghai or Canton. I therefore engaged myself, temporarily, in other employment—that is, I have been acting as companion, philosopher, and friend (professional) to a young gentleman called *Sir* Theo Mustard, whose late father was a millionaire in Leeds, England, and whose uncle, now guardian, sent his charge to see the world, expense no object. I must admit that *Sir* Theo Mustard is not perhaps altogether fortunate—or even normal—in mental equipment, and only occasionally showed a keen interest in the

79

beauty spots to which I guided him. We traveled to the
Yangtze gorges; to Nanking; to the Holy Mountain; to the
model prison, Peking; to call on the Governor of Mukden;
to the Chinese drama; to spend one week in Seoul; to the
Kongo-san; and finally I escorted him, with valet, to the
train in Harbin which will carry him to Berlin. In Harbin
Sir Theo Mustard and I parted with mutual expressions of
good will and——"

"To Seoul?" exclaimed Seryozha.

"Yes, Seoul, a fine old-world city, called by some the
Peking of Korea. Of course my professional escort was paid
for with a very handsome salary, but, most unfortunately,
I received bad advice about investments in Harbin, and,
to make a long—I mean—in short, I found myself
stranded in Manchuria with scarcely a——"

"You have been to Seoul?"

"Yes, I have told you. I went to Seoul with Sir Theo
Mustard and spent there a very enjoyable week, since there
Sir Theo Mustard was afflicted with ear-ache, which obliged
us to stay longer in that picturesque old capital than we had
intended. The ear-ache arose, I think, from an otherwise
most successful afternoon we spent in the Seoul museum.
It made a great impression on Sir Theo Mustard, for he
several times referred to Seoul by name, even after we had
reached Harbin——"

"Do you know the way from here to Seoul?"

"Certainly I do. I have a great gift for studying maps,
railway guides, and other schedules, and in Nanking I was
able to show Sir Theo Mustard a chart showing our exact
future movements — times of trains — expeditions — names
of hotels — curio-shops, etcetera — foreshadowing every detail up to the last moment of the trip. Of course it was impossible for me to anticipate the ear-ache, but apart from
this——"

"Will you please come with me and visit my mother

and my father to tell them about Seoul?" asked Seryozha.

They both stepped backward from the balustrade with such alacrity that they trod on two bare Chinese feet on tiptoe behind them.

"Certainly I will come and visit anybody," said Mr. Chew. "As soon as I saw your face, Mr. — er —, I felt we should be friends. I was right."

"Have you met a gentleman called Gavril Ilitch Isaev in Seoul?" asked Seryozha breathlessly, as they walked side by side up the street.

"Isaev? He keeps a small but respectable hotel in Seoul, and, curiously enough, I stayed there for a night or two, since the Japanese hotel was full when we first arrived — or rather, it had only one suite disengaged, which was occupied by *Sir* Theo Mustard and valet."

Seryozha's dog bounced into Anna's kitchen, and when Anna saw it, she thought, "Thank God, he has not gone away forever, after all."

"Mamma," said Seryozha, "I have brought Mr. Wilfred Chew from London."

"From London?" exclaimed Anna, and instantly left the room. For she was still wearing only her cotton bodice and petticoat, and there was a bottle-green velvet dress, sixteen years old, waiting in a tin trunk for just such an occasion as this.

She took twenty minutes dressing herself and frizzing her hair, and as — self-conscious, hopeful, and flushed — she came to the open door of the living-room, she stood for a moment outside and heard her husband saying to Seryozha in Russian: "Tell him politely that we are poor and could not possibly afford two yen a day above his keep. But tell him that he shall share and share alike with you — he shall be treated, in fact, like my own son, in addition to a little salary of twenty-five sen a day ——"

Anna tightened her lips and came in. She was flattered

and astonished to see the brightening of Mr. Chew's smooth, mobile face as he saw her.

"Ah, Mrs. Malinin, I presume," he said. "It has seemed long waiting for you, but ladies must be waited for—I remember this in London. I am so interested to hear that you also know London. I have been for four years a law student in London—Middle Temple . . . you of course know Middle Temple—and I was called to the bar there eight months ago."

"Ah yes, the bar of London," said Anna, eagerly. "I am very ignorant of most London matters, but I know of course there are many bars."

Mr. Chew accepted this innocent remark as a joke so readily that it might almost have been guessed that he had made it himself more than once. When he smiled, Anna noticed his solitary gold tooth and thought that it looked like the royal box glittering in the middle of the row of ordinary boxes at the opera. So she said: "And the opera of London—oh, how happily I remember it! I have been to the opera four times with a lady called Honorable Mrs. Atkinson—there has been 'Siegfried'—'The Valkyrie'—'Magic Flute' and 'La Bohême.'"

"I also knew a family called Atkinson," said Wilfred Chew. "Edward F. Atkinson, but I don't like him much—such a conceited chap—I worked in the chambers on the same stairs for four months and he scarcely spoke . . . simply because he was the son of a solor—naturally anybody could get briefs in such circumstances——"

"To me," said Anna, after a partially smothered hiccough which showed how deeply excited she was, "the scenery of the opera is very, very happy, Mr. Chew—in such scenery one has never been so unfortunate as to see all—do you understand?—there is always a round the corner or an over the hill which one has not seen. How very, very happy it is to me, to know that there has been a round the corner—

that I have not seen — even if it is only made with woods and paints. England, to me, Mr. Chew, is a big, big *round the corner.* . . . More happy than possible happiness — yes, no?"

"Now there," said Mr. Chew, "I should scarcely agree with you entirely, though of course I have had many happy hours in London. But to a young man carving out a career the work was often hard, Mrs. Malinin, and English people — with the exception of a gentleman like Reverend Mr. Oswald Fawcett — are nearly always snobs ——"

Anna, her burning eyes fixed upon his tooth, said: "Yes, yes, Mr. Chew. And the pillars of this opera-house — do you remember? — all gold and twisted — so" (for a moment she seemed to think that she could twist her fat upraised forefinger into an imitation of barley sugar) — "like . . . like . . . pillars of that thing — how do you call it? — horses-merrily-go-galloping-round on the Hampstead Heath. These go-rounds are very, very good things, I think, but Betti was being sick afterward in the hot tent."

Old Sergei and Seryozha sat back in their chairs, their hands folded across their diaphragms, proud of their wife and mother, listening hopefully to this loud and genial conversation, though they did not understand very much of it. During a short check, Old Sergei said in Russian, "My love, do you not think that Mr. Chew would be just the man to ——"

"Kensington Gardens, too, is good," said Anna, bounding in her chair. "Each day, at half past eleven, Betti and I have walked through the Kensington Gardens as far as Queen Cleopatra's Needle ——"

Wilfred Chew started as if stung. "There is some mistake, surely, Mrs. Malinin. Cleopatra's Needle is not in the Kensington Gardens."

"Yes. But yes. A little spike in the middle of the Kensington Gardens."

"This is the Albert Memorial."

"Tcht, Mr. Chew! King Albert's Memorial is very well known by me. I make no mistake. A very, very big spike — King Albert in middle — bull — elephant — lady at corners. It is all known by me."

"Nevertheless, Cleopatra's Needle is, beyond question, on the Embankment of the river Thames, Mrs. Malinin."

"Tcht, tcht!"

"Anna my dear," said Old Sergei. "It has just occurred to me that we might induce Mr. Chew——"

"But I *know* the Kensington Gardens very, very good, Mr. Chew. Each morning have I walked to that little spike, builded in a pink stone, very shining——"

"Ladies always know best, Mrs. Malinin," said Mr. Chew, archly. "But in this case——"

"Ah tschah! But I have *seen*——"

"Well, well . . . you ladies must have your own way. Reverend Mr. Fawcett used to say, 'Always allow a lady the courtesy of the last word, Wilfred.' So let us say Cleopatra's Needle had wings and flew every morning at half past eleven to the Kensington Gardens to make her bow to you, Mrs. Malinin."

Anna, only half understanding, rocked backward and forward in restored satisfaction, patting her fat knees with every forward swing. But as she did so she became secretly more and more doubtful of the accuracy of her memory of Cleopatra's Needle. Her pleased face clouded slowly as the doubt crystallized, her rocking was gradually braked and stilled by inward questionings. There was silence in the room.

"Annitchka my dove," said Old Sergei, rapidly, in Russian. "Mr. Chew has just come from acting as guide to a young English nobleman, and it has occurred to me that we might persuade him to look after our Seryozha on this trip down to Seoul——"

Anna sighed.

"I know you are not very anxious that he should go, my love, but Mr. Chew's fortunate arrival must surely alter your view to a certain extent. It almost seems as if he were sent by God to us in our difficulty. He actually knows Isaev — has been staying in his house. If I understand your conversation rightly, he seems to know your friends, the Honorable Atkinsons, in London, which must give you pleasure. Also, it seems to me very probable that he is of the same family as my old friend Colonel Chu Wen-chou (whose father came from Canton also, you remember) and——"

Wilfred Chew, listening with bland blankness to the Russian, caught the names. "Ha — Atkinson — Chu — Isaev — all this talk of families and mutual acquaintances. . . . I was telling your husband, Mrs. Malinin — (in joke, of course) — that he must remember that he is not seeking for a tribe or family to go with his son, but simply for a reliable companion — and *that*——"

"Oi, tcht!" said Seryozha in English. "Please let my papa be satisfied in the way he wishes. This talk of families is good talk for him — it makes him glad."

Anna sighed again, and heaved in her chair.

"It is natural," said Old Sergei, half apologetically, half reproachfully, "that I should be glad to find that my son's companion comes of an honest and good stock. I always respected Colonel Chu and, although his father came from Canton, the colonel was never seduced by Bolshevik influence, so rampant in that part of China. Anna my dove, I am sure you agree with me that, all things considered, this is an opportunity that should not be missed."

Anna's eyes were fixed on her son's face. Seryozha's mouth was open and his face, unusually pale, was lighted up with a half-incredulous hope. Anna imagined how that tense white look would crumple up at a word of discouragement from her. It would be like pricking his poor, silly, feverish, puffed-up heart. After all, why shouldn't he go? she thought, deliberately letting her rigid mind go limp. People went on such journeys and returned; and if their mothers had feared the worst for them beforehand, that in itself was a sort of insurance that the worst was not to be. She began looking forward to watching Seryozha's face, three minutes from now, when she should have said yes. Now she only uttered an ambiguous grunt.

"The only question is, the expense," said Old Sergei. He turned to Wilfred Chew and said in English, "We poor mans. Two yens every day too much. I pays twenty-five sens every day. Also I pays all foods and beds."

Wilfred Chew smiled engagingly and shrugged his shoulders, holding his head on one side. "Between gentlemen, Mr. Malinin, there should be no bargaining. But surely one yen a day, and all expenses, would not be too much to ask. You must remember that I am an educated chap — not a common vulgar guide, so to speak ——"

"*Speke!*" shouted Anna, a sudden glare of inspiration burning up the whole problem in her mind. "This spike in Kensington Gardens is called Speke's Needle."

"Ha — Speke!" said Mr. Chew, faintly, for he had been severely startled by his hostess's full-throated roar. "Ha! no doubt, yes . . . Speke's Needle. . . . A renowned judge, of course, Speke. . . ."

The discussion came to a standstill for a moment, but Anna, her mind now cleared of distractions, was her keen self again. "One yen a day we have not got," she said, abruptly. "You see, Seryozha, it is not your mother that prevents. The thing is not possible. You know yourself what we have and what we have not."

"Of course," said Old Sergei, in Russian. "If the interest on my two hundred yen should by now have reached a considerable sum, we should be able to afford to pay — say —

fifty sen a day now and, when the money was in our hands, give Mr. Chew something extra, proportionate to the services he will have rendered us."

"If there will be more money for us in Seoul," said Seryozha, to Chew in English, nerved by the crisis to speak thus crudely in spite of his shyness, before a young man so superior, "my father will give more money to you. He speak fifty sen a day *promise* — at the end more, perhaps."

"My salary for acting as escort to *Sir Theo Mustard* —" began Wilfred Chew. Then, as he saw a mulish finality written on the faces of all three Malinins, he added, "but there, life is full of such contrasts. I will escort your son for fifty sen a day and expenses, on the understanding that if he obtains the money with interest from Mr. Isaev, I can claim ten sen on every yen obtained over and above the two hundred yen."

"Well . . . Annitchka?" said Old Sergei, faintly.

"I should have to wash out all three of his shirts," said Anna, her eyes suddenly full of tears. "And I must have time to patch the knee of his best trousers. . . ."

Seryozha remembered one of his mother's English idioms. "Tschah! All this bibbing and tuckering . . ." he said. Then, with a loud creaking yell of joy, he rushed into his mother's arms.

CHAPTER SIX

SERYOZHA AND Wilfred Chew began their journey in a
happy sunlight swimming with swallows. Neither Seryozha
nor Wilfred saw the birds. And indeed, birds are transparent, I think, like the safe anonymous shapes of sheep on
hillsides or policemen at city crossings; these things are part
of fitness; they are so native to the air that they become
glass to the attention. An eagle is different, of course; no
one ever looks through an eagle; a piece of the sky is re-
served for him, and he moves into his place as a king moves
to his throne, with every eye upon him.

"I think it is three meters from this to that," said Seryozha, becoming for a moment an eagle, spreading his arms
to an imperial stretch and pointing his beak to the sun.
Unfortunately, his feet unexpectedly remained on earth and
tripped over a stone.

"Three meters is nothing for an eagle," said Wilfred, who
was thinking on rather a large scale today. He was feeling
exuberant because Anna had listened to him so gladly. Poor
Wilfred, everywhere a foreigner with too much to say,
living either with people who could not understand his
speech or with people who did not want to, might be said

to be the one lonely resident of a spiritual city of Babel. Not only was his world afflicted with a hopeless confusion of tongues, but also, the towers of elaborate talk he built, though always designed to reach heaven, only attained a level high enough to give him a depressing view of his audience scattering abroad beyond recall. But Anna had shown herself a sort of honorary compatriot in his lonely city; her understanding, linguistic and spiritual, had been perfect. She had spread herself like a desert, as it were, thirsty for the shadow of his high place. From time to time, to be sure, she had blossomed forth with some trivial and inadequate prattle about her own womanish conclusions and experiences; nevertheless, the atmosphere, on the whole, had been unusually *right*. Wilfred, that optimistic architect of battlemented follies, had been for once free of the feeling of straining to get his toppling themes buttressed up to some kind of completion in the presence of strangers either wholly untutored or else prepared for flight.

Wilfred and Seryozha felt as if they were walking backward for a moment as they compared their progress with the sweeping speed of the eagle's shadow across the valley. But they marched stoutly on. The river, broad, polished and set in a pale bed thinly shaded with pink-twigged osiers, ran beside them through the clear light. The whole broad valley was so clearly lighted by the white sun that every stone, tree, and village on the yellow-green mountains stood out with the flat significance of such details in a good nineteenth-century chromo-lithograph.

The colors of the Koreans' clothes were like bright pins all over the valley, catching at — almost scratching at — the indifferent sight. Koreans in Kanto are worn by custom to the same fine transparency as birds and other lovely and common furnishings of the scene; they are to the eye what the gentle ticking of a clock is to the ear. Yet today, since it was a Korean holiday, the Korean wanderers were so gayly dressed as to catch even an accustomed eye. Favorite colors were arsenic green, poison pink, apple green, and a cheap crude blue — all very unflower-like colors, yet they sowed the roads and fields and paths with an effect of flowers. The little Korean girls wore wide, semi-transparent, gaudy skirts hung from the shoulders by embroidered braces — and they wore nothing else. The little boys wore red-flowered silk Eton jackets ending abruptly at the fifth rib — and they wore nothing else. *Décolleté* for girls down to the waist — *dejambé* for boys up to the navel. In either case, if the purpose of clothes is to conceal, the purpose was most inadequately fulfilled; if the purpose is to decorate, decorated indeed the wearers were.

The distant paths, plaiting, splitting, and raveling like threads on the hillsides, invited the eye. Some paths look as if they lead away and never come back, but these paths, spotted with gay holiday-makers, seemed to lead *in* — to lead home — or, at least, to lead out into the flowery sunlight under promise of leading home again soon — home to nights of good food, good digestion, good sleep, and good wives. Comfortable little domestic paths, in spite of their dancing informality.

Round every Korean grave — each a mere bunker on a grass slope — a group of merry descendants chatted, laughed, and ate. It must be delightful for the dead to know that the grassy lumps beneath which their bones lie are rendezvous for joking, feasting friends — are just extensions of the scenes of their living hospitality, now made immortal like their souls. It must be good for the lonely dead to know that their names will never be a wet blanket on laughter and horseplay, and that once a year they may count on being hosts and householders once more.

"These heathens," said Wilfred Chew, "have no proper respect for the dead. They don't appreciate the awful position of a dead man after a life of heathenism and sin."

Seryozha thought a little. It always irritated him to hear any criticism of what was physically natural. "Let them be, let them be," he wanted to say. "Let them be — why — simply because they *are*." But he could not remember any English words that would express this feeling. "Nyet sin," he said, vaguely, waving his hand vaguely toward the sinner-speckled hills.

"You mean," said Wilfred, who always felt it was his business to explain to people what they meant, "that the heathen cannot help their dreadful darkened condition, if they have not been given any opportunity to see the light. But, Mr. Malinin, every heathen now, I believe, has heard the message of Christianity. Schools like the Wesleyan Academy at Yueh-lai-chou — though not all, perhaps, quite so excellent — are everywhere. Devoted teachers of the Word travel upon bicycles, donkeys, Ford's motor-cars, trains, junks, steamboats, and Peking carts in all directions among the heathen — though I admit that men of such great saintlike influence as Reverend Mr. Oswald Fawcett are rare. Look at my own case. At the age of thirteen I am called to my father's side — my father was a very wise man, an official in the Sanitary Department of Canton, spending the retirement of his well-earned old age at Yueh-lai-chou. 'English,' says my father, 'is the business language of China. Christianity is a part of English. You shall learn English at the Wesleyan Academy and so be fitted for a life full of advantages. Christians have many advantages in this life.' Reverend Mr. Oswald Fawcett, when I told him this, laughed his usual merry, hearty laugh and said, 'Not so many as in the life hereafter.' Be that as it may, look at the result of my father's wise Christian ruling. Instead of being a hopeless sinner and perhaps a mere merchant or clerk in Canton, I am taught the Holy Bible by a man like the Reverend Fawcett, as well as clean morals, manliness, mathematics and a thorough grounding in English history and literature, with special attention to the plays of William Shakespeare. By this preparation and moral grounding I am enabled to pass the London Matriculation ('Matric,' we London scholars say), and to become a student in a London Inn of Court. I am proposed by the well-known bencher, Mr. Winkworth, K. C., and seconded by his renowned colleague, Mr. Weston-North. I eat my dinners——"

"You eat some dinner?" asked Seryozha, suddenly drawing a *pirozhok* out of his pocket and sitting down to eat it. "Dinner . . . a most good plan."

A look of intense spiritual hunger came over Wilfred Chew's face and he swallowed once or twice, as if calling his useless words back into his throat from the unheeding air. Anna had made a packet of rice-filled *pirozhki* for him and he stood eating, swinging his weight from one foot to the other, looking hungrily from Seryozha's face to the hills and back again. Yet even utterance uncomprehended was a relief to him, though it was rather like playing squash racquets against oneself. After a moment, therefore, Wilfred began again to utter, with his mouth full, on a rather lower note than before, as he watched Seryozha's face wistfully for some possible freak of understanding.

"Yes, I eat my dinners. Twice I eat with three other men, namely, Williams, Banks, and Feathers. Feathers invites me—he is very pressing. He says: 'You must join our mess, Mr. Chew, I will not take no for an answer.' So of course I bow pleasantly and accept the politeness. When I sit down among them, they say, 'You do not drink wine, Mr. Chew?' I say, 'No, gentlemen, I have been brought up by Reverend Mr. Oswald Fawcett to consider alcohol as a moral danger.' Feathers, who was not really, I think, a moral man, says, 'Good egg! (this is a London expression of joy). That's just as I thought,' he says; 'there'll be all the more moral danger for us.' Of course he was merely joking. Nevertheless, they did not invite me to take wine again, shewing that my words made an impression of moral determination on them. Indeed, Mr. Banks once said to me, 'It has meant a good deal to us today, Mr. Chew, to have a teetotaller in our mess.'"

Seryozha was familiar with the English word "moral" by now, for he had known Mr. Chew three days.

"It is pity you have not seeing our singing girls of Chi-tao-kou," he said, happily, feeling that he was at last in the swim of this flood of information. "Some are not too bad. The little Matvievna — her skin is most white. Before, when I was young, I thinked, I shall marry her, but after, I find yist only singing girl. A most merry girl."

"Christians should avoid such women," said Wilfred Chew, seriously. "They are a moral danger. If you find self-control difficult, Mr. Malinin, you should pray — or perhaps marry."

"Oi! marry . . ." said Seryozha, spurting out crumbs of *pirozhki* as he laughed. "I have money *nyet*. I give all to my mamma."

His heart, however, warmed to Wilfred in response to this tribute to his maturity. Certainly, he thought, once a man is safely away from his home, the world takes him for the man he is.

"One could marry with a certain amount of worldly wisdom and still remain a Christian," said Wilfred Chew. "For instance, there is a very delightful young lady of your own race — Miss Ostapenko — who lives at Mi-san, near Seoul. *Sir* Theo Mustard and myself, when motoring from Seoul on an expedition, asked at Miss Ostapenko's father's home for some water for the radiator, and were invited to stay to tea."

"Ostapenko . . . ? How is her father called?"

"She is Miss Tatiana Ostapenko. Her father is called Pavel Ostapenko, Esquire."

"Tscht! Tatiana Pavlovna. She marries nobody. Alexander Petrovitch Weber speaked about her. She is many times betrothed; she is many times saying this, saying that; she is not good for mans. Alexander Petrovitch say she has betrothed seven times — he say that Tatiana is married, perhaps, to a devil. Devil is inside her. He speak so. He speak, yist better to be dead nor to be betrothed to Tatiana Pavlovna."

"Oh, that is ridiculous! I noticed a sort of shyness about her, but who knows what is in the heart of a pure young girl? She is certainly extremely pure. And perhaps of an ice-like nature. Yet she is considered beautiful. As a Chinese I should not think her beautiful, but as a Londoner, I can see that she is a little like the late Queen Alexandra (widow of the late King Edward Seventh) in features. Also, Mr. Malinin, she will have a fortune. It is good for a Christian to make friends a little with the mammon of unrighteousness, though not, of course, to the point of serving two masters."

"It is more good not to be dead," said Seryozha. "I like better to be alife with Sonia Matvievna nor to be dead with Tatiana Pavlovna. I have speak much with Alexander Petrovitch Weber these last days in Chi-tao-kou. He speak like this: 'Tatiana Pavlovna not good. She is like dead. With her a man must not be alife. She make a man dead, like a devil.' Alexander Petrovitch speak also: 'She is finish of me. She has taken away my life.' He was nice chap, too. I hope he will soon be alife again. I speak to him about Sonia Matvievna. He speak, 'So? She is easy to love? So?'"

Seryozha mimicked young Weber's long-drawn-out "So-o-o-o?" with a question sound at the end of it. "I speak: 'Indeed yes, she is most easy indeed. More better nor a devil.' And so I think. My papa speak: 'I think this girl Tatiana Ostapenko is perhaps child of Pavel Nicholaievitch Ostapenko, the cousin of my papa's uncle's wife. Pavel Nicholaievitch always has been bad boy — his child is perhaps bad also,' my papa speak. 'Seryozha, do not be making any visitings to such bad people,' my papa speak. I am the one son of my papa and my mamma — I wish not to be maked dead by devils. I do not love devils."

"There are cures for devils," said Wilfred Chew, thoughtfully. As he spoke, a vague picture of banners and smells disinfecting devil-haunted Chinese houses floated before his eyes. Almost immediately this picture was replaced by one of himself bringing back a gloriously enriched Seryozha to the threadbare, anxious little house in Chi-tao-kou. A Seryozha married to a beautiful heiress. Old Sergei would surely forgive disobedience that led to such a result. And what about the agreement? Ten sen on every yen over and above two hundred yen, he thought — and wished he had it in writing. Then he thought, Russians pay matchmakers, they say, very much as Chinese do; would not old Ostapenko be prepared to make it worth a man's while to find a good husband for a girl with seven failures behind her?

Wilfred Chew was quite without guile. His Christian upbringing had really planted a kind of charity to all men in his naturally affectionate heart. It was part of his vanity to be good — not only to seem good. He would most certainly have been very sorry to disappoint the Almighty in His (doubtless) high expectations of Wilfred Chew. Still, it was also part of his vanity to be prosperous — and surely this was also part of the Almighty's plan for him. For instance, Wilfred's genuine love and reverence for the Reverend Oswald Fawcett had not prevented him from making a good profit, on commission, out of Mr. Fawcett's passion for buying trashy brass "curios" from the shopkeepers of Yueh-lai-chou. Why should it, indeed? There is so often a point in a Chinese deal at which the seller sells for a little more than he had hoped and the buyer buys for a little less. A fraction of that little less — that little more — is the natural prerogative of the mutual friend, be he Christian or heathen. This was so much a commonplace in Wilfred's mind that he had never even dreamed of considering himself a less disinterested disciple of his reverend idol for making pocket money out of the latter's ignorance of the value and quality of brass. So many worshipers have profited out of the weakness of idols, after all. But of course Wilfred did not think of it in this way. He simply wanted to be not only a good Christian, but also a good business man.

He was already quite fond of Seryozha. After all, the boy was of conveniently silent habit, and even, occasionally, seemed impressed by what was said to him. Wilfred was by now for the most part resigned to not expecting much more of an obtuse world than this. He was like the secretary of an impoverished charitable society — satisfied if he got one ambiguous acknowledgment to a score of appeals.

The *pirozhki* were finished. The teeth of the travelers being now at rest, their feet could plod on. Wilfred wisely said no more about the heiress of Mi-san, for the present. His English law experience had taught him that there were limits to the persuasive powers of the voice, and that explanation was sometimes better dumb. Wilfred spent the afternoon trying to give his companion a rough summary of Roman law, Constitutional law, Criminal law, and Real Property and Conveyancy. He was just passing on to the material of the final examination — Common law, Evidence and Procedure, and Equity, to the tune of a low song from Seryozha — when they realised that Pa-tao-kou lay below them — the village in which they intended to spend the night. They had just climbed over a shoulder of cliff that overhung the river. The roofs of the Korean village lay like a shuffle of brown leaves beside the river. The sandbanks in the broad river looked almost the color of violets in the late night — all the subdued color of the valley, indeed, was overlaid with this smoky violet glaze. The early preparations for sunset were nobly ungorgeous. The sky was a striped bursting confusion of steel and silver — gleaming silver spilled down from a low cloud-masked sun in concentrated pools on far gorges. The most brilliant concentration of all was hidden by a steep broken crag a dozen miles away, so that the crag was backed by a diamond glow, though its topmost rocks were brushed by clouds. The glow behind it was like the radiance by which one might know a holy city—or like the mist of white spray that rises from the unseen deep pool that receives a waterfall.

Seryozha was very hot and looked the hotter for the forensic coolness of his Chinese friend. Sweat patched Seryozha's brown smocked blouse, his yellow hair was lank and damp, the sockets of his eyes were polished with sweat like well-greased ball-bearings. Yet he led his companion at a cheerful run down the dusty zigzag that sloped to river and village level. From the bottom of the hill the track into the village ran between the river and a narrow deep-set irrigation ditch. Along the track a bullock cart plodded to meet the travelers. The cart's wheels splayed out like knock-kneed legs; there was no room even for the cart's own stunted shadow between the wheel and the ditch. Slow floating leaves and sticks in the ditch met and swam through the cart's shadow, as ships might meet a storm cloud. The Korean driver of the cart was asleep in the bottom of the shovel-shaped, woven-withy basket that formed the body of the vehicle. Wilfred Chew, accustomed to the implacable demands of traffic in cities, prepared to jump the ditch on to a dike that bordered a ricefield. There seemed to be no other alternative. But Seryozha had no respect for wheels or hoofs as opposed to the pedestrian's rights; he was also still under the way of his rush downhill. He flapped his arms like a kite and with a loud "Boo-boo!" threw himself toward the bullock. His dog joined in the charge with a supporting shout of "Boo!" The astonished bullock, without altering its sullen and meditative expression, completely lost its head. After curtsying wildly right, left, and right again, it swerved, sprawling, aside and jumped into the river, choosing, it seemed, dishonor

rather than death. The jolt of the wheels, whisking over the
humped bank of the road, detached the basket body of the
cart from its chassis. The driver, still asleep, remained curled
up in the basket on the water's brink, like the infant Moses
ready for a rather improbable Pharaoh's daughter, while the
bullock, dragging only a wooden skeleton on wheels,
ploughed up and down in the shallows. Its world had come
to an end. The string in its nose was loose; there was no
cruel safe god to tell it what to do. It shrugged the yoke
from its shoulders and, now naked and unattached, swam
hysterically out into deep water.

Seryozha, doubled up on the road, squealed and cracked
with laughter. His dog, always glad of a chance to show itself
amphibious, pursued the enemy into the water, shrieking
with delight. A crowd of Korean and Chinese men and boys
was instantly present, laughing, arguing, and wailing in vigor-
ous tenor voices. "Eck-eck-eck!" they cried invitingly to the
bullock, but the harassed beast, trying to escape the dog,
swam outward, swam inward, and was caught by a strong
current and carried downstream. It would have given one of
its horns, now, to find firm ground under its feet and a firm
burden behind its tail, but it did not know how. Staring eyes
upcast, nose wide open, curving about foolishly in the current, it swam right and left, right and left, on the strong
dragging current. All the villagers ran downstream after it.
Only the driver remained, asleep in the basket. Seryozha
stood over him, laughing still. His dog, rashly refusing to re-
linquish the chase, was now helpless, too, being snatched
downriver like a hooked fish. Seryozha went on laughing;
his dog was expected to look after itself, though by now it
looked a mere flea on the great pale body of the river.

Wilfred Chew stared scornfully down at the sleeping Korean. "Ai!" shouted Wilfred in the man's ear. "Ai—ai—
ai!" He bowed himself down, almost pressing his nose to the
small black horsehair top-hat of the sleeper and screamed

98

"*Ai!*" It was alien to Wilfred's Chinese instincts to slap or shake the man. But Seryozha knocked the poor fellow's little hat off. This effected a slight movement of the eyelids of the carter. Communication was now held up, as usual, by the lack of a common language. But, gallant as ever, Wilfred wrote in large Chinese characters on a page in his notebook "Bullock — Floats — Away." This composition was flaunted before the twitching eyelids of the semi-conscious bereaved man.

Opposite the village, the bullock and the dog ran aground on the same sandbank. "Eck-eck-eck!" yawped the watchers in honeyed voices. Only a side strand of the river divided the sandbank from the mainland. The water flowed gently here, and both the marooned animals could have negotiated it easily. But the struggle and strangle of their arrival had frightened both; the bullock had too little imagination and the dog too much, to allow them to contemplate a new aquatic venture for the present. The bullock, still feebly shaking its horns at the silver emptiness round it, stood drooping, puffing, blowing its nose, splaying it legs, firmly rooted on all that seemed left of its old, obscurely known, obscurely trusted world. The dog, sobered and wet, squatted, panting, on the furthest possible promontory of the sandbank from the bullock. It was sick of bullocks. Obviously it was thinking, "Lord! what a companion to be marooned with on a desert island!"

"Come," said Seryozha, after whistling indifferently to his dog and being interrupted by a new giggle — though his cheeks felt quite strained with giggling already. "Vot hotel? Let us enter."

As they passed the crowd of men, women, and children on the shore — now some forty strong — all shouting, "Eck-eck-eck!" the bullock on the sandbank suddenly decided to settle down, a bovine imperialist claiming kingship over a new-found land, with only one subject — and that one a rebel. The bullock knelt down clumsily on its forelegs first, and remained for a few puzzled, uncomfortable seconds with its behind tilted up, feeling densely that something still remained undone. Then it remembered its hindlegs, and folded them awkwardly. It sat like a carpet bag on its wet bald island, looking through its thick eyes across the water at the crowd of yelping gods. The dog ran to and fro on the bank, wagging its tail winningly at the river, as if hoping to persuade the obliging stream to part its waters and leave a dry crossing for a poor dog's exhausted feet.

Seryozha and Wilfred entered the inn and threw their bundles on the kang. The proprietor, with a gray stubble of hair on a thin head, sitting on his haunches in the middle of his mud floor, smoking a very slender pea-size-bowled pipe, bowed as they came in. His wife, tottering across from the fire on stiff bound feet, brought each of the guests a cup of tea. The door became entirely blocked by spectators, coming from the sight of a Bullock on a Sandbank to enjoy the finer spectacle of Strangers Drinking Tea. The smell was very thick, but smoke partly drowned it. It was not a very inviting end to a day's journey, but Seryozha, it must be remembered, had never known a real hotel. He had never seen a bathtub, a bellboy, a real brass bed, a parquet floor, a poster advertising a seaside resort, a revolving doorway, a lift, or an Axminster carpet. He had never eaten either à la carte or table d'hôte, or leaned against a mahogany bar. Fleas he was accustomed to, bugs he disliked, lice he drew the line at — but he had never within his memory lived in surroundings in which any of these intruders could cause any considerable surprise. The Pa-tao-kou inn, therefore, seemed to him as tolerable as, say, the Red Lion, Bobble-under-Ouse, might seem to the average commercial traveler — a very so-so place, affording at least the luxury of a good deal to grumble mildly at.

Yet for Seryozha there was something decidedly wrong

with the place for the moment. A blankness in the region of his ankle-bone . . . a silence . . . no panting in the background of the hearing . . . no wagging in the corner of the eye. The panting of Seryozha's dog was to him what the ticking of a clock is to another man; he did not notice it when it was there, but felt uneasy without it. He walked to the doorway. The dog and the bullock, meek and resigned, still passively colonized the sandbank. The last spears of the sunset pricked the river.

"I am hot," said Seryozha, wiping his flushed face with his sleeve. "I shall swim in this river." It would be bad for the dog, he somehow felt, if he admitted that its plight mattered to him.

"Have you brought a bathing costume with you?" asked Wilfred.

"*Schto?*"

"A bathing costume? A garment for swimming purposes?"

"*Schto?*"

Wilfred clicked his throat. Seryozha pushed his way out through the crowded door and stumbled down over the rocks to the river's edge. He pulled off his clothes with a cheerful frankness and walked into the water. The crowd of villagers followed him from the inn, their eyes never leaving him. They added to their numbers, they shouted for their friends and families to join them—especially at the moment when his astonishing nakedness burst upon them —but they could not leave him in order to advertise the entertainment, for fear lest they might miss some item which might never be repeated. And their enthusiasm was rewarded. About seventy of them were able to watch a spectacle that had never before been seen in Pa-tao-kou— the spectacle of a White Man Swimming in the River.

The water climbed up Seryozha's body as he waded deeper and deeper. The garment of delicious coldness, as it wrapped itself higher and higher about him, seemed to be piped by a wire of almost-pain, a steel hair of ice or fire, climbing up his legs and his body. His thirsty skin gloried. He threw himself flat in the water, his open mouth just held above the surface. He felt strangely level with the world's floor. All perspective changed to fit eyes only six inches from world level instead of the usual six feet. He saw the darkening sandbanks like clouds, the bullock and the dog like giants, wild geese resting on far distant sandbanks like tall electric gray ghosts.

"Mr. Chew! Mr. Chew!" Seryozha's voice came with a curious clang across the water to the inn.

Wilfred came rather nervously out on to the shore, but seeing that he need not yet see that Seryozha was naked — since six-sevenths of that nakedness was modestly submerged — he looked relieved and shouted thinly in reply.

"Mr. Chew," called Seryozha, ploughing this way and that, "tell them — yist some fishes in their nets. I see a jumping." A thin this-way-and-that bristle of poles, supporting fishing nets against the current, straggled in the middle of the side stream.

Poor Wilfred felt almost a fool. However competent one may feel to address a jury, it is a fact that one is not trained at the English bar to act as communicating medium between naked fellow-men fifty yards away, and peasant compatriots with whom — in spite of their nationality — one has no word of common language. Nevertheless, Wilfred patiently jotted down a few hieroglyphics in his notebook and showed the paper to his Manchurian host. The host, after breathing loudly yet affably for a moment on the message, sketched a dozen characters in reply.

"He says the nets are not yet cleared," shouted Wilfred, self-consciously. "They are usually examined after sundown."

"I will examinate in a minute," shouted Seryozha. Wilfred averted his eyes as Seryozha, tipped with sunburn, began to walk up the far shallows to the sandbank, looking like an ivory saint on which coarse copper extremities had been stuck as a blasphemous joke. The dog threw itself upon him; cries and barkings of joy clanged across the water. The light was growing very quickly dimmer now. Outlines that were sure at one moment must be guessed at in the next, then believed in with the heart of faith, and finally only remembered.

Seryozha was fairly clear to the spectators as he roused the bullock from its rest. The bullock's behind rose first. Then it indulged in its usual pause, trying to remember what came next. But as Seryozha rushed at it with a facetious cry, its forelegs were inspired and straightened themselves with a plunge. The worried creature took to the water once more, abandoning its new kingdom without wagging a horn. Twilight blurred it; it was there — it was here — no, it was there — it was suddenly much nearer than any one had expected, splashing meekly up out of shallow water toward the village.

Seryozha could be heard whistling to his dog, exhorting it with a kindly curse. Then there was a gentle flipping noise of swimming. The dusk drew veils across the white blurred water.

Suddenly there was a noise of turbulent water, a squeal — "Oooo-eeee!" from Seryozha, and then bubblings and churnings and snortings only.

"What has occurred?" quavered Wilfred. "Mr. Malinin — are you involved in some calamity?"

A snorting as of restricted fountains, waterspouts, and whirlpools, was the only answer. The sound, coming across calm water, had a brittle, urgent quality. Then a bubbling squeal from Seryozha. "Yist big fish!"

"You must return to shore immediately, Mr. Malinin," wailed Wilfred, walking excitedly to the river's edge and pawing the sand like a thwarted horse. "Your parents would highly disapprove. . . ."

The bubbling and churning continued. Seryozha's dog came ashore near Wilfred, and began barking anxious injunctions in the direction of the struggle. A few half-forgotten, almost atavistic, Cantonese curses burst from behind Mr. Chew's English gold tooth. The words were like dark unheard-of deepsea creatures being churned to the public surface by some profound convulsion of nature. "Return — return," he wailed, trying to feel English again.

And suddenly, out of smoke-colored blankness, Seryozha returned. With a sudden loud breathless laugh he walked out of the water, towering tall in the dusk, clasping a large fish to his stomach. The fish cramped itself in curves from side to side, goggling voiceless o-o-o-s at the sky.

"Yist this most big fish catched outside the net," gasped Seryozha. "The nets have catched him by his skin. He has bited me."

He threw the fish on the rocks, where it whipped and lashed itself about, taut and terrible, mouthing its suffocated appeal. "I think," said Seryozha, pulling his trousers on, "that we shall soon be biting him. *Fkuzna!* Good biting, yes — no?"

"I did not know," said Wilfred Chew, examining the dying fish gravely, "that salmon could be plucked out of rivers by hand in this way. In England, I have heard, people fish for such fish with tame flies tied to rods."

Seryozha spouted river water out of his mouth, hawking crudely in his throat. He then sucked his bleeding finger and spat a little diluted blood. "In China," he said, shrugging himself and dancing a little to make his clothes hang easily on his wet body, "salmons are rare to be caught so, round their waist. Never before, I think. This was a misfortune to salmon — the net have catched such little cracks of his skin — so." He touched the straining gills and then stood up and looked down, feeling, as he always felt after such deeds were done, that he had spoiled a joke. A smiling salmon in the water had become solemn and sorry now on land — because of him. "He bited me," he murmured in doubtfulness and obstinacy. "Now I shall be biting him."

"Such a fish would indeed make a successful dish," said Wilfred, who had no such qualms. He did not really know that animals were alive. To him they were either ambulant food or else inferior substitutes for wheels. Sometimes they were just *things* with a smell, like dogs. "Yet, Mr. Malinin, legally the fish does not belong to us."

Seryozha began arguing with the innkeeper, whose nets, it seemed, had originally detained the fish. The fish, one gathered, was not for sale at all; perhaps the innkeeper had been considering having it stuffed for his wife's delight; perhaps he would have given it to the pigs. Seryozha, however, expressed the opinion that the fish should not only be sold to him, but sold very cheap, since he had gone to the trouble of bringing it out of the water (thus saving the innkeeper a trip in his boat), and had, in addition, been actually injured by the fish. Seryozha suggested that the innkeeper was lucky not to be asked to pay for the damage caused by his dangerous and uncontrolled fish. It then appeared that the fish, on second thoughts, might be sold as supper for the travelers — but at an immense price. Argument continued. The price began shrinking, like a flower from which the petals were being plucked. I buy it — I buy it not — I sell it — I sell it not. . . . Finally Seryozha said, "I have buy the half of this fish for eighty sen."

"Which half?" asked Wilfred.

"Is this important — which half?" exclaimed Seryozha, surprised but willing to be informed.

"Very important," answered Wilfred, judicially.

A new argument began between Seryozha and the innkeeper. After about ten minutes Seryozha said, "I have buy the behinder half of the fish for seventy-five sen. The before half shall cost ninety sen."

"The behind is better for our purpose," said Wilfred. "You can clean the fish and I will cook it."

The fish was divided by lantern-light, on the inn *kang*, in the presence of about thirty witnesses.

"Take the heart and the liver and the gall," said Wilfred, "and put them up safely."

"*Nyet* good," said Seryozha, wrinkling his nose at the mess in question.

"Please do as I advise," said Wilfred, sharply. "It is most important."

Seryozha, making a slightly mutinous noise in the back of his nose, wrapped the heart, the liver, and the gall of the fish in a piece of newspaper. "It shall smell," he said.

"Some smells are good."

"This smell *nyet*."

"Goodness is a comparative term."

"Oi-oi!" said Seryozha.

The fish, as Wilfred began to cook it, became a kind of trysting-place for all the delicacies of the village. Water chestnuts, garlic, sweet corn, peppers, young greens, tender white roots were brought in by business-like outsiders and bought by Wilfred for a few sen. The smell of cooking became a smell that ought certainly not to be omitted from Paradise.

What would heaven be like, in fact, without happy empty stomachs and the smell of a good supper getting ready? thought Seryozha, as he sat in the doorway and watched the stars of heaven. A half-moon was rising above the rice-fields; its reflection swam like a fish in the water of the rice-fields, appearing and disappearing, striped and coy, among the blades of rice — a fish swimming very deeply and secretly. There was enough light to show the rice, bleached of its

jewel-like green, all upright, all still, brushing the sight upward like soft fur. Softer than the softest fur, pearly pale
like a Persian kitten's fur.

Seryozha stared at the lovely world, feeling cooler and
cooler after his hot busy day, thinking of nothing. Yet all
his senses, all his limbs and members, were straining after
rapture; his ears were open for a great harmony; his eyes for
some light they would never see; his tongue and his throat
were tense to utter some unspeakably true word; his feet on
tiptoe for a leap beyond the starriest athlete's dream; his
stomach was hungry for some super-food, his sex sense aching for nothing less than a goddess. The moon and the stars
seemed like little seeds of some stupendous flower — seeds
sterilized, embalmed in a coffin built of the limiting substance of space and thought. Seryozha panted, stirred, panted
again, spat. . . . "I am hungry," he said uncertainly, after
some time, turning to Wilfred.

"The fish is now prepared," said Wilfred, glittering with
the excitement of success.

The fish was indeed good. Seryozha drank some *samshu*
with it. "I wish there is a singing girl in this village," said
Seryozha. From time to time his chewing was checked by
a surge of silly memory in his mind, that made him clasp
his stomach in an ecstasy of giggle and blurt a high cracking
ha-ha into his dish. Then he found that he was sitting on
the newspaper packet that contained the heart, gall, and
liver of the fish.

"Ah, tschah!" he exclaimed, annoyed. "Mr. Chew, to
what use is the heart and the liver and the gall of this fish?"

"You remember," said Wilfred, "we were talking about
devils. Well, the smell of the heart and liver of such a fish
is a cure for devils. If a devil or an evil spirit trouble any
one, we must make a smelly smoke of these things before
the man or woman, and the party shall be no more vexed."

"What party?" asked Seryozha, stupidly.

"Well . . . a cold woman, for instance," said Wilfred, after buzzing dubiously to himself through his teeth for a moment. "Coldness in a woman means that a devil is in her, and the devil can be frightened away by any husband that takes proper precautions."

"Ai-ai!" exclaimed Seryozha, feeling that he was acquiring useful knowledge. "Inside such women yist devils! Tcht! tcht! So here is magic—to make smells against devils. Mr. Chew, is this Wesleyan magic, yes—no?"

"It has nothing to do with religion," said Wilfred, stuttering a little in confusion, as though the Reverend Oswald Fawcett had laid a hand on his shoulder. "Religion is one thing, medicine is another. Chinese medicine is one of the most ancient and profound studies in the world. Western science has proved more and more the real wisdom behind Chinese medicine."

"Oi—medicine!" sighed Seryozha, nodding several times and thinking of castor oil. "I understand. Yist medicine, nyet magic. You know such plenty Wesleyan things, Mr. Chew, I have forgotten you know also Chinese things."

"Well, every Chinese knows from early childhood about the devils that obsess human beings. No religious education can alter that knowledge. And also we know it from the Bible, too. The apostles were taught to drive devils out."

"But with smells nyet," said Seryozha, not sceptically, but anxiously. He enjoyed acquiring unusual knowledge.

"With smells is one way," said Wilfred, firmly. "Devils cannot live in smelly smoke. In the western hemisphere also, in old-fashioned times, Papists burned those who did not accept their faith. For the same reason, I think. They burned the body, and so the devils, not liking the smell, fled away. But now, though Christians may not burn the body, there is nothing to forbid them from stinking devils out."

"Indeed nyet," agreed Seryozha. "It is all most wise. I shall remember. The heart and the liver of a salmon—yes?

But the gall — it is not a right smell, yes — no? Shall I not then throw away this gall? Yist to no use."

"The gall is extremely useful, too," said Wilfred. "It cures blindness." He was raking away in his memories of the servants in his father's compound at Canton.

"Blindness!" cried Seryozha. "My papa is blind."

"Some blindness," said Wilfred, cautiously, "is incurable. Other forms can be cured by surgical operations. But a Chinese doctor once told my old nurse that out of one hundred cases of blindness in his town, he was able to cure ninety-two by a course of treatment that involved a massage of the eyeball with the putrefying gall of a fish."

"Oi! Yoi! Yoi!" said Seryozha, astounded. "Ninety-two. It is very many. I shall hold this in my mind."

And he kept the lucky sticky little parcel closely beside him on the *kang*. But he did not, that evening, hold anything very much in his mind. A tingling, humming restfulness spread over his body; noble aspirations, happily attainable, surged in his contented brain; he felt that he had two pairs of eyes — one seeing charm and beauty in the watching brown faces of the coolies at the door, the other recognizing dreams and secrets in the shapes of shadow, the angles of the smoky little room. His head recovered with a wrench from a slow pendulum droop that he had not noticed had begun. He lay down with his head on his bundle on the *kang*. His feet must have dreamed they were walking again, for he woke with a jolting sense of stumbling over something. "A little stone," he thought, drowsily, "with a devil in it." Then his sleeping still feet went on secretly walking — walking — walking — throb — throb — throb — carrying his comfortable body into darkness.

CHAPTER SEVEN

TATIANA'S MOTHER, Varvara Alexeievna Ostapenko, sat in her garden, embroidering silk in bright colors. Varvara was a tall woman, thin and melancholy, with a dark birthmark on one cheek. She had a slow and anxious awkwardness of body; she held her head up often, as though listening, walked on tiptoe, and when, as now, she rested, never leaned back for more than a few seconds. A few seconds slackening and then again there she would be, listening, with her face up, as though expecting a call.

The garden, which had been made by their Japanese landlord, seemed built, fitted together, rather than grown. Curves of asymmetrical disciplined branches looped from sky to ground; the green in-bent horizon of the garden looked like handwriting against the dazzling sky. A young reddening maple, a pine, a Japanese cherry tree, and a stunted self-conscious cedar laid down careful shadows at one another's feet in a sort of cold courtliness. There were no flowers except Michaelmas daisies frothing in a mauve mist over the brim of a streaked glazed blue urn in a corner of the garden. Flying seed-pods, gossamers and birds seemed like untidinesses in the air of a garden where even the shadows were studied. The September heat of the plain boxed in the garden as though in a glass case.

A thread of sound like a flute—the sound of Tatiana whistling—from somewhere in the house, seemed to run like a rill of coolness through the garden.

"Tanya whistles like a boy," thought Varvara. She imagined Tatiana as the girl must look as she ironed in the washing-shed outside the house—whistling in time with her ironing. "She must be hot, though," thought Varvara. "There is no draught in the shed." She imagined the light diamond mustache of tiny drops that appeared always on Tatiana's upper lip when she was hot—a little delicate hint of heat that, in that still girl, took the place of the raw flush, the bloated mouth, the hair askew, the stare-eyed goggle that in so many other women and men are the symptoms of over-heating.

The three members of the Ostapenko family were always very conscious one of another. Their craving that each should be justified, even when wrong, that each should be worthy of each and appear worthy even when unworthy, that none should be hurt or humiliated, even when deserving of rebuff, amounted to a kind of chronic soreness of heart. They all almost hated and quite loved one another —savage in the disappointment of their own hopes of one another, and savage in their anger against outsiders for being disappointed. They had an overbearing family egoism; they felt as if they were set apart, as if they should be judged by a standard different from that to which other families conform. Each thought the other two, for instance, more beautiful than ordinary beauty; even Varvara's birthmark seemed to her husband and daughter a sort of hallmark of queer beauty. Only Pavel Ostapenko felt real vanity about himself; Varvara and Tatiana each felt it for the other two. In themselves they were more proud of the things they did not do very well than they were about their gifts. With one half of her mind Varvara knew that her designs for her embroidery were not worth the exquisite stitching she put into them. The designs were childish and ungainly — not simple enough to be primitive, not clever enough to be sophisticated. Criticism of her designs, therefore, could make her tremble with anger, and pointed praise of her stitching was almost equally humiliating. She knew — and refused to admit — that she was an interpreter, not a creator, in everything, but she refused to be praised for anything less than creation.

In the same way, Tatiana's only vanity was her whistle. It was sweet and most flexible and versatile; she could give it either the ogling quality of the saxophone or the cold veiled purity of the flute. It was always impeccably accurate. Her ear heard words in the air which, running through her senses, not through her brain, came out as tunes through her lips — wandering, passing, blind tunes that never went forward and never came back. It was a foolish and tiny skill, much more akin to a bird's song than a human sound; the sound mixed lightly with the cooing of doves and the whistling of larks — it had none of the interrupting, creative quality of most human melody. Tatiana did not feel that she should be applauded for her whistling, but she herself enjoyed it intensely. It was very close and clear in her own ears and filled up all the lonely space about her. She heard it almost as though it were space singing, not herself, and she looked forward to it whenever she set herself to work with her hands in an empty place. She valued this knack of hers far more than she valued her straight and vivid beauty. She had grown weary now of having her beauty praised, since such praise was always the prelude to a demand — to one of the dangerous approaches she dreaded.

There was a side gate to the garden, opening under a twirl of tufted pine branch. By the care with which the latch was lifted Varvara knew that her husband, Pavel, was a little drunk but not very. Varvara looked at him with a sourness that came of expectations disappointed. The trouble was that she had invented a Pavel Ostapenko for herself, to which the actual Pavel seldom conformed. She was a Procrustean wife.

Pavel looked uneasily at his wife as he pulled at his little red beard. He used his beard as though it were a kind of tab by which to pull his mouth open; tugging at his beard, he pulled his jaw down — snapped it up again — open — shut — open — showing fine teeth and an uneasy tongue.

"I have some news," he said, looking down at his wife, rather relieved to be about to put his uneasiness and rancor into words.

Varvara had decided deliberately to sulk a little. She felt that a cold silence now might make him drink one glass less next time.

"I have heard something," he began again, "that makes me as uncomfortable and guilty as though it were my own fault. Oh, Varitchka — that poor boy, Sasha Weber. . . . I was fond of him. He has cut his throat."

"Sasha!" exclaimed Varvara, shocked out of her resolve. "But he has left Seoul. . . . How do you know? . . . Who heard?"

"Soloviev heard from the boy's mother. He had reached Chi-tao-kou, just over the Chinese border. . . . Evidently he found life unbearable, after all, though he made a show of indifference." Pavel's tears — for he was an emotional drinker — spilled suddenly over his cheek-bones.

"It is not our fault. It is not our fault," said Varvara, huskily. "What nonsense to cry as if it were our fault! A boy's folly still remains folly, even if he is dead and will never be a fool again — poor little fool!"

Ostapenko pulled his jaw into a few more gapes. His eyes — brown irises entirely surrounded by whites — glared in a frightened way at his wife.

"Up to now I have tried to think of Tanya as a dear girl — a too charming, too lovely girl. . . . Every lovely girl, I have thought, has these adventures . . . fascinating danger to the young bloods . . . fatal gift of beauty . . . the kind of thing great-aunts in the 'fifties suffered from — love-tokens, duels, rivals sending rosebuds — you know what I mean — quite natural. . . . Now, suddenly, Varitchka, I don't believe it is natural, or pretty. There's something wrong. Something unnatural. Something *unhealthy*." He said the last word almost in a choking voice. Health was one of his vanities.

"Unnatural? Unhealthy?" exclaimed Varvara, stitching in tense jerks. "What is unnatural? What is natural? Only the majority."

"Well, youth is natural . . . and girlishness . . . and warmth and motherhood . . ." Pavel was shading his eyes with his hand, and from beneath his little finger tears that seemed unwarranted by the matter of what he said ran down his face. "There's something about our Tanya that kills decent young creatures like Sasha Weber — even if they don't cut their throats or join the Chinese army. Look at Piotr Isaev; look at Boris Andreievitch, or Stepan. One can't wag a finger at all this and say, 'A-ha! the saucy chit!' O God! that's the trouble — she's not near enough to be saucy. You can't smile at a thing a hundred miles off."

Ideas that looked like the long-ignored truth seemed to come with appalling clarity into Pavel's humming, giddy mind. He seemed to see his daughter all at once as a stillness, an interruption in loud and moving life — something pale suspended like a ghost, just higher than the ground — about which gay coarse heavy-footed life moved in vain, moved and dodged, seeking for glances from eyes that stopped warm hearts beating. A little figure of death surviving life. And this was his daughter. Her existence seemed to him, in his present mood, an insult to the life that dizzied him in himself. "What kind of a creature have I begotten?" he croaked. "Something that is a woman and is not."

"There you are," said Varvara, fiercely flattening the silk upon her knee. "There you are! Why should everything be a woman or a man?"

"What do you mean — men — women? What else is there? Out of men and women comes life — the only life there is."

"Tanya is living."

"Tanya — ah, tschah! — she is living." He was silent, listening to the sound of Tanya's whistling. "Yes," he said, after a moment, in a different voice, "she is living." He paused for some time, waving his head a little as though his eyes were trying to follow the twirl of a rather giddy world. "But because of her, Sasha Weber is dead."

"Not because of her, exactly," said Varvara, slowly. "Because of a collision between new things and old things . . . Sasha Weber comes at the end of something old — Tanya comes at the beginning, perhaps, of something new."

"A bad beginning," said Pavel, "since it seems our line is to stop with her. I don't know what you mean, Varitchka. And whatever you mean, I'm sure it is unhealthy and ugly."

"Everything's unnatural when it begins. Everything's ugly when we haven't seen it before."

"I don't know what you mean. It is Tanya's duty — it is every woman's duty — to be natural and warm and young, not to suck life out of warm natural young things and remain cold as a cat herself."

"We don't know what is the duty of new things," insisted Varvara. "Perhaps they haven't any. Anyway, new or old, they're all natural."

"What is she, then, you silly woman, if she's not the thing

we know—a young woman, born to bear children?"

"Perhaps she's a *thing*," said Varvara. "That maple tree's
a *thing*. A man can love that without wanting to get into
bed with it. Listen."

Tatiana's whistle fluted, stopped again, shaped itself into
an unthinking trill or two.

"Listen," said Varvara, "whose voice is that? That's a
thing's voice."

And as she applied this cruel word to her daughter, the
word became somehow a word of praise—a proud word. It
seemed suddenly common to be anything but a *thing*.

"Ah, tschah!" snorted Pavel, striking the trunk of the
little maple tree with an outflung hand. "It is absurd. I have
been talking nonsense. So have you. Tanya's just an un-
awakened child. The little minx. She has no understanding
of her effect on men. Perhaps the shock of hearing of Sasha's
death and knowing it to be the result of her childish heart-
lessness will—Tanitchka!" he shouted.

Tatiana in the ironing-shed heard his voice with an
urgency that almost stopped her heart. She was so lost, so
inclosed in her cooing forgetful space, that his voice seemed
like a shot suddenly unwarrantably fired in time of peace.
Her finger was jerked by surprise from the handle of the
iron she was using and pressed for a second on the scorching
metal. The pain of the finger sprang up her arm. After the
first second, her burnt finger was interesting to her—a
possession to be studied, to be proud of. She began prodding
it, squeezing it, to make it hurt more. The skin thickened
and whitened on the burn; she looked at it closely, feeling
the finger grow hotter and hotter—more and more apoplec-
tic, as though it were so full of blood that it would burst.

"Tanya!" roared her father again from the garden.

Tatiana left the iron burning a sheet and went out of the
shed, through the house, and into the garden.

Her father stood with his arm crooked round a bough

of the little maple, like one with his arm round the shoulders of a friend. He looked at Tatiana anxiously, breathing heavily. Her mother, sitting rigidly, jerking at stitches, did not look up.

"I heard a piece of news today," said Pavel, "that may interest you. Or it may not."

"I expect it will, papasha," said Tatiana in a drowsy voice. She stood rocking a little on her feet, torturing her throbbing finger.

"I expect you hardly think it worth while to remember Alexander Petrovitch Weber," said Pavel, who had become very angry again directly he saw his daughter. He fixed on her his characteristic glare that islanded his irises in startled white. "Sometimes it seems to me that you don't distinguish between one young man and another. I suppose you think they're all alike in their folly—and none worthy of your highness's attention. My God!" he shouted suddenly, "it would do you good to be raped by one of them."

Tatiana pinched and tore at her agonising finger.

"Alexander Petrovitch is dead," he said. "He cut his throat. Just before he killed himself he wrote to his mother that his death would relieve you of a nuisance."

"That was ridiculous of him," said Tatiana's mother in a matter-of-fact voice. "It was also very spiteful and theatrical."

"At any rate, you wouldn't waste a tear on Sasha Weber, of course," said Pavel to his daughter, choking with anger. "Sasha knew that, of course. But he was mistaken, poor fool, in thinking that you would feel anything so active as relief, wasn't he? Why should you feel anything at all? What does it matter to you that a living young man is dead?"

Tatiana looked at her finger. Through the nail, she noticed, the red blood showed purple. Things were hurt, things died, blood ran into burnt fingers and out of cut throats. Containers of uneasy blood, that's all we are. Big and little, male and female, two-legged, four-legged, six-legged, many-legged, winged and creeping, wise and foolish, we slide and stride and wiggle about the world until something called death lets the blood out, to be soaked into the ground, to be dried into the air, to form again in other containers. . . . Why should there be any of this merging between one skinful of blood and bones and another? Why can't we get used to the loneliness of having separate blood? Pitchers may go to the same well, be dipped, and come home full, clinking handles, tinkling together, but always separate, each with its dreadful integrity complete, its inviolate solitary storm of contents. Not till the pitcher is spilled is there a merging — a cold, loveless merging into thirsty space. These images, quite clear but wordless, passed across the screen of Tatiana's sight as she looked at her finger, cramping the muscles round her eyes till her forehead smarted. "Why do I feel my finger and my forehead hurting, and not the wound in Sasha's throat?" she thought all at once. "What is it that feels one wound so much and another not at all?"

The maple tree rustled as Pavel shook it with his tense arm. His arm was aching to beat his daughter, to break up her exasperating stillness. "I suppose you don't know why this unhappy young man killed himself," he croaked.

"No," said Tatiana. She knew that he had killed himself by way of revenge on her — he had told her that he would, but she did not know why. What were two *me's* to each other, that one should be so necessary to another? A sort of accident, it seemed, happened in young men's blood that made them think that two *me's* could be kneaded together into an *us*. Most of them probably lived to find it a mistake. Only dear Sasha had incredibly thrown his *me* away — poured it out of a cut throat, because he could not double it into an *us*. Here in this generous world were a million million *me's* — a million million columns of lonely blood and bone. There was no such thing as a real *us*.

"Except the Siamese twins," said Tatiana aloud, absent-mindedly.

Pavel boxed her ears.

Varvara got up from her chair, her face twisting, her mind profoundly disturbed. "Oh, what a complicated family I've got!" she thought, proudly. "You must stop and think, Pavlik," she said, in a dry, urgent voice. "Think. Think. It's impossible to make things one way that really are another. Tanya is Tanya, whether you like it or not, and you know, when you're sober, you like it. She has as much right to be herself as you have—and even if she hadn't, you couldn't change her, either by hitting her or in any other way. She couldn't change herself. She's alive."

"Yes, and Sasha's dead," shouted Pavel. "He had just as much right to be alive as she has. More right, because he was natural. He was a man. He should have begotten sons. What is this *thing* we have called our daughter? A *thing*— a lifeless *thing*—killing live men. . . . What about our grandchildren who have a right to be born? A *thing* that's not alive is preventing men and women from being alive. She's cutting us off from our grandchildren. Five times— six times—seven times—she might have been married; she might have been turned into a live woman—a live mother —a live wife. Her face, her body—her woman's face and body—they're lies. . . . Yes, she's crying now—she looks almost like a woman when she cries, doesn't she—but it's all lies. . . ."

Tatiana, her head still bent over her hand as though she were obsessed by the phenomenon of her burnt finger, was crying violently—her shoulders jerking, her mouth squared, the muscles round her eyes quivering, tears springing down her cheeks and chin. She was rigid with anger against her father because he was invading her—his words were fettering her, just as his hard hands had clapped an ache round her head.

"And Piotr Gavrilovitch — whom she promised only a month or two ago to marry — where is he now? Gone — turned out, I suppose, since all her promises are lies. I suppose she said, You foolish Petya, that promise of mine was a joke — a *thing's* promise. . . . Eh? Eh — ? Answer me, girl."

"What do you want her to answer, Pavlik?" said Varvara, standing within an arm's-length of her weeping daughter, but not touching her.

"Answer me, girl. Piotr Gavrilovitch, the last young fool you lied to — you showed him the door, I suppose, when you'd sucked him dry. He's not coming back any more, is he?"

Tatiana shook her head.

"No, of course not. I suppose you said to him, You can go and cut your throat now, Petya, as Sasha did. The joke is over, you said — till another softhearted young fool comes along. It's a joke you've played too often, you little snake. I tell you it's a stale joke. I wonder you can sleep at night. What about Boris, who went to Shanghai? His father never heard from him again. Did *he* cut his throat, too, do you think, or just starve to death? It doesn't matter to you, of course, does it? What about old Soloviev's son, Stepan? You didn't manage to turn *him* out of his home, but I hope you're proud of what you did do, for I've never seen him sober since he left this garden for the last time. What about Vanya, whose eye you nearly blinded for life at that kissing game when he was having a bit of fun? What about —— Good God, girl!"

For Tatiana was suddenly laughing. She lifted her eyes at last from her clasped hands and laughed. A picture of a sort of centrifugal burst of young men bouncing from one center had come into her mind. Like a flock of rabbits running from a weasel — jumping off cliffs, plunging into streams, turning head over heels in panic, springing under railway trains — a bomb of furry fugitives bursting as the result of one puny little spark of life inside a separate bag of fur. Certainly *seven* was too many to cry over. Over *one* — each one of the seven — tears might be shed. Tatiana knew that as soon as she was quiet again she would be imagining the cruel look of the knife in poor Sasha's sight — the feel of its pressing edge on his tender throat. But now — seven voices singing in silly unison, "Good-by forever" — seven twangs of breaking hearts like the snapping strings of balalaikas. . . .

The father and mother stood and looked at their giggling child.

"She is right," said Varvara after a moment, with a brisk, hard look, as she folded her sewing. "Seven is too many to cry over. Seven is like the chorus in comic opera. You go and lie down, Pavlik; you are over-excited and you talk nonsense. There is no reason why Tanya should try to be any different from what she is. If seventy lovers instead of seven came along, it wouldn't be her fault if none of them was the right one. Perhaps she's just more particular than the rest of us." . . . She looked at her husband with a wry, unnatural archness. "Or perhaps she's not the kind of girl that marries. It's only a habit that makes men and old virgins think so much of love and marriage. . . ."

Varvara stopped speaking, overcome with a sort of despair. All this pain, this weeping, this shouting, was like a blot upon perfection — a blot that must be at the same time erased and accepted by her. This storm must be outwardly stilled, yet inwardly justified; it must be part of the air of the house now — and yet it was leaving ruin in its path. Ruin must henceforth decorate the garden. Part of her pride in the family's perfection must be Tatiana's imperfection, just as Pavel's drunkenness had become a subtlety — an Ostapenko essential — misunderstood though it might be outside. She knew that her husband was often drunk, but ignorant outsiders might think — well, they might think

that he *drank!* She knew there was a fundamental perversity,
a passional lack, in her daughter—but, with so many disappointed and spiteful lovers about, Heaven knew what the
neighbors might say. They might call the child frigid, un-
desirable, likely to live and die alone. One must fashion
these potential weapons into stones to strengthen the ramparts of family defense.

"What have you done to your finger, Tanya?" she said,
awkwardly.

"I burnt it on the iron."

Pavel was walking a few steps here and a few steps there
in the hot shade of the garden, clasping and unclasping his
hands, mopping his dripping forehead. "Butter," he said.
"Butter is good for a burn." Thinking of his Tanya—his
claimant for Ostapenko immortality—burning her finger on
an iron gave him a sharp pain in the pit of his stomach,
though he still longed to beat her and make her scream.

"It is very sore, I suppose," said Varvara. "If you come in
I will put something on it."

"Butter—butter——" murmured Pavel, rather wildly.
He was wondering why this business of Tatiana's disappointed lovers had seemed to him so important just now.
By what logical steps had he reached his present condition
of agitation and anger against his daughter? Everything
seemed unnaturally separated in his mind now: the talk in
the drinking-house with old Soloviev, the news of Sasha's
death at Chi-tao-kou, the sudden discovery that the leaves
of the maple in the garden had turned gold, Varvara's comment on Tatiana's whistling, Tatiana's tears, Tatiana's
laughter, Tatiana's burnt finger, Tatiana's need of a good
whipping, Tatiana's need of butter, his own need of a wash
and a good sleep . . . each of these facts seemed static and
ready-made in his mind, none growing out of any other.

Alone with Tatiana, Varvara said as she bent over the
wounded finger: "Your papa is over-excited . . . the hot

weather. . . . His disappointment is natural. Sasha Weber was the son-in-law he would have liked."

Tatiana's throat tautened as she imagined a knife at a throat. Yet really Sasha's suicide hurt her just about as much as her burnt finger hurt her, no more. Her thoughts were intermittently free of either injury; they played with the shape of the sunlight on the floor, with the angular lines of her father's coat hanging on a chair, with the blowing, casual design of gusty gold sand blowing across the paper screens. Chairs, tables, cupboards — heavy props for heavy Russian bodies, supports for heavy Russian possessions — looked oddly in the light flat Japanese gold-and-white room. They were like vulgar plums in a cake or cube of light sweet air. The alcove that in a Japanese house should hold a flowery suggestion of an altar framed Katya's sewing-machine. Tatiana could almost see the surprise of that room, finding itself patched with such heavy shapes and shadows; finding itself looking out at a frank spotted world through the crudeness of glass windows, instead of veiled by the subtle blindness of paper windows set into fretted frames. Though Tatiana was so well used to the room, she saw it freshly today because she remembered that Sasha once knocked his head against the frame of this door. He must have felt the bruise as now she felt her own burnt finger; her own head, she remembered, had ached for an hour in sympathy with his, just as now her throat tingled and throbbed to the slash of a knife against his throat. The strange prisoner *feeling* still puzzled her — that prisoner, filling his prison with such a flame of superfluous life, pain, and joy, that the neighboring human prisons are almost set alight. And then — suddenly — dead — cold — no feeling — no message from the prisoner ever again. Six months ago the results of the contact of Sasha's skull against a door-frame were a curse, a blue skin, an hour's soreness, a little headache, a lot of grumbling, sympathy from Tatiana, a chronic caution when entering by that door afterward. Now, Sasha's bones could beat against hard stones . . . no protests of skin and blood, no complaint from his quiet lips, no anger in his brain, no sympathy needed from friends and lovers. No sympathy — no sympathy needed; no wandering love whistled in by a master from far fields. She was safe now, she thought, from one more invasion. Sasha could never make her feel guilty again — guilty for being Tatiana Ostapenko.

Her finger was throbbing, her head was aching from her father's blow. She still felt coldly angry with her father — and yet proud of him. He had attacked her spiritually and physically, and yet, she thought he was so splendid, so queer, so much more colored and individual than other men. He was a part of her; for the moment she hated him as she might hate one's own rebellious limb. "A lonely and wild father," she thought, "hitting his daughter because she would take no lover. How rare! how Ostapenko!" She would not have contradicted an outsider's view of her father. "A simple tipsy man," you might have said, and so he was. Yes, simple with a precious Ostapenko simplicity; tipsy as a poet without words. . . . Even ordinary derogatory words could be twisted by each Ostapenko to feed the family sense of apartness.

"Well," said Tatiana, "Sasha's safe and dead now." Her finger hurt so much, as her mother touched it, that she could almost have wished to die of this injury as Sasha had died of his. Tatiana's body was always morbidly sensitive to pain. Little pains, that in other people seemed easily dismissed from attention, often demanded real fortitude of her. That was why she was so much preoccupied with the thought of pain — why she invented stories about pain and death in the night to make her body thrill.

"My darling," said Varvara, in inquiry, not in criticism, "have you no feelings for other people's sufferings? Do you not mind very much about poor Sasha?"

Tatiana listened, a little confused. The two questions seemed to her to be quite separate. Minding about a person — no. Minding about people — well, nobody could feel more actually than she felt the very feelings of people, animals, insects, things, ghosts, even the air bruised by shadows.

"No mamma, I haven't any heart," she mumbled, feeling this to be the safest claim.

Varvara registered this as a confirmation of a new piece of Ostapenko peculiarity. Her daughter had no heart. Well, were hearts necessary? Men and women — especially women — had been judged too much by their capacity for love. This was because people who love, propagate, thought Varvara, and transmit their vulgar standard of love from generation to generation. Just as rabbits transmit their bobtails. Bobtails are a conventional rabbit standard. A rabbit with a long curly tail would be feared, shunned, trampled to death, so the innovation would die untried, unbequeathed, abortive. But its death didn't prove the essential wrongness of long curly tails for rabbits. Genius was probably often heartless. But genius did not often propagate. Strangeness meant physical mortality, so strangeness was rare, never reborn, always new in every manifestation. All the stupid things — cruelty, prostitution, womanly modesty, conventional religion, conventional morality — only survived so rampantly because of the excessive fertility of the stupid.

"Well," she said, lamely, "people with no hearts have no babies."

"People with no hearts," said Tatiana, "can be the mothers of — oh — all sorts of things." She had a vague feeling of tremendous posterity — mountains, clouds, tigers, spiders, flowers, cities — all giving birth. . . . But even as she spoke she knew that this feeling was an easy and false consolation.

Varvara sighed and went out. Tatiana went to her room, her finger greased and bandaged and the more painful for having been treated so seriously. She stood rigidly, looking toward the window. To look out of her window was, with her, almost always a prayer or an act of praise to some unknown God. The window was like the face of God or of a lover to her; she studied every line and shade, as an adoring lover studies a face, or a believer a miraculous manifestation. She marveled so over living things, simply because they lived, moved, breathed, grew, begot, conceived. Yet she was accused of killing, of treachery to that strange quiet empire, the law of which is the beating of the heart. She, who valued things for their independence of herself, for their incomprehensibility, for their magical remoteness — she who so slightly intruded even upon her own life — was reproached for intruding on the lives of others. All the world outside her window was jeweled with impeccable life — and she, trusted in the treasure-house, was a convicted robber. She set her eyes and her face toward that world, but a voice in her heart was crying: "Take me out of the earth, that I may hear no more the reproach. . . . If men who lived are dead, why should I, who never lived, have the right to breathe when every breath I take is a lie? Or if I must live, let me *live* at last, let me be a woman alive, as these animals around me are animals alive. . . . Let me no longer see only — let me *be*. . . . It ought to be easy to live," she thought, desperately, breaking off her prayer and dragging her eyes from the bright window. "Even a worm in the earth can live. . . ." Her finger throbbed and burned. She looked at it, pinched it. "Oh, you liar!" she said.

She went down from her room, through the sunny kitchen and out through the ironing-shed into the yard. She noticed the iron standing on the sheet as she had left it, and, lifting it up, looked at the angular heart-shaped burn on the linen. The sheet was not spoiled in Tatiana's eyes; the mark was symmetrical, shapely, and of a fine sienna color. The thing, in fact, was simply branded with a signature of oddity.

She left the iron tilted upright, and thought that it looked like a creature begging forgiveness for the sin of printing a private and unlicensed mark upon its world.

She leaned on the gate of her father's yard, looking out at the valley, at the crisscrossing paths, the yellow mud-walled houses, the tree where she had parted from Piotr Isaev, the last of her lovers. She leaned one cheek on the top bar of the high gate, and looked at the world sideways, under the blurred arch formed by the bone of her nose and brow. Seen sideways, thus framed, everything in sight looked separate and significant — to be seen by itself. The barley looked as if it were being brushed upward by an impossible perpendicular wind. The soft hills changed their angles and were now built of precipices down which the clouds rolled like avalanches. And, as if the freshness of this sideways view quickened also her hearing, she could hear with a sudden urgency the starlings in the big tree preparing for autumn flight. They were making that curious wailing whistle — almost like a miniature howling — that starlings utter in their migratory restless mood. And as soon as Tatiana noticed this sound, she could see that almost every leaf in the tree had a bird behind it. The tree was as full of movement as a bonfire; whistling curled up from it like smoke.

Tatiana felt an arch tweak at her instep. She looked down and saw that all the chickens in the yard, thinking that her presence meant a meal, were gathered about her feet. Each hen looked incredulously at the unexpectedly uneatable dust about her feet, first with one eye and then with the other. Tatiana, watching them, putting thoughts into their narrow heads, presently became aware that, leaning on the gate, she had opened it a little, and the disappointed hens were wandering out into the road.

Tatiana, dancing on her toes as she always did, ran out after them, and as she did so, a further block of hens squeezed out with a rustle and a cackle. "Chok-chok-chok,"

she called, throwing imaginary grain in the gateway. A few
hens went in and a few more came out. "Supposing they
were men," thought Tatiana. "Men that I was trying to
lead—like Joan of Arc—to some great enterprise. I should
have to fail, with such silly rebels as these behind me." Her
supposings always promoted her to a first place. "Friend, go
up higher" was always the note of her imaginative orgies, although in actual life she never asserted herself. But in her
imagination she never knew herself as a mere Tanya.

In her mind, now, the indecision of the hens was as articulate as her own predicament. "What does she want us to
do?" she thought for the hens. "This way—that way—
which way? I'm trying to do right, but—what is right? Oh,
what a puzzling world this is, outside our gate. . . !"

With a good deal of flurry and worry Tatiana drove the
chickens—all of them but three—back into the yard.
There they were, that group of cackling conservatives, trying to collect their wits after their daring excursion into
novelty, scratching feverishly at the dust and, in their excitement, hardly looking at what their scratching had turned
up. Tatiana thought they all must have that bathed, naked
feeling that comes on getting safely home after a new experience. But she had no time to enjoy their relief, for the
three exceptions were hurrying away into the world. They
believed that they were being chased by a perfectly unconscious and absentminded donkey which was carrying a load
along the track, side by side with its small boy tyrant. The
three hens hurried from side to side of the track, confusedly
flattering themselves that so far they had cleverly outwitted
their pursuer.

Tatiana looked at the misunderstood donkey lovingly and
wondered if all devils were devilish by mistake. She pulled
the mild devil's dusty ear as she ran by.

The hens redoubled their efforts. Two devils were evidently after them now, they thought. They had entirely for-

gotten which way the peaceful cabbage-stalks and fish-heads of home lay. Their lives had suddenly become one huge delirium. Tatiana giggled as she ran. Who would have thought that three hens could run so fast and so far. She imagined her mother saying to her father, "Where can our Tanya have got to, Pavlik? Can she have gone to weep on Sasha's grave at Chi-tao-kou?" And then the efficient Japanese police telephoning, "Anoné . . . anoné . . . *mushi — mushi — anoné.* Your daughter was last seen climbing the rocks of the Umi-Kongo in pursuit of three hens. . . ."

Every time Tatiana burst into a wily gallop, hoping to outrun the hens in one spurt, the hens did the same and outran her. It was a hopeless situation; Tatiana wasted a lot of breath in giggling.

Passers-by were quite unhelpful. None of the Koreans on the road lifted a finger to shock the errant fowls into a return. The only Korean that helped at all did it unwittingly. He was lying quite drunk on his side near the ditch, his top-hat tilted over one temple; he was singing in a smiling little whine to himself, and when the hens found themselves looking into a human face on a level with their own beaks, they very nearly decided to turn back. But on second thoughts they made a wide detour and hurried on.

But about a hundred yards farther on, the hens met two pairs of boots which danced menacingly about the road, while voices thundered, "Chok-chok-chok." The hens turned back. The odds were too heavy — devils before and devils behind. How can hens die better than facing fearful odds? Almost any way — much better — thought the hens. Tatiana, close on their tails — for the hens were getting tired — saw for a moment only the boots of the approaching strangers shuffling helpfully in front of the hens. Then she managed to seize one hen by the wing and snatch it to her bosom in a storm of flying feathers and dying yawps. The

other hens rushed round in circles. They were caught by the
strangers.

Tatiana had an impression of clumsy size in the man nearest to her, but she hardly saw his face because at that moment all the sky became full of birds, keeping a vast rendezvous in the sky. Thousands and thousands of birds decided
at that moment to fly back to their lost summer; thousands
and thousands of them merged into a great giddiness against
the blue—a wind for the sight. Their thousands of twit-
terings and whisperings ran together into one wide shrill
sibilance; the rustlings of their countless wings were
smoothed into an illimitable breathing. It was impossible for
even Tatiana to think thoughts into such a multitude; it
seemed they must fly in a kind of democratic ecstasy or
trance, they must think with a multiple *me*, an ego spread
thinly over the whole sky like butter on bread.

Tatiana, dazzled and giddy, watching the birds, heard
one of the strangers talking what seemed to her to be English, and in the midst of the unknown words she caught her
own family name. She looked then at the two men with the
shocked, half-insulted puckered look with which she instinctively met any approach—a look of, "Sir, pray unhand
me." She saw Wilfred Chew's gold tooth. Where had she
seen that strange thing before? Of Seryozha she only saw
that his eyelids were very much tucked in under the brow
bones, and that his hair was bleached and rough.

Seryozha saw very much more of Tatiana than she saw of
him. A feeling of quick interest seemed now to establish
itself in his mind with the familiarity of an old feeling,
though he had not realized that he had paid much attention
to the talk of either Alexander Weber or Wilfred Chew.
She was a little too odd-looking for his rather childish taste;
her face was too white, her hair too dark a red, her eyes too
light and wide. Yet he felt instantly in touch with a new

and manly experience; the expression of her face, puckered, he thought, against the sun — though really it was against himself — seemed to be laughing and young, but laughing through a mist. There was something in her eyes that reminded him of his father's blindness — or, he thought, of that queer glare in the moon's face that gave him, on a clear night, that sense of inexplicable hunger. She was bowed a little on one side to hold the horrified chicken under her arm; she looked like a child trying to hide a forbidden toy, bending askew, alert to run. There was a just visible twitching of the muscles under the soft bluish skin below her eyes. This still creature could move, then; there was a flutter in this stone.

"This, Saggay Saggayitch," said Wilfred Chew (who had, you see, made an advance in intimacy), "this is Miss Tatiana Ostapenko whom I mentioned to you once or twice before. She, unfortunately, in common with the rest of her family, speaks no English, but I believe she will remember that we had the mutual pleasure of meeting, some time ago, when I called on her father with Sir Theo Mustard. Kindly recall this to her mind in Russian."

Seryozha at once withdrew his eyes from Tatiana, since he was about to address her. He looked at a stone on the ground, at the vanishing cloud of birds. "This Chinese fellow says you know him," he mumbled.

"I remember," said Tatiana, remembering suddenly. "He came in a motor-car with an imbecile English lord."

"She remembers, does she not?" said Wilfred, complacently. "I thought she would. I was right."

It was impossible for Tatiana to carry three hens under two arms. She carried one, Seryozha carried the other two. Tatiana walked a step in front — she was never quite with any one. Seryozha did not look at her. He slouched along, looking at his shoes — the toe of one of which was completely worn away — looking down at the hens. The hens were looking at each other across his lower chest with an unexpectedly calm expression. Seryozha, who suddenly felt much cleverer than usual, remembered another English idiom. "Look," he said to Wilfred, "Mrs. Hen say, 'Keep stiff upper beak, sister.'"

He swung along, pleased with his wit, looking at everything except Tatiana. Nobody said anything else.

But just as they passed the village tree, emptied now of its birds, Tatiana looked up and, with one little dancing step, broke the rhythm of their silent walk. And Seryozha looked at her then, looked at her straight young back, her headkerchief, which had slipped back to her nape, looked at the clothes and trifles that incased her — the comb that held her red hair, the faded blouse, the full, uneven cotton skirt, her brown bare legs, her feet shod with cloth shoes. He saw these things clinging to her slim dancing body — this rustling cloud of faded cotton swinging round her body. She didn't know that little tape was showing at her neck he thought gently. She was suddenly real to him, because he could imagine the homely habit by which she would put on those touching clothes — a comb here, a button there, and then a look in the mirror to see, anxiously, if everything was pleasant and decent. That little tape, the day-worn look of the hem of her skirt, the dust on her blunt Chinese shoes, humbled her charmingly in his sight. He strutted behind her; the hens seesawed under his arms, sharing involuntarily in his swagger.

CHAPTER EIGHT

PAVEL OSTAPENKO lifted his dripping face from the washing-basin and looked out of the window, blinking his staring eyes. Two unknown young men with Tatiana — no, on second thoughts, one, for the second was a Chinese. "Funny," thought Pavel. "I seem to have seen them both before." "Varitchka," he called hoarsely to his wife in the next room, "where have we seen these young men before?"

"What, more young men . . . ?" moaned Varvara. She looked between the flowers in the window at Seryozha and Wilfred. Seryozha was squatting down, launching the hens into freedom, as though they were little ships. Like little ships in full sail they sprang away from him with wings out and bowsprit necks craning. Tatiana, watching them, had a simple hen's relief written upon her face. Her fingers fluttered like rudimentary wings.

"The Chinese," said Varvara, "is the man who came in once, with an Englishman and a French valet, when their car broke down. We gave them tea, you remember. We could only talk to them through the valet. I remember the Chinese because of his one gold tooth. That Russian lad is a stranger to me. So he is to you, Pavlik. You are muddled today. How could you ever have seen him before without me?"

"Yes, I have. His face is absolutely familiar. It is something about that line from jaw to ear; something, too, about his eyes—the lids so deeply tucked in. Who can it be?" He turned Seryozha's face about in his memory as one turns an unopened letter, testing one's instinct, yet refusing to prove it by a simple practical act.

"I have it," said Pavel. "That boy is exactly like my sister's husband's cousin, Sergei Dmitrivitch Malinin. He had those eyes and that carriage of the head, exactly. I knew him when I was a child and he was this lad's age. I may have met him once or twice later, too. He was in my brother-in-law's business in Moscow. This boy's height and build and coloring are all quite unlike—yet the eyes and the jaw. . . . I never saw such a likeness. Sergei Dmitrivitch was a silly lad, I see now, but I thought a lot of him then, because he could move his scalp and his ears by themselves—his hair slipped all of a piece right back, like this. Ah, tschah! I can't do it. . . . How well I remember. . . . I used to say, 'Wobble your hair, Seryozha,' and he always did it for me. I think he was flattered by my admiration of his skill."

"Your cousin Sergei Dmitrivitch," said Varvara, assent dawning in her face. "The man who said that the seat of the soul was in the nape of the neck? He came to supper with us, in Moscow, soon after we were married. It must be twenty-five years ago. I have never forgotten the way he fingered the back of his neck as he talked, as if he were encouraging his soul. Yes," she said, leaning tensely between the fuchsias in the window, "I can see what you mean about the eyes of this boy. But it must be imagination, Pavlik."

Tatiana came in. She felt almost as if she had created Seryozha; it was quite important to her that her parents should approve of this new Russian that she and her hens had conjured out of empty air on a Korean trail where no new Russian had been heard of before. Russians in Far Eastern villages are so well used to living in water-tight communities that they forget there are such things as strangers of their own race.

"A Russian young fellow is here," said Tatiana. "And a Chinese who says he is the one that came with that imbecile Englishman whom you taught to say *Za Vashe zdorovye papasha*."

Pavel was now feeling that exalted feeling that comes just after a drink and just before the reaction. He went to the door sparkling with handsomeness and enthusiasm. Seryozha, in the yard, still showing off a little in case some one might be looking out of the window, was making his dog jump over an upraised stick.

"Come in! Come in! Come in!" shouted Pavel Ostapenko. "It is seldom we meet strangers of our race — seldom indeed that we have the pleasure of——"

Wilfred Chew pushed in front of Seryozha and shook one of Pavel's two generous outstretched hands. "You will remember me, I feel sure, Mr. Ostapenko," he said in English. "I had the mutual pleasure of calling here with a gentleman called *Sir* Theo Mustard, of Leeds, England, about a month ago. And now I introduce another gentleman——"

Pavel laughed breezily. "Tell your friend," he said in Russian to Seryozha, "that I can't speak or understand English. I can understand it written down, because I have to depend for news on the English newspapers, but spoken it means nothing to me." As usual, his pleased voice made this ignorance sound like a virtue or a cleverness. The spontaneous reply to the tone of Pavel's voice explaining one of his shortcomings would have been, "Well, well — I congratulate you. . . ."

"Where do you come from, my dear sir, and may I know your name?"

"We come from Chi-tao-kou," mumbled Seryozha, feeling too large for the door as he was drawn in. Wilfred Chew, coming across the sitting-room between the two big Russians, looked like a cocoanut palm between two oaks.

Then Pavel said, "Do you know my cousin, Sergei Dmitrivitch Malinin?"

"We know him," said Seryozha, with the young boor's natural instinct to begin by being disobliging in the giving of information. He added to Wilfred in English, "They speak, do I know my own papa?"

This was the kind of joke that appealed to Wilfred. That some one else should not know something that he himself knew, seemed to him essentially flattering and amusing. (One notices the same ready sense of simple fun in a rustic, directing a stranger through his village — "Turn by Winkler's Corner. . . . What, you don't know Winkler's Corner where Mrs. Thompson's mare fell down dead last year? Well, it's opposite the Glebe Field. . . . For goodness' sakes, you don't know that, either?" etc., etc.) Wilfred Chew laughed with delighted hissings, because these simple Ostapenkos did not know that Seryozha was his father's son.

Pavel was baffled by Seryozha's uncommunicative manner. "Is Sergei Dmitrivitch in good health?" he asked, though he really wanted to say: "What's the matter? Is my old cousin dead or has he turned you out of doors, young man?"

"He is in good health," said Seryozha, and added, indifferently, "He is my father."

"Well, well!" shouted Pavel, leaping up and clapping his hands about Seryozha's shoulders. "My dear, dear boy, you don't know what it means to us in our exile to have a kinsman walking in like this. We haven't heard anything of any of our kin since the revolution, and though your father and I are only distant cousins, I used to have the greatest admiration for him. Can he still move his ears and the hair on the top of his head?"

"He has no hair to move, now," said Seryozha. "And he isn't merry enough to do that kind of thing now. He is blind."

"Blind!" Pavel's emotions, always a little exaggerated by the excitement of a drink just over or that of a drink to come, at once materialized in the form of a tear in each eye. "Ah, poor man! poor man! Blind! . . . I am very tender-hearted. Excuse me."

"Explain me what he is saying," said Wilfred, anxiously. But there was no time, for Pavel went on:

"Blindness — the most terrible of all afflictions, especially to a man of your father's sturdy independence of character. . . . He used to be so kind to me when I was a young boy and he a youth about town in Moscow. His hair, falling backward, looked like an accident. Lord! How I used to laugh! And now he is blind. Ah, how carefree children are . . . how little they know. . . ."

His beautiful deep voice, uttering these sad words, seemed to bring to the minds of all three Ostapenkos the unearthly and tragic glamour of a remembered Ostapenko childhood. Egoists always have unhappy childhoods, and always look back on them in an agony of rapture and emotion. The eyes of both Varvara and Tatiana were wet at the thought of the laughter of little Ostapenkos, unconscious of a threatened doom.

"They are all crying," said Wilfred, feverishly. "Explain me, please, Saggay Saggayitch, what is being said."

"It is curious how all members of our family — mine and no doubt yours, Sergei Sergeievitch——" Pavel included Seryozha's family as a polite afterthought, "are haunted by this sense of doom — this atmosphere of tragedy — from birth till death, and always a tragically sudden death, mind you. A hard-drinking, hard-riding, passionate, gloomy, sen-

sitive, tragic breed. . . ." He rolled these delicious words
in his throat, drew himself up to his full splendid height,
and glared at Seryozha, as though scorching into his young
kinsman's intelligence the baneful splendor of his connection with the tragic Ostapenkos. "This air of doom — your
father's blindness is a fearful example of it — seems to affect
even those who come in contact with us. My daughter's
betrothed, Alexander Petrovitch Weber —— By the way,
were you still at Chi-tao-kou when that tragedy culmi-
nated?"

"What tragedy? You mean when Alexander Petrovitch
lost his papers?"

"He lost his life," said Pavel. "He cut his throat."

Seryozha caught his breath and looked at Tatiana. There
seemed to him to be no spontaneous connection between
this live young woman and that dead young man. For he
had an extravagant respect for life; unconsciously, he en-
shrined it as a holiness. The power of movement, the sight
of movement, and the feeling of movement were his trin-
ity.

Tatiana rubbed her hands slowly together and passed the
tip of her tongue across her lips, looking here and there,
but not at Seryozha.

"It is certainly a curse," boomed Pavel, standing swinging
his weight from one foot to the other, almost as though he
were dancing. "It is part of the family curse which you and
we, as kinsmen, share. Tanya has had seven admirers, and
all have felt the force of the family doom. We are certainly
accursed. . . . If you were not a cousin of ours — and thus
involved in any case — I would advise you to keep away
from us, young man. Ostapenkos affect all who approach
them."

"Kindly explain what he is saying, Saggay Saggayitch,"
twittered Wilfred.

"That case of champagne, Varitchka my dear," said Pavel,

"may be said to have been long waiting to be opened in honor of a kinsman."

Varvara, frowning with excitement, went out of the room, and as she passed Seryozha she said in a low voice to him, "Sergei Sergeievitch — you mustn't judge her by love."

Seryozha turned quickly and looked after her, gaping. "Well, these are queer birds, these Ostapenkos," he thought, and had an impulse to step to the door and shout after his hostess, "I don't intend to."

"What did Mrs. Ostapenko whisper to you, Saggay Saggayitch?" cried Wilfred, rumpling his thick black hair in a frenzy of thwarted enthusiasm.

"Alexander Petrovitch," said Pavel, "was my darling future son-in-law — the ideal son-in-law. Sometimes I think, Sergei Sergeievitch, that women exist only to suck the blood out of men. . . . Excuse me a moment. . . ." He could hear that Varvara was looking in the wrong place for the champagne.

"Please, please, what is he talking about, Saggay Saggayitch?" said Wilfred desperately, as their host went out.

"Oi . . . about mans . . . and womans . . . plenty things," said Seryozha. He was looking blankly at Tatiana's reflection in a looking-glass. It was an old dark glass that made everything seem twilit and leaden — even Tatiana's bright hair.

Tatiana, crouched over something on the table, said, "Have you ever noticed that there are always pictures of spotted deer on all Japanese match-boxes? Sometimes in one attitude, sometimes in another, but always under a little tree. I wonder why."

Seryozha did not know why, so he only grunted humbly. Wilfred Chew, feeling anxiously that an opportunity for wit or sentiment was being missed, leaned forward, grinning with all his teeth, and said, "*Horosho*, Miss Ostapenko, *horosho, horosho.* . . ." *Horosho* was the only Russian word he knew, and of course it was an enthusiastic and ambiguous one. Poor Wilfred, it was torture for him to be left out of talk.

Pavel came back with the hurried gait of one who has thought of several good things to say while he has been away.

"Women, Sergei Sergeievitch, are like a kind of dry rot in a man's world," shouted Pavel, who was suffering from one of the momentary spasms of dislike of women that come to a man who lives alone with devoted women to whom he is reluctantly devoted.

"I must say, I don't understand this grumbling at things for being things," said Seryozha, feeling very manly. "You can't grumble even at a louse for being a louse; only if it pretends to be a beetle — then you can grumble. Or if it bites you, you can grumble at the bite. But bite or no bite, it is what it is. I don't think women are dry rot, or anything but just women. They do what they were born to do, just as we do and lice do."

"You are like all young people in these days, cousin, full of contradictory arguments," said Pavel, genially, without giving attention to a word Seryozha had said. "I'll tell you a story out of my own experience — a story that always seems to me to typify the mean part women play in men's affairs. Excuse me a moment while I open this bottle. Tanya, the wire-cutter."

Tatiana, without rising and without lowering her eyes, which were fixed in a kind of blurred stare on the match-box on the table, pulled out a drawer close to her. She was for a second obliged to focus her eyes on the contents of the drawer as she selected the wire-cutter and handed it to her father. Then she fixed her blurred, trance-like gaze on her father. He was half turned away from her toward the guests, and she could see the layer of healthy fat at the corner of his jaw, his cheek, the side muscle of his neck, and even his ear, wobbling as he talked. She thought, what an inconceivably over-elaborate use we make of these strips of flesh — our lips, our tongues, our hands, our feet . . . praying, singing, telling lies, explaining philosophies, opening champagne bottles, making watches and guns, dancing, treading out grapes. . . . What a complicated destiny for something that is, after all, nothing but *meat*. . . . The natural thing for lips to utter is a grunt, thought Tatiana — a kind, calm grunt like Seryozha's. Yet there was the flesh on the sides of her father's skull all quivering like a jelly to no purpose, the bones all shaking anxiously with superfluous effort.

Pavel poured out three glasses of champagne for his two guests and himself. Wilfred shook his head vigorously. "I never touch alcohol," he said. "Its dangers have been so well explained to me by Reverend Mr. Oswald Fawcett. And, Miss Ostapenko, I see, does not touch alcohol, either."

Pavel hesitated and then poured out half a glass for his daughter. His attention was drawn by this to Wilfred, and he said: "Your friend might be interested in my story too. What a pity that he speaks no civilised language."

Wilfred, feeling that he was being referred to, bowed excitedly several times.

"About ten years ago," said Pavel, settling down. "Or wasn't it ten years ago? Anyway, at the time the Japanese and Americans were at Vladivostok, I happened to be buying ponies in Mongolia. Wherever there is war, Sergei Sergeievitch, somebody will be ready to pay for horses, and horses are my skill. All Ostapenkos have an eye for a horse. Some people have skill in writing poetry, some in starching evening dress shirts. I have skill in horses. Those little Mongolian horses are excellent in their way — the English race them and play polo with them in Shanghai, I believe — and in the war I found it several times worth while to go down into Mongolia, leaving my wife and baby in Vladivostok, and buy direct from the Mongolian breeders.

An amusing expedition, that; the Mongol horse-breeders are decent, hospitable men if you treat them fairly, though — God! — they smell! They live in tents and feed you on mutton — mutton — mutton — cooked sour, somehow — nothing but mutton (except that once I found a horse-tail in the big family stewpot. Lord! I can tell you I went out and vomited)."

"What is all this about, Saggay Saggayitch?"

"He eat sheep and horse's tail," said Seryozha, and poor Wilfred, astounded, fell back in his chair, trying to hook this information on to anything that had gone before.

"At the time I crossed the border into Mongolia, the out-of-the-way districts were hardly affected at all, as yet, by the revolution or its after effects. Once one got away from the railway zone, one was off the track of politics. So when I returned into Siberia, with fifty good ponies, I was surprised to come across a troop of Red cavalry — the offshoots of Boudeny's activities, I suppose — under the command of a scoundrel called Ivanov."

"Bolshevik horses," said Seryozha in English, seeing Wilfred drawing breath to bleat another hopeless appeal.

"Now I, Sergei Sergeievitch, am an unsentimental man without any prejudices. I am always ready to receive new ideas. My skill in horses is my only fixed idea. Perhaps I shall shock you by saying that — at any rate at that time — though I had steered clear of politics my sympathies were rather with the revolution than against it. Twenty years before, my younger brother had been sent to Siberia, as a student, for speaking at a meeting in Moscow. I never heard of him again, and naturally that had made an impression on me that was hostile to the Tsarist regime. I always behaved as a good and cautious subject of the Tsar, of course, still, I was open-minded about a change of government. So that when I found myself, without warning, in a camp of Red soldiers, and was detained, with my four Korean grooms, I was able to face Ivanov without prejudice or panic. 'General,' I said, 'I'm a man of no prejudices. I'm not afraid of you, and I tell you straight out, I can see that most of your horses are worn out and only fit for a merciful bullet, and that half your men don't know how to put a saddle across a horse properly or ride the beast when saddled.' Ivanov was astounded at my *sang-froid*. 'Hmph!' he said."

Pavel's voice was quite enough to make himself the hero of his story, unaided by the sense of his words. He quoted himself in a voice of noble clarion courage, and Ivanov in a barbarous snarl. The *hmph* of Ivanov whetted Wilfred's appetite for explanation to an almost unbearable keenness.

"My goodness gracious! Saggay Saggayitch, what does that *mmpp* mean?"

"He speak, Bolshevik has bad horses."

"But this story cannot be *all* about horses," wailed Wilfred.

Pavel, however, swept on: "Well, of course, Ivanov could see at once what kind of man I was, and, in a word, he not only promised to buy my horses, but, since he was likely to be in that valley most of the hot weather, employed me, informally, to lick his detachment into shape, both horse and man. It *was* a job. As a rule, our peasants have what I call 'horse sense,' but those louts — my God! — they must have been brought up with newts in a swamp or polar bears on an iceberg. They simply didn't know which end of a horse was which."

"I thought you said this story was about women," said Seryozha, who had been rather touched by Wilfred's last cry. . . . He added aside to Wilfred, "He speak still about horse."

"Wait," said Pavel, with a breathy laugh. "The women will come — they always do, curse them." He poured out more champagne. He felt very much alive, as he always felt when he had been more than half drunk and, after a period of irritation and partial sobriety, had begun to drink again. He tingled with a glorious heroism; every muscle, every nerve, every thought felt bright as a sword, after a little hour of rusty eclipse. "They were waiting to be reinforced by some artillery before tackling a stray independent party of White military engineers and miners, in a high mining village in the mountains. The Whites were in a very strong position. The only way up to the village was up a very steep ravine, or in a little dangling gravity trolley on a wire (which had, of course, been cut by Ivanov). The village must have been quite fifteen hundred feet above valley level; you could see it like — like — well, like the gold crown on a tall tooth, if you can imagine it, clamped, one might say, on a tiny peaked plateau. A couple of machine-guns could, and did, easily defend the pass. It was a difficult job for Ivanov, and he was particularly anxious to put it through because Colonel Rodin was said to be in command up there — a colonel of engineers who had given a good deal of trouble up and down that region. The place, too, was a regular magnet to all the miners of White sympathies in those mountains. The only thing Ivanov could do for the present was to stop their valley water supply — an elaborate hydraulic business that fed several of the mines from the river. I remember it being constructed several years before by an American mining engineer. Ivanov, of course, put that out of action, but still they held on, so they must have had mountain streams up there, or pretty big emergency cisterns."

Wilfred bounced in his chair, performing a little impromptu dance on his buttocks. "What is all this about, please?"

"They stop water-pipe," said Seryozha, and Wilfred, though profoundly puzzled, was at least relieved that the story had left the subject of horses.

" 'My dear Ivanov,' I said, 'excuse me, but you simply don't know the kind of people you're up against. I know this region; I know these miners; I know dozens of the men in charge of these mines; you're up against something as stubborn as the mountains themselves, given just these kinds of conditions. They're adventurers, these miners, and that means they're individualists, and that again means that in ordinary circumstances every man is for himself — they're not the "shoulder-to-shoulder" kind, when nothing threatens them; they'd as soon break a man's nose as shake his hand. Sometimes they're the sons of political exiles, and sometimes they've lived in these mountains so long that they've almost forgotten their mother tongue. They don't sing pretty songs about Holy Russia, or go, with clean faces, to church on Sunday. But once something *does* happen to bring them together (and you may depend on it, Stepan Rodin knows how to handle them), well, I tell you they'll never give in. You know what Rodin is — people say he's the son of a priest, you know, and only the adopted son of old Rodin, and I bet he's made a holy war of this. . . . What's more, I'll bet they've got a priest in that village, praying night and day while we sit here, to a little packed church. They've got their women and children to defend up there, too, and that always makes a difference. Once these fellows remember God — once they feel they've got God behind them — well,' I said (and it was a funny thing to say to a Red anarchist like Ivanov), 'God *is* behind them. . . .' You see, Sergei Sergeievitch, I remembered I was a religious man myself. Political reform is one thing, but I was sick of the blasphemy and filthy twaddle in that camp. I don't see why you can't set up an enlightened government and still worship God. Well, that's what I said, anyway — and it was disastrous for me."

The good-natured Seryozha realized that this part of the story would certainly interest the student from the Wesleyan Academy. "In such high mountains they are praying to God, he speak," said Seryozha, and was rewarded by Wilfred's look of bland, if blank, gratification. Wilfred's glass of champagne was strangely empty. Wrapt away in his emotional prison, he had been absently sipping his wine all this time, for lack of anything better to do with his lips. It was at this point that Wilfred was inspired to get out his notebook and his fountain pen and begin to write in English in his insipid clerkly hand. The plot of Pavel's story, as it filtered through to Wilfred, was so very exiguous as hardly to be able to engage even the most optimistic attention, and Wilfred had thought of another way to reëstablish himself in the center of the stage. Hardly had he put pen to tooth when, as by a miracle, his glass was full again. He wrote earnestly on, sipping his wine, sucking his pen, writing again, and only rarely lifting up his voice to inquire affably after the progress of the story.

Seryozha was getting bored. He looked at Tatiana across the stream of her father's voice that ran between them. She seemed to be getting smaller and smaller; she was sinking lower and lower in her chair. She was really trying to be unobtrusive — to be part of the twilight — because if her father should notice her, she was likely to be sent to help her mother and Katya in the kitchen. Tatiana, when still, was very indolent, afraid to break a spell of peace; when moving, she moved ardently, she danced, she ran. Now she hardly breathed. She listened to the story, lending her faint changes of expression to the changing phases of the story — frowning for Ivanov, tossing her head for Rodin, assuming a delicate insolence for her father's defiances. She and Seryozha, all the time, looked at each other across the river of talk with eyes endowed by wine with a sort of magnifying intensity of sight.

Pavel was opening a third bottle of champagne, but he did not stop talking. "What I said made Ivanov uncontrollably angry. I've often thought since that he must once have been a man of simple orthodoxy, before Bolshevik propaganda filled his stupid mind. That would account for his anger at what I said; one is always more annoyed by hearing something one might once have said oneself. He said a good many things about my infecting his sound men with outworn superstitions — treason to the Soviet — you know the kind of thing . . . and then he literally kicked me out of camp — unarmed — without a kopek. He'd got my horses, mind you, and not a penny did he pay for them, the dirty scoundrel. 'You can carry a message to your friends, sitting trusting in their divine cockalorum on that mountain top,' he shouted. 'You can tell them that with the hot weather coming on and their water supply in my hands, they'd find it wisest to change sides. . . . You go there and tell them that and stay there,' he said. 'Perhaps I'll pay you your money when you bring them all down, all with your tongues hanging out, ready to lick our hands for a drink. . . .' I really think he wanted me to carry that message — that's why he let me go. Anyway, I went. I couldn't do anything else. His men had taken all my money and papers and my grooms had disappeared. I just thrust my chest out and walked up the pass — as well as I could for a kick one of the dirty brutes had given me on the ankle. The defenders wouldn't waste their machine-gun ammunition on one lame man. I shouted, 'Don't shoot,' and waved my arms, and they let me come. They searched me, and then I had a talk with Rodin. Would you believe it? there were some quite good-looking women in the village — Russian refugee women, I mean, not the miners' wives — refugees who'd drifted there in Rodin's wake, I suppose. . . . Everything was upside down in those days. My God! they were hard up for water. There was a little cascade in the ravine, but it was almost dried up, and their cisterns were almost empty. No likelihood of rain, either, and, of course, not a drop coming up from the valley. Ivanov had seen to that. People were allowed to drink by measure. I saw a woman faint in the street, the day I got there, and next day a young fellow had a kind of fit. I liked Rodin, and he saw at once what kind of man I was. We found we had friends in common. I was with him when a group of men — the village storekeeper, the publican, a couple of mine agents, and some such outsiders, came and asked him to give up the village or take his soldiers somewhere else. 'Better give up than die of thirst,' they said. 'We'll have to give up some time, at this rate. You said we were to trust in God, but he doesn't send us water, so it couldn't be much worse for us if we put our trust in Red Ivanov.' Rodin said, 'Wait five days' — just like that — 'wait five days.' He said it so confidently and so mysteriously that the deputation thought he'd got some idea up his sleeve. When they'd gone I said, 'My dear Colonel, what in the world do you expect will happen in five days? The Second Advent?' 'Oh, anything may happen,' he said. 'I never look more than four days ahead; the fifth day is the one I can't see, so I always expect a good deal of it.' And that day, while he and I were talking, Julia Arcadievna sent to ask Rodin to spare her a few minutes. She was the widow of a man who'd died of sunstroke during the retreat across Siberia, and there she was drifting east with the refugees, and had somehow drifted here — one never knew where people would turn up in those days — but she was absolutely virtuous, my dear Sergei Sergeievitch, absolutely virtuous."

Seryozha shifted in his chair, his big limbs tired of still-ness. He became aware that a certain activity in the slowly spinning room was to be identified as the appearance of dinner. He saw the bottles fly upward to allow for the laying of the cloth and then descend again, upright, like angels. He saw blue plates settling like leaves upon the cloth. The movements of Varvara and the servant were like a little controlled wind making all these orderly displacements.

"What does *dobbri-dyet-il-niar genstchina* mean?" asked Wilfred, but not in the manner of one who really wants very much to know. His notebook, like the bottles and glasses, had been mysteriously snatched to heaven, a white cloud of cloth filled his sight, and now the notebook alighted again, ready for use, with a full glass of champagne beside it.

Seryozha could not remember the English words for a virtuous woman. "*Nyet* singing girl," he said, uncertainly.

Katya, the servant, leaning over Pavel with a plate, said: "Have you heard the news, Varvara Alexeievna? Piotr Gavrilovitch has joined the Chinese army. He wrote from Mukden yesterday. I heard it from Olga Ivanovna's niece's woman."

Pavel glanced with vindictiveness at his daughter. "Ha, Tanya! News about your Petya. That disposes of another of them, doesn't it? Tanya, you are listening to my story, aren't you?" He went on: "Well, Sergei Sergeievitch, when this virtuous woman saw Rodin, she said, 'Stepan Stepanovitch, what have you said? Five days? You have given God five days to save us in. What blasphemy to set such a limit. If faith can sustain us for five days, why not five hundred? Surely we can wait on God's will for longer than five days.' 'There's such a thing as being too thirsty to trust in God,' said Rodin. 'There's such a thing as having too dry a throat to pray with. Not for people like you and me, Julia Arcadievna, but for the ordinary ruck. Even five days is something. If you pray for us, perhaps something will happen to help us, even in five days.' He had a great admiration for Julia Arcadievna. I always say myself that women are in the way when there's fighting to be done. If it hadn't been for all those women and children, we could have given up our position and tried our luck against Ivanov's men in the valley. They outnumbered us, of course, but they were a poor lot, as I knew. Still, Julia Arcadievna was a damned handsome woman, and intelligent, too. She said: 'I've got an idea. I won't tell you what it is. If it fails, nobody but me loses anything. So don't ask me any questions, but come to the head of the pass tonight, Stepan Stepanovitch, and wish me luck.' 'Why, where will you be going?' 'Don't ask questions, I tell you. I've always thought I was born to be a spy.' Would you believe it, Rodin thought so much of that woman, he let her go. He even told me he had great faith in her. It's wonderful how good looks in women go to men's heads. Wonderful," he repeated in a different and savage tone, turning his white glare on his daughter.

"Rodin was a curious fellow — a fine-looking fellow, but quite bald," went on Pavel, stroking his own thick auburn hair, glad to establish superiority over the hero he spoke of. "Plenty of hair on his upper lip, but none on his head. He and I went to the sandbag barricade at the top of the pass that evening — for by that time he trusted me absolutely, and certainly it wasn't likely I should hold any more with these revolutionaries after they'd behaved like that over my horses. At sunset Julia Arcadievna, with her little Korean maid carrying a parcel, came mincing down the pass. Good lord! — what a change! She'd put aside all her widow's blacks and there she was in a sandy-colored Paris-looking frock with red embroidery, and no hat or veil to hide her pretty yellow hair. She looked stunning. She'd rouged up her lips and blacked her eyes a little. She'd a way of opening her eyes suddenly very wide as she looked at you. . . . 'Let your gunners and sentries know I shall be coming back in four days, Stepan Stepanovitch,' she said. So she went. She went in the evening, I suppose so that she could pretend to Ivanov's men that she'd slipped away unseen down the pass."

"Well, did she come back?" asked Seryozha. The widow, Julia Arcadievna, sounded to him almost too mature to be

interesting. He imagined a brazen hard-bosomed blonde of
thirty—almost an aunt's age. Seryozha could just remember meeting his mother's sister in Russia before the revolution, and women admired by older men always ever since
appeared in his mind's sight as shrill, plump, vivacious old
women of twenty-nine or so.

"Yes, she came back," said Pavel, looking almost alarmed
at the climax of his story. "She came back on the evening
of the fourth day, with a parcel."

"Well . . . she went away with a parcel didn't she?" said
Seryozha.

"Yes . . . but this was a different parcel—bigger and
heavier. She opened it in the presence of Rodin and me
and a lot of the men, on the terrace looking over the valley.
It was wrapped up in an ordinary army blanket. It was
Ivanov's head."

Seryozha snorted with surprise. "Ivanov's head! How had
she killed him?"

"Tschah! I leave you to imagine. In a woman's way, of
course. Poor devil! Playing on his manhood. That's a
woman's way, Sergei Sergeievitch. And what do you think
she told Rodin and me? That she hadn't actually slept with
Ivanov. She hadn't even given the poor beast that satisfaction. Lord! it was a disgusting thing to see her holding up
that head—all bloody it was—with both hands, smiling a
smug, rouged, womanly smile."

"Well, what happened? I suppose the revolution didn't
stop for lack of Ivanov's head," said Seryozha, prosaically.

"No, but the troop moved off in the dawn of the next
day. I watched them go—little lolloping specks in loose
formation. I knew why, of course—they were nothing but
raw louts; only Ivanov held them together; they were lost
without him. Some of our miners went out along the mountains and sniped them when they came to the narrow head
of the valley. They even got back some of my horses."

Varvara watched her husband. Only she knew how little of his story was true, and she did not mind. On the contrary, the story seemed to her a wonderful and brilliant fruit to have grown out of the seed of a little drab anecdote about a miner's Yakut woman who went out spying. Nobody was like Pavel, thought Varvara. He was her contribution to the sum of things — and, through him, Tatiana. She made no other contribution, and therefore had no other return. She sat self-contained, contributing no smile, no wit, no generosity, no money, no tyranny, no song — none of those forms of invested capital which alone pay dividends of friendship, fear, gratitude, love, or power. Nothing comes to the heart that hasn't first gone from it; Varvara knew that. But she didn't mind, because Pavel and Tatiana were her songs, and the voices of Pavel and Tatiana the returning echoes of her songs.

"Is this the end of the story?" asked Wilfred, noticing a silence, in spite of a slight fogginess of perception.

"Yist. She cutted off Bolshevik head."

"Good!" said Wilfred, feeling himself at last in possession of the facts. "Horosho, horosho," he added, nodding brightly to Pavel.

"Did you listen to my story, Tanya?" asked Pavel, suddenly turning on his daughter.

"Yes, papasha."

"A good one, wasn't it?"

"Good, but perhaps a little long," said Tatiana's mother, hastily.

"I'm glad, at least, she kept herself clean of him," said Tatiana between trembling lips.

"What?" roared Pavel.

The usually restrained Varvara suddenly made a great noise, clapping her hands, rapping the table, speaking in a shrill brisk voice: "Do you know what we are going to have for dinner? A gosling — a gosling in honor of our young cousin." She looked desperately at her husband and spoke more loudly still: "Oh, so good — you'll never guess how good, Pavlik! . . . You've all been talking so long, you men, that Katya and I had plenty of time to roast it to a turn. A gosling — a gosling — *oh* so good!" She banged the table for her husband's attention.

"What is she saying?" asked Wilfred, startled.

"She speak, we bite goose for dinner."

"My goodness gracious!" breathed Wilfred. "I thought she was announcing some calamity. So loud." He looked ruefully at his notebook, for the sudden noise had caused his shocked hand to make a little blot in the middle of one page of his neat writing.

Pavel, though his impulse of anger was a little softened by the goose, would not allow his attention to be entirely distracted by his wife's irrelevance. "Very well done, Varitchka. A gosling. Very good. But, Tanya — *what* was your comment on my story?"

Tatiana was silent. "Tanya made no comment," said Varvara.

Yet in Seryozha's hearing was ringing quite clearly the comment that Tatiana had made. *I'm glad, at least, she kept herself clean of him.* What a curious word — *clean* — he thought, and his thoughts went round and round it in a slow spin. *Clean — clean — clean* . . . women *clean* of men — men *clean* of women. He was young enough to be very impressionable by words, and the word *clean* did not strike him as being a euphemism for something much less attractive. On the contrary, in his present thin-spun, rarefied, wine-blessed mood, it seemed to him to express an ideal of some sort. That was the word that fitted his own rare moon-washed feeling — that hunger in the presence of quietness and color for something that would not appease the demands of either stomach, brain, or sex. Poor Seryozha! He almost recognized that hunger of his at that moment, though he could give it no other word than *clean*. It was his body hungering to be free of talk and understanding—hungering to be a bit of world, a blade of grass, a tiger—anything that was not dirtied by talk and thought. Everything between men and women was dirty—except one thing. "That girl—one could *eat* that girl, and remain clean," thought Seryozha.

He was obsessed with the image of hunger, since the gosling had been mentioned.

"Tanya," said Varvara, clearing away the *zakuska*, "come and help me dish up the goose."

The two women went to the door. As Tatiana passed Seryozha, he expected her to smile at him; he felt so sure that an understanding had been established between them, that she would be grateful to him for so keenly appreciating her word *clean*. But she did not smile at all. She walked past him, meeting his eager eyes without a change of expression, grave, blank, as though thinking of something else. And so strange was the chill that this blank look gave him, that his memory, shocked, threw back to the context of her remark, and he knew instantly that he had entirely misunderstood her words. *She kept herself clean of him.* By clean she meant cold, dead—all life was dirty to her. Her ideal was coldness. No tiger of life could hunger for that white unsmiling ghost. Seryozha thought, "If I had her, she'd melt like ice in my arms—she'd be *clean* of me, then." The word *cold* occurred to him many times—*cold* —*cold*—*cold*—before he realized what it suggested to him, and then he got up, a little unsteadily, and followed mother and daughter toward the kitchen. In the passage he paused beside where his pack of possessions hung on a peg. As he unstrapped the buckle of the pack he heard Wilfred, in the sitting-room, begin to entertain Pavel Ostapenko in a bright voice. Wilfred was not sober enough to mind that his host did not understand a word that he was saying; his automatic reaction to the silence was an impulse to emit information. Pavel was not sober enough to mind not understanding, and in any case he had something else to think of.

"The Japanese police, Mr. Ozz . . ." said Wilfred, "show themselves indeed marticrats—(marticrats? Yes, mautonets)—to travelers crossing the border, and at one point I really began to think, I really began to think that I really began to think—oh, well, Mr. Ozzabanko, you know all that without really beginning to think—I mean, without my telling you. But being a barrister-at-law of the Middle Temple, London, I could say to them. . . . And the Diamond Mountains—Kongo-san—though honeysuckled with soup—I mean soupstition—su-per-stit-ion—Saggay Saggayitch said 'Buddhanok on every up-look,' twelve thousand peaks, you know, but not really more than—well—what would be a conservatory estimate?" He began to think very deeply.

Seryozha in the passage took out of his pack the little smelly package that contained the heart, gall, and liver of the fish he had caught at Pa-tao-kou. It was in a perfectly disgusting condition, yet to Seryozha the smell was a smell of fate and magic; everything that Wilfred had said about it seemed to fit the circumstances so well. Blindness. Woman's coldness. Real magic indeed. The thing *must* have other powers besides its powerful smell. With his claspknife he cut a small piece from the heart and another small piece from the liver, and then, wrapping the rest in its paper, he replaced it in his pack. The two small flabby chunks he concealed in his hand and, striding into the kitchen, dropped them in the fire.

"What a curious smell!" said Varvara at once. Tatiana, pouring sauce into a bowl on the table, made no comment. She held her body too upright—almost bent a little backward; her head was high and she was looking down over

her pale cheeks at the sauce as though she despised it.
Really she was thinking of Seryozha's skin. As he had stood
for a second at the fireplace, she had noticed that the skin at
the back of his neck was not pitted or pimpled like Sasha's
or Petya's. This meant a great deal to her. His neck was as
neat as the fur of a dog, or the charming behind of a well-
kept horse, she thought.

The servant, Katya, seized the dish that bore the gosling
in her brawny bare arms and carried it towards the sitting-
room. Varvara followed with the vegetables.

Tatiana still stood at the table, but now, instead of looking down at the sauce, she looked sidelong at Seryozha,
soberly tightening her lips.

"Why do you look like that, Tatiana Pavlovna?" asked
Seryozha, holding the corner of the table, for he felt extremely dizzy.

Tatiana was silent for an unexpectedly long second, and
then, "O Christ!" she exclaimed in a high sudden voice.
"Can I not even *look* like myself without being asked questions — without surprising somebody, offending somebody,
hurting somebody's feelings, making somebody reproach
me? Even if I do nothing — good or bad — only just *be*
— my *being's* not allowed."

"Who doesn't allow it?" asked Seryozha, swaying over
the table toward her, feeling very uneasy.

"You — papa — mamma — Petya — Sasha. Why do you
look like that, Tanya? Why do you *do* like that, Tanya?
Why are you alive in *that* way, Tanya? Why aren't you
alive in *this* way, Tanya? What can I do less than just be
born, breathe, and at last die? I'm not attacking, not pretending . . . I just *am*. I only ask to leave you all alone
and be left alone."

"Oh, not be left alone, surely!" exclaimed Seryozha,
shocked to imagine such a small creature growing old alone.

"No, not to be left alone any more than a common

sparrow is left alone because it is a sparrow," said Tatiana, violently. "Just to be allowed to walk on the earth in my natural way, as a sparrow is allowed to fly in the air. No bird cuts its throat for the sake of another bird. No father bird nags at his egg for just lying quiet in the nest."

They both smiled for a second or two at this.

"I could leave you alone," said Seryozha. "God knows it's a thing I ought to understand. I only want things to walk about and fly about by themselves. . . . I like my dog to go on laughing at his own jokes without me. . . . What am I saying? I'd never cut my throat for anybody, Tatiana Pavlovna."

"Come, children, come," called Varvara from the sitting-room.

But as Tatiana and Seryozha, carrying plates and sauce, joined their elders, Pavel said, "Here's this snake of a daughter of mine . . . here's this virtuous murderous heroine coming back with the head of a new murdered lover in her hands. Here's this——"

"Pavlik! Pavlik! Think! Think!" said Varvara, in a low violent voice.

"Come, everybody," she added, clapping her hands with a relapse into her unnatural shrill vivacity. "Gosling to eat —good gosling to eat. Come and eat gosling."

"I won't eat," said Seryozha, suddenly seizing the end of the table and bending, with an insolent but tremulous grin, toward his host and hostess—"I won't eat until you say I can marry Tanya. Please, Mr. Chew, help me. Oh, but, damn it, he can't speak the language! Well, there it is. . . . Pavel Nicholaievitch, may I marry your daughter?"

"God bless you, why not?" shouted Pavel. "I've told you the truth once and I'll tell it to you again. She's been be-trothed seven times and all seven men are dead—dead, aren't they, Tanya? Or if not all, what do you care? She kills lovers for pleasure. She bites them when they kiss her.

She slits their throats when they touch her. She cuts off their heads when——"

"Pavlik! Pavlik!" said Varvara. "*Think!* You are talking nonsense."

"Well, you can't say I haven't told you the truth, young man. My daughter's a snake. If you want a snake for a wife — God bless you, boy, you can follow the rest. I'll dig your grave in my meadow tomorrow. Nevertheless, for the present, be merry . . .'"

"I won't eat till it's all properly arranged and signed," cried Seryozha, bravely, though his heart sank. This was the first transaction he had ever made all by himself, and he felt dimly that it was not being made in the grown-up, business-like way he would have wished to boast of to his mother. "Mr. Chew, listen. Ah, tschah! Mr. Chew is asleep!"

For Wilfred, overcome by the wine, sat forward, his body telescoped upon itself, his elbows wide, his hands clasped upon his plate, his chin on his hands. His eyes had been shut, but now, as he heard his name, he opened them and rolled them roguishly at Seryozha. He opened his mouth, too, and waved his tongue, but no words came forth. He tapped his notebook with an idiotic significance.

There was a pause. Varvara looked nervously at her speechless guest. Pavel did not seem to notice Mr. Chew's unusual demeanor, but he drew the notebook from beneath his guest's plate and focused his frowning eyes on it at arm's-length, inviting Seryozha to read over his shoulder. With care, Pavel, who was accustomed to reading English newspapers, could read what Wilfred had written. It was this:

THIS INDENTURE made the twenty-seventh day of September One Thousand nine hundred and twenty-eight BETWEEN SERGEI SERGEIEVITCH MALININ of Chi-tao-kou in the Province of Kirin Manchuria timber worker (hereinafter called

the husband which expression shall unless the context otherwise determine herein include his heirs executors administrators
and assigns) of the first part TATIANA PAVLOVNA OSTA-
PENKO of Mi-san Korea Spinster (hereinafter called the wife
which expression shall unless the context otherwise determine
herein include her heirs executors administrators and assigns)
of the second part WILFRED CHEW (CH'U WEI-FU) of
the Middle Temple London England Barrister-at-Law (hereinafter called the Agent which expression shall unless the context otherwise determine include his heirs executors administrators and assigns) of the third part and PAVEL NICHO-
LAIEVITCH OSTAPENKO of Mi-san in Korea Equitable
Merchant (hereinafter described as the settlor which expression
shall unless the context otherwise determine herein include his
heirs executors administrators and assigns) of the fourth part
WHEREAS a marriage is intended shortly to be consummated
between the husband and the wife AND WHEREAS the said
marriage has been arranged so to be consummated as aforesaid
at the suggestion and with the assistance of the agent NOW in
consideration of the services rendered and to be rendered (at
the desire express or implied of the parties hereto other than the
agent) in the premises by the agent THIS INDENTURE
WITNESSETH that the settlor agrees to pay to the agent on
the consummation of such marriage as aforesaid the following
sums (that is to say) Y100 (one hundred Yen) in consideration
of his services in arranging the said marriage and Y50 (fifty
Yen) in consideration of professional services in the negotia-
tion preparation and execution of these presents AND in consideration of the natural love and affection of the husband for
the wife and of divers other good and valuable considerations
him hereunto moving and enabling THIS INDENTURE
FURTHER WITNESSETH AND IT IS HEREBY AGREED
AND DECLARED AS FOLLOWS
1. The said husband agrees to accept the said wife as his wife
and to support her as such in that state of life to which it

has pleased God to call her to have and/or to hold to love and/or to cherish until death do her part (NOTE fill in formal parts as respects wife)

2. The husband further agrees in consideration as aforesaid to settle on the said wife by will or otherwise within a reasonable period of time the sum of Y250 (two hundred and fifty Yen) at present at his disposal and/or under his control in the Bank of Chosen Seoul.

3. And in consideration of the love and affection of the said Settlor for the said wife and in further consideration of the natural gratitude of the said settlor to the said husband for offering the said marriage in spite of the 7 (seven) previous unfortunate circumstances the said settlor agrees on the consummation as aforesaid to pay as dowry the sum of Y2,000 (two thousand Yen) to the said husband

Nothing in this Deed shall disentitle the said agent from receiving any sum of money thereunder or from charging his reasonable professional fees in connection therewith IN WITNESS whereof the parties hereto have hereunto set their respective hands and seals the day and year first above written (NOTE Query add clause re agent performing Wesleyan marriage ceremony query Y25 fee)

WILFRED CHEW, Barrister-at-law.

"But I don't understand," said Pavel, suddenly realizing that he was drunk. "Have we talked about this before?"

"Not we, but he," said Seryozha, sheepishly. "He talked of it several times—being a friend of both of us. I took little notice of him, as at that time I didn't consider myself a marrying man. He's a good chap, Chew," added Seryozha, sentimentally. "Of course being a Chinese and a lawyer, he must drive a bargain. But he is a good honest chap. Twice he lent me his blanket, when I was cold after swimming. I shall sign this. I have sworn not to eat until I have signed something, and I am very hungry." He wrote his name on the paper, his tongue-tip writing in the air above the pen.

"We will not sign it till tomorrow," said Varvara. She could not read the agreement, but she was dubiously watching her husband's glazed red face.

"Tanya and I will sign it now," said Pavel, the uncertain lines of his face stiffening all at once to obstinacy. "It's not every day one gets the chance to have a hero for a son-in-law."

He splashed his signature under Seryozha's large blotched name. "Tanya," he added, putting the pen into his daughter's hand.

For a moment Tanya wrote with it on the air, as though in a dream. Her father and mother watched her. Seryozha paused childishly, with his mouth full, to watch her. Her lips were set in a little smile. She leaned back in her chair and looked down her cheeks at the paper. Then she wrote her name in tiny letters — Tatiana Pavlovna Ostapenko, and under her name she suddenly drew a little alert picture of a sparrow taking flight.

Her father looked guiltily at the signatures and the drawing. He folded up the paper and put it in his pocket. "Ah, tschah!" he said, as he seized a new bottle of champagne. "It means nothing. We still have tomorrow. . . . Varitchka, let's eat your goose."

CHAPTER NINE

From the moment of Seryozha's departure from Chi-tao-kou, Anna's world seemed filled with an entirely new air. One would have said that Seryozha must have filled the house as completely as a snail fills its shell — so convoluted, so entire was the emptiness he left, from floor to ceiling, from wall to wall. Out of doors, looking through Anna's eyes, one would have guessed her son a bright obscuring light — so bleakly new and hard and shadowless was every leaf, every hill, every silly angle of the street, lacking even the possibility of his presence. It was a world lit, as it were, by indirect lighting under low clouds, instead of by the honest bland sun.

Anna's son, ever since his birth, had always been within a few miles of her, and now those few miles, empty of him — a cube of featureless summer air — boxed her in, a prisoner. She could not spontaneously imagine his return. With a mental effort she could invent elaborate scenes of his homecoming, but she knew them to be artificial, knew them to be constructed with ingenuity rather than with faith and hope. Such scenes were always shattered by her conviction of premonition. "Absurd! . . . He will never come

back. . . ." Every inch of the earth is, after all, so dangerous.
Here, where we stand, a minute or a million years ago, some
heart failed. There, at that point to which our dear love is
hurrying, the lightning struck, the germ of plague was born,
the tree will fall, the flood will surge, the murderer will
stab — a minute or a million years hence — a minute or a
million years ago. Living is a matter of missing death by a
hair's-breadth or an æon — it doesn't matter which — and
dying is a matter of coincidence. If we knew the past and
the future of every yard of every path we tread, or of every
stone our dear love's foot turns over as he goes, where should
we turn for peace? Once we have realized the billions of
deaths and horrors that have been, the billions that will be,
every inch of the world seems soaked in blood. Every inch
of the world, it seemed to Anna, was haunted by the ghost
of a son whose mother had let him go. "Even at this very
second, perhaps, his foot is lifted for his last stride."

"Why should you be so pessimistic, Annitchka?" asked
Old Sergei, who had rather relaxed his attitudes during this
period of acute domestic discomfort, and lived now in an
emotional deshabille, content to be seen as Old Sergei
Malinin at last. "Hundreds of young men have made the
very journey that he is making and have come back safely.
Indeed, our Seryozha is doubly safe, since he has a reliable
man with him." He spoke to reassure himself as well as his
wife, since her chronic conviction of a fatal presentiment
affected him, too. He kept secretly in his pocket a knotted
string, making a new knot for every day that brought no
news of his son, in order that he might not have to irritate
his wife by asking her to verify his calculations by the calendar. Apart from this tiny effort of ingenuity, Old Sergei
had become, in a few days, very much more helpless than
ever before. The necessity for posing as a father being now
past, he had shrunk and withered into immobility, as flowers, dry and forgotten in the empty vase, hardly respond, ex-

cept by an unlovely rattle, to the moving air that used to swing their bright heads. Old Sergei expressed by his wistful avoidance of authority his craving to be at last old, to be nursed, to be pitied, to have nothing more expected of him.

"Ah, why did you send him away?" said Anna, turning on the old man. "He was our life — our crutch; we're nothing but a couple of old bags of bones without him. You know what a dangerous, lawless country this is for a Russian, yet you were so greedy to add money to money. . . . Why, money's dirt compared with the safety of our Seryozha. The money we had was enough; we lived very well; we were happy enough."

"Don't worry yourself so, Annitchka. It's folly to worry so — besides, it worries me. The boy's not gone far; he'll be back again in no time; we shall see him one of these days coming in at that door as usual — or rather, you'll see him, since I am so afflicted."

"I shall never see him again," said Anna, looking at the door, trying to force her imagination to reconstruct the prow of his long shadow, coming in at the door, like a ship into harbor.

"Oh, very well, then, worry — worry. You take pleasure in worrying both yourself and me. Cry yourself sick if you like."

But Anna was not crying. She never cried. Her eyebrows were hitched up, her forehead strained into wrinkles, there was a little taut pain in the top of her head; these things, with her, took the place of tears. Sometimes she could almost have prayed to her muscles, Let go! Let go! Let go! Her eyes, her brow, and the little sore tiptoe yawning feeling inside the top of her skull seemed to be caught, hooked, seemed to have forgotten how to relax.

Poor Old Sergei was certainly a most uncomfortable old man at that time. His wife could hardly bear him, and yet she was not so cruel to him as she would have liked to be.

Kindness was, as it were, at each extremity of her behavior to him; the core of her feeling was kindness and she tossed an exasperated kindness from her finger tips. This surface kindness made her buy him things he liked to eat and serve them with muffled curses, which, being misheard by him, she would change to words of half-ironic gentleness. But between the core and the surface of her mood there was a dark, tortuous area of weariness and hatred of his plaintiveness, his meanness, the contradiction of life that he was. In this intervening confusion of her nature she suffered a sort of contrariness, a doubling back, that made her challenge herself unconsciously to be cruel — to try him a little more — a little more — a little more (will he stand it?) — a little more still (almost like a murderess daring herself to press a trigger) — till he would suddenly feel the prick of her insult, and lose his temper and his dignity. Then she would feel acutely guilty, talk to him gently with elaborate harmlessness, answer his meandering talk for a little while, until the obscurely revengeful impulse came back to hurt him again — a little — a little more — a little more still. . . .

She would wrench his rheumatic fingers with a half-deliberate pinch as she guided his hand to his food, and then, when he cried out, impulsively and genuinely beg his pardon, pretending, even to herself, that it had been a clumsy accident. She would sit and look at him, grinding her teeth because he was not his son, and all the time make wounding or humiliating retorts to his plaintive prattle. He was not very acute and did not often perceive that he was being worse treated than usual; he only thought that Anna seemed clumsier and stupider than usual, more misunderstanding in her talk and more abrupt in her movements. And, seeing his obtuseness, that strange contrary cruelty in the soft Anna would gloat over its opportunity — the tormenting of a creature too silly to recognize the instrument of torment — "how safe . . . no one will ever know of this

. . . no one but me . . ." Then, in the night, she would suddenly wake up, frozen with self-disgust, beat her head with her palm, and throw herself upon her husband, crying: "My darling, I'm sorry, I'm sorry! Forgive me. What a beast I am!" To Old Sergei these violent night-scenes of remorse were much more disturbing than the subtle discomfort of his days.

In order partly to be away as much as possible from her lonely house, and partly to save her old husband from herself, Anna pretended that she had a lot of work to do for Mrs. Butters during the first week of Seryozha's absence. Really the preparations for the Butters baby were finished now, and Anna was only needed at the mission once a week to help with the darning and mending. Yet every morning, after breakfast, she would murmur a vague word or two about Mrs. Butters's sewing and disappear, leaving bread, cheese, and beer ready on the table for her husband's noon meal. Old Sergei would sit drooping alone all day in the street doorway. He had charge of the sale of a few packages of cheap Russian and Japanese cigarettes, matches, sweets, biscuits, bottles of lemonade and clay pipes that were arranged on a couple of trestles outside the living-room door — the last *rigor mortis* of his dead shop. But only two or three customers a day spent a few sen on his goods and all day he would sit, half in and half out of his door, listening to the shouts of Korean and Chinese children playing, listening to the thin whine of the Japanese photographer next door singing over his work, listening to the clop-ker-clop of the senseless facetious gamboling of the mission kid in the yard behind the house, listening to the unfailing accompaniment of wails, cries, and squeals of thwarted and hurt animals that is always in the background of the hearing in every Chinese town. Sometimes the lonely old man would spend hours trying to lure within reach a dog that he could hear panting and snuffling and snapping at flies and ticks

across the street. With a bait of crusts or show of imaginary
food, he would patiently fish for the animal, only for the
pleasure of touching its rough neck and shoulders when at
last it trusted him enough to approach him — touching its
mangy ribs, its furtive tail, feeling the drip of sweat from its
hanging tongue, assuring himself morbidly of the presence
of another prisoner like himself, another life within another
lean, sad, and elusive body.

The first day of Seryozha's absence, Anna's only impulse
in leaving her home was to walk a little way along the path
that he had trodden. Perhaps she might see the print of his
big shoes or find something that he had dropped — the stub
of a cigarette or the paper that had wrapped *pirozhki*. Perhaps she might learn something about him from a Korean
peasant or Chinese peddler who had seen him passing by.
At any rate, she could see things that he had seen — notice
the patched crops upon the hills, the sharp rocks that slit
with a short gash of foam the smooth-running surface of
the river, the thin shade under which he had perhaps rested,
the bloomy dazzle of reeds in the shallows, the fantastic
duplication of crags — reared in groups, as nearly alike as the
chimneys of one house — halfway round the horizon, the
farm dogs that must have barked at him, that great scrawny
sow, dragging her unbeautiful dugs through the dust, that
must have made him laugh yesterday. Probably he remembered, when he saw that, that his mother had once said that
the fat pink mission school on the hill, flanked at right
angles by a neat row of little pink mission houses, looked
like a sow suckling its young. She felt for a moment as if
she were actually sharing a laugh with her Seryozha, and she
stood staring hungrily at the sow until the poor beast looked
almost embarrassed.

Then she noticed, sitting on a stone near the river, that
young Russian who had lately walked up from Seoul —
Alexander Petrovitch Weber. This young man, a plain,

sad, gawky creature enough, radiated beauty in Anna's eyes, because she knew that he and Seryozha had met. Seryozha had even brought him to the house the day before yesterday when she had been busy over the washing. Seryozha had, she believed, liked him, and this boy had doubtless been delighted by Seryozha. It seemed as if some scrap of Seryozha's darling personality had been grafted upon this young man.

She therefore walked towards him, feeling fat and humble and ungainly, as she had felt ever since she had lost sight of Seryozha. She must be tentative and a little self-conscious with every one now, since there was no one in Chi-tao-kou to justify her existence — no son before whom she could feel, "Well, I mayn't be beautiful, but this splendid creature calls me Mother." She approached Alexander Weber, conscious of her waddle and of her splay shoes, one of which was slit over one toe to accommodate a corn.

Alexander Weber was very tall and lanky, black-haired and sallow, with a big nose, abrupt cheek-bones and generally prominent features — among which an assertive Adam's apple seemed to hold its own, almost as though it were a second attempt at a chin. He had a very gentle look in his dark eyes — a look which he withdrew from the river and focused, as though with difficulty, on the approaching Anna.

"My son — Sergei Sergeievitch Malinin, you know — started for Seoul yesterday."

"I know," said Alexander, rising politely, though indifferently, from his boulder. "I thought of going with him."

"Going with him? Why, you have only just come from there, surely!" said Anna.

"Yes," said the young man, dreamily.

"He hasn't anything like the spirit, the vitality, of my Seryozha," thought Anna, gladly. She added, aloud, "Had you hoped to find work in Chi-tao-kou. I'm afraid there is little for Russians to do here, especially for a young man like you, that would be worth while. Is that why you thought of leaving so soon? Or are you not well lodged?"

"I am on my way up to Harbin," he said. "There is always a chance of a job on the railway there. Oh yes, I am well enough lodged. I am with Nikitin, the *droschki* man. He even let me earn something yesterday, driving an American missionary to Erh-tao-kou in a *droschki*."

"On your way to Harbin?" exclaimed Anna. "Why, you have just said you considered going back to Seoul."

"Yes," said Alexander, straying into his dream again. "I am not really sure what I want to do."

"Perhaps you have left some one you are fond of in Seoul, and are worrying about her," suggested Anna, gently. "Your mother, perhaps." A mother, it seemed to her at the moment, was the only thing that a young man could reasonably worry about.

"Yes, I have left my mother," answered Alexander, patiently. "But she has other sons. I have left my betrothed, too. Or rather, she *was* my betrothed; she is not so now. She is a dreadful creature."

"A dreadful creature?" exclaimed Anna, surprised.

"Yes, dreadful. Would you believe it, Anna Semionovna? — she — she forgets in a minute — even while you are speaking — what you are speaking about. She will say — 'One moment, Sasha, I must just take this basket to my mother,' and one waits — waits — waits — half an hour — an hour — and at last one goes to find out what has happened. There she is, whistling, shelling peas in her mother's kitchen. 'But, Tanya,' you say — and then you see that she has forgotten. Forgotten that I was waiting — that I was in the middle of telling her something — I — her betrothed! Sometimes, too, when I meet her unexpectedly, I can see that, for a moment, she doesn't know who I am . . . even the face of her betrothed she has forgotten. It is not to be borne."

"How extraordinary!" exclaimed Anna. "What a heartless woman."

"Heartless! Heartless, you say! She is as heartless as death. She is not alive. Sometimes I think she really hates anything that is alive. And it is not as if she were really very irresistible. She can't afford this behavior—if she doesn't look out she'll never get a husband."

"Perhaps that would be as well," said Anna. "Since she couldn't make a man happy."

"Happy! Happy, you say! She is death to any man that loves her. Seven men have loved her—and where are they now? She has a pretty face, certainly, but any one who loves her loves death. One may walk side by side with her and feel that a river runs between her and oneself—like remembering some one who is dead. She has red hair and very thin hands. Once I took hold of her hand—caressingly, as a man does take the hand of his girl—and when she tried to snatch it away, I held it—in fun, you know—surely a man may do that. . . . Anna Semionovna, she *bit* me—really deeply—in the wrist. I was quite revolted. I walked away. After half an hour she ran after me. She holds her head like this . . . and her hair comes unpinned when she runs. She runs very lightly. When I heard her coming, I thought: 'Well, at least something is gained. She can be near enough to a man to be angry with him—and then to come and beg his pardon.' And so she did beg my pardon—but what do you think? In begging my pardon she shook hands, lightly and politely, as one would shake a stranger's hand . . . then she drew her hand away, and seemed to imagine that no hurt remained. . . ."

"Well, you are well rid of her," said Anna.

"Yes, indeed," replied Alexander, instantly far away again, fixing his gentle, black, shortsighted gaze across the river.

There was a pause.

"Of course a moment of passion like that is not *live* passion, as it would be in a live woman. I'm sure it is not a sign of life. No man has ever seen a sign of life in her, though seven men have loved her — poor devils. Her hair is a bright dark red; that is supposed to be a passionate color for a woman's hair — but like the rest of her beauty, it lies. She is always polite. She can whistle to bring tears into your eyes — so soft — so strong — though of course whistling is not a suitable gift for a woman. But she's not a woman — that's why she's death to a man. I say, 'Whistle for me, Tanya,' and she whistles — for she is most polite and kind in doing whatever little thing you ask of her — but it is not for me she whistles; she whistles for the sky — for something far away. Such a girl, who can do nothing but whistle, and talk about cold fancies, and shake hands, and bite a man who has a right to caress her — well, her beauty is wasted, isn't it, Anna Semionovna? If you can call it beauty; I am not even sure that one could call her beautiful."

"She is not worth another thought," said Anna.

"No, indeed," said Alexander, looking at her with wet eyes and a guilty half smile. "It is a joy to be away from her, and to be with full-blooded men and women, after knowing such a dangerous ghost of a girl."

Anna had for several minutes been bored with the subject of Tanya. "What a pity that my son left Chi-tao-kou just as you arrived. He could perhaps have found you work in the timber-yard. There are so few young fellows of his own age in this region for him to have as friends. Though you are a little older. Still, you would have liked him, I am sure, if you had known him better."

"Yes, it is a pity. It is a terrible pity that I did not think of going down to Seoul with him. I wish I had. I wonder if he will go by Mi-san."

"I never heard of Mi-san," said Anna. "Is it one of the towns on his way to Seoul?"

"Almost on his way. Not more than, say, twelve hours out of his way if he goes on foot. If he goes by train, it is about three hours' walk from the railway."

"Well, why should he go there? Is the place of any special interest?"

Alexander, feeling that perhaps he had mentioned Tanya two or three times too many, and might have led this old woman to suppose that he was romantically interested in the hated girl, assumed an odd, secretive manner. "I do not think Mi-san is in the least interesting," he said. "To be sure, there are some mounds which — well, a Russian horse-dealer whose name I do not care to mention — a man who lives there — says are prehistoric and must contain relics of the past. But what live man cares for such dead things? Then there is a magic well which the Koreans say cures a thousand and one ills — but I think every sick man who drinks there must be suffering from the thousand and second ill — for I have never heard of a cure. What is more, Mi-san is a downright *ugly* village; one large tree, to be sure — but trees are commoner in Korea than here in Manchuria. The houses there are common-looking, the street filthy and dusty. A particularly unattractive village indeed."

"Then I am sure Seryozha will not go twelve hours out of his way to visit it. He has seen too many ugly dirty villages."

"No, certainly he will not. He would be much wiser not to. I only mentioned it because, if one starts from Seoul by the late tourists' train — the Gensan train — one can arrive in the small hours at Choan-san and, by walking quickly, be in Mi-san by breakfast-time, spend two-thirds of the day there, and walk back to the railway in time to catch the tourists' day train back to Seoul — in this way only missing one day's work."

"But Seryozha would not dream of doing such a thing to visit an unattractive village in which he knows no one." Anna looked at Alexander, her fat face screwed up with pity for this sad, gawky, inferior substitute for a son. "Perhaps, my dear, Mi-san is where your horrid Tanya lives."

"Tanya? What Tanya? Oh, I had forgotten her," said Alexander in confusion. "Ah yes, now I come to think of it, she does happen to live at Mi-san—I mean Tanya, this dreadful girl I mentioned to you. What of it? One knows so many girls . . . they all have to live somewhere. . . ."

Anna saw his Adam's apple moving up and down. His very plainness seemed to her, in her over-sensitized mood, most heartbreaking.

"Alexander Petrovitch," she said. "Won't you come and live with my husband and me while our son is away?"

"Good God, no!" said Alexander, shutting his eyes as though he had been struck. "I mean—excuse me, Anna Semionovna—I hardly know what I am saying. I meant to say, thank you very much for your kindness, but" (his voice broke as he realized that he was being pitied) — "but I must stay with the Nikitins. I am not very well just now. . . . I have a touch of dysentery, I think. This pain in the pit of my stomach goes on and on. . . ."

"You could have Seryozha's room," said Anna, ardently, hiccoughing with anxiety. "I can make a kind of gruel with arrowroot that would——"

"No—no—no!" said Alexander, and swung his clasped hands, as though in an agony of prayer, up from between his knees to his chin and down again. He looked intensely away across the river, and beat himself on his big mouth to steady his lips. After a long moment he said, in a high firm voice, "Have you ever noticed how few young Korean girls wear blue? They wear pink, green, yellow, white, but never blue. They don't seem to have noticed how pretty a young girl can look in blue."

"No, they don't wear blue," said Anna, sighing gustily. "But Chinese young girls wear nothing but blue."

"Ah, but they wear trousers. Chinese coolie cloth made into trousers has an ugly effect. Stiff and ugly — not swinging out when they dance or run. . . . Besides, they don't wash it enough to let it fade to that cloudy . . . cloudy blue. . . ." He sat so long without saying anything more that Anna realized that she might as well leave him.

"Well, Alexander Petrovitch," she said, feeling nothing but a useless, clumsy old woman again, "remember that I invited you. . . . You may change your mind. . . ."

Alexander did not seem to have heard her. His eyes were fixed upon her stockings, which were of a light gray. Alexander felt that he was haunted by light-gray stockings — since Tatiana always wore them. Every woman seemed to flaunt a cruel parody of Tatiana's slim dancing gray legs, and every time he saw gray legs he felt as though something emotionally final had happened — whether hopeful or hopeless it was impossible to say. It was as if Tatiana had stepped across his vision. Even the station master at Gensan, by wearing gray socks, had stabbed Alexander Weber's heart hot and cold. Even the piers of the dock at Gensan, bleached with sun and sea, had made him feel, "Is she coming — has she gone?" though he did not realize why.

Anna walked away. The sow was now suckling her ten ridiculous little balloons of babies, but taking no notice of them — not fussing about them with the loving attentiveness other mothers show. The sow's soul seemed to be lost in that huge mound of a body; her body was an outlying region, only very sparsely colonized with the germs of consciousness, only nominally under the government of some little vital citadel of egoism in the soul of the sow. That great swollen body did what it had to do — conceived young, suckled its young, rooted its jaws drearily in mud, shoveled food in under its snout, moved the stiff, overburdened props of its legs — but all these dull doings were uninspired by spirit. Only the tail, knotting and squirming tautly, seemed to have some more direct communication with the sow's remote inner life.

Anna laughed delightedly as she imagined herself nursing ten little Seryozhas. "With any other husband I should have had four at least — even though I was thirty-five when I married," she thought. "Then I could have kept three at home with me all the time, and Seryozha could have traipsed off as far as he liked."

Then suddenly she began walking home very fast, tearing at the armholes of her dress because they were too tight for such rapid movement. She had remembered that Seryozha had not packed the little phial of castor oil she had filled for him out of the big bottle. She made a wild plan to hire a *droschki* and get Alexander Weber to drive it. Seryozha and Wilfred would by now be about halfway from Pa-tao-kou to their night's stop — thirty miles from here, perhaps . . . a *droschki* with a good horse. . . . "It is most important," she assured herself. "Castor oil has saved lives before now. I could leave the old man plenty of cheese and bread, and get that Lai woman to come in and heat up the potatoes tonight. . . ."

She hurried into the kitchen. Old Sergei was sitting at the table, running his fingers through the heads of a bunch of zinnias he had picked in the yard.

"I am going to drive after Seryozha," said Anna, in a hasty, defiant voice. "It is *most* important. I can get a *droschki*. I shall only be away till tomorrow noon, I dare say. . . . He left something *most* important behind . . . that little bottle of castor oil. It might easily be a matter of life and death — eating at these filthy Korean inns. . . ."

"The castor oil?" exclaimed Old Sergei, looking dizzy. "He took the castor oil with him. He was packing his pack in here while you were cooking *pirozhki*, and he said, 'Tell mamma I have put the castor oil in, since she makes such

a point of it. Look, in here——' he said, forgetting that I
cannot look at castor oil or anything else."

"He forgot it, I tell you," shouted Anna, in a wild voice.
She rushed to the shelf which had been the rendezvous of
Seryozha's accumulation for the journey. She stood looking
at the bare shelf for a moment, in a silence broken only by
one loud sad hiccough. "Then, if he didn't forget it, why
didn't you tell me before, you old fool — you silly old fool
— you heartless old fool of a father? But why should you
care? You send your only son away into the desert without
a qualm — selling him for money — for a paltry two hundred yen. . . . Why should you care if he lives or dies? Or
for me, the child's mother — why should you care if I eat
my heart out with worry?" She stood in the middle of the
kitchen, quivering, bending toward him as though she would
strangle him.

Old Sergei, a little frightened, began to make the low
humming noise between his lips that he used to make when
they were first married, to soothe her when she became excited and nervous. She had been a slim young woman then,
and he, gentle and always a little dense about the causes of
her agitation. They used, in those days, to cling together in
the dark, after a disquieting day, to the sound of that silly,
compassionate humming. It soothed her now, though she
seemed rather annoyed to be soothed. With a surrendering
quick sigh she went away into the bedroom and, after a long
period of silence there which her husband dared not interrupt, returned and cooked the supper, talking only rarely,
alternately insulting him and apologizing to him.

But every day she escaped from home in pursuit of
torturing reminders of her son. Sometimes she would stand
in the gateway of the timber-yard by the river, watching the
straining bullocks pulling at logs, watching the tilted trees
on trestles being sawed by one man below and one above,
watching glistening satin logs being hauled out of the river,

176

watching finished planks being built into bristling wigwams. Sometimes she walked to an orchard that tiptoed on the slope of a hill, to see a little freak of a glimpse of very distant Korean mountains, wedged into the jumbled puzzle of Manchurian ups and downs. Sometimes she went to the mission garden to watch the children of Mrs. Butters's and to gloat over every pimple of their inferior complexions, every missing tooth in their whining little mouths, every ungraceful angle in their rickety limbs, every detail that flattered her memory of her fine son. She was very kind to the mission children during those days and spent a whole afternoon mending their toy pedal motor-car. "Your children are so very little, Mrs. Butters—perhaps it is healthy to be so little, perhaps my Seryozha was always too big—I dare say he was six inches taller than Dickie, when he was so old. It is pity that Dickie cannot carve woods—my Seryozha did always carve small ships in woods—but you are right—perhaps it is dangerous to do things with knives. Your children can play with motor-car—this is more modern—my Seryozha must always *make* something. . . . This motorcar—see, it is broken—the horn cries no more, it is in two bits—the back side has come undone from the sit-downupon. When my Seryozha was nine he shall have mended this—but never mind, Dickie, I will mend it for you—because I also have a little boy, I will glue the bulge of this horn to his tootle—I will glue this back side—and so Betti and Dickie shall be as safe—as safe—as safe as in their lovers' arms. . . ."

"Indeed, much safer, I hope, Mrs. Malinin," said Mrs. Butters, frostily, drawing her children away toward the house.

Sometimes Anna would seek out young Alexander Weber and make anxiously prosaic and useless suggestions about his problem. "Well, if you love her, my dear boy, marry her. . . . Well, if you feel like *that* about her, forget her.

. . . Occupy your mind with something else. . . . Have you tried fishing in our river? Well, dear Alexander Petrovitch, why not go back and ask her — ah — you are tired of her — well, make up your mind — you can't have it both ways, you know. . . ." All the time she cursed herself. "How useless I am. Being a mother has taught me nothing about how to comfort a young creature's sorrow. Any other woman would know what to say to him." Yet she heard her own reasonable, tiresome voice again, "Well, if you still love her, why not ask her to marry you . . . ?" Indeed, a practical friend can always easily cut the ground from under the feet of sorrow, but sorrow, as Anna knew, remains reared up in the heart that harbors it; without a leg to stand on, there it stands, as tall and terrible as ever — silly sorrow that will not lie down — the ghost that cannot be laid — casting its shadow where no ground is.

A day or two later, when Anna came in from mending socks and boasting of her son at the mission, she found her husband in great agitation, fumbling in his bureau among his threadbare Sunday clothes.

"We must go, Annitchka, and help . . . a terrible thing has happened. . . . Oi-oi! poor boy! poor boy! . . . Yet what a wicked presumption it is to take one's own life. . . . Oi-oi! what a terrible thing to happen . . . !"

Anna gave a loud, furious cry, instantly imagining Seryozha dead with a stain of blackish blood in his yellow hair. She could not speak; she took Old Sergei by the arm with a cruelly tight grip, and tugged him away from his occupation, feeling impelled to prevent any one from doing anything — to stop everything in the world happening — if Seryozha was dead.

"Alexander Petrovitch has killed himself. . . . Little Mitya Nikitin came just now to ask us to go over — the boy cut his throat. . . . Little Mitya says there was blood creeping out under the door; Nikitin saw it when he got up this morning, though they heard no sound in the night except a sort of cooing that they thought was owls — Elyena Ivanovna said, 'Owls! I never heard an owl before in Chi-tao-kou.' And then, in the morning, blood coming under the crack of the door in the shape of a long spoon, little Mitya says. Of course they tried to rush in, but the door was bolted — they had to break it open so violently that the bolt flew across and broke the window, and Nikitin, falling inward, nearly tumbled over the body, because it was just inside the door. Young Weber was quite dead. Little Mitya says he was lying with his head thrown right back and his throat gaping, looking widely upward, as though at an airplane, his mouth open, one hand thrown up, as though pointing, the other holding his razor. . . ."

Anna sank down on a chair, leaning on the table. She could hear inside her head a loud keen sound as of steam escaping. Her first thought was: "Well, now Seryozha cannot die — now that he has once been dead in my thoughts and has risen again. He is safe now." She sat breathing heavily, and gradually, as the shock passed, she forgot that ultimate crisis of her fear and began to feel that young Weber's death was the most terrible thing that could have happened today. She began to remember that the day had been mounting up in a sort of crescendo to disaster; the milk had been sour, a chicken had been killed by a cat, by some freak of absence of mind she had opened the wrong door in the mission compound and found Mr. Butters at prayer with a friend — she imagined now that she had suffered an overwhelming sense of foreboding on hearing the mission children teaching their puppy to die for its country — "Dead — dead — Spot — dead. . . ." Anna was persuaded that the whole day had been climbing up to death, like the note of the rain-bird — higher and higher, sharper and sharper, cracking, straining, higher and higher, till the voice splintered in a wild horrible peal and was still.

Alexander Weber was now promoted in Anna's mind to the status of a thing truly loved and terribly lost, and this process automatically involved a paroxysm of self-reproach on poor Anna's part; "I could have said — why didn't I insist? — if I had been wiser — I might have said — I might have done . . ." and now there he was, his blood running like a messenger out into the world, with a message of tacit reproach to a world full of blunderers.

Anna noticed that her husband had found and put on his old only Homburg hat. This hat, which Old Sergei scarcely ever wore, was his tribute to the solemnity and excitement of death. Like the screw top of an engine out of regular use and seldom assembled, it lidded a creaking, rusty organism, rarely set in motion but now profoundly pulsing and pounding, the reawakened essence of vitality running like a vapor from end to end of the feeble obsolete casing that inclosed it.

"Where are you going?" asked Anna, huskily. "I think you sit here and wait for disasters."

"Well, we ought both to go and help, I think. The boy was of our race. Besides, he left a letter for you. Elyena Ivanovna has it."

He clung with both hands to her arm as she led him through the streets. His body hung back, for fear of stumbling, but his spirit urged haste for fear of missing something. He was always in a hurry to be near the dead, forgetting that the dead are the only friends who can be really depended on to wait for us.

The Nikitin tribe, a group of promoted peasants — three or four inter-related families living in a maze of Korean houses that almost amounted to a hamlet — was divided between sentimentality and resentment, in the matter of Alexander Weber's suicide. They had laid the body of the young man, as though it were in disgrace yet might hope to be forgiven, in a room in an outlying house. The grandmother of the various families, a very aged, crumpled, ivory creature, watched over the body, trimmed the candles, and read — or seemed to read — from the Bible, though much of what she mumbled was a half-remembered rigmarole, for she never had been able to read easily and was, in any case, almost blind now.

Alexander Weber lay on the bed, looking astounded. The bluish lids now covering his large, sunken, meditative eyes did not modify his expression of amazement. His lips were set in a tautness that was not so much a smile as a suggestion of an attempt to whistle through his teeth. "I'm not listening to you," that mouth seemed to say, provocatively. "You can say what you like — you can't annoy me now. I'm simply not listening." His neck was rigidly bandaged with clean cloths, and this gave him a stiff, stuffed, shrugging look, like a skeleton George the Fourth. After so much talk of blood, it seemed to Anna that everything looked very wan — very thoroughly drained of color. The white bandages, the white clothes on the young man's bleached body, the pale light of the candles competing with the cracks of denied daylight, the scrubbed boards, the wilderness of sheet, the quietness, the featureless old voice mumbling — everything seemed pale, stilled, and suspended.

Anna had snatched up, as she left her own home, a little silver cross that had been left to her by an old aunt long ago. It had little sentimental meaning for her, but she had so few possessions that, if she had thought a little longer, she would perhaps have found that she could not spare it. Now, however, it was in her hand; she had looked at it several times, on her way through the streets, not committing herself to sacrificing it, yet dedicating it to sacrifice . . . teaching her hand to give it away. And now, without saying anything, she laid it on Alexander's breast above his clasped finger tips. "Easy to do — now," she thought, self-reproachfully. "Everything I do is always easy and obvious by the time it occurs to me to do it." But she was glad that she had laid her cross on his breast. That was the right, womanly thing to do, at last. She heard one of the Nikitin nieces making a little clucking sound of approval beside her, and was soberly relieved to have made no mistake in giving her gift. The cross made a little shining, definite meaning to the blank picture; it slipped into place as the moon slips into a blind evening sky, when the sunset has been drained away.

Old Sergei stood at the room door, hungrily craning his face toward the dead youth. "Shut away," murmured Old Sergei, hoarse with the excitement that death always aroused in him. "Cut off—shut away. How *curious* it all is! . . . All the little things lost—his tastes in food, the jokes that amused him—how curious! Even perhaps a little plan that he had to buy himself a blue tie in Harbin or to see Charlie Chaplin in the cinema—all lost—nothing could be more lost; if you offered a reward of a million rubles, you could never know those things now. How *curious!* Perhaps there was something his whole heart was set on, yesterday—and yet, if it happened today, he wouldn't turn his head to look."

"No," said Anna. "If she came now, he wouldn't turn his head to look."

"How curious—how curious—how very curious," whispered Old Sergei, trembling with elemental bewilderment, "that he should make no sound. If he had left this room a thousand years ago, the room couldn't have lost his voice more completely. I haven't seen a dead man since I was blind, you know, Annitchka, and I had forgotten that dead men don't breathe. Come away—come away now, Annitchka. I can't bear to hear no breathing. It's so very curious. Where is that breath? Where are the words we should have heard from him today? Oi! how terrible not to see a thing so silent! Death is more explained by eyes than by ears, Annitchka. Listen—I simply couldn't *touch* a dead man, now that I can't see. It would be like . . . cold meat. . . ."

"There is no need to touch him," said Anna, indifferently.

She did not move, and Old Sergei, clutching her arm, leaned forward, listening to the stillness that frightened him, glaring with his useless eyes. They stood for a long time, as though in a dream. Anna had strayed into a mood of peace. She almost didn't care, now. Here was one unhappy boy's unhappiness quieted, and her own happy boy left alive to enjoy his strong, hopeful life — undisturbed by such a destructive thing as the love of women. God was not dead. If the two boys had changed places — the happy one cut off in his happiness, the despairing one preserved in his despair — she would have thought, "This is typical of the contrariness — the non-sense of divine decrees." Often Anna felt obliged to suspect the divine wisdom, but now she gladly admitted a kind of profound sense — even in omniscience. That blood-sucking woman — whatever her name was — had missed one splendid and indispensable victim, and drained this poor drooping boy of his life. Seryozha was the more valuable, and he was safe. For Seryozha, thought Anna, a mother and a dog were enough. Neither she nor any other boy's mother would ever find Seryozha sitting on a stone, glaring as if in a trance at a swift river, talking — talking of a cruel woman, as though his tongue had forgotten all other words, as though his thoughts' grooves were worn too deep for change, as though his heart were bound to a ghost — like a story she had read somewhere about a prisoner bound to a corpse. Well, something like justice had been done. Seryozha was safe from love, and this desperate boy at peace at last — dead of that same love.

Now, now no longer sealed
In a thin pent body,

Mine are the windy fields
And the long halls of the wood;
I, who was loved and held,
Am now as cold as God.

The lover and his bride
Burn in a narrow flame.
We who have died
Keep no such tryst with worms.
Our sleep is wide,
Being in no man's arms.

One of the women of the house touched Anna's arm and gave her a letter. Anna's name was written on a rather bulging envelope.

The letter said, in rather a stilted manner,

Esteemed Anna Semionovna, I have decided to finish a life which is no more interesting to me. I am twenty-four years old and I am convinced that life has nothing more to offer me. I have always held the philosophical opinion that a man of experience has a perfect right to take his own life when, in his mature opinion, he has had his fill of experience. I don't know whether I may have mentioned to you that I have been very badly treated by a woman (if woman she can be called), by name Tatiana Pavlovna Ostapenko, and you may perhaps think that I have been weak enough to let her heartless behavior prey upon my mind, and that this is the cause of my death. It is not so, I assure you. Her repudiation of my honorable affection, though unreasonable, could not, of course, affect very seriously a man of my philosophical temperament. On the contrary, I am glad to think that my death will relieve her of remorse for her conduct — for she has a tender conscience, though she has no heart. She will think, "Well, poor Sasha is safely dead, now. I need worry about his sorrows no more." For she *did* worry — with a cold uneasiness. Perhaps when she is a lonely old woman she will worry again, but for the present she is welcome to get what satisfaction she can out of my death. In reality, my life and my death are my own affair, and women have had no influence on either. I should like to leave her my little gold compass which I have wrapped in a sealed packet in my pack, though it may seem ironical that I should leave her the thing I valued most in life, since she valued me not at all. Nor I her very much, really. I leave to my mother Maria Nicholaievna Weber, my money, seventeen yen fifty, and the rest of my possessions. Except my watch, which I leave to my younger brother, Konstantin Petrovitch Weber, with the advice that when he grows up he confine his love affairs to the caresses of Korean singing girls — they are safer than the kindness of virtuous women.

I should be grateful, Anna Semionovna, if you would kindly send the inclosed letter to my mother, as above, at 2 Takezoecho Ichome, Seoul, and apportion the belongings found on my person and in my pack as above directed. I hope you realize that I did appreciate your kindness to me, though I may have seemed at the time rather absent-minded, owing to some business affairs that were engrossing me. In reality I enjoyed the various amusing and interesting chats we had together.

ALEXANDER WEBER

"Well," thought Anna, biting her lips defiantly as she read this letter. "It *couldn't* have been my Seryozha. It *couldn't*. It's ridiculous to compare the two boys. One was half a man and the other is a whole boy. No woman could suck the blood out of my Seryozha, especially a woman whom all her lovers call death. Besides, he is most unlikely to meet her — twelve hours out of his way. Why should he meet her? There must be hundreds of Russians in Korea?" She looked at Alexander's stiff suspense-filled face, and some inward dismissing finger in her heart pointed him away — away — to be hurried into the earth — to be buried with

his dangerous secret of love — to have that mouth stopped
that talked so constantly of his cruel love — to have that
wound of love cauterized — to isolate a contagious heart in
the cleansing grave.

But as she walked home, with Old Sergei clinging to her
arm, tears ran down her face and she sobbed aloud. "Oi! it's
just that all boys are alike," she said, roughly and brokenly
to her husband. "The same number of fingers and toes . . .
the same silly hearts . . . the same busy soft bodies . . .
all the boys in the world are really like one huge silly young
body. . . . Yet Seryozha's still safe. I can't care much about
this poor Alexander." As for Alexander — let some other
mother worry about him. She, Anna, had given him her
aunt's silver cross — and so — away with him!

"We must help the Nikitins to arrange for a decent
funeral, even though he did kill himself," said Old Sergei,
fussily. "There was a nice plot of ground next to Alexei
Vassileievitch's grave, wasn't there? Shall you leave your
aunt's silver cross on his breast, or did you only lend it to
him?"

"My aunt's cross? How do you know I put my aunt's
silver cross on his breast? You did not go near him."

"How do I know? How should I not know? I saw it, of
course." He was abruptly silent for an astonished moment
and then said, "Anna — I saw it."

Anna's thoughts always ran in such a bustling hurry along
grooves worn by her own experience that for a moment she
did not realize the significance of his emphasis — in spite of
her first feeling of disconnection between the remark and
her reason. He saw it — well, why was that nonsense? She
had seen it herself. Why not? He saw it, yes — he saw it?
He — saw it? But he was blind!

"How could you have seen it?" she said, irascibly. "How
could you see anything? Tell me, how did you really know
it was there? You didn't touch him — you said you couldn't

bear to and you didn't. What do you mean, you silly old man? How did you know about the cross? Explain. Don't make silly mysteries."

"There is no mystery. I *saw* it," said Old Sergei. Then the impression began to dim and he added: "Yet, no—that's absurd. How could I have seen it? Let me see—how *did* I know it was there?"

Anna's mind could only digest everythings or nothings. There was no *sometimes* in her schedule, only *always* and *never*. The suicide of Alexander, and her own sense of failure, had inspired in her that futile, sore irritation left by a happening that cannot be revoked—that craving of the heart to say, "Let's pretend it hasn't happened," when the brain answers, "But it *has*. . . ." The heart crying, "Come back to yesterday—yesterday he lived," and the brain insisting, "No. Face today. Today he is dead. . . ."

"Oh, you old nuisance!" said Anna, while even as she spoke she recognized her accusation as false and unfair. "I believe you can see all the time. You have been pretending blindness all these months, just to be tiresome and make us pity you. . . . Look, walk by yourself now, you old hypocrite. You can see perfectly well. Let go of my arm." She threw his clinging hands away from her arm and walked furiously away.

Old Sergei was left in the middle of the street, flapping his arms like a child. He threw all his tremulous householder's dignity away and began bellowing: "Anna! Anna! Help! Anna, are you a devil? Annitchka, I am lost—I can't see. Annitchka darling, help me! . . ." Several Chinese peddlers, shocked and amused at this loud scene between a male and female Big-nose, stood still to watch.

Anna came back to him and snatched at his hand, almost crying with hatred of herself and him: "Tschah! Come along then; come along, you old fool."

"But, Anna, I swear you are wrong," twittered the old

man, wild with relief at her return, clinging with both hands
to her wrist as he stumbled beside her. "Annitchka, I swear
I am no hypocrite — I am blind — you can see I'm blind.
The doctor said I was blind. I can't explain about the silver
cross, but I am not lying about my blindness — I swear it
— Anna — believe it — believe it — believe it!" he cried,
shrilly. Her harshness had sent him abruptly back into his
childhood again, he shook and pinched her arm, like a
naughty child, in a panic of insistence. The Chinese peddlers walked slowly behind them, laughing, fascinated and
embarrassed.

"I shall go straight to the hospital," said Anna, obstinately, "and talk to the Japanese doctor and ask him what
really is wrong with your sight . . . whether it is possible
that you are simply pretending, all these months, to be helpless. He called it *hysterical* from the first. . . . I shall ask
him what all this means — I see — I can't see — I see — I
can't see. Tschah! you old baby. . . ."

And she did, after leaving him on his own threshold, walk
to the hospital, having nothing else to do, and ask the Japanese doctor to explain this curious intermission in her husband's blindness — if genuine blindness it was.

The Japanese doctor was a very sparkling young man who
had studied medicine and psychology in Chicago. In spite
of his American education, he still preserved that contradiction or quibble in social convention characteristic of his race,
which obliged him continually to hiss inward politely
through his teeth for fear of seeming to exhale in the presence of a stranger, yet allowed him to hawk and cough ex-
plosively every minute into that stranger's very eye.

He thought poor fat untidy Anna very uncouth, but he
bowed to her neatly and repeatedly and was delighted to talk
about his most treasured case — Old Sergei. He was less delighted to hear about him, for, though he spoke beautiful
English, he understood very little, unless it was written

down. This is a peculiarity of the Japanese as linguists — all have tongues, but few have ears. A Japanese fellow traveler may give you an exhaustive account of the geological history of the Cheddar Gorge, and yet face you with a blank baffled bow when you ask him to pass the cheese, please.

"You say he saw something — a horse, I understand."

"A cross on a dead man's breast."

"Ah, you say he is dead. Well——"

"No. He has seen a cross that I have given to a dead man."

"Ah, he has seen a dead man. I see by my notes that this interest in funerals is characteristic of the patient. I understand everything now. This glimpse of a dead man is most illuminating, missis." Even while he was speaking he decided to write an account of Old Sergei's case to the magazine of the medical school at which he had studied. He saw Anna through a sort of veil of anticipated printed words of flattery. . . . "Doctor K. Morimoto of the Chi-tao-kou hospital, Kanto. . . . Interesting observations by Japanese psychologist. . . . Notes of an illuminating case. . . . Doctor K. Morimoto's new light on hysterical amblyopia. . . . Doctor K. Morimoto, the rising young psycho-pathologist. . . ." The doctor felt obliged to speak loudly to Anna through this happy fog of hopes and compliments which dazzled his gold-rimmed glasses, she seemed to him so pleasantly dimmed. Yet he bowed automatically in her direction, feeling vaguely grateful to her for having an illuminating husband. "This matter bears out my first diagnosis, thus proving it to be perfectly correct. Your husband could, I am convinced, be cured of his pseudo blindness by psycho-analysis, if Chi-tao-kou could produce an analyst who shared some common language with the patient. Nothing, however, could be less helpful than the analysis in Japanese of a Russian patient who had no acquaintance with the Japanese language by an analyst who was unable to speak Russian. Your husband, when attacked by business and other misfortunes, and finding his position as independent merchant and paterfamilias threatened by the police and other dangers, takes refuge, unconsciously, in a reversion to the helplessness of the child, a claim for protection in this case established by blindness. Hysteria, you must remember, missis, is an affliction like any other affliction; it must not excite our contempt or irritation; it must be treated as a real affliction. Your husband is certainly not consciously deceiving us all; his Unconscious is simply tired of the responsibility of being the head of a family in such difficult circumstances, and, by wrapping itself in such a disability as blindness, claims the protection, so to speak, of his family — a protection that cannot be withheld from a blind man. I see, by referring to my notes, that your husband has long had an interest — amounting almost to an obsession — about the duty of honoring the dead of his own race. So, being brought into the presence — I think you said — of a dead Russian today, his Unconscious allowed itself — if I may so speak — a little holiday from its protective business of blindness, and gave him a glimpse — which he did not at once realize was a glimpse — of what so profoundly interested him. This craving to see the dead man being satisfied, the protective armor of pseudo blindness is resumed."

"The old liar," blurted Anna.

The doctor's Unconscious wrapped itself in a protective armor of impenetrable Japaneseness. "Yes indeed, missis. You must simply consider your husband for the present as a genuinely blind man, though his physical sight is unimpaired. His Unconscious is determined not to see until it is safe for it to do so, as it were. It will not allow him to be thrust back into the ranks of well and hearty men who take charge of their own affairs."

"The old coward," snorted Anna.

"Indeed yes, a most interesting case," mused the doctor. "It only needs to be rounded off by a cure."

"It certainly does," said Anna, ominously.

But on the way home she resolved to be more patient with her old coward. She heard with horror in her remembering ears her own rough harsh voice and his gentle martyred bleatings. "Did ever any woman commit so many sins as I?" she exclaimed, secretly, stamping and snorting along the street. "Never a minute passes without my having to be sorry for something I did the last minute. I must have been mad to treat my Old Sergei so—even if he had been the worst old husband in the world. And he's not the worst—he's only just an old fool—and he's fond of me." But her conscience could not let even this description of him stand. She began tenderly to remember him as he was when she married him—a thin, fanciful, conscientious bookkeeper in a Russian firm in London, a member of a high-thinking debating society, and interested in moths. He was always rather like a moth himself, she thought, but a nice, ivory-colored, clean one. He had been devoted to his gay, noisy Anna. He had always been ready to cover up her mistakes and comfort her conscience. She had married him —(Good God! was it possible?)—she had married him because she thought he was so wise. But the fact that he had proved not to be wise seemed to her now endearing. If he had been really wise he would not have remained devoted, she thought with a humble hiccough, to a fat blunderer like herself.

And so she went on thinking in remorseful circles until she got home, and then she heard her own voice saying, "I went to see the doctor and he says your blindness is all hysterical lies—all lies—do you hear? You needn't trouble to lie to me any more, now that I know. Ah, tschah! I brought you a packet of English cigarettes to smoke, you

old liar . . . !" And she threw the packet rudely on the floor
at his feet. Old Sergei humbly crouched to grope for it, but
Anna squatted down herself to pick it up. Their foreheads
collided. "Devil take you, you old fool," said Anna, and she
helped him into a standing position and patted him, a little
too hard, on the back, uncertain whether she did it in exas-
peration or friendliness.

In this precarious way the days went on, piled themselves
heavily together to make a week — a fortnight. When Old
Sergei had ten knots in his string, he began to say, reasonably, "He really *might* be back today; it isn't likely, but he
might."

At the end of a fortnight they received a letter from
Seryozha to say that he had married Tatiana Pavlovna
Ostapenko.

It was a very bald letter. Seryozha was not a literary boy.
Anna found it when she came in from a long walk out into
the country — out on to the road by which she hoped to see,
far across the valley, two distant figures returning home.

"He has married that woman whom Alexander Weber
called death," said Anna, putting down the letter. Now she
knew why the outlines of young Alexander's body had
seemed so empty and expectant to her. Seryozha had been
drawn away, like life through the door of a wound, drawn
across deserts to love death, drawn by the lure of a ghost —
a cruel ghost who sucked life. That was the end of Anna's
son. He had been stolen away, to lie at last dead, far from
home, married to death. That blank that was Alexander
had been waiting — to be filled by Seryozha's glowing body.
Anna's eyes, unprompted by her sense, now filled in a *him*
in the place of the *it* that had lain on Nikitin's table — that
pale death — that wan vision — that *thing* only casually
labeled Alexander Petrovitch, as it might have been labeled
with a number — that obscurely anonymous seventh

doomed lover of a ghost. Anna knew now what dear color that pallor waited for—the bright dead face of Seryozha —astounded, desolate, haloed with white, alone, and married to death.

"My son is dead. Now I care for nothing—my son—since I have let you go—the light of my eyes. . . ."

CHAPTER TEN

THE NIGHT of the goose and champagne — the night of Seryozha's arrival at the Ostapenkos' house — seemed the longest night in the whole realm of time — a sort of Methuselah of a night. The days of a man's life, thought Seryozha, are of different ranks — counts, princes, fat bourgeois days, rough peasant days — but this was a grand duke of a day, a giant of rank, quite outside the standard of ordinary days. Each royal minute was like an hour, each hour like a crowned year. All the other days of his life should bow before this — the day that promoted him to be a king, to be married, to drink champagne.

Wilfred's great day, which, for some little time, may be said to have been in eclipse, rose again when the goose was served. Wilfred, on being tactfully roused by Seryozha and led away to put his head under the pump, assumed a guiltily bright manner, to prove to the world, and to the absent Reverend Oswald Fawcett (who was Wilfred's conscience) that he had not drunk any wine to speak of. He did not notice that his legal document had disappeared from in front of him; he hardly remembered having written it, though it remained a settled plan in his mind; his tongue felt a little knotted and uncertain, but that did not matter, since scarcely any one would have understood anything he said in any case. He enjoyed the goose.

Varvara's goose took three and a half hours to eat. It was half past eleven when they finally could eat no more, and even then there was no childish suggestion of going to bed. The day was recognized by common consent as a great day, and allowed to occupy its throne indefinitely. It scarcely seemed to the happy and excited Seryozha to move at all. Half past eleven when the goose was finished and, hours later, only twenty-eight minutes to twelve. The time that had elapsed since his proposal to marry Tatiana had been accepted seemed so enormous that he was as well reconciled to it as though his parents had arranged it in his childhood. Age had matured and mellowed it to the status of a reasonable sanctioned thing.

He found Tanya more and more beautiful each minute, and each long minute gave him time to learn something new and delightful about her face. At first it embarrassed him to look at her across the brown hill of goose carcass that stood between them, because she, on her part, never took her eyes off his face. But after a while he found that somehow, though her eyes were on him, their two pairs of eyes never seemed to meet. She seemed to be looking at him in a blind way, as a painted picture looks, and he could watch her without self-consciousness, as one might bravely cross glances with a painted queen. Seryozha had never in his life had such an opportunity to look at a beautiful girl. He had no words to say all the things he noted about her. "Supple," he thought, anxiously, "clean — even — ivory — bones like carved curves — hollows under cheek-bones, carved again — something pulling outer corners of eyes down and lips up — accurate — keen — sun always dazzling eyes. . . ." He saw that her skin was like faintly tinted ivory, but, never having approached real civilization, was not surprised at that pale gloss that would have showed you or me that Tatiana had never come in contact with a powder puff.

As for Tatiana, she had never seen that odd animal, man, presented in such fair colors and with such striking inoffensiveness of detail. I dare say that the fact that Seryozha had never yet needed to shave (though he *did* shave, sometimes, on Sundays, when his mother was unusually forgetful of his manliness) had, at the beginning, more part in his fascination for her than any other factor. He seemed to her so well sewn up in his nice skin. Men, she had always found, were such a clumsy piece of work compared with animals. They were so flawed, so pitted with pores and discolorations, so smoky, so hot, so shiny bald or sticky-haired — like a child's stitching on canvas, whereas any animal was like Chinese embroidery on silk. One had only to compare the face of a Korean beggar dog — crawling with ticks, yet honest, finished, and sinless — with that of a Korean beggar man — rotted away with mean and complex depravity . . . one had only to compare the fine eager beam of a thirsty horse bending to drink from a pool, with the leer of a Russian approaching his glass of beer — to see the essential golden rightness in an animal's face and to admit the spoiled spotted thing that man is. Seryozha seemed to Tatiana as flawless and bland as an animal, and she watched him with real delight and imagination, as she often watched her father's young horses running from end to end of their field. Life beamed from Seryozha direct — not refracted among distorting human angles. Whatever he did would be *right*, Tatiana thought, just as whatever an animal does is right. Sometimes dangerous, perhaps, sometimes surprising — but always right. And always lovely, if one looked at it *not* through the complicated spoiled lens of human eyes. Something about an animal was always mercifully far away — by itself, even if the animal was in one's arms, demanding attention. Something about man was too close, even if that man was far away, even if he was dead in a far country, dead of his own intrusion. Something about Seryozha would always be far away, thought Tatiana, even if his breath were on one's cheek — something in him would be part of the sunny, sweet, dumb world, happy and living by itself, like a galloping colt.

Pavel Ostapenko's voice trumpeted on. Hardly a word he said was true, but every word exalted him or his family. He was like a motor engine which, by running, charges continually its own battery. The more his lips uttered his own praises, the more was his listening heart charged with an exquisite accumulation of vanity, and the more self-flatteries did his lips find to express. Seryozha was by now quite established as a grafted twig upon the towering Ostapenko tree. The divine word Ostapenko now included Seryozha and his parents, and the whole great branching growth brushed the clouds.

Neither Seryozha nor Wilfred drank any more wine. This was partly because Pavel Ostapenko had by now drunk so much that he continually forgot to fill any glass but his own. But it was also because Seryozha was warm with a glow of glittering responsibility; he did not want to lose himself in folly and sickness tonight; he was gloriously happy as he was, and everything looked as happy as a flower. He felt that he had climbed to a pinhead peak of happiness, and that to go any farther would be as stupid a descent as to retreat — and almost as impossible. As for Wilfred Chew, the spirit of the Reverend Oswald Fawcett was reëstablished on his disciple's inward throne. Wilfred felt sure that he had not yet done anything wrong. Surely a good Wesleyan could join in the harmless feastings of his friends — especially if the language bar prevented any other sociable interchange. Champagne up till now had been labeled Good Fellowship. But the happy emergency of Good Fellowship being over, the liquid part of the feasting now became alcohol and even moral danger. Wilfred, really anxious to be good, was made aware of the necessity for this change of labels, by noticing that he was talking, involuntarily, in a rather peculiar way. Every time he finished a sentence he clicked in his throat and resolved prudently to say no more. Then, the next minute, that hard-worked and usually impeccable servant, his tongue, would start unexpectedly on a new piece of strangely twisted and thwarted information.

Varvara Ostapenko sat divided between a resentful conviction that her husband was drunk, and a resentful fear that the strangers might have the impertinence to notice that he was drunk. There were drawbacks in being married to such a rare creature as her husband, she thought, and one of the drawbacks was the commonness of the people who dared to pass their common secret judgments on his rarity. Drunkenness was an Ostapenko oddity that she allowed for in the Procrustes frame of her wifely pride, but every time her husband got drunk he got drunk in a slightly different way, and she had to use her ingenuity to lop off something here about his behavior, and stretch something there, to fit her angular, inelastic standard of Ostapenkoism. She felt the necessity of presenting to strangers the sight of each Ostapenko neatly fitted into this frame — "and criticize anything if you dare!" Pavel's romantic lies were part of her standard for him; his arrogance, his belching, his forgetfulness of his guests' needs, his occasional rancorous references to his daughter — were excrescences that needed shaping into conformity, and at every example of these unlicensed eccentricities, Varvara looked furiously at Seryozha and Wilfred to see if they had dared to see or hear.

But Seryozha stared only at Tatiana, and Wilfred was listening only for loopholes in the talk into which he might squeeze some uncomprehended remark of his own. So presently Varvara felt that she could trust her rare drunk Pavel alone with these gentle strangers and go to bed. She took Tatiana's hand to lead her away.

The mutual stare of Tatiana and Seryozha had, it seemed to them, blown a sort of thin glass globe inclosing them — a glittering loneliness in which a miracle of dumb familiarity had been possible. All round it the humming sound of Pavel's talk had only served to make their apartness more private. Seryozha was even able to leave enough of his unneeded brain outside this crystal bubble to allow him to answer with a suitable grunt the tone of any of Pavel's remarks that sounded incomplete without a complementary guestly grunt. But all the time he and Tatiana felt as deeply sunk in themselves and in each other as puppies must feel in one litter in the straw while the bustle of the stable goes on above them. And now, by Varvara's action in rising and taking Tatiana's hand, their glass house was shattered, their mindless drowsy warmth of shared life was startled into a tiresome awareness.

The women were gone. The royal day had doffed its crown.

Pavel Ostapenko's talk now imposed the tiresome necessity of being understood. There was now nothing for Seryozha to bury his attention in, except his host's voice — nothing to watch except those staring, rufous eyes, that little gold-red beard being pulled and pushed like a latch to open and shut busy jaws, the blouse flapping open to show drops of sweat among the thick auburn hairs on his breast.

Directly Varvara and Tatiana had gone, Pavel, also noticing their absence, responded to it by talking about his wife.

"A wonderful woman — my wife — Varvara Alexeievna," he said. "I wish I could be sure that our girl would make you as good a wife as her mother has me. Lord! how sorry I feel for some of my friends with their scolding wives — wives who set themselves up to be their equals — wives who gad about in silk stockings—wives who get drunk—wives who can't even roast a chicken decently. You know, there was quite a romance about my marriage with Varvara Alexeievna. . . . She was a milkman's daughter, and of course my people wouldn't hear of such a match for me. We Ostapenkos are intensely proud—but also, mark you, intensely romantic—chivalrous—disinterested. If one of my family gives his word, well, he'll keep it as though it were a lawyer's bond. Well, that's what my father hadn't reckoned with—he wasn't allowing for the romantic chivalry I inherited from him and the impulsive, passionate, quixotic line behind him. I won't conceal from you that my father had reason on his side; I could have made a most excellent marriage with the daughter of one of my father's oldest friends—a fine plump girl with a big dowry and broad hips and shoulders, who loved me to distraction and would no doubt have borne me half a dozen sons to carry on my name, instead of one puny hen-chick. It would have been a good match, and I won't say that I was blind to its advantages—but, 'No,' I said—'no, papa, I can't go back on my word——' "

"Translate to our host, Saggay Saggayitch," Wilfred suddenly said, speaking very carefully, "how much I admire his taste in furning—in fursh—in furnaces—in furnishing what is usually such a comfortless place—a Japanese house. It is almost English, almost 'sgood as the first-class boarding-house where I stayed in Bloomsbury West Central One, while a law student. Such strong chegs to the lairs, and all so costly as I can see with half an egg—half an eye."

" 'Poor little Varvara Alexeievna loves me, papa,' I said, 'and counts on me. I've given her my word and I'll marry her like an honorable man.' Well, there was a terrible passionate scene—typical of the scenes in our family, for we were no milk-and-water lot, I assure you, when roused. But in the end my father saw I was determined—a twinkle

came into his eye and he said, 'By God! Pavlik, you're a true
Ostapenko, no doubt about that——''

"And tell him, too," added Wilfred, "that even in England I never saw before a mustard-pot in the shape of a
howl — owl — though I once saw this bird in person when
going to Ascot in a flus, buttering through the woods one
evening. Fluttering — through — a wood — in-a-bus."

"I married Varya, as you might say, if not exactly out of
pity, certainly out of chivalry — poor soul. I knew she was
not likely to have any other offers — a poor milkman's
daughter, and so thin, and with that birthmark. But Lord,
she was — and still is — devoted to me. She knows her luck."

Pavel's face was the face of a man who had never had a
setback. His features were set in lines of happy certainty;
his mouth looked entirely brave against self-doubt; his
tongue did not know how to stumble. Only his eyes, anxious
and roundly staring, looked as if they feared attack — as if
he had to open them widely in order to collect evidence that
all that he said was believed and appreciated. His eyes chal-
lenged you to say that he lied or was mistaken in anything,
and if you had expressed a doubt, he would have piled evidence on evidence, false witness on false witness, lie upon
lie, perjured oath upon oath, completely forgetting the
foundation of truth on which such a toppling edifice of af-
firmation is most safely built. Until at last you had to admit,
"Well — yes — if you assure me of that, and that, and that,
and swear to it so solemnly, of course I must believe you that
this is so," and only then did his round eyes relax, blink,
look safe again. You were convinced; that was all that mattered; he had obliged you to admit that he was right.
Whether he *was* right did not matter — that he had lied
from the beginning did not matter — you had said that he
was right, you accepted his truth, though it was no truth.

"I must say," went on Pavel, "except in one matter, I've
never had to regret my impulsive and chivalrous decision.

Varya's been a wonderful wife to me (I can see it now looking back) except in one particular. The exception I leave
you to imagine, my dear boy. You're young, but you know
life, and you know as well as I do there are certain things a
decent man doesn't give away when talking of his wife.
Nature—and a man's nature especially, mind you—shocks
her, seems to her improper. She has tried to adapt herself,
poor soul; she sees quite well that such freakishness and
prudishness make a woman an unworthy mate for a manly
man. But fundamentally, it's still there. . . . It accounts for
much of the oddity in our Tanya's nature. Tanya, our only
child, has inherited her mother's nature, though her coldness has a different aspect. . . . Tanya doesn't think anything improper—indeed, her mother and I have often had
to check the freedom with which she describes her observations of animals. She doesn't examine realities enough to be
shocked by them—she just feels far away from physical
realities. She is, you see, of an unhuman nature. (I'm not
concealing anything from you, my boy, I don't think it
would be fair.)"

He fixed his round eyes on Seryozha all the time, as if, in
spite of the complacent set of his mouth and carriage of his
head, he was expecting Seryozha to say: "O Lord! Pavel
Nicholaievitch, you are a liar!" But of course Seryozha said
nothing of the sort. He sat in a dream, half listening to his
host, half remembering the lost face of Tatiana. He rubbed
the bridge of his broad shiny nose wisely. Of course he knew
that parents never know anything about their children.

"Saggay Saggayitch," said Wilfred, "you say nothing. As
a friend you will 'llow me to suggest, would it not be better
to show a little more vivivacity with this kind gentleman,
Mr. Ozz. You don't talk enough, my dear chap, you don't
make the bezz of yourself. Your future may hang on making
bezz of self."

"When I say unhuman," went on Pavel, "I don't mean

anything against the child's temper. She has the sweetest temper, the tenderest heart. . . . She gets her sweetness of nature from my side, of course. She's a dear girl and perhaps love will teach her a great deal. I used to call her a fairy when she was little, and now sometimes I'm tempted to call her a fairy still, but I'd say it in a different voice now. It's been a great pain to me. I counted so on a family of robust sons and daughters to hand on my good old name to. . . . They're a man's immortality, his children and his children's children. . . . However, my dear boy, it may very well be that the right husband for Tanya may get the right results with her. One never can tell. Even icebergs melt under some sun or other, and Tanya, as I say, isn't an iceberg emotionally . . . she has my blood in her as well as her mother's, and therefore she has her own brand of passionate feelings, like all her breed. She signed that paper with a very good grace—allowing for the natural shrinking of a young girl—and in a sense she is already your wife, with her own eager consent, mark you, which is further than any of the other lads ever got. That paper was drawn up by a professional lawyer, and declares you man and wife. You couldn't ask for a better paper than that." He was silent suddenly, pouring himself out some more wine.

Nobody spoke for several minutes, not even Wilfred. Wilfred's head was nodding; his eyelids and chin were dropping. The clock pointed to half past twelve and Seryozha was proud to find that he was not sleepy.

Pavel began speaking again in a voice of rather defiant surprise. "Just now I said 'In a sense Tanya is your legal wife.' But of course really there's no in a sense about it. She is your wife. That document was drawn up by a professional lawyer; we have all signed it in the presence of Varya and Katya as witnesses. What more could we do to make a marriage legal? There is no priest of our Church available—besides, you and I are too modern to feel the need of the

Church's interference in practical matters like this. In Paris
— London — New York — a legal paper, duly drawn up and
signed, is enough for a legal marriage. Why should we expect more in Mi-san? My boy, you're a married man. Congratulations!" Doubt came into his strained eyes again.
"Really I don't know what else one could want to make the
thing correct and in order — lacking a priest. It's not as if
there was any unwillingness on either side — you both
signed of your own free will, at your own suggestion. She
gets a good dowry. You'll find me a generous father-in-law.
All we Ostapenkos are generous to a fault. Your father,
Sergei Dmitrivitch, will be delighted at such a good match
for you — a dowry of two thousand yen is not to be sniffed
at, and there'll be more later — and he gets a lovely daughter-in-law into the bargain."

"The paper is legal all right," said Seryozha solemnly,
speaking to the shades of his father and mother, and pursing
his face into a man-of-the-worldly look. "As legal as possible.
Mr. Chew is a famous lawyer in London. He never would
write an illegal paper."

Wilfred, opening his eyes for a moment, found the eyes
of both Russians fixed upon him. He was one who always
put the best construction on any ambiguity, and that two
Russians should look at him implied some pleasing compliment just uttered in their outlandish tongue. He bowed
pleasantly in answer to their look. But bowing, which he
always did thoroughly and briskly, being always quite sure
of his occasion, now started a ball rolling in his head. Something went on bowing by itself inside his brain; the room
bowed round him — or rather curtsied, in silly acknowledgment of this something inside his head that went on bowing. Was his outer skull really wagging? he asked himself in
some consternation. Could this uncertain ball be the head
of Wilfred Chew, Esquire? A slight bump as his forehead
hit the table showed him that his head, though unusually

independent, was still attached to his body, but, since the forehead was on the table, he might as well let it stay there. "Then they will think I am simply asleep," he thought, cunningly. "Any gentleman may go to sleep without being thought morally affected." It was quite outside his plan actually to go to sleep. His pretense of sleep took on an aspect of revenge, almost, in his own mind as he shut his eyes. "Well, if people *will* talk Russian for six hours without a break, they can't be surprised if their superiors seem to go to sleep." He listened upward, as it were, feeling that he was turning his ears like a dog—listened to the sound of Pavel's talk. It sounded like shyok-shyeh-shyok-shyeh, and in Wilfred's ears it swelled and dwindled like the humming one hears when under chloroform, or like the wowing of an airplane engine in the sky.

While he was still marveling at the fact that this contagious bowing craze seemed to be affecting his hearing and making sound bow too, a sudden startling silence fell in the room. The light inside Wilfred's eyelids changed from scarlet to deep purple. Some one must be taking the lamp away. Heavy feet trampled cautiously out of the room, the rhythm of their tread adjusting itself to the rhythm of Wilfred's throbbing attention. Tramp-ti—tramp-ti—tramp-ti—and then a check, and a woman's voice "Ah *Pavlik!*"—a voice of almost unbearable disappointment.

Wilfred lifted his pendulum head only enough to be able to lean his chin instead of his brow upon his hands. His head might actually roll off if he should rear it unsupported into the swinging air again. Across a glimmering silver plain of lampless tablecloth, he saw a perfectly still golden scene framed in the doorway. Pavel Ostapenko, holding the lamp a little crooked but not dangerously so, stood facing his wife in the passage, his eyes stretched to an alert glare, like a squirrel's eyes. Varvara, in a blue cotton kimono, stood defiantly across the passage, watching her husband with a defiant dark look. Her wine-colored birthmark looked like an eccentric shadow thrown by a more ominous flame than the lamp's light. Seryozha, against the opposite wall, was drawing a little parcel from his pack. "The fish's liver and heart," thought Wilfred. "He is going to face the devil in that red and white Tanya woman. She sleeps behind that door at the top of the little matted slope out of the kitchen. I saw her go in when I was washing at the pump." "*Pavlik!*" cried Varvara again with a low violence of voice, but her husband took one step towards her, took Seryozha's arm and pointed over his wife's shoulder — "At the devil's door," thought Wilfred. Varvara put both her hands in her mouth, cramming all her fingers between her lips as though frantically trying to tear them to pieces. She looked like a witch, grinning fixedly through the fringe of her fingers. Pavel began talking again. Wow — wow — wow —, heard Wilfred. Wilfred's heavy eyelids dropped like a curtain on the bright scene, and when next he half lifted them there was no light except the light of the kitchen fire, blurring and quickening on the passage walls, like breath dimming a window-pane. There were distant voices in the kitchen. Wilfred's perceptive senses became mixed in a drowsiness, and the voices became a cloud, a curious menacing cloud like a wing, each spasm of sound a feather in the wing — the whole flaked cloud coming nearer and nearer on a wind that blew in regular throbbing gusts. Before this wind all the trees in the world bowed, and all the leaves on all the trees were blown so as to show their white linings — white flecks showing silver in a moonlight that streamed from no visible moon. The moonlight had a breathless quality, in spite of the wind. Everything in the world was flawed and burnt with sparks of white; all the stars of the sky, fleeing from that stupendous winged dragon of a cloud, were lying dying in agony in the dust, like fish thrown up by a great departed wave. Trees, houses, deserts, and mountains were caked, clogged, with dying, gasping stars. The pursuing cloud strode across the sky; one could hear now the approaching boom — boom — boom of its wings. And Wilfred, sweating with excitement, addressed the jury, though his voice was a little thick. "I know how you bind dragons, gentlemen," said Wilfred. "With one hand you take them behind the gills and with the other behind the wingpits — (wingpits? Well, armpits. Why not wingpits?) Yes, with the other firmly under the wingpits and thus they are perfectly helpless." He said this bravely and the jury was obviously impressed. The jury numbered thousands — their little silver-white faces upturned, all over the twilit limitless hall. One must be brave before such a crowd of puny dying white faces — yet, as the wide earth-shaking booming of wings drew closer and closer, Wilfred wondered whether he could really master so frightful an enemy single-handed. Boom! *boom!* ʙᴏᴏᴍ! BOOM! — the monster was upon him; it had only a little blank disc for a face — how much more terrible than gnashing teeth and flashing eyes! Wilfred suddenly shouted in such a great voice that the strong wind was checked and the galloping cloud thrown back on its haunches. *Asmodeus. Asmodeus. Asmodeus.* Now what? thought Wilfred, mad to show his own monstrous power. One hand pinching the gills and the other the soft bending ribs (a lizard's ribs), a twirl . . . round and round the sequin-scaled body whipped the rope, flipped skillfully by Wilfred's heroic hand. "I am bound — I am bound — I am bound," piped the little fading disc that was the demon's face. But, oh, the scales were cold. They burned like naked ice. The great icy body leaped, squirmed, and writhed like a hooked fish. Here, a limb struggled loose — Wilfred lashed it with another loop; there, the tail began sweeping free — it was bound before more than a paltry million stars had been annihilated; here, a claw reached out and was instantly netted. The vast faceless thing heaved, powerless, agonized. . . . Yet, what was that — boom! *boom!* вооm! BOOM! again? Was some outlying coil breaking free? A scarlet air was blinding the world, a scarlet pain was riveted like a helmet on the hero's brow. Walls, a table, lamplight, a smell of roast goose — little dazzling homely things imprisoned him. Here was the room again, safe now from its terrific menace. Pavel Ostapenko was coming in with the lamp. He would want to hear the news of Wilfred's victory, of course, yet it was difficult to talk through such a taste in the mouth — such a band of pain round the skull.

"I bound Asmodeus! I bound him!" cried Wilfred. "Ah — my head! my head! . . . Yet I bound him — Asmodeus. . . ."

Ostapenko sat down at the table and buried his face in his hands.

"Where is Saggay Saggayitch?" asked Wilfred, thickly, feeling the need of an interpreter.

"Sergei Sergeievitch? Oi! where — where?" groaned Pavel in English.

This unexpected proof of linguistic sympathy encouraged Wilfred to begin to tell Ostapenko about his dream in detail. He never could quite believe that people really didn't understand English. Incomprehension was a sort of coyness on their part, which brisk treatment might help them to overcome.

But Ostapenko only replied by groans; only when Varvara came in did the talk begin again, and then, of course, in no more intelligent language than that outlandish Russian. Shyeh-shyeh shyok-shyok wow-wow — as though by its pulsing it was measuring off the seconds of this endless night.

"Don't Russians ever go to bed?" thought Wilfred. Clasping his aching head without disguise, he got up and stumbled over to the sofa. None of them cared that he had bound Asmodeus for their sake. By the way—why *Asmodeus?* He lay down on the sofa and was instantly drowned in profound dark sleep.

"You needn't look at me like that, Varya," said Pavel, raising his tired face. "It seems to me you have lost your senses. Here we have a charming and eligible young man —a kinsman of my own—whom our daughter has chosen willingly as her husband——"

"Pavlik—*think.*"

"Well, my dear, I'm not jumping to any conclusions. I'm only asking you not to be so sure that your daughter shared your own ignorance as to the actual significance of that paper she so eagerly signed. She has plenty of sense, and she must have realized that one doesn't sign lawyers' papers without committing oneself to something. She realized from the first, I think, that it made a married woman of her. She was probably waiting and wondering, in her room—a neglected bride——"

He paused to listen for that urgent, "Pavlik—*think*" again, but it did not come. Hearing no protest from his wife, he allowed his always self-sufficient mind to nurse the illusion that he had prevailed. Varya believed him—and why not? He had told her the truth. The paper was binding, the marriage sanctified by lawyers' law, according to Western European custom if not Russian custom. He was not accustomed to imagining what lay behind other people's silences, nor had he any ears to hear things that were not uttered. His roving telltale eyes, however, refused to look at his wife.

His voice began again with a challenging confident sound. "Tanya's consent means the more because she is by no means easy to please. . . . Seven betrothals behind her, all broken by her own overfastidiousness and whims. Here we have the pair, obviously falling in love at first sight, like the story books. Here we have Sergei Sergeievitch only too willing to overlook the unfortunate chops and changes of the past (which we have not concealed from him), proposing for our daughter most ardently, and Tanya at once showing an equal eagerness to be his wife. Here we have, most fortunately, on the spot, an English-trained lawyer of a high degree of learning, kindly arranging for us a legal marriage paper such as is daily drawn up in London or Paris or New York or any other sophisticated city — a form of marriage which, in the absence of a Russian priest, is the best we can possibly hope for. How very very much more fortunate we are than those Russian families — we know many of them — who in these hard times, for lack of any religious marriage facilities and too ignorant to obtain legal help, have to dispense with any ceremony at all, however naturally moral, modest, and respectable they may be. We, on the other hand, have a paper, properly signed and in my safe keeping, and if things go wrong I now have a means of protecting my daughter——"

"I can't hear their voices in the kitchen now," said Varvara.

"Well then, we must suppose they've done all the talking they want — in the kitchen," said Pavel with a blustering uneasiness. "But, Varya, listen — what other marriage ceremony can you hope for? What would satisfy you? True, in old Russia nothing short of a ceremony in church would have contented us (little as I, a modernist, believe in these superstitions). But we are not in Russia now. We are exiles. We must no longer feel provincial and Russian in our prejudices. We are citizens of the world now. What is good enough for sophisticated modern people in the great cities of Europe must be good enough for us. We must move with the times. There's nothing else for it. Angels aren't likely to come down and conduct an orthodox Russian marriage service for us. That paper, I assure you, satisfied me, a business man, as being comprehensive and legal. You can't read English, but I can, and I read every word of it. In it Sergei Sergeievitch swears to be a faithful husband to our Tanya, to support her as long as they both live, to provide for her in case of his death, to take her to his home and treat her as what she is—his legal wife. What more can he do? He has signed the paper—you saw him do it. The lawyer had signed it already. I have signed it to show my approval and my willingness to do my part—give our girl the dowry that we always meant to give her, and pay for the valuable services of the lawyer. Tanya signed it with her eyes open. I feel perfectly satisfied about it."

"Then why were you groaning just now as I came into the room?" asked Varvara.

"Why . . . well, I'm tired, of course, and overwrought. One has one's feelings as a father, and one's only child's marriage night is an emotional experience for any parent. Even though I am perfectly satisfied that the children are man and wife, and that—— Well, Varya, what's the use of arguing? I gave in to you on every point you mentioned. I let you have a talk alone with the child—and I don't believe you did anything more helpful than cry over her. I admitted the sense of your suggestion that young Sergei shouldn't immediately take her away from her home, and he willingly promised to stay here for a fortnight, so as to allow the little creature to adapt herself to marriage in the comfort of familiar surroundings, with you and me at hand. And you saw how Tanya accepted what I said. She was listening attentively to me, I could see that, though she never has a closely attentive look; and if she was staring at her husband all the time, well, isn't that natural, in a young bride? And then, when I had explained to her gently that by signing that lawyer's paper the marriage had become a legal thing and that her husband was now entitled to some proof of her love and duty, did she protest? My dear Varya, you irritate me inexpressibly when you look like that. I ask you, did she? Compare her behavior tonight with what she did when Boris kissed her at the kissing game — with the fuss she kicked up when Sasha Weber pressed her to marry him before the end of the summer — with her screaming hysterical fit when Petya Isaev kissed her in the garden on her birthday. Well, I ask you — what did she do tonight when she came back from her weep with you? She walked across the kitchen to her husband and just said his name, Seryozha — just like that, in a soft voice — *Seryozha*" — (Ostapenko wheezed a restrained falsetto). "Why, Varya, what's the matter with you? You yourself were convinced at the time. You said to me, 'Come away, Pavlik, it's their affair, after all. Let's leave them to work it out together, whichever way they wish.'"

Varvara was shaken. "Can it be really all right?" she asked of the witnessing air. She was so well accustomed to thinking that everything had an odd contrary rightness of its own, if an Ostapenko thought it right. "Oh, Pavlik — if you would only come free of these words and *tell me* out of your own heart if it's all right."

He went on talking. She had known he would never come free of words. He could not. She knew the expression of his mouth — the set of lips determined to convince by words alone. Even when she asked him, as she often did, to *think* — Pavlik — *think* — she knew it was impossible for him to think as well as talk — to go behind his own plausible words, to compare them with the facts in his own brain, and trim his argument to the shape of his inmost conviction. She knew that words were in themselves the stuff of his conviction — he believed what he said, instead of saying what he believed. Yet this was Ostapenkoism; she did not criticize it; words were his genius, she thought. Outsiders might say that he quibbled, but his wife shaped his quibbling to fit into her pride in him. Only Pavlik could quibble as superbly as he quibbled. Only Pavlik could make a thing actually true by proving ingeniously that it was true. He could mold truth. She began to see that this elaborate quibble about Mr. Chew's paper was sealing the paper itself with an actuality, a significance, that it had not seemed to possess. The paper had floated as negligibly as a dead leaf into Varvara's notice, and now here it was, transmuted by Ostapenko argument into a heavy lawyer's parchment, a thing to be kept in the safe, a thing solid enough for the future to be built on. It blew in like a leaf and settled like a stone. Pavlik's talk and magic had turned the blowing fancy to stone — to the cornerstone of the house.

Varvara was in the grip of reaction from her first moment of furious anger with Pavlik and her suspicion of him. When she had first seen him walking toward the kitchen threshold, pointing out Tanya's door to young Sergei Malinin, all her faith in him had seemed for a moment to be cracking. At that moment she could have torn him to pieces; he was something namelessly hideous — naked of words at last. Now that he had clothed his intentions with their usual fine wrappings of explanation, she felt like a child who, in the dark, thinks it sees in a moving shadow at the door a bogey arriving frightfully to devour it — and then in the next moment identifies the thing as the sweet familiar shadow of its mother and feels incredibly safe again. Varvara felt the remorse such a child might feel — remorse and sheepishness, for having so mistaken that loving shadow, misheard that dear step, repulsed with panic a friend so tried and so trusted. Must she not make up for her first panic of misunderstanding by understanding with double intensity?

It was the more possible for Pavel to convince Varvara, because she felt herself, in this matter, on his ground, not her own. She had no illusions about the incompleteness of her own nature, though she would have resented bitterly any suggestion that an outsider could see her lack of life.

Living with the ebullient Pavel had taught her secret humility. She therefore attached no moral superiority to her fear of love—no *you ought not*—only an *alas, I am not*. Her natural instinct, even if Tatiana had been married with every possible rite of orthodoxy, would have been to lie awake with tears of horror throughout her daughter's wedding night. This she recognized as morbidness, and was therefore the more inclined to distrust her own almost unbearable instinct of reluctance to believe in the sudden significance of this lawyer's paper. Paper blessing—church's blessing—archimandrite's blessing—God's blessing—her answer to each or all would have been—*No*—*no*—*no*—*not for my Tanya.* . . .

Among Ostapenkos, she was accustomed to being more sober but less inspired. She had felt essentially right as she barred her husband's path to her daughter's door, but she was used to feeling right, yet knowing herself wrong. The strange rather than the reasonable must be her accepted standard. The breath of sobriety she introduced was an irrelevance, in this strange family she loved.

Yet—in this case—Tanya—that white baffling door of Tanya's fortress to be knocked upon—to be assailed with such abrupt news from the strong thick world of men. . . .

"I'll just stand in the passage for a minute to listen if I hear voices," she said. "He may be arguing with her, trying to persuade her against her will. He's just a boy—it's difficult for him. Supposing she's crying. . . . She cries so quietly. . . ."

"A funny thing," said Pavel, "to be expecting to hear the bride crying on a night like this. . . ."

Varvara stood in the passage for a minute or two. There was no sound. She turned. Through the front door, left open for coolness this hot night, she saw the houses of Mi-san roofed with silver; she heard the distant barking of a dog sounding like a beating on copper. The alchemist

stillness transmuted to bright metal the polished leaves of
the zinnias and shrubs in the garden. The sky shone like a
spangled dragon's wing. There were even stars in the dust
of the street—a dust of stars, too, over the brick material
of the frame of the door, and stars in every spider's-web.
After all, she's just another flower in another garden,
thought Varya dreamily, another starry seed on the wind,
blowing home to earth. She was thinking wordlessly; she
was seeing a vision of the breaking of dear loneliness, the
breaking of the virgin round world by the forces of fire and
water and wind, the breaking open of strong remote mountains, breaking into chasms and seas, craters, valleys and
peaks—the dumb world breaking with a song of thunder,
and broken, being clothed with intention at last—clothed
with snows and flowers and blue veils of ice and deserts of
corn-colored sand and feathers of fire—a world the richer
for its broken integrity. To make a statue was to break a
stone. Being alive was a breaking of death. To become
something was to shatter the peace of being nothing.

Come home—come home—come home, Tanya. . . .

Varvara roused herself with a start, finding her lips parted
to utter a call. She went back into the living-room and
found her husband groaning again, his head in his hands.

"What is distressing you so, Pavlik? You are so sure it is
all right, and yet you moan and mourn."

"Tschah! I don't know. Leave me alone. No, I'll tell you.
I'm not worrying about our Tanya—she's all right. She has
to grow up sooner or later, and she showed more feeling
about this boy than she did about any of the others. I'm
sure we were right to strike while the iron was hot. No, I
worry about the boy—a decent bright boy—and my
cousin's son, too. What if it were really true that there's a
curse on any lover who comes near our Tanya? We couldn't
say we hadn't had full warning—she really has sucked the
life out of every one of the lads who were attracted by her

good looks. Supposing it really is a fact that there is something deadly in her icy pretty looks. Supposing we find this nice boy dead by her side in the morning. . . . What should we say — how should we explain it? The neighbors would all say — 'well, you've had fair warning, haven't you? It's as good as murder.' One can't disregard such a possibility. There's something so very strange in the perfectly consistent string of disasters that has followed each of her affairs — disasters to the lads themselves, I mean. I've heard of such curses" (Pavel always had precedents ready). "I knew of a nice old woman — very rich, very quiet, very good-natured and considerate — whose servants always died before they had been in her service a year. She was obliged at last to go and live in a hotel at Yalta, and even there, they say, the chambermaids kept on developing mysterious diseases. There are such cases — it's no good shutting one's eyes to them. There certainly is something fatal about our Tanya's effect on men — there isn't a single one of her admirers that hasn't reason to regret ever having set eyes on her. Sasha's dead; Isaev, in the Chinese army, is as good as dead; young Stepan Soloviev is a hopeless sot; Boris threw up a respectable job to go and be a pimp in Shanghai; Vanya seems to have gone entirely off his head. One can't ignore all that, Varya, one can't say it's coincidence — it does look like the work of some kind of devil that possesses our girl. Have we thrown away the life of this nice boy, Sergei Sergeievitch? His affair has gone further than any of the others — the curse would affect him more immediately and fatally. . . . Oh, Varya, I have a dreadful premonition . . . I have a terrible feeling that in the morning we shall find him dead — and Tanya icy and quiet as she always is, no sorrier than if she had crushed a spider by mistake. What could we say? How could we explain it to his father and mother?"

"It's the night makes you have such fancies, Pavlik," said Varvara. "Two or three o'clock in the morning is always the time when people who can't sleep have their dreadful fancies."

"Two or three o'clock in the morning is when people die," said Pavel Ostapenko, shuddering. "O God! what have I done that my only child is so cursed that I have to fear so for every one who comes near her? What a silence is in this house, Varya! One can hear no sound of life at all."

"One couldn't, anyway, from here."

Ostapenko looked at the clock. "I wonder why people die in the small hours. I wonder if it's because all the demons of the night have gathered strength out of the dark by then."

"No, certainly it isn't. It is because the pulse beats most weakly then."

"Yes, but the demons of the night perhaps seize that opportunity. Perhaps people always die then for that reason. The dead never come back to explain to us the deadly wiles of demons. O God! perhaps the boy, even as we speak, feels something freezing his heart, and thinks: 'They told me the truth about this haunted girl. Why wasn't I wise in time?'"

"Perhaps you are a little tired, Pavlik," said Varvara. "Or even a little—— Well, you know, Pavlik, you drank a great deal of champagne."

Pavel groaned again. His sense of guilt about his insistence on the consummation of the marriage had strangely disguised itself, transferred itself to a fear for Seryozha's safety. His imagination was very strong when dealing with the inhuman and mysterious, although it could never penetrate a fellow mortal's skin and show him a glimpse of the reasonable and sensitive hearts of his neighbors.

"Why don't you go to bed?" suggested Varvara. "You are doing no good by sitting up—only tormenting yourself."

Pavel rose to his feet and left the room so promptly that Varvara looked after him in surprise. She was not accustomed to having her suggestions so instantly followed.

After a moment she rose, too. She looked down for a minute at the sleeping Wilfred. His mouth was wide open; his gold tooth looked ashamed with so much uncovered pink and cavernous mouth round it; as a rule, its glory was enhanced by the discreetness of its glimpsed glitter. "How hospitable we are to our visitors," thought Varvara with a faint sneer, looking down at Wilfred's helpless sagging face. Then she went to her bedroom, pausing a moment in the passage to listen to the silence.

Her husband was not in their bedroom. She lay down on the bed in her kimono, and shut her eyes. In the glimmering steel light of early dawn, the dark mark on her cheek looked like a third sunken eye.

She opened her eyes an hour later to find that her husband was still not by her side. As she went back along the passage to look for him, he came in at the front door, looking exhausted and wretched leaning on an earthy spade.

"Why, Pavlik, where have you been? You are all earthy —look at your hands. You look so tired. . . . What have you been doing?"

"Oh leave me alone—don't nag at me! . . . Oh, Varya, I have such a terrible presentiment of evil to that boy. I'm sure she breathes death . . . the more I think of it, the more sure I am. . . . We are as good as murderers . . ."

Varvara sighed. "Oh, Pavlik, how obstinately fanciful you are when you have been drinking. Now *think*—think of the ordinary everyday world; think of our dear little Tanya learning to knit socks for you, learning to ride a horse, helping me to make the beds and to shell peas. . . . Demons don't live in such simple things. Here is Katya—she shall make us a cup of tea each."

For the first beam of the sun, aiming like a wary archer across the red plain, always woke Katya to her work. The energetic old woman had no alarm clock; she relied on the sharp tip of the first ray to pry her little red eyelids apart.

"A cup of tea," she repeated after Varvara, opening that kitchen door which had been such a tiptoe secret all night, and stumping briskly into the kitchen.

Varvara stood in the front doorway, watching the sun rise — watching the sun climb surefooted up straight rails of red cloud.

Pavel followed Katya into the kitchen. "Katya, you know our little Tanya was married last night," said Pavel in an uneasy whisper, pinning the old woman's attention with his wide sharp eyes.

"Married!" exclaimed Katya shrilly.

"Pssst! Yes, married — by this Chinese guest who is a lawyer and knows the London way of marrying without a priest."

"There is no such thing as marriage without a priest," began Katya loudly.

"Devil take you, old woman, I tell you there *is!*" said Pavel, convulsed for a second with fury by this bluff attack on his edifice. "Tanya *is* married. She is a wife, legally. She is in that room there with her husband — and with my blessing, I tell you. Do you think I should not be the first to make my only daughter's honor safe? Don't be such a fool, old woman, but listen to me. You know Tanya — you've known her all her life. You know she's not like other girls, quite — easy in love, accustomed to kissing and flirting. I want to know if they're all right — I must know — and I daren't look in — I daren't. . . ."

"Pavel Nicholaievitch, you've been drinking. Why should you want to spy on a man and his wife — if man and wife they are? . . ."

"They are — they are!" cried Pavel frantically. "I swear they are legally man and wife. . . . It's only that I have a presentiment. . . . Katya, be a good woman and just open that door a crack — just peep in. . . . I must know the worst now. . . . I daren't look myself. . . ."

"Ah, tschah!" said Katya. She waddled up the little matted slope and listened at Tanya's door. "There's no sound," she said.

"No sound!" echoed Pavel, terrified. "Ah, dear Katya, just open the door a crack, very quietly, tell me how they look."

Alarmed and shocked by his wild manner, Katya cautiously opened the door a very little, and put her fat red face to the crack. When she turned her face it was creased into a sentimental smile. "I must say they are a pretty pair," she said, as pleased as though she had had a hand in the creation of their beauty. "As pretty as fairies, asleep in each other's arms, his lips to her cheek . . ."

"O my God! Safe! Safe!" cried Pavel, and rushed down the passage, calling: "Tea—tea! Varitchka, where's my tea?" Then he ran like a boy back into the kitchen. "Katya, you might tell Yi to fill up that deep trench he will find in the garden to the east of the poppy bed."

"I can see it from here," said Katya. "It looks like a grave."

"Yes—yes. I thought I might want to bury some rubbish today. . . . But I don't want it now. Tell Yi to set to work on it at once. . . . O God!" he cried, running back to Varvara. "Varitchka, can't we praise God or something . . . ?"

CHAPTER ELEVEN

Seryozha's dog, all netted with spiders' webs and glazed with dew, stood in the doorway, collecting with a high nose the too faint traces of Seryozha's vicinity. The smell of putrefying fish clinging to Seryozha's pack in the passage-way cheered the dog a good deal; it knew that smell by now as part of the family. The house seemed to be empty of everything but air, and this happy patch of smelly air was a sort of ghost of Seryozha — the next best thing to the presence of that solid and glorious being. The dog stood for a long time with its nose pressed very hard to a spot on the floor on which Seryozha had dropped, hours before, a small shred of fish liver. For quite a minute, the bereaved dog licked this spot slowly, romantically, like a melancholy epicure.

Slanting from the windows were shallow barred slides of sunlight, down and across which raced and blew and eddied the little light glittering typhoons of dust stirred up by Katya's recent sweeping. The pale floor mats were a rectangular maze of sunlight and shadow; and flies seemed to browse in these square fields of sunlight like cattle seen from an airplane. Now and then this restful illusion was broken

by one fly rising and flying petulantly away as another one
alighted. A sequin-blue butterfly with a long tail flew uncertainly in from the garden, its shadow dodging across the
fields of sun and dikes of shade, and settled on Tanya's blue
cloak which hung on a peg. It opened and closed its wings
slowly before its shadow, like a queen trying on a new
dress before the glass. Summer morning danced in the
house, but, to the dog, human bustle alone spelled morning—and human bustle was disturbingly lacking here.
There were so many strangers in the house—the blue
butterfly, a couple of thistledowns riding high across the
ceiling, a muddy spade with a rather dead section of worm
on it, leaning against the wall, a riding-whip smelling of
horse, a noisy bee that hovered about the dog's shrinking
ear, an insolent brown hen on the threshold—all strangers
—no friends—and the dog loathed strangers. Strangers so
often have stings, like bees, or sticks, like beggars, or kicks,
like horses; they never smell right.

A smell casts no shadow before; dogs, therefore, who are
led through life by the nose, have to be intensely conserva-
tive. They can tolerate no new departures because they can
know no destinations. Seryozha's dog, though trying to be
brave, felt as far away from its own tried and trusted circumstances as a man might feel who found himself the first to
set foot on the moon. To the dog this house seemed as
shimmering and appalling and silent as the moon; this
bright gloss of sunlit air, speckled with smell-less strangers,
lacking the immediate familiar smell of known gods, was
as lifeless as the brittle bodiless glare that lays gray shadows
at the feet of the moon's starved peaks. Traveling from
place to place, one carried one's own exciting, flying world
along with one; somewhere close in front of one's thrilled
nose was home, or something like home; somewhere close
behind one's tail was one's own tramping homespun god.
But arrival at Mi-san had meant to the dog an elaborate

homelessness. That little spot of concentrated rotten fish smell on the floor was all that was left of home.

Tiptoeing on stiff suspicious toes into the living-room, the dog was much pleased to find Wilfred Chew lying asleep on the sofa. As a rule, the dog thought nothing of Wilfred, but this morning the man could certainly be promoted to the rank of an encouraging smell. The dog pushed its nose into Wilfred's eye, savoring the blessed tang of something known before. Wilfred, with a loud groan, turned over, flinging his arms across his frowning shut eyes, and the dog whipped its precious self away to the other side of the room, fearing a kick.

A very small piece of goose skin, which, under the table, had escaped Katya's active brush, comforted the dog for a moment, and this snack inspired the lost animal to go to the kitchen. It knew where the kitchen was; any dog could find a kitchen, even in the moon. Katya had gone to market. The kitchen door at the end of the passage was ajar, and the dog pushed in. In a bucket by the pump it found a priceless treasure of goose bones and gravy-splashed scraps.

Seryozha, coming with a dazed, quiet step into the kitchen, saw his dog and loved it as he had never loved it before. That dusty brindled back seemed to shine with a light of blessed familiarity. Seryozha's tired eyes, looking at it, seemed to be stroked with a kind of home balm. He stood still watching the dog, his consciousness numbed — as it always was — by the thrill of seeing an animal enjoying itself by itself, unaware of his presence. To watch his dog smiling and snorting into its bucket of ambrosia almost made him feel as if this old worried Seryozha were standing here watching his young self, careless and apart — his young lost self, enjoying something as this old watching Seryozha would never enjoy anything again.

The dog looked up and saw Seryozha. It cringed and crawled toward him, expecting a kick for thieving, and

Seryozha, beaming at it, gave it a little soft kick to oblige it. While he focused his eyes exclusively upon it, blurring from his sight the strange surroundings, he could imagine himself that young happy Seryozha again at home in his mother's kitchen. He could pretend that he would look up in a minute from the dog's delighted writhings and see the white pansy face of that old clock in the marbled case on the dresser — that kind foolish dial with the six rubbed out — look up and see that it was time to go to work again — to begin another safe known day.

Seryozha, with the dog hurrying triumphantly at his calf — almost pressing its front teeth against his calf in its anxiety not to lose him again — went out through the kitchen door. He crossed the walled Japanese garden and went out into the acre or so of Ostapenko estate, half of which was a vegetable garden and half a railed inclosure for horses. A Korean in his white puffed clothes — looking like a cream cracker — was filling up a trench in the earth of the garden, and Seryozha, loathing the man because he was the only man in sight — and a stranger — put as much distance as possible between them and sat down on the edge of a little stream that ran at the foot of the fence. The high grass, tufted with wild blue geraniums and scarlet lilies, hid Seryozha from the world as he sat down, dangling his feet over the stream. His dog, pressing its seat as near as possible to his, sat down, too, and blew great hot loving breaths into his ear.

Seryozha threw his arms round the dog's neck and cried into its shoulder.

For the first time in his life, Seryozha was shaken — shaken in his stalwart anonymity — called home to self-consciousness by a sort of earthquake of the heart. He had been invisible, he had been a matter of course, he had been too close to see, he had been a hollow yet satisfactory person labeled Sergei Sergeievitch Malinin. He had no more known the creature that moved behind that name than he had known the shape of the bones that moved beneath his flesh and skin. The only mystery about the anonymous blank life that lay behind the name Sergei Malinin was found in the repeated utterance of the name itself, curiously enough. A delicious poised strangeness perched on the peak of the soul, when one said that name — Sergei Malinin — Sergei Malinin — a hundred times over. This slippery transparent Seryozha, through whom, as it seemed, one could see the sky, was a hill of glass on which no bird but that winged mystery of his own mesmeric name could find foothold. As for love — women's love — friend's love — self-love — a hill of glass afforded no hospitality to such flying visitors.

Now, this earthquake intrusion of a trespasser had shaken him awake — had forced him to turn and meet himself. He was recognized as a man, as he had longed to be recognized; he was traveling, far from his mother, as he had longed to travel; he was married, by his own expressed wish, to the most beautiful and gentle girl he had ever seen. And he felt the lonely fright of a chicken outside the egg, of a fledgeling outside the nest, of a weaned puppy refused its mother's warm teats. He shook with a fevered longing to go back — to go back into safety — to be warm and careless in little yesterday again, instead of turned loose in this wide draughty today, with no guide but his own reluctant maturity.

Seryozha tried to dislodge a stone in the bank with his heel; he kicked it spitefully, as though he were trying to demolish something menacing. Growing up, then, was a trap; he had been lured into it by an exquisite decoy and must spend the rest of his life pressing his face against iron bars. There was Tanya, the decoy, a prisoner with him — still exquisite — still his. But Seryozha had never felt the need of a friend or a comforter — had never yet desired reinforcement against himself or any one else; he had not

known that even his mother's affection was valuable to
him — he had thought it contemptible, quite negligible —
though now he saw it tenderly as part of the furniture of
little safe yesterday. He had a mournful senseless vision of
himself now, spinning a whipping-top in the street of Chi-
tao-kou — a game that needs no partner. And here was
Tanya — a spray of orchids handed to a person who needed
both his hands for the whipping of his top.

What was that Mr. Chew had said about cold devils?
There were no devils, really, but there were strangers. As a
boy, yesterday, Seryozha had never noticed strangers. Now,
it seemed, a stranger could trespass — could lie in one's
arms all night and yet never be known, never be simple,
forgotten, easy, taken for granted. He must live uneasy,
now, he must come inside himself and think. This was the
result of the cold presence of strangers; no magic smoke —
no heart and liver of an enchanted fish — could exorcise
that trespassing presence.

Seryozha's body was not accustomed to being used by
thought. It scarcely knew how to behave while thinking.
His heel kicked and kicked at the stone, and when the
stone at last fell with a splash into the stream, his body
felt innocently triumphant, and his lips began to whistle
by themselves — a low, flat whistle.

His dog was greatly cheered by this sound, and still more
delighted to be suddenly pushed off the bank into the
water. Seryozha's body, having achieved one splash, desired
another. The dog laughed in the water, rolling its entranced
eyes upward, and, finding that it could not jump up to the
top of the high bank again from the hampering water, ran
gayly a few yards down the current to a point at which the
stream flattened out into strands of sand and shallow bubbling rapids over pebbles — a perfect working model of a
Manchurian river. Seryozha's eyes — always alert for miniature things — noticed the fidelity to fact of this toy river.

And his eyes remembered the spring in Manchuria — that rolling golden lark-shrill Manchurian spring that was, to him, home and yesterday. He remembered tremendous auburn distances and wide tender curves of marbled colors in varied earth — yellow deepening to orange — orange to red — red paling to sandy — sandy to cream — with here and there the faint green flush of pricking grass — and on every rainbow hillside, a white spot of Korean moving slowly along the edge of a growing parallelogram of new-furrowed land behind a yellow blob of bullock.

"Ah, tschah!" said Seryozha, throwing a stone at a bird. The stone rustled and ricocheted through the bush beneath which the bird sat, but the bird scarcely moved. "A funny thing," thought Seryozha. "A bird that's not afraid of a stone. . . ." He took off his shoes and splashed across the stream. The bird — a sparrow — looked at him with an anguished round eye, but it scarcely moved. Seryozha put his hand over it, loving it as soon as he saw it was too sad to be his prey. Caked round one of its claws was a ball of clay as big as a walnut. The bird must have alighted unwarily on some unusually wet adhesive surface — it must have been involved in some combination of circumstances outside common bird-experience — so now it went hopelessly encumbered, a crawling thing about the grass instead of a brown flash in a tree. Seryozha took out his pocket knife, and with his cautious clever blunt hands began flaking off the hard-baked mud, sliver by sliver, till first one little scaly knuckle appeared, then another. The anatomy of birds' claws he studied by comparison with the free claw, so that the point of his knife knew where to be bold and where delicate. The bird's eye, bright and silly as a sequin, remained fixed upon him; its little bones, wrapped thickly yet unsubstantially in a warm padding of feathers, seemed swooning in his hand. After half an hour's delicious mincing work, the whole claw was free; the knife had made no mistake. "Stand up, bird," said Seryozha impatiently, as the bird reeled on his wrist. Its freed claw remembered, hesitantly, how to grip; it tautened its body, threw a glance of sharp loathing at its savior, and flew a few yards. "Oh, get away now, bird," said Seryozha, and threw a stone at it.

"The darling thing," said Tatiana's voice behind him. "It thinks itself so clever." She stood in the long grass, biting a blade of grass, her head bold and vivid against the faint blue morning sky. "It thinks it used your knife so neatly — made a fool of you. It thinks you were trying to eat it or something, and freed it by mistake because it was so clever. It's laughing up its wing at you."

"It was very kind of me to take so much trouble about a little idiot of a bird," said Seryozha, throwing stone after stone at the bird as it fluttered from branch to branch of a low tree. "You praise these silly beasts so, but, say what you will, we're better friends to them than they to us."

"Oh, of course . . . but what are friends, after all? Just messy things. . . ."

She wondered why he looked so sulky. Had she grieved him? Ought a wife to be somehow different? She thought alternately. "Well — it's what I am — he must take it or leave it . . ." and, "But was I wrong? ought I to have been different?" She was in two worlds — her heart away in its solitary and exciting wilderness, her body watching for a signal from her lover, and desperately ignorant of how to obey the signal when it should come.

Seryozha was sullenly thinking, who were these two persons discussing nature? Sergei Sergeievitch Malinin, a married man, and Tatiana Pavlovna, his wife, two grown-up people with interesting thoughts. What if he sprang to his feet now, and ran home? He thought of Sonia Matvievna — that easy squeaking creature in Chi-tao-kou. Her conversation was all giggle — one giggle for yes — another giggle for no — no giggle ever meant anything so complicated as a discussion of a sparrow's reaction to an act of human helpfulness. Then he remembered the consenting Tanya of last night. Sonia Matvievna would have had only a giggle for that, too.

"Ah, Tanya — Tanya — come closer. . . ."

She knelt by his side at once and kissed him lightly on one eye. His dog, inspired by this, rushed upon him and kissed him, much more clumsily and ardently, on the other. They all laughed.

Seryozha stopped laughing rather soon. In fact only the dog went on. It was insensitive to atmosphere, and knew nothing about the domestic changes in divine Valhalla since yesterday. Tatiana stopped laughing and watched Seryozha's face. Even the kiss hadn't been right, she could see.

Seryozha blinked the eye that she had kissed. It felt shocked by that light, quiet kiss; the eyelid fluttered by itself like the skin of a horse's shoulder. He supposed that he was hungry, though he wasn't quite sure. The skin of his face felt disappointed. His ears listened for some loud vulgar shout or laugh. Girls were fun, and one was fun to girls. Yet Tanya, though so lovely, so darling, was no fun — nor did she find him fun. What, then, was between them — something more exciting than fun — or nothing? Now, for instance, she suddenly seized his hand. Why should she do this, if it were no joke to her? Why should she want to hold his not very clean hand — so quietly, so seriously? Her thin hand seemed to need no pinching — no activity at all. He held it, with a surprise that gradually changed to pleasure. Vaguely, with no recognition more articulate than a faint prevision of serenity, he began to know that this quiet taking for granted was at least as fit a sequel to last night's strange joy as the restlessness and roguishness of Sonia Matvievna would have been. Something was born between Seryozha and Tanya at that moment — a taking-for-granted for two

—a doubling, instead of a halving, of anonymity and un-
consciousness.

"Do people ever have breakfast, in Korea?" asked Seryozha. The sun was quite high. This visit seemed to lack
landmarks, somehow. And he had promised to stay for a
fortnight. Was it only perhaps hunger that made him feel
that he would never be at home in life again?

They walked toward the house. Seryozha's dog led the
way. It hoped that their destination was the bucket full of
goose scraps, and writhed winningly at the back door. But
Seryozha and Tatiana walked to the front door and into the
living-room.

Pavel Ostapenko sat there, leaning over the still sleeping
Wilfred, looking rather like the Doctor in Sir Luke Fildes'
picture, but not feeling like that at all. Pavel was haggard
and cross. At the moment of his waking, the thought had
broken on his brain like a clap of thunder: "What will happen when Chew wakes up—sober? What if he says the
paper is *not* legal?" Pavel, of course, had not for a moment
entertained the thought, "What if I were wrong?"—but
only the much more torturing doubt—"What if he *says* I
was wrong, and tells the others so?" He had spent an uncomfortable hour wondering whether the impossible could
happen—whether Pavel Ostapenko could be accused of
having made a mistake. Every voice in the house, except
one, could now be depended on to say, "You were perfectly
right, Pavel Nicholaievitch," and that, of course, was just
the same as *being* right. But, unfortunately, the one voice
that remained, so far, silent in this necessary chorus was an
indispensable one. And still more unfortunately, the lips
that should form these vital words were sealed by intem-
perate sleep, and the understanding that should evolve the
utterance could not be reached by Ostapenko logic, however eloquently expressed, even had it been awake. What on

earth was the Almighty about, thought Pavel irritably, to create such a superfluity of human beings who were unfamiliar with the language that Pavel Ostapenko could use so skillfully. Unless something was done, an unthinkable emergency would arise — Pavel Ostapenko would be humiliated in the eyes of his inferiors. It followed that Pavel must somehow, in some language not yet invented, have a talk with Wilfred before any one else had a chance to do so. Pavel must be ready with a sufficiently persuasive argument to induce Wilfred, the moment he awoke, to admit — "You were perfectly right, Pavel Nicholaievitch, in the course you took," and to confirm this opinion triumphantly before the family.

Pavel sat with one elbow on his knee, glaring and breathing hotly at the innocent blank face of Wilfred. Beside him on a table were one hundred and fifty yen in notes, a Russian-English dictionary, an elementary English grammar, an illustrated history of the Russian Empire, several large sheets of paper covered with English words in wavering block letters, and the deed drawn up by Wilfred the night before.

"Tschah! Go away," whispered Pavel, irascibly, to Seryozha and Tatiana as they came hungrily in. The foolish interfering creatures might awaken Wilfred prematurely, and Seryozha — the interpreter — would then have the dangerous first word.

Varvara, hearing the young people come in, joined them at the living-room door, carrying a tray. "Breakfast, Pavlik," said Varvara. "It is eleven o'clock."

"Devil take you all!" said Pavel in a furious whisper that scraped his throat. "Who in the world wants breakfast at this time of day? Can't you leave the poor devil to finish his sleep in peace?"

Varvara, carried forward by the slow impetus of her grave assumption that breakfast was needed, put the tray on the table before she turned to her husband in surprise. "Who wants breakfast, you say!" she echoed. "Why, Pavlik, every one wants——"

Pavel rose to his feet in a shivering paroxysm of anger, and waved his clenched fists in the air. Varvara snatched the loaded tray up just in time to prevent him from seizing it and throwing it through the door. With the tray in her hands, she recovered her hard calm manner. "Pavel Nicholaievitch is rather tired this morning," she said to Seryozha and, squaring her angular shoulders, she led the retreat from the room.

Pavel was left with the prostrate Wilfred, whose plaintive expression suggested that he was locked in a prison of disquieting dreams. One could almost see his teased brain beating at the closed shutters of his eyes.

"Should I not wake him?" Pavel asked himself. "He isn't enjoying himself, wherever he is."

But just as he leaned forward to say some urgent awakening word, the door opened and Katya, the servant, came in, with an expression of——"Leave him to me; I'll manage him." Seryozha's dog bustled after her. It thought the stout kitchen-smelling Katya a most delightful woman, and innocently mistook her for its hostess.

"Pavel Nicholaievitch," said Katya, "you must allow me to lay the table for breakfast. It is——"

Pavel rushed upon her with a roar, all his teeth showing, arms and legs sprawling across the air. The outraged old woman fled a few paces, then tried to make a stand in the passage. But Pavel slammed the door in her face with such a bang that the dog squeaked as it fled, believing itself shot.

The noise half roused Wilfred, yet, in spite of the discomfort of his dreams, he was reluctant to wake. He rolled about on the sofa and buried his face in the cushion, trying to drive his struggling consciousness back into the safe imprisoning corridors of sleep again. Pavel stood over him. "Curse him!" he cried. "He must be doing it on purpose."

He seized the cushion and dragged it from under Wilfred's head. Wilfred substituted an arm for it. Pavel dragged the arm away, too.

"Awaken, Mistah Chew, awaken!" he shouted. He had looked the English word up in his dictionary.

An obstinate sealed look came into Wilfred's face, then a look of petulance, then a distortion of the most unspeakable agony, then a light of beautiful resignation, then a recollection of the Reverend Oswald Fawcett. Wilfred opened his eyes, himself again, though rather a melancholy self. "Hrrgh?" he inquired in a strangled snort, disappointed with the waking world.

"Is time of breekfast," shouted Pavel, feverishly consulting his English notes. "Mistah — quick — awaken."

Wilfred lay with his eyes wet and callow in their puffed sockets, like new-born kittens in their lair. His gaze was fixed with a tranced expression on a spittoon; one would have said it was his dearest treasure.

Pavel thrust a sheet of paper between Wilfred's eyes and the spittoon. Wilfred took a minute to adjust his drowsy focus, and then he recognized his own writing on the paper. It was the indenture he had drawn up last night. So it had not been a dream, thought Wilfred, surprised.

Pavel pushed his red beard close to Wilfred's face and said very loudly in pidgin Russian — for he had forgotten most of the English words he had prepared, "Eta — bumaga — horosho — ah?"

"Horosho, horosho," mumbled Wilfred, vaguely, feeling flattered by the word of approval.

Pavel, encouraged, produced another sheet of paper — his own composition this time. "Tatiana Ostapenko and Sergei Malinin marriaged good ? ? ? Is it? This Indenture Witnesseth true? Is it ? ? ? R.S.V.P. Very Importance."

Before Wilfred had time to achieve full understanding of this last message, Pavel — nervous lest the man should prematurely shake his head — thrust the Russian history before his guest, open at a picture of the wedding of Peter the Great. "All same?" shouted Pavel, in a sweating frenzy of suspense and mental effort, rapping his finger first on the picture of the wedding and then on Wilfred's draft of the deed.

"All same — all same," said Wilfred, heartily, though still uncertain what was required of him.

Pavel, more and more hopeful, yet still in an agony lest some one should come in before understanding was complete, positively prodded the deed, indicating — so forcibly that Wilfred's kneecap below was quite bruised — the four signatures — Wilfred's own, Pavel's own, Seryozha's and Tatiana's.

"Married good, is it? All same church," he rasped into Wilfred's ear, consulting his notes again. "Very importance because this night they have sleeped ensemble like marriaged. Now fornication not, is it?"

Wilfred now understood. His brain cleared and began reviewing the results of this premature acceptance of his drafted agreement. His eyes cleared and saw a pile of ten-yen notes on the table. He woke up wholly. He read his draft through carefully, his tongue, as well as his bright eyes, leaning out of his head with a creator's eagerness.

His first thought was regret that these impetuous people had not waited for him to show what he could really do in the way of drawing up an agreement. This scribble was nothing; it had a blot in the middle of one page; it did not do Wilfred Chew, Esquire, of the Middle Temple, London, any credit at all. Besides, added an afterthought, it was quite worthless. There were no witnesses to the signatures, and very little substance to the matter. Yet — what of it? These were decent people, who were made happy by believing themselves decently folded within the limits of the law. Law-abiding people only too anxious to abide by even this exiguous semblance of the law. *Outlaws craving to be in.* Supposing Wilfred, as he thought loftily, annulled by a sceptical word this marriage that he had accidentally made, much disturbance of mind would result — and no advantage. "Morally it is a real marriage," thought Wilfred. "And it must be God's will, since God has not provided these poor barbarians with their orthodox machinery for getting married." He felt conscientiously that he was, in this instance, an instrument of God's will. In fact, since the law, as represented by Wilfred, had more to do with the making of this marriage than Heaven had, he felt himself to be in the position of chief justice in this crown colony of Heaven. His it was, not God's, to exercise, as it were, the discretion of the court in this case. Reverend Mr. Oswald Fawcett would surely be the last to wish quibbles of church or law to destroy these innocent barbarian illusions. Supposing a baby were to result from last night's naïve precipitancy, would it not be a misuse of Wilfred's supreme power to make the poor little thing illegitimate by a careless word?

While Wilfred thought all these things, his eye dwelt blankly on the pile of ten-yen notes on the table.

"Are all the parties concerned in the agreement prepared to carry out the various undertakings named?" asked Wilfred, sternly.

"*Schto?*" asked the anxious Pavel, his chestnut eyes almost leaning out of their sockets. Perhaps, he thought, the whole crux of the matter depends on these unknown words that he is saying.

"Have all the signatories expressed their honest intention of abiding by all the provisions of the indenture?"

"*Schto?*"

Wilfred clicked in his throat. For a second he considered tearing the silly old paper in half. Then he pointed to the clauses that dealt with the money payment. Pavel's eyes, like a thirsty proboscis, sucked in the information indicated.

Wilfred gave Pavel time to reabsorb the idea under examination, and then leaned over, took the pile of notes, and counted out on to his own knee one hundred and fifty yen.

"Horosho — ah?" yelled Wilfred.

"Horosho — horosho," replied Pavel in a rival bellow.

"Then in this case the *bumaga* is perfectly *horosho*," said Wilfred, throwing himself with abandon backward on the sofa, to show that the matter was settled.

"Horosho — ah?" queried Pavel, making sure.

"Horosho, horosho."

"*Bumaga horosho* — ah?"

"Horosho, horosho."

"Horosho."

The storm of sibilant uncertainty died down. Everything was all right. Everything was safe. Wilfred and Pavel sat and looked at each other, a little tired but with glorious faces.

Then Pavel leapt to his feet and threw open the door to let the world come in. "Breakfast — breakfast," he shouted in Russian, clapping his hands like a kindly sultan summoning slaves.

Varvara and Katya and the dog surged in, without rancor. Tatiana and Seryozha were late. They came in, hand in hand, as Pavel, Varvara and Wilfred began to eat. All three of their seniors looked at them for a moment in an odd silence.

Tatiana had the sense that they — two humble victims of a strangeness — were offering themselves tentatively to these eyes. She often had this pitying sense that comers-in were on approval, shrinking behind the transparent, hopefully decorated, adjusted screen of their faces. "Will I do? This is the best *me* I can show you. Will it do?" Egoists were even more touching than altruists. Her father's precarious challenge to criticism had often wrung her heart. Now here she was — vulnerably visible herself — she who had been unconscious — bodiless — invisible all her life. Here she was at the mercy of eyes, having dangerously taken body on herself through the big solid body of Seryozha beside her.

It was as though the old story of the magic cloak of invisibility had been reversed; by wrapping her water-clear impersonality in this wide cloak of reality that Seryozha was, she was seen — seen — a woman at last — obliged to offer herself for acceptance or rejection by the eyes of strangers — obliged to ask humbly for tolerance, from eyes.

And as she looked at Seryozha going shyly round the table to his place, hitching up one shoulder awkwardly as though one of his legs were heavier than the other, patting down the brassy crest of hair on the crown of his head, she felt almost as if she were in his body, protecting it from the cold challenge of eyes — as if she were with him inside his too visible body which quailed, yet hoped for the best — which preened itself, yet feared rebuff. She felt herself the true traditional wife — helping him to strengthen his ramparts, arming and encouraging the tender *I* inside that tough body.

And when Seryozha said to her father, "Thank you, I won't have any honey," Tatiana could almost have cried, so suddenly obsessed was she by the thought of that *I* — alone all its life till now — hoping for the best possible results from its little notions of making itself charming — or at least inoffensive; trying to feel confident of victory in its humble struggles to impress itself; keeping its body clean, its nose wiped, its mind wistfully yet imperfectly adjusted to the minds of others; walking in and out of the presence of strangers, saying, "Will I do?" and then, "Did I pass?" When Seryozha said, "I won't have any honey, thank you," she saw him clinging forlornly to his rights and prejudices, daring to refuse honey, to like ham, to be different from other people, presenting himself cautiously as an individual to the round ruthless eye of her father.

Seryozha, unaware of the pathetic picture he was presenting to his wife, ate a very hearty breakfast and felt better, in
spite of a slight spasm of indigestion. His father and mother
were on his mind; he believed that he was pitying them, but
really he was homesick for them. How could he combine
the keeping of his promise to Varvara — to stay at Mi-san
for a fortnight — with his determination to get home as
quickly as possible? And there was that money still to be
fetched from Isaev in Seoul. His life seemed to him now so
complicated that he sweated a little all the time. He gave
inarticulate consideration to a letter that he would write to
his mother — Dearest mamma, I am married to Tatiana
Pavlovna Ostapenko. . . . That wouldn't take long; he
knew how to spell all the words. In the meantime, he drew
Wilfred aside.

"My mamma and my papa, Mr. Chew, they thinks I
come back soon."

"Well, you will, will you not?"

"Nyet. Pavel Nicholaievitch speak me I wait here fourteen
day."

"Very hospitable, I'm sure."

"Da da da. But I speak him, Yes, I *shall* stop."

"Well, it is for you to say."

"Nyet. My papa and my mamma thinks I come back
more soon."

"Well really, my dear Saggay Saggayitch, I cannot grasp
your difficulty. It is impossible for you to be in two places
at once."

"Most impossible, indeed. Nu, if I shall wait here fourteen
day, then, after, I must go to Isaev to speak him to give me
my papa's money."

"Well, what of it? That was what you came for, primarily,
was it not?"

"Yes indeed, very primarily. Yet yist too long time. My

papa and my mamma very sad. Fourteen day here. Three four day Seoul. Ten day walking to Chi-tao-kou. Too long time."

"Well, why not make a quick trip to Seoul today or tomorrow, get your money and come back here?"

"But I speak Pavel Nicholaievitch and Varvara Alexeievna most certain sure I wait here fourteen day."

"We seem to be arguing in a circle, my dear chap," said Wilfred, still anxious to be helpful, yet conscious of a deadlock.

"Mr. Chew, I give you my papa's paper. You go to Seoul and speak Isaev give you my papa's money. So you bring back to me this money and after fourteen day, we go home."

"With the greatest pleasure, my dear Saggay Saggayitch," said Wilfred Chew, immediately.

CHAPTER TWELVE

"This is very kind of me," thought Wilfred Chew, as he sat in the Seoul-bound train. The train lurched through the black world with an open-throated, gasping roar. "I really seem to be a kind of guardian angel to these Russians. . . . What would they do without me?"

As he thought of the Reverend Oswald Fawcett, who had warned him against every sin except complacency, the hundred and fifty yen that Ostapenko had given him seemed to lie not exactly heavily but perceptibly on his bosom. The money was a foreign body in his conscience, like a splinter of shell in a soldier's flesh. "There is nothing wrong in being paid for one's services," Wilfred replied to the shadow of the Reverend Oswald Fawcett. Poor Wilfred! his conscience was already a naturalised alien in his Chinese body. And now must his Chinese lips turn traitor and serve this Wesleyan conscience? His brain — Chinese born — London trained — sought a compromise. "Men are sometimes made use of, surely, by God for His purposes . . . used, in fact, as angels or heavenly messengers, in answer to the prayers of unhappy people. Yet those men, so used, still have stomachs that must be filled — futures that must be provided for. . . . Why, don't you remember, Mr. Fawcett? there was a time when we prayed for more blankets for the school, and that very afternoon, in walked a coolie with a present of army blankets from the Dutch Consul. That gift was none the less Heaven-sent because we had to tip the coolie for bringing it. Money must pass — even between angels — especially when honestly earned. . . . What else is money for? Money isn't always mammon — it is sometimes just simple food and lodging. To continue upon the earth at all, we guardian angels to simple barbarians must be paid — must be fed — must be kept alive. . . . Of what use is a dead guardian angel to any one?"

Wilfred, as a sort of challenge to the impassive ghost of Mr. Fawcett, elaborated this heavenly-messenger idea, which his mission training showed him in quite a literal aspect. An angel was to him as concrete as, say, a duck-billed platibus; he had been taught to believe in the actual existence of both, though neither had, in fact, crossed his path. "Perhaps," thought Wilfred, suddenly beginning to combine his mission-bred trustfulness with a sort of home-made mysticism, "I am literally an instrument of Heaven, born exclusively for that purpose, brought into the world to straighten out the lives of these good Russians. How could you prove the contrary? Perhaps the angel that came to the Virgin Mary was an angel in the body of the local equivalent of a pre-natal-care district nurse (no, Mr. Fawcett, it is not an irreverent thought — an angel in such a manifestation would be none the less an angel — why not?). For an angel to be visible, a body is necessary, and a body, being a worldly garment, must have a worldly justification. A minister, who lives, eats, is paid his salary, dies, rots away in the grave, you say is God's representative in any community . . . how then should God clothe His messengers — His materialized answers to prayer — in any other than a human body? How could those blankets have reached our school without a coolie to carry them — probably a coolie who was looking forward to his dinner. How could old Mr. Malinin receive his money from Seoul, or acquire a beautiful heiress for a daughter-in-law, without me? In all probability, many prayers rose up to heaven at the same time, and combined to elicit *me*, the common answer to all these prayers — old Mr. Malinin's prayer for his money; his prayer to be cured of his blindness (for the rubbing with putrefied fish is a tried remedy and may yet be successful); young Saggay Saggayitch's prayer to see the world; Mr. Ostapenko's prayer that his daughter after seven failures might find a suitable husband; Miss Ostapenko's prayer that the curse of unwomanly coldness might be taken from her . . . all these prayers, probably, rose in one breath to the Throne, and God sent one ingenious combined answer — me. . . ."

Wilfred threw himself back on the vibrating railway cushions, defying the shadow of the Reverend Oswald Fawcett to find a fallacy in this modern and lucid argument.

"And if I — Wilfred Chew — was born, educated in the Wesleyan Academy, enabled to study law in the Middle Temple, London, and be called to the Bar, simply to accomplish God's purposes for these poor helpless Russians — if this was God's idea of a suitable education for His messenger — shall I be ashamed of supporting myself by means of the wits and the education that He has given me? Shall I refuse fair payment — prostitute the advantages God gave me — become a beggar? You will be saying next that I should have refused the rather ample traveling expenses Saggay Saggayitch handed to me on starting. Traveling expenses are necessary, even to an angel — if that angel happens to be traveling in human form on wheels. . . . Just so, similarly, God *meant* me to receive this commission" — he smacked the wad of notes on his bosom — "for drawing up the agreement and arranging the marriage — just as much as He created me — an answer to prayer — in human form and adorned me with education."

There was no one else in that section of the compartment, and Wilfred took out the wad of notes and began counting them. The money, he was sure, was well earned; the notes had a righteous texture against his finger tips; and yet, as he ruffled them, he had a feeling that the shadow of the Reverend Oswald Fawcett in front of him was counting something *beyond* the notes in Wilfred's hand — and counting that something with a reproachful eye — counting the intentions, the financial hopes of Wilfred — ghosts of notes not yet paid. "And what I say about this money I have in my hand," persisted Wilfred to the reproving shadow, "applies with equal reason and force to the commission I intend to charge on the money I have been empowered to secure in Seoul. A just commission is in no way open to criticism. What is it but a dividend paid on that capital which we call education? Yes, it is true that the people I am acting for are ignorant people, incapable of checking my transactions. . . . For that very reason I feel that the trust is sacred — that I am a mouthpiece for babes and sucklings — that it is for me alone to appraise — justly and temperately — the value of my services, and to reimburse myself with an honest moderation. If I were to leave the amount of my commission to that old Mr. and Mrs. Malinin — the one so confused and senile, the other so ardent and exaggerated — they would almost certainly offer me far too much — probably the half of their fortune. Even at that they would, definitely, gain by their association with me. But no — I will refuse everything that the unthinking ardor of gratitude may inspire them to offer me; I will turn away my face, kindly but firmly, as a messenger of God should, from all extravagant offers of reward. 'No — *no*,' I shall say, and nothing will turn me from my determination. Now — to enable me to afford this perfectly correct attitude — what am I to do?

What but pay myself, on a logically worked out basis, my exact commission on whatever I may get over and above old Mr. Malinin's expectations — my exact commission — and not a sen more. The trust of these innocent barbarians in me is a challenge in itself; I would not betray it for all the silver in the Bank of Chosen. I intend to secure, on their behalf, as in honor bound by my divine trusteeship, every sen that I can. I am perfectly aware that old Mr. Malinin would be quite satisfied — quite unsuspicious — if I returned to him with the original two hundred yen plus perhaps five and twenty yen as interest. He has no knowledge of the workings of compound interest. Shall I content myself with satisfying his innocent and humble hope? A thousand times no. I will make a rich man of him — the comfortable founder of a prosperous family. My errand shall be successful beyond his wildest dreams. As an answerer of prayers I will give good measure, pressed down and running over. And who shall say that, for this useful service, I am not entitled to a fair percentage . . . purely as a *defense* against the old man's extravagant gratitude? 'No, Mr. Malinin, no — I do not need a sen more than what I have earned. Keep your money. Prosper righteously. Good-by.' . . . I shall then withdraw like the heavenly messenger I truly am, leaving behind me all prayers answered, all troubles smoothed away. . . ."

He threw himself back in his seat again, licking his gold tooth almost as though he were delicately showing the tip of his tongue to the ghost of the Reverend Oswald Fawcett.

"Oh nonsense!" he thought. "Why all this talk? After all, I am Chinese. Commission is the very lifeblood of China, yet Chinese are the most honest and trusted business men in the world; the honesty of Chinese business men is proverbial — even in Bloomsbury I have heard talk of it — yet every Chinese business man takes his commission as a matter of course."

He scanned the ghost again, and still his expatriated heart was not satisfied.

"Why, can't you see how pure my intentions are toward the poor idiots? I *like* them — I am genuinely fond of that lumpy young Saggay Saggayitch. I really do mean well, and will *do* well by them. . . . Why, look, I am traveling second class at this moment — not first. . . . Well, no, of course I shan't exactly give back the difference — not in so many coins — yet traveling second in this way will allow me to spend more in Seoul on my employer's behalf. This in itself shows how disinterested I am. I *know* that I am sent by God to help them. I have proof of it, as follows: I have received direct promptings from Heaven. For instance, that fish — even while Saggay Saggayitch was in the water catching that fish, I suddenly felt quite clearly that I had already dreamed that very scene; I knew at once that the heart, liver, and gall of the fish were to be preserved as gifts from Heaven. God sent that fish — having caused it to be miraculously caught round the waist (a most exceptional method) by Saggay Saggayitch, and I was warned in advance of the miracle by means of a dream. What does this prove? Does it not prove that I am God's messenger to them? And not only that; I am genuinely fond of them; I wouldn't do them out of a sen. No, I *wouldn't*. . . ."

The first light of dawn gave a curious false emphasis to various insignificant details in the compartment — to inequalities in the stuffing of the cushions — to spittoons — to smears on the window-glass — to dust and dreary ornamentation. The ghost of the Reverend Oswald Fawcett faded from Wilfred's moral sight as the light grew stronger and picked out more and more prosaically the details of his surroundings. He leaned back, feeling justified and sophisticated, and looked out of the window. Brown bat-wing villages, shadeless and lightless in the diffused drowned light of dawn, clung to the miles of dry green and yellow land. The first cooking-fires were being kindled in the clay stoves outside the cottage doors; smoke breathed in a cool blue haze through roofs. Scarlet peppers, spread out to dry on the roofs, looked almost grape-blue with the dew on them — though when the sun should touch them they would wake to a Christmasy vermilion. Mountains — their earth wine-red as though clothed in heather — cut the intensifying line of the horizon into a jagged zigzag. Out-of-doors always seems more essentially out-of-doors at dawn — not, as in the busy afternoon, a mere extension of man's indoors. There was that aloofness — unstained by humanity — about the cold paling twilight of the land, that one sees in a wild animal's eyes.

Wilfred had replaced his well-earned money in his breast pocket, but he still held upon his knee four papers that armed him for his errand. Now, by that same first ray of the sun that lighted the eastern aspects of the western mountains as though they were candles, he reread these papers, in order to clarify his anticipation of the next few busy hours.

The first paper was a Power of Attorney signed by Old Sergei in favor of Seryozha. It had been drawn up by Wilfred himself from memory. Wilfred, of course, had only a haughty barrister's recollection of such a pettifogging paper as a Power of Attorney, yet, as he ran his eye over it, he congratulated himself on having composed an impressive echo of the real thing.

Know All Men by these presents that I Sergei Dmitrivitch Malinin of Chi-tao-kou retail merchant Do Hereby Constitute and Appoint my son Sergei Sergeievitch Malinin of Chi-tao-kou timberworker my true and lawful Attorney for the purposes hereinafter expressed that is to say In my name to receive the moneys deposited by me with Gavril Ilitch Isaev of Seoul hotel-keeper in July one thousand nine hundred and eighteen for investment in his business namely two hundred yen and interest accruing thereto and to give an effectual receipt therefor. And I hereby declare that this Power of Attorney shall be irrevocable for Twelve Calendar Months from the date hereof.

In Witness whereof I have hereunto set my hand and seal this fourteenth day of September One thousand nine hundred and twenty eight. Signed Sealed and Delivered by the above-named Sergei Dmitrivitch Malinin in the presence of Anna Semionovna Malinina of Chi-tao-kou housewife.

Of the other papers, one was a note in Russian from Pavel Ostapenko to Gavril Ilitch Isaev, introducing Wilfred as the trusted friend, legal adviser, and man of affairs of Pavel's cousin, Sergei Dmitrivitch Malinin, explaining young Seryozha's non-appearance in Seoul, inviting Isaev to come to Mi-san for a few days and drink the health of Pavel's newly married daughter, and cordially hoping that the news from Isaev's traveling son, Petya, was good.

The third paper was written in English by Wilfred and signed by Seryozha. It ran:

DEAR MR. ISAEV. Since it is impossible, for reasons explained by my father-in-law Mr. Ostapenko, for me to proceed to Seoul in person to discuss with you the final settlement of the transaction that took place between you and my father in July, 1918, I am placing my Power of Attorney in the hands of my father's friend and legal adviser Mr. Wilfred Chew of the Middle Temple, London, and should be much obliged if you would consider him as my father's agent in my stead, and either place in his hands the two hundred yen which you most kindly invested for my father on his last visit to Seoul and the interest accumulated during the interval, or else (and this would give me much pleasure) come yourself to Mi-san thus killing two birds in one bush, namely settling the financial transaction in person and enjoying my father-in-law's unstinted hospitality.

The fourth paper was a greasy and laconic memorandum of receipt in Russian. Anna had translated it for Wilfred as simply, "Received from Sergei Dmitrivitch Malinin on July 12, 1918, two hundred yen for safe keeping. Gavril Ilitch Isaev."

Seoul looked excited and glittering in the morning light. The sight of large, efficient-looking buildings and large efficient-looking English and American tourists made Wilfred strut, feeling himself a man of the world returned at last to his world.

He found his way, without difficulty, in a rickisha to the Isaevs' hotel, a transformed Japanese inn. Like all Japanese houses lived in by non-Japanese, it had lost its light, kite-like look — it was an architectural bird with clipped wings. Wilfred strolled up the steps, an upslanting cigarette in his mouth, and found Isaev in the hall, reading a Russian newspaper.

It was Wilfred's misfortune always to remember people much better than they remembered him. He remembered Isaev as a human frog, a squatting pyramidal person with a moist shiny skin, and an immense slit-like mouth always gasping obscurely for air. Olga, Isaev's wife, was not present, yet Wilfred remembered her with an equal exactness — a padded person, plump breasts padding her neat dress, secret cushions padding her neat hair, puffed smiles padding her cheeks. On her devolved all the acquiescences that Isaev never uttered; his attitude was a chronic No and hers a constant Yes. Wilfred had counted on laying his business before man and wife together. To find only Isaev present set him back a little, but he began with his usual affability, "We have met before, Mr. Isaev. My name is Chew, Wilfred Chew, barrister, of the Middle Temple, London. I hope I am fortunate enough to find a room disengaged once more in your comfortable hotel."

Isaev nodded uncertainly. All Chinese looked alike to

him. His spectacles were made of very thick convex glass. He had a very thick and conspicuously shiny face; everything about him was thick and shiny. Attention was called to his surface in every way. Somehow Isaev could scarcely be imagined as hollow like other people; there could hardly be room for a brain between the thick walls of that skull, or space in that square inflexible breast for a heart to bound or flutter. His nose was a simple mass of shiny flesh, pierced by only the smallest and most rudimentary nostrils. He held his head back to look at Wilfred over his newspaper, under his spectacles, and across his wide sallow polished cheek-bones.

"We have a room," he said in English. "How long for?"

"I have business in Seoul that should not keep me long. My business, as a matter of fact, Mr. Isaev, is with you. Can you spare me half an hour now? Excellent. We have, as I mentioned above, met before. . . . I was in Seoul only a few weeks ago, acting as secretary-companion to an English baronet, *Sir* Theo Mustard—you may have heard of him. However, in order to give our acquaintanceship a more personal flavor, allow me to hand you this note—a letter of introduction from Mr. Pavel Ostapenko of Mi-san."

Isaev took the letter with distaste and, holding his head up and the letter down, read it across the intervening area of his face.

"I hates Pavel Ostapenko," he said, simply, when he had finished it.

"Really!" exclaimed Wilfred, pleasantly. "Well, I can understand that there might be room for more than one opinion about his peculiar personality. He is a man of very strong character and such men commonly make a strong impression one way or the other. However, his letter will at least show you that I am no man of straw, being recommended by a substantial member of the community such as Mr. Ostapenko, you will admit, is, though his personality may not have a universal app——"

"His daughter is a bitch," said Isaev in the same flat remote voice.

"Well well," said Wilfred, still courageously bright. "As to that, again, there might be a difference of opinion between friends on the subject of Miss Ostapenko, who is, like her father, an individuality both marked and——"

"She is a bitch."

"You really think so? Well, your decided and original views on Miss Ostapenko's charm will no doubt add interest to the news I believe Mr. Ostapenko gave you in his letter. Miss Ostapenko was married only two days ago to my young friend Saggay Saggayitch Malinin. The name Malinin is, I believe, famil——"

"This bitch treated my son very bad," said Isaev.

"Indeed I am deeply sorry to hear it, my dear sir," said the tireless Wilfred. "I remember hearing Mr. Ostapenko describing your son as a particularly fine young man. He is, I am sure, a credit to you, and though he may temporarily have fallen a victim to what is called in London 'Cupid's darts' he will——"

"Because of this bitch," said Isaev, "my son have joined the Chinese army."

"Indeed! Well, you know, boys will be boys. Your son is not the first fine young man who has turned from disappointed love to a military career, and—mark you—made good. . . . The soldier's profession is, after all, considered an honorable one, especially in your country, and I have no doubt that your son will distinguish himself and rapidly gain promotion. Perhaps, indeed, he will some day be able to look back with self-congratulation on his association with the Ostap——"

"He is losed," said Isaev. "We have losed our son. From

the Chinese army Russians never come back. She is a bitch. The whole Ostapenko family is a bitch."

"Ah," said Wilfred. He clicked in his throat and a baffled tragic expression filled his face. Then, like a railway engine that has bumped against buffers, he drew several breaths and, having shunted himself out of this unpromising siding, started briskly off again on a new line.

"But this is all by the way. Perhaps I had better come to the business which brought me here. I will take a chair, if I may. How delightfully the morning sun illuminates this room! I referred just now to young Saggay Saggayitch Malinin. His name — or rather his father's name — is, I believe, familiar to you."

"Never in my life."

"It will occur to you in a minute, I am sure, when I recall the circumstances. A busy man, I know, cannot afford to overstock his memory with unnecessary details. This Saggay Dmitrivitch Malinin, now a retail merchant in Chi-tao-kou, Manchuria, once paid a visit to you a long time ago — ten years ago, to be exact, in July, 1918."

Isaev was silent. Language had been given to him for the purpose of obstructing his fellow-men — not coöperating with them.

"As I think I have already mentioned, Mr. Isaev, I am a barrister, of the Middle Temple, London. Mr. Malinin has constituted me his man of affairs. Having, by my advice, executed a Power of Attorney in favor of his son, Mr. Malinin commissioned me to accompany this son to Seoul in the capacity of legal adviser — since young Saggay Saggayitch has had no experience in business matters — in order that I might make everything clear to you, and satisfy you as to the details and authenticity of his business with you. I hope I make myself clear?"

There was a long silence.

"I hope, Mr. Isaev, that you take my meaning."

"I not understand one word what you speak," said Isaev, looking at him craftily.

Wilfred suddenly became wholeheartedly discouraged. The language bar again. He had no doubt whatever of his capacity to achieve anything at all that a fluent use of the English language could bring about. But remove words from a talker and where is he? This stopping of ears, by means of incompatibility of language, against a talker, is like the stopping of earths against a homecoming hunted fox.

Luckily, at this moment a half-seen piece of furniture, upholstered in striped linen, just inside an inner doorway, suddenly quivered, became human, advanced toward them and turned into Mrs. Isaev. She said something hastily in Russian to her husband and then remarked cheerfully in English to Wilfred: "Ah — you were here before, staying with us. Wait — I remember your name — Mr. *Chew*, is it not? We are glad of seeing you again, Mr. Chew."

Wilfred, although he realized she had been listening and might have gleaned this information from what had been said, preferred to feel that he had made an enduring impression during his last visit. "A charming woman," he thought, building up her, as we all do, from that single flattering aspect of her that faced himself.

Just as a palæontologist builds up a whole mountainous prehistoric beast from one bone, so we reconstruct our neighbors from a mere glimpse of a ghost. We are doomed to live among ghosts just as surely as we are doomed to see through our own eyes only. All are ghosts — these lovers — these enemies — these passers-by. . . . We see them through the distorting lens of vanity. We traduce our neighbors by the senseless names of friends — of enemies; we divorce them from their realities, bereave them of body, cut them off from their destinations and starting-places, make homeless ghosts of them. If they love us, they are darling ghosts to us; if they injure us, they are bogeys. Yet

all the time something that is not a ghost lives at home —
far from our sight — dark, changeless men and women
built of blood and bone and burning egoism, creatures that
neither love us nor hate us — nor even know our names —
things that are, not things that are seen by us to be.

Wilfred lived his life largely backwards. The scenes his
optimism anticipated glowed so gloriously, sparkled with
so flattering a success, that the reality was almost always a
diminishing, an anticlimax, a dim and inexact rendering of
the bright foreseen event — like the creation of a defective
memory, or like the telling of a good story by one who has
forgotten the point.

This, the entrance of the acquiescent Isaeva, was the point
at which the curtain rose on a scene that Wilfred had already rehearsed on the stage of his hopeful fancy. There
had been nothing wrong with the rehearsals; here was the
first public performance. Wilfred's forward-hearing ear could
hear his own voice reasonably explaining the circumstances
of his mission — Old Sergei's loan and his wish for its return; he could hear Isaev's voice grunting agreement,
Isaeva's voice confirming and gracing the accord. Wilfred
could never anticipate counter-arguments to his own logic;
it was too faultless. He was not, therefore, surprised to hear
the expected sound of success beginning — a coo of agreement from Olga Isaeva in reply to a grunt in Russian from
her husband.

"Of course we remember Sergei Dmitrivitch Malinin
very good," she said in English. "My husband has not at first
understood your pronouncing of the name. Sergei Dmitrivitch — how good did he behave to us!" It was almost impossible for Olga to speak without a smile, it seemed. "My
husband knows business very good, but he speak English
not so good. I can help you perhaps with my so poor
English. You speak English so very good yourself."

"It is no merit," beamed Wilfred. "I have been educated

at the Wesleyan Academy in Yueh-lai-chou. I have also studied law for many years in London, and was called to the Bar there. I carry papers from Mr. S. D. Malinin which I should like to bring to the notice of Mr. Isaev and yourself. I am sure you will remember that, ten years ago, when Mr. S. D. Malinin visited Seoul last, Mr. Isaev was so kind as to take charge of two hundred yen which he undertook to invest for Mr. Malinin in whatever way he thought fit. This was because Mr. Malinin did not think it safe to carry his money in cash back to Chi-tao-kou (where there are no banking facilities), the times being then troublous."

The couple murmured together in Russian for a moment, the wife's face still armored by a smile and the husband's by flat stupidity.

"My husband remembers this time quite good, Mr. Chew, but it was not quite as you think, he says. Sergei Dmitrivitch, who has been the brother of my husband's oldest friend in Vladivostok, has gived us this sum — about two hundred yens — in gratitude for my husband's friendship with Mr. Malinin's brother who has died. When Sergei Dmitrivitch comes here we are very poor — our life is not good — we have runned away from the Bolsheviks — we have nothing. We live in a small room here in Seoul and we say, 'What to do — how to live?' Then Sergei Dmitrivitch says, 'You shall make a hotel. I shall give you two hundred yens because you are friends of my brother who has died. You shall borrow from the bank. Your hotel shall be good; you, Gavril Ilitch, are good with business — you, Olga Ivanovna, can cook good. Your hotel shall therefore be altogether good.' Oi! it was goodness that caused the good Sergei Dmitrivitch to give us this money. It has been the beginning of our hope."

"It was certainly the act of a friend," agreed Wilfred, a slight shadow crossing his face as he heard this unrehearsed interpolation. "Nothing in this life is more encouraging than

the way in which—if we live Christian lives—our friends
come forward when we are in trouble and reward us for
our past good deeds by trusting in our schemes sufficiently
to invest in them. Without such friends, what should we
do? How true is the Gospel saying, 'It is better to give than
to receive.' Yet in this case, Mr. Malinin saw that it was
better still to *invest* than to *give*—since, in investing, one
enjoys the combined pleasures of giving *and* receiving. His
timely investment in your future placed your delightful
hotel on its feet or rather foundations. I am very glad that
you so deeply appreciate the friendliness and faith that he
expressed in your business soundness by placing his savings
in your care. This friendly spirit makes business so much
easier. His was certainly a Christian act, and, since we are
all Christians here—Greek Orthodox being no doubt but
another expression of similar great truths to the Wesleyan
faith in which I was brought up—I am sure you will be
sorry to hear that Mr. S. D. Malinin, who was such a good
friend to you in time of need, is now in very poor circumstances himself. He is a victim of blindness, and also of the
local unrest in Chi-tao-kou which has caused his shop to be
looted and his business most seriously affected. In fact, he
has scarcely a bean, and it is for this reason that he is obliged
to employ me in order to withdraw from your business the
capital he invested in it ten years ago, together with interest
accruing to same. Up to now he has been more than satisfied to leave the sum accumulating, at compound interest,
in your competent hands. A sum of money—I see by this
little ready-reckoner of compound interest which I bought
at a money-changer's on my way here from the station—
doubles itself in ten years. Mr. Malinin's capital, therefore,
must by now amount to over four hundred yen."

"It is a mistake," said Olga, her smile becoming a little
fixed, as though there were an invisible clamp at each end

of her mouth. "Sergei Dmitrivitch, a so good man, must not wish to take away his good gift from us."

"Mrs. Isaev, the mistake — a quite unimportant one among friends, but one that needs to be rectified at once — is on your side. I have here a paper, signed by your husband and given to Mr. Malinin, acknowledging the receipt of the money 'for safe keeping.' Your husband will remember signing this, I am sure. No one would sign such a paper in acknowledgment of a mere gift."

Olga referred this to her husband in Russian, and, since he did not reply, she understood that he could not deny the authority of the receipt.

"May I please see this paper?" she said, charmingly. "You explain all so very good, Mr. Chew, yet it is good also to see, in order to understand yet more good."

Wilfred spread the crumpled ten-year-old piece of paper on the table, pinning it down with a delicate finger and thumb, since, even among smiles and Christians, a man of law is always prepared for the worst.

"Ai — two hundred yens — good — good," she cooed, vaguely, as she leaned over the paper. Her fingers made a curious snarling gesture towards it which surprised Wilfred. "A charming and sensible woman," he thought, "but a little nervous."

Isaev got up heavily and walked with a straddling gait across the room to look. The receipt was just as he remembered — just as he feared.

"Two hundred yens . . . to keep safe . . ." he sighed after a long silence, during which he returned to his chair. The clumsy impersonal settling of his wide buttocks in his chair looked as though some solid shiny Buddha in a large invisible grasp were being balanced on its pedestal again.

"Two hundred yens . . ." repeated Olga, turning her smile upon Wilfred again after a murmured word or two with her husband. "Well, perhaps we have make little mistake about the good gift — we have thought Sergei Dmitrivitch a so good friend; he has said, 'It is a gift,' and we could not believe he shall ask to take away his gift. Now we understand. This is not friendship — to give a gift and then to take away. It has not been love or gratefulness. It has been business. Our mistake has been because we have loved Sergei Dmitrivitch."

"It was the beginning of your prosperity, my dear Mrs. Isaev," said Wilfred, throwing his hands apart and looking round as though to reintroduce her to all the family possessions in sight — the spittoons, the ornate buffet crowded with bright bottles, the pots of ferns, the wobbly wicker tables, the blackwood chairs, the posters of the South Manchurian Railway and the British American Tobacco Company on the walls. . . . "What more could a friend do than help you to reach this luxury?"

"To say this is not good, Mr. Chew," said Olga archly. "We have not luxury. We are poor. Yet my husband will, perhaps, when he is able to do without so much money, send two hundred yens to Chi-tao-kou, if Sergei Dmitrivitch, poor man, is now not in good position. Perhaps next year we shall try to afford to do this."

Wilfred, by some freak in the angles of two mirrors in the room, had just caught sight of his own neat seated form in profile. Some of us, when we do this, have the feeling that we have caught ourselves out, that we have accidentally trespassed behind our own vanity. Not so Wilfred. He never caught himself out. All that he saw in that reflected Wilfred Chew who sat over there unconscious, as it were, of being looked at, pleased and encouraged him, buttressed him in his confidence. English clothes — a neat auburn tie just showing under the profile of the round chin — English Panama hat held in a refined hand upon the knee — English words parting those superior smiling lips — in that encouraging mirror Wilfred saw before him truly an angel on a mission of guardianship, a success among failures, a water-lily among frogs—all, in fact, that he hoped to be.

"Mr. and Mrs. Isaev," he said, in a rather sharper voice, "there is no use in this beating about of birds in the bush. I speak now as Mr. S. D. Malinin's man of business. If you will think again, you will see that this is not a matter of two hundred yen to be sent in charitableness, when it can be spared, to a poor chap in China. This is a matter of the immediate withdrawal of a certain sum of money, Mr. S. D. Malinin's capital, from your thriving business, together with the interest that has accumulated in ten years. You have used this money, successfully and skillfully, in the building up of your business, but it is not your money and never was. It is perfectly easy for me to prove that hitherto there has been no consideration given in return for Mr. Malinin's two hundred yen. It was not a gift, and was never mistaken for a gift—the terms of the receipt preclude that. Therefore it was an investment on which, though dividends have been earned, none have as yet been paid, and none demanded up till now. Here is this little book on compound interest which I mentioned before. According to that, since the time expired since the investment was made is just three months over ten years, the sum in question should now amount to four hundred and nine yen sixty-five sen. In the name of Mr. S. D. Malinin, therefore, and of his son, Mr. S. S. Malinin, who holds his Power of Attorney, I demand the immediate return of this money—namely, four hundred and nine yen sixty-five sen. There is no matter of opinion—nothing good-natured or bad-natured—this is simply a business matter, and we are business men and woman who know that what must be must, and what doesn't *want* to be can be *made* to be."

Both Isaevs looked at Wilfred astounded, Olga's amiable mouth dropping open and her husband's grim slit welded more tightly shut. From now on, a curious contradiction began to make itself felt — that Olga's radiant acquiescence somehow obstructed settlement, while Isaev's superficial intransigeance had the effect of advancing matters.

"You are a so good man, Mr. Chew," said Olga. "I know you will not be angry when I tell you how much you mistake. We are *not* prosperitous. We are full of misfortunes. That fire in our kitchen last year — oi! how misfortunate. We have losed three hundred yens' worth of our kitchen properties — saucepan, boiler, dishes, ice-box — all losed. Truly this is Sergei Dmitrivitch's money that is losed. . . . When he has given the money, he has said, 'This two hundred yens will pay your kitchen properties. . . .' Now kitchen is burnt — Sergei Dmitrivitch's money is losed. Poor Isaev — poor Malinin — it is truly misfortunate for both. . . ."

Wilfred smiled a little insolently as he sat leaning forward, swaying his hat between his knees with his right hand, like a snake-charmer at work. He made no reply to Olga's appeal. "A pleasant enough woman," he thought, "but rather a fool."

Olga rose from the arm of her husband's chair and fetched three glasses and a bottle of port wine. "Mr. Chew, you must please arrange this matter more good for us. You are our friend, too — see, now, you will drink with us. My husband cannot give this large number of yens — even if enemy puts him in prison, he cannot give. But you are not enemy — you are friend. I drink — Za Vashe zdorovye — I drink to you. It is business of lawyer and friend to arrange matters for his friends."

"Well, well," laughed Wilfred, a little self-consciously. "I admit that the few odd yen and sen make the business a little petty. Mr. Malinin has given me *cart blaunch* (blank card) in the matter, and I should feel justified, I dare say, in accepting on his behalf the round sum — four hundred yen.

Mind you, in a court of law I could easily establish a claim for the full amount — but this is not a court of law, it is simply a business matter discussed between two friendly parties who have no wish to injure each other by the bloody chopping off of a legal pound of flesh like Shakespeare."

The Isaevs started nervously at this sudden change to the butcher's vocabulary. They watched his mesmeric swinging hat.

"Four hundred yens *not*," said Isaev, after a moment.

"Where is Sergei Sergeievitch?" cooed Olga. "Did you not speak that he has come with? I am sure he is good friend like his father — like his uncle. . . . He will ask you, Mr. Chew, to arrange this matter more good for poor us. Why is he not here?"

"As to that," said Wilfred, buoyantly, "nothing can be easier to explain. Here is his letter. He is at Mi-San, having been married on Thursday, and hopes you will come and attend the subsequent festivities."

"Married to Tatiana Pavlovna," said Isaev. "The bitch."

Olga's white teeth showed in a widening smile. "Then he is married to a not good girl, Mr. Chew. Because of Tatiana Pavlovna our son is now not good boy — gone away from us — soldier in Chinese army. Surely Mr. Chew, you shall not ask us to help with our moneys to pay for this marriage — to help a not good girl who has behaved not good to our son — that she may have a husband." Olga laughed, an open-throated laugh as though she had been outlining a delightful program. "Must our family's money help Tatiana Pavlovna who has harmed our family? Surely, Mr. Chew, you are too good and too clever a man to say this."

"To begin with," said Wilfred. "It is not your family's money. It is Mr. Malinin's. To continue with, even if it were a fact that the money might help toward Saggay Saggayitch's wedding expenses, you should surely be the last to complain. Surely your dearest wish should be to hear of the marriage of this young lady you do not like, and her departure from Korea. Miss Ostapenko, having become Mrs. S. S. Malinin and taken up her residence in Manchuria — in a remote and inaccessible village, Chi-tao-kou — what then prevents your son from returning to his home? He went away to escape her — he will return once she is removed."

"Petya return?" said Olga, putting her knuckles to her mouth with an incredulous gesture.

"Without a doubt. She has been a rose in his flesh. Or, as the proverb says, a rose between two thorns — one thorn being removed, he turns to the other. . . ."

Once more the exuberance of his vocabulary baffled his hearers. A butcher at one moment — a botanist the next — and yet, all the time, a lawyer really. Still, what he had just said made a great impression. It was a fact that Petya had said that Korea was not large enough to hold himself and Tatiana Pavlovna. Emptied of Tatiana, presumably, it would be just the right size for their son.

Isaev reread Ostapenko's letter and, with the murmured help of his wife, Seryozha's English note. Olga sat upon the arm of his chair, her round cheek leaning toward his sparse hair. Wilfred walked over to show them the Power of Attorney. Their three heads bent together and they looked like an affectionate family group. The Isaevs could make nothing of the Power of Attorney, and still less after Wilfred had explained it. Isaev now realized that he was going to pay that money — or most of it. His slow brain was like a ship that does not answer readily to the helm, but which, when the continued insistence of the helmsman's hand affects her course at last, applies herself with an obstinate and heavy exaggeration to the new direction. Isaev's mind was obsessed now by the necessity for haste — by the fact that

the bank would close early on Saturday. Only by going to
the bank soon would he be able to conclude this tiresome
necessity for talk and thought, and be left in peace to finish
this Harbin newspaper account of a delicious scandal in the
family of an ex-general.

Olga also knew now that the money must be paid, and
she could scarcely endure the knowledge without screaming.
Underneath this comfortable and well-filled outer woman
was a straining, insatiable emptiness—a sort of spiritual
sucking in, like the inhaling draught at the mouth of a sea
cave. Olga had never given a gift or consented to a surrender
in her life. Her charming and gentle eyes—always alert behind their charm—wove a kind of web about her as she
walked the world—a web into which a flying miscellany
blundered—in which nothing came amiss—and from
which nothing ever escaped. Nothing ever went out of her
predacious heart or hands. Even her love for her son, her
tolerance of her husband, were predatory. Unswerving and
ravenous purpose had arranged her face in those attractive
and receptive contours, just as nature gives some tropical
flowers a sensuous yet implacable appeal that lures insects
into their trap. All Olga's cupboards were filled with a great
treasure of rubbish; her heart was stored with accepted gifts
—willingly or unwillingly given, but never returned and
never paid for. Nothing came amiss—a bribe, a compliment, an act of reluctant obedience, a gift of money, a gift
of old newspapers, a declaration of love, a couple of celluloid hairpins left behind in a drawer by a guest. . . . She
went through her cupboards by day, thinking, *mine—mine
—mine;* she went through her heart by night, still thinking, *mine—mine.* . . . And every time her eyes rested on
her ugly husband, she saw him as a fixture in her house, a
symbol of property. She saw his hand as an extra hand of
hers—a hand that must, on her behalf, receive money from

strangers, carry that money to the bank, and push it over the counter into safety — but never write a check unless that check were written to earn more money.

And now, to think of something labeled *mine* suddenly changing its label to *yours* — to think of that cramped auxiliary hand of hers forced to detach two or three hundred yen from the darling accumulation, to receive nothing in return except a dirty little forgotten slip of paper, made Olga's heart swell with helpless fury. Yet still her smile corked up the ferment within her.

"I could give," said Isaev, slowly, "one hundred and fifty yens today and, after not many months, perhaps, a hundred other yens. More than two hundred and fifty yens *not*."

These words hardly seemed to Wilfred to make sense at all. Forgetting for a moment that he was a heavenly messenger, he wondered how the old frog could not understand that *eventual* repayment was not — from Wilfred's point of view — repayment at all; that money handed over to the Malinins when Wilfred should be not there but in Shanghai, perhaps — London, perhaps — Timbuctoo, perhaps — might just as well be peanut-shells, for all the good it would do to the principal in the case — Wilfred Chew.

"My dear Mr. Isaev," said Wilfred, licking his gold tooth between puckered lips, "let us talk sense, please. You are not now buying a pianola on the instalment plan; you are returning to an investor his capital, with the interest due. *Due*, I repeat, that is to say, to be paid now. It is not a matter of next year or some time. Here I have a little piece of paper which it is to your interest to redeem. The moment my client's money is in my hands I give you this piece of paper. You burn it. You are free of debt. You snap your fingers on the nose of the world. If you do not choose to hand over the money, I replace the little piece of paper in my pocket and have recourse to the law. I am a lawyer, your friend as well as Mr. Malinin's, and I assure you that you will have to pay in the end. Well, why not now? Why this undignified haggling? As I said before, Mr. Malinin would adjust his convenience to yours to the point of suggesting a round sum — four hundred yen — instead of his exact rights. This sum I should take the responsibility of accepting on his behalf, but——"

"*I* should — *I* advise — *I* accept —" Olga archly mimicked him. Just as the work of a camera is, some think, a glance from the evil eye, so this sweet vehement parody of Wilfred's voice seemed like the subtle curse of an evil tongue. "Mr. Chew, it is *not* our friend Sergei Dmitrivitch which speaks; it is *you*; it is you that wish to take the money from poor us; it is *you* that speaks — that has power to arrange how much. Sergei Dmitrivitch is many far miles away from us——"

Isaev interrupted her; "Da-da-da, Olga, he speaks. Why should he not speak? He is friend of Sergei Dmitrivitch — he speaks for him. Sergei Dmitrivitch is our friend. I hope then Mr. Chew will be so kind to be our friend, too. Mr. Chew, please think — like *our* friend — like Sergei Dmitrivitch's friend — how this matter can be finished. I treat you like friend. You are my guest here — my friend. As long as you stay here — two day — three day — I charge nothing. You are a *friend*."

"It is most hospitable of you," said Wilfred, rather frostily. "But on second thoughts, when we have settled this business I think I will not stay in Seoul. If we can reach the bank before it closes, I feel I ought to take tonight's train back to Mi-san."

Isaev's face was quite animated now. He was like a pyramid tipped with sunrise.

"Well, whether yes or no, I invite you like friend. If you speak no, still remember my hospitality has money value and what I offer to friend I do not take back. One week in my hotel I offer — one week, I think, twenty-five yens. See,

I make you my guest if you go away — if you stay — it is all the same — you are my guest and friend." He laid twenty-five yen on the table beside him. "We shall better finish this matter now because the bank will shut door. Did you speak two hundred and seventy-five yens?"

"My dear Mr. Isaev, I did not. On the contrary. You mis-heard me. I may have mentioned the sum of *three* hundred and seventy-five yen. This would I think be a reasonable compromise."

"Oi-oi! Mr. Chew — remember how rich Sergei Dmitri-vitch will be soon; he has now very rich son, married to that bitch. Plenty money — I think Pavel Nicholaievitch pay plenty money to have his daughter married at last. Sergei Dmitrivitch — now so rich — will not be made angry by little matters. Fifty yen more — fifty yen less — it is nothing to a man whose daughter is rich bitch. I also am business man — I am not made angry by small matters. If you come to bank now, I give you three hundred and twenty-five yens — thus all are glad — all are still friends."

Isaev got up. Wilfred got up. Olga remained sitting on the arm of Isaev's chair, her fine eyes fixed on the two ten-yen notes and the five-yen note on the table. Wilfred, his affectedly wandering attention having been recalled by a murmur from Isaev, picked up these notes with a polite embarrassed laugh and, after flipping them about in the air for a moment to show that they were entirely irrelevant — in fact, nothing at all — put them in his pocket. Olga's eyes were thus released from their spell. She looked wildly round the room for a minute and then followed the two men to the door.

"Are you also coming to the bank with us, Mrs. Isaev?" asked Wilfred, cheerfully. "It is indeed a fine morning for a little constitutional (as we call a walk in London)."

Olga gave a vague laugh and followed them into the street.

Wilfred and Isaev walked side by side, Olga a dozen paces behind. She looked intent, like a spaniel scenting game — she was following the scent of receding money.

"I still hope," said Wilfred, "to persuade you to accept the invitation of Mr. Ostapenko and Saggay Saggayitch to return with me to Mi-san and take part in the marriage rejoicings — and to satisfy yourself by eye that the dangerous young lady, Miss Ostapenko, is securely spliced."

Isaev made no reply. The necessity for affability was over. He walked with an effort, heaving his heavy body, breathing asthmatically — not only through his mouth and nose, but also, apparently, through his goggling eyes. Bicyclists, the most insidious danger to life in the Japanese Empire, slithered and glittered round him like eels round a rock. As he waddled across the wide shadow of one of the old serene squat gateways of Seoul, one could imagine that just so would the gateway itself advance behind its massive shadow, should those great red plaster bow-legged flanks be spurred with life.

The door of the bank was a triumphal arch for Wilfred. He was genuinely delighted to have secured a reasonable sum of money for that innocent old dotard, Sergei Malinin. He was pleased to have done well for himself, too — twenty-five yen here, a hundred and fifty yen on the marriage, his expenses during these weeks, and fifty sen a day, and finally the promised ten per cent on the unexpected hundred and twenty-five yen he should bring back. Over two hundred yen altogether — and all earned in a perfectly correct Wesleyan manner, thought Wilfred, looking defiantly right and left along the hygienic perspectives of the bank. And he saw, drooping courteously over the far end of the counter, in conversation with one of the Japanese clerks — the Reverend Oswald Fawcett! To be sure, Wilfred knew as certainly as he could know anything that Mr. Fawcett was at present on a walking tour in the English lake country. Yet there he was—or at least here, in the bank, was one—an angel—a ghost—clad in the limp duck suit affected by Wilfred's dear pastor—wilting, stooping, seeking support, giving, even across these wide spaces, the impression of being defective in eye, in teeth, in complexion, in hair, yet somehow armored with a sort of pale pre-Raphaelite brightness. . . . "A vision—a vision," thought Wilfred, and stood frozen, face to face with his conscience across the throne-room of Mammon. By a sort of divine imperialism, the foreign conscience, sitting uneasily in Wilfred's Chinese nature, armed itself, just as Shanghai—that anomalous growth grafted upon a Chinese mudbank—in time of trouble, blossoms forth with Aldershot machine-guns. So, in the brain behind Wilfred's narrow bright eyes, the still small voice of conscience said, with the faint Lancashire accent that distinguished Mr. Fawcett, "Wilfred Chew, what would Jesus say?" There was, unfortunately, no doubt what Jesus would say. Jesus was an Oriental like Wilfred himself, as Wilfred had often thought—but an Oriental who never seems to have had any idea of the value of money. With one's brain, which is Mammon, one earns money; with one's heart, which is Jesus, one gives it back. It is lucky, thought Wilfred's slightly mutinous brain, that the voice of the heart *is* still and small, and not too often heard, for to obey it is expensive—and when that still small voice is heard, it is heard above all greater noises—across wide spaces filled with the clinking of money.

Wilfred hurried, borne on charmed feet, to the side of Isaev, who was leaning his iron diaphragm against the mahogany flanks of the counter.

"Take this twenty-five yen, Mr. Isaev," mumbled Wilfred in an uncertain hurried voice. "I made a mistake. It is part of Mr. Malinin's capital. Three hundred and fifty yen—that is the sum due to my client."

Isaev's brain moved slowly, but his hand accepted the

money and laid it upon the sheaf of notes already on the counter.

"Be so kind as to give us an envelope," said Wilfred to the Japanese cashier. And when the envelope was brought, he added, between lips still slightly trembling, "Be so kind as to give us a stalk of sealing wax."

The flaming stick of wax, like the flaming sword of the angel of Eden, barred Wilfred away from his treasure.

"Now I will write," he said, and he wrote on the sealed envelope, "Contents: three hundred and fifty yen, being Sergei D. Malinin Esq.'s capital returned in full, with interest, by G. I. Isaev, Esq. Signed, Wilfred Chew." He put the bulging envelope in his breast pocket and handed Isaev the original receipt. Only then did Wilfred's eyes seek along the counter for the vision of his conscience. The figure was gone. A slight radiance seemed to Wilfred to remain.

But on the steps outside the tall figure of a stranger stood, wagging a ridiculous sunshade at a rickisha — obviously the figure of a Frenchman, with a long drooping mustache and the pulled-down bloodshot eyes of a bloodhound. Wilfred saw at once that this was his angel; from within that crumpled duck suit, that sallow skin, his vision of the Reverend Oswald Fawcett had glowed. "Certainly — certainly — it was a vision; a miracle purposely dazzled my eyes — otherwise I could not have made such a mistake. Ah, I have been good, I have been good." Wilfred's happy heart chanted. "It shall be said of me — 'Well done, thou good and faithful servant.'" His happy heart, washed by the sacrifice, sang, as it were, in its bath.

At the foot of the steps Olga Isaeva stood, her eyes glowing at the two men from a rigid face. "The money is paid?" she asked in a high soft voice of her husband.

"Da-da-da," said Isaev calmly, and showed her the returned receipt.

"Tschah! you filth!" shouted Olga suddenly, and spat at

Wilfred's waistcoat. She turned to her husband and slapped his face, shouting a few shrill confused insults in Russian. Then words failed her. "Ah — ah — ah!" she screamed, and swayed about, wringing her hands. Several rickisha coolies, foreseeing that this curious seizure would end in physical collapse, came and laid the shafts of their vehicles invitingly at her feet. About forty Japanese bicyclists alighted and stood round the party. The Frenchman, thanking God that he was French, bowled away in a rickisha; the thin prancing brown legs of the coolie, seen from behind, seemed to be attached, in skittish incompatibility, to the long drooping torso of the passenger.

Olga disregarded her public. She strode over the rickisha shafts and hurried away down the street, still ejaculating, Ah — ah — ah! and slapping her clenched knuckles of one hand into the palm of the other.

Wilfred was paralyzed with astonishment. Feeling quite sure that Olga Isaeva liked him, he could only suppose that she was suffering from some kind of fit or convulsion. Isaev stood looking mildly at the tattered receipt in his hand, as though wondering whether something in its wording had provoked her. He remained on the lowest step of the bank for a few minutes, as though built there, the thin, craning coolies standing round him like scaffolding. "My wife is sometimes a little bit angry . . ." he said.

After a moment he began. "Tonight my wife will——" and stopped, evidently feeling that what he had begun to say was not worth finishing. Then he said, firmly, "I think I come with you to Mi-san tonight, Mr. Chew, yes — no?"

CHAPTER THIRTEEN

WHENEVER PAVEL OSTAPENKO knew that he was likely to meet a friend, old or new, he always automatically inquired of himself whether the meeting was likely to do him credit or no. "Is everything all right? Does he appreciate me? Has he lately seen any one who might have criticized me or told lies about me? Have I told him the same story as the one current here?" And as soon as he received Wilfred's telegram from Seoul, announcing his immediate return to Misan, accompanied by Isaev, Pavel, testing in his own mind the newcomer by means of this third-degree questionnaire, was annoyed to be obliged to answer, "No. There is danger here. Isaev may very well withhold the requisite smile as he greets me — may even be discourteous. He imagines he has a grievance against my family; he blames his son's downfall on my daughter. He once called me — (Pavel's very inmost voice sank to the veriest inmost whisper) — a *windbag*. Something must be done about Isaev."

Pavel, of course, disliked Isaev for disliking him, yet he was so sure of his own superiority that his dislike was entirely impermanent. Simply, the man's disease — dislike of Pavel — must be subjected to immediate treatment and cure. To be deeply offended at being called a windbag, one must suspect uneasily the truth of the indictment, but Pavel had no such suspicion. The man Isaev had made a ridiculous and offensive error — and of his error he must be convinced as soon as possible — not by reproach, but by eloquent proof of Pavel's essential non-windbagacity. The matter of Tatiana's guilt, though still urgently in need of readjustment, was less urgent than the windbag misunderstanding, since Tatiana, though certainly a limb of the Ostapenko tree, was an outlying limb. A man, for instance, would be less offended by criticism of the shape of his little toe than of the shape of his nose. Indeed, alone with his daughter, Pavel would have detached her from the Ostapenko body altogether; in speaking to her he would have admitted — and even insisted on — her guilt in the matter of the jilting of young Piotr Isaev. But in speaking to Isaev, Pavel would instinctively graft his daughter on to the main Ostapenko trunk once more, and swear to her inviolate blamelessness of any interference with young Isaev's peace of mind. And he would prove it too (with as much ease as he could, in Tatiana's ear, prove her guilt) — prove it to his own satisfaction, and perhaps to the resentful father's. When speaking neither to sinner nor sinned against, Pavel would not entertain the question of sin or justification, truth or lie, at all. Truth was non-existent, unless he was engaged in propounding it; in words lay his entire standard of truth, morals, and behavior.

Much of Pavel's life, therefore — since words were his standard — was spent in getting his word in first. It was, for instance, necessary for him to see Isaev before any one else in Mi-san should see him. If their first meeting since the family estrangement should be a public one, Isaev's Ostapenko heresies might be expressed in the hearing of Ostapenko believers before Pavel's doctrine of reassurance should have time to take effect.

"What on earth is the old fool coming here for?" thought Pavel, irritated by the necessity of riding fifteen miles to the railway station on a very hot day. "I only invited him because I took for granted he wouldn't come — and because I thought the courtesy might loosen his purse-strings to my young couple's advantage." However, he could not afford to question the stark necessity of seeing Isaev alone first. Of course the old snake had probably poisoned Wilfred Chew's ear already, but incompatibility of language had, one hoped, been a safeguard to a certain extent. Besides, Wilfred was a Chinese, and his approval didn't matter so very much.

Pavel, never indolent, was as tireless in defense of his vanity's interests as is a fish-hawk in providing for the inmates of its nest. Before Sunday morning was a morning at all, before the first knot of the parcel that contained this coming week had been cut by the first blade of the sun, Pavel was awake, was forcing the sleepers of his household to be awake, was shattering with a hurrying candle this precious blank dark nothingness between last week and next week.

Seryozha, in the little room behind the kitchen, woke up and sat up, as the noise of a heavy foot stumbling over a heavy metal thing tore him from sleep. He lighted a match; it was just past half past three. He lit the candle and sat for a few minutes, clasping his big knees, looking down at the sleeping Tatiana.

She looked so proud, asleep; her mouth was loosened from its waking anxious, gentle smile, to a slight exquisite sneer. Her cheek-bones almost looked like shrugged shoulders. She seemed almost crafty now, as if she had escaped, by wiles and cunning, leaving this pale contemptuous dummy in her place — had escaped and was free now in a trackless wild. Tatiana always looked forward to sleep, although she loved life so much. On waking every morning, she was impatient to be quickly up and living, to get the day soon begun and soon ended, every morning being, to her, a promise of another night and new dreams. The hither bank of every river that we must cross is but a promise of the farther bank—a promise that gives us courage to swim out boldly into the current.

Seryozha looked at her face almost resentfully; he was vaguely conscious that to call her from sleep would be to recall her from a palace to a cottage—and the knowledge hurt him. Her pretty mouth, stopped by sleep, seemed more ruthlessly frank now than when day parted it to say kind, tentative things. Now, asleep, she admitted that most of the words she knew were not to be said to him. Waking, she disguised her refusal by uttering always *invented*, not *known*, words—words of timid conscientious love, warmth, interest, consent—words spoken only from a tender heart, not blurted with the lips of a vital body.

With Tatiana, Seryozha was forced to be conscious of himself. Even side by side with a far-away, sleeping Tatiana, he was obliged to confront himself with naive comparisons, to blunder about among clumsy thoughts of right and wrong. In spite of her remoteness, she had introduced an unwelcome immediacy into his self-knowledge. Being a married man was, for him, to be married to a new critical, shrewish self, that called attention to the slowness of his understanding, the poverty of his experience, the prosaic quality of his love, the size of his hands and feet. . . . And Tatiana stood between him and this new, carping, fretful self, in the guise of an ineffectual friend and peacemaker—murmuring unconvincing, yet exquisite, reassurances, gently decrying injustices and misunderstandings between that newly-married, ill-assorted couple—Seryozha and his soul. And, having flattered both contestants with a tender courtesy, she was gone—a peacemaking neighbor gone to her home, her duty done, leaving Seryozha and that new inward domestic tyrant eyeing each other suspiciously—

"Was that right? — was that clumsy? — did that sound
stupid?". . . Oh, never to be alone again. . . .

Seryozha, clasping his knees, looked at his hands. The
knuckles were red and not very thoroughly washed. His
right thumb was made unshapely by a deep old scar. He was
not old enough — first, to value and then to forget the very
thickness and strength of his body. The first stage — the
stage of living unconsciously in his big body as though it
were a twirl of air — was left behind him forever. In the
second stage he now was — the stage of feeling responsible
for, yet betrayed by, his great limbs and hungry organs and
appetites, as a child is embarrassed by the companionship of
a gross aggressive elder brother. Soon he would arrive at the
third stage — the simple serenity of size, the stage at which
the big bones and little soul — lion and lamb — lie down
together dreamlessly in their lair.

But now he looked at his scarred useful thumb and sighed.

He got up, and after pulling on his shirt and trousers with
a feeling of disgust at their homespun and stained look —
a look he had never noticed before — he went into the
kitchen and found Varvara and Katya prodding a morose
reluctant fire, and Pavel standing over them with a candle,
elaborately repressed curses filtering through his beard.

"I am going to the station to meet Mr. Chew and Gavril
Ilitch," said Pavel. "Some one has to take a couple of horses
to the station for them to ride, and it would seem discourteous, I think, to send a servant only." He gabbled a little
because he did not want Seryozha to offer to come with
him. The whole expedition was arranged largely for the
purpose of protecting his son-in-law's illusions about Ostapenko perfection. But in any case he needed no audience
for the feat of dialectics which was to lure the errant Isaev
back into the fold of Ostapenko orthodoxy. He would not
even have let his wife witness the meeting between himself
and a doubtful admirer; he supposed that she had never

seen him humiliated. "I leave you, son, in charge of our women-folk," he added, boisterously, to Seryozha. "The only pair of trousers in a bundle of petticoats — a great responsibility. . . ."

Seryozha stretched his mouth automatically to filial acquiescence. This robust paternalism was much easier to cope with than was the jejune and bloodless nagging of his own father. Arrogant complacency rebounds from the attention, but false pathos bores into it, like some unwholesome parasite.

Yet when, just as the sun, though still invisible behind a neighbor's roof, threw stripes of gay fresh gold all over the plain, Seryozha came out to watch the departure of Pavel, the servant Yi, and the four horses, he was filled with an almost uncontrollable longing to go too. Pavel's jocose reference to the trousers and petticoats had somehow made almost articulate Seryozha's momentary weariness of women.

Seryozha stood watching Katya giving confused, strident directions to Yi, the Korean servant, about a skein of yarn that she wished him to buy in the town through which the railway ran. Yi, though he had exchanged his billowing white robe for a white riding suit with no superfluity except a discreet drapery about the seat, still retained his horsehair hat — a truncated edition of the traditional Welshwoman's hat, but as small as a doll's. It tottered like a belfry on the steeped skull-cap that lidded his narrow skull, and gave him a look of tapering neatness — like a well-sharpened pencil. Katya, seen in contrast with that impassive skeleton, typified all that was most exasperatingly *petticoaty* about women. She fluttered, she wobbled, she sweated, she squawked; streaks of hair shook about the mottled nape of her neck. The lumps of her body were encased in a buttony, patchy, hooky, stitchy material, like turnips in a sack. Above all she *talked* — she wanted something, and wanted repeated assurances that what she wanted would be brought to her.

"*Bunamayesh? Bunamayesh?*" she yawped to the silent Yi, nagging at him to acknowledge her authority — as women always nag, thought Seryozha. Always their petticoats, their hair, their scent, their bosoms, their voices *stuck out* from them, encroaching on space and air, imposing an aura of artificial excitement and complexity on life. Men, calmly concave men, walked neatly, sleekly bounded in their decent bones, doing what must be done. These were not the words of Seryozha's thoughts, but he looked at the great this-way-and-that fuss of women's footprints on the dewy grass between the door and the road, and glumly reminded himself that only a few purposeful, large, well-aimed marks showed the men's traces. Of course this was largely because the purposeful feet of Pavel remained still, nobly rooted in manly authority, while his voice commanded women to fetch this — go there — do that — no, not that, *this* — no, not this, *that*. . . . And of course it would be fair also to add that Tatiana's feet had not smirched the dew at all, because they were in bed. Indeed, Tatiana's encroachment on the world, as Seryozha could not but have admitted, was slighter even than the manliest man's. No intrusion can aspire to a point more discreet than the vanishing point, and Seryozha's wife could hardly diminish much more the reticent trace she left without erasing it altogether. Yet a vague sense of his own injustice and poor logic did not make him look with more tolerant eyes on the anxious, hurrying flutter of Varvara and Katya. Indeed, his irritation with these harmless women was merely a revenge for the irritation with men which Tatiana did *not* confessedly feel. It was a revenge for the gross look that his scarred spatulate hand had taken on in his own eyes, since that hand had been married to the brown, unflawed, flexible strip of bones and muscles that was Tatiana's hand.

And when at last Pavel could find no more orders to give to his two women, when at last his long legs were astride of the dancing mare and Yi had scrambled up on to the back of one of the impatiently following horses, Seryozha could bear it no longer. He ran after the party and swung himself astride of the last spare horse. "I'm coming too," he said, grinning at his father-in-law.

Pavel, taken unawares, could think of no explicable reason why the boy should not come, especially as Yi shouted his willingness to walk home and so leave all four horses free on the return ride. It was amazing, thought Pavel, how inconvenient people were. Nobody ever respected the subtle integrity of Ostapenko plans. Simply because it was impossible to explain those plans to common people, common people found them easy to thwart.

Seryozha's happy and charming look, as the boy set his eager horse to canter down the trail, suddenly touched some forgotten softness in Pavel's heart, however — it was almost like a homesickness. "Oh, let him come," he grumbled to himself. "I can think of some way to have a quiet talk with Gavril Ilitch."

The way lay for the first half-hour along narrow dikes between rice-fields, and the horses must dance — with a slightly sidewise gait — in single file, Pavel now at the head of the procession, Yi and the spare horse behind him, and Seryozha at the tail, so that talk was impossible. The toppling dike shook under the bouncing tread of sixteen hoofs—shook frogs and dew and dragonflies out of the grass into the flooded fields below. The frogs had vermilion stomachs and grass-green backs patched with black. The dragonflies were sequin blue. The frogs and dragonflies sprang out from the dike's brink into the sunlight; they glittered together between one's eyes and the dazzling water, like splinters of kingfisher color.

Seryozha's dog, bursting with happiness, floundered in and out of the water, snapping genially at frogs, dragonflies, pigs, butterflies, bullocks, ponies, and even clods of mere

earth in a frenzy of joy. It was a kind dog, but in its excitement it rushed at a brood of day-old chicks near a cottage
and set them blowing about the trail like an explosion of
yellow thistledowns. It could have swallowed them as one
swallows yellow gooseberries, but the hen, completely selfless, instantly made herself terrible — a super-hen — with
spread ruff and taut spread wings. Masked thus, she rushed
at the enemy, positively roaring with heroic anger, clapped
the dog about the muzzle with her wings and after pecking
at its eyes, almost thrust herself into its mouth. The dog,
extricating its teeth from this ardently offered sacrifice, hurried sheepishly away, pretending to be engaged in some new
and worthier chase, but really humiliated — put to flight by
the ridiculous and splendid bird.

The trail in front began lifting itself up out of the rice-
marshes on to higher land, like a water snake coming out to
bask in the sun. No rice, no farms, on the hill — it was an
untamed hill, furred with velvety, rather sun-dried grass.
Man's only marks upon it were oblong or square patches of
canary-yellow buckwheat here and there, and the headstones
of old forgotten Korean graves, like worn-down tree-stumps
bristling from the roots of their red mud and grass mounds.
As the horses cantered up the diagonally mounting trail,
and Pavel, twenty yards in front of Seryozha, reached the
top of the ridge, the older man's rather heroic bright head
and upslanting beard towered against the sky. An instant
later, all the riders seemed to attain to the level of the low
rising sun, and their endless slim elastic shadows laddered
down the soft slope as far as the farther valley — seven-
league stilts, straddling a dozen distant rice-fields at a stride.

"A fine climate and a fine country," said Pavel, who was
always exhilarated and fortified in his pride by finding himself on a horse's back. He looked down complacently at his
titanic shadow — as big as a rainbow. "Why don't you stay
here, Seryozha — settle down here and help me with the

horse business? I'll write to your father and explain how it is. He'd be delighted, I'm sure, to have you so well settled."

"Oi — no — no!" said Seryozha, startled. He added, childishly, "You promised I could go home after a fortnight."

Pavel looked at him, surprised. "Why, my dear boy, you're a free man! You can go when you please — after Thursday week, of course. We asked you to undertake to stay with us till Thursday week, in case poor little Tanya might feel — Well, thank God, things are going well. Still, you've given your word not to take the child away till Thursday week, when the fortnight will be up. After that, of course you're free to go home or anywhere you like — but I can't understand why you should want to. Much more opportunity here, in well-governed Korea, than up north, among Chinese brigands in Kanto. And I could be useful to you here. I'm in very good standing with the Japanese; this horse-breeding idea really was an inspiration on my part. The Japanese have such short legs themselves, they'll give any price for long-legged horses. How often have I tried to get a likely cob off on a policeman five foot one high; but, no — a taller horse — a taller horse, please. . . ." He imitated the polite hissing of a Japanese. "However, I'm here to supply the demand, and if the Japanese police start using giraffes, I shall be on hand to breed them, you may be sure. They know me now as a man who never lets them down over a horse deal. If you come into the business you could learn the Japanese language and——"

"Oi, no, no!" said Seryozha. "No, but let me go to my father."

His father, though tiresome, puny, and ugly enough, seemed to him at this moment more part of the dear ugly furniture of his home than did his mother. With his father beside him, as with his claspknife or his dog, he could feel himself effective, dignified, taken for granted, not to be sur-

prised unawares into childishness. With his mother he could
not always feel this. She was near enough to him to trip up
his pride, to prick his youth to self-consciousness, to rouse
him to effort. It was quietness, non-adventure, that he hun-
gered for just now — to feast his eyes on the disfigured face
of the home clock, on the little crooked window of his bedroom at home, on the helpless, humble, unwandering figure
of his father — these were his cravings. He sought everything that was sure to be there — everything that could be
depended on not to be suddenly strange and humiliating.

"Go to your father, then," said Pavel, curtly. "I can tell
you, though, when *I* was your age . . ." And for an hour
and a half he *did* tell him.

The ridge climbed higher, and though the day grew
brighter, the valleys, being more deeply sunken, were filled
with mist — slung with a canopy of dark steel-colored mist,
which presently the sun would first polish to bright silver
and then roll away altogether. Flowers of a deep brooding
gentian blue burned deep in the grass. Far away, a monstrous pyramidal stalagmite of mountains craned to meet a
stalactite of far-flung clouds. Foothills, like dispersed ripples,
lay about the great central wave of land — gathered themselves, higher and higher, about the multiple toppling head
— like an immense tidal wave, towering above tributary
waves to overwhelm the valley. The clouds, an inverted
pyramid, seemed to reflect this piled accumulation; there
also, in the sky, were the foothills, the swelling base, and
the apex of the cloud range, as though the sky were a mirror,
answering the stormy earth.

"The Kongo-san," * said Pavel.

Their trail ran out upon the spine of a sharp spur of hill,
and it seemed impossible to believe that horsemen could
ride down from such an airplane flight of land. On three

* Diamond Mountains, sacred mountains of Korea.

280

sides — to right, to left, and before — distant fields, rivers,
villages, and groves, seen under the horses' chins, were flattened down by a wide weight of glass air. Yet the path which
led the riders, as it seemed, over the brim of this high grassy
world into the air, proved to be a reasonably tame descent —
a fluent series of zeds and esses, zigzagging and looping
down the fluted sides of the hill, in easy, if twisted, gradi-
ents.

By the time the instructive tale of Pavel's youth had
brought him to his first business triumph — ("I said to him,
'No, my dear sir, that's where you're wrong. I may be half
your age, but I've kept my wits about me and you can take
it from me. . . .'") — the hoofs of the four horses were
rattling over the bleached, water-worn stones of a dry river
bed on valley level. Sandpipers found an innocent sport in
fluttering invitingly in front of the pursuing dog's nose; their
chicks, nearly independent now, were still obedient enough
to heed the mew of command and be frozen into black-and-
white pebbles, impossible to identify. A couple of little boys
were herding pigs among the boulders, and screamed with
pleasure at the artless dog's confusion.

The father of the little boys came out of his thatched
shed to watch the riders. Pleased by their rich look, he hailed
them, and, dragging a yellow ground-melon from the tangle
of his garden, shuffled toward them, peeling the fruit as he
came. So earthy was the hand in which he held up the fruit
that black smears were printed all over the pale peeled flesh
of the melon. Yi, the servant, shocked at such manners, reproached his compatriot. The peasant, laughing at his social
faux-pas, pulled round his even dirtier coat-tail from behind
him, and held the fruit in that. Pavel, delighted at the
friendly subservience of the Korean, took the fruit and ate
a few mouthfuls of it, nodding in a princely way at the man.
Juice and seeds were tangled in his red beard. When he was
on horseback, it was evident that he would have made a

good king. His chestnut eyes, directed downward at humanity under the proudly lowered lids of a man raised up, lost their staring, round, appealing look. They no longer expressed, "You *must* believe me" — they took for granted that you would. He spilled a coin or two out of his flat casual palm as he stuck his heels into his horse's ribs and clattered away.

"I shall never be as grown-up as that," sighed Seryozha, riding humbly after him. And he longed the more fiercely for his own poor inferior old father, as one might long for even a false word of encouragement.

Pavel was still dealing with his triumphant twenty-fifth year when the party reached the station. Seryozha's impression was that his father-in-law had matured extremely slowly, but no detail of the process remained in the young man's mind. The station, a humble, flat affair — a mere wooden box on the edge of a couple of metal stripes, distracted Pavel's attention from his recital.

"Here we are," he said. "Only twenty minutes to wait. I timed that very neatly."

The mud strip that acted as platform, was empty except for a Korean woman, who squatted on the ground, crying loudly. Her head was crowned by an elaborate arrangement of napkin that might have been the pride of a suburban butler. Wisps of dusty hair clung to her tear-wet cheeks and she carried a crying baby bound upon her back. Seryozha looked at her with distaste. "These women. . . . Leave them behind in one place, they crop up in another. Always demanding attention . . ."

"What can she be crying for?" he asked.

Pavel took no notice of this. "While we are waiting, I will ask about your journey back to Manchuria," he said. "I want Tanya to travel as comfortably as possible. It is her first real journey since she was a child, and the parting from her parents is bound to be rather a strain, so I want her to be well looked after." He began talking about the details of the journey — sleeping berths, hotels, steamers, orders telegraphed ahead. . . .

"Oh, I shall never be man enough to arrange all that," thought Seryozha. And equally, he felt he must not be child enough to let Wilfred Chew undertake everything.

While Pavel talked in Japanese, with a patronizing affability, to the hissing station-master, Seryozha stood near the weeping Korean woman. He wanted either to strangle her or to stroke her dirty neck — it was impossible to be sure which. As he looked at her, his dog bustled up with its usual "So-sorry-I'm-late-I-was-detained-on-business" manner and licked the woman hastily on the ear. She screamed and pushed it away. Seryozha looked at his dog fondly, admiring its *savoir-faire*. "What about my dog?" he asked Pavel. "How will it travel in a sleeping berth?"

Pavel laughed good-naturedly and spoke to the station-master again.

"You will have to put it in a crate and send it as freight," he said, "if you think the creature's worth taking home again. But if you like to leave it with Yi at Mi-san ——"

"My dog can't travel in a box," said Seryozha. The dog cramped itself coyly at his feet, realizing that it was being talked about, but naïvely confident that the talk was kind.

"Nonsense! All dogs travel like that here. It's a rule on Japanese railways." Pavel spoke inattentively, for he was straining his sight toward the far sun-dazzled spot where the ostensibly parallel railway lines defied geometry and converged on the horizon.

"Well then, I shan't go home by train," said Seryozha. "I shall walk."

"What *do* you mean?" asked Pavel. His attention, suddenly recalled, whizzed down the slippery widening perspective of the railway line from the horizon to his son-in-law. "What do you mean — you'll *walk*?"

"My dog can't travel in a box," said Seryozha, between nervously rigid lips.

"My daughter can't travel on her feet," said Pavel, glaring at him in amazement.

There was silence, bounded on the one hand by the continuous duet of the wailing Korean mother and child, and on the other by an insect-like twanging resonance, the sound of the approaching train. Pavel guarded the rather precarious integrity of his last word as the train approached. He knew it had not convinced his incipiently mutinous son-in-law, but still, as long as silence followed it, it could be considered as the last word on the subject. And now the roar of the train might be counted on to drown any further impertinence.

The train's roar swelled and swelled, just reached the verge of the unendurable, and then broke, like a schoolboy's voice, into a falsetto of hissings and steamings, as the train stopped.

Wilfred and Isaev climbed down. Pavel hurried toward them; here, the first word rather than the last, was the important one.

"Excellent, excellent," he shouted, seizing Isaev's slow hand. "Old friend, you are welcome. You give me the greatest pleasure." He tried painfully to be economical of words — terse and manly of voice. Windbag was a charge that an amiable taciturnity must disprove. But he could not resist adding something more — and something more — and something more after that. Nothing but words ever occurred to him as relevant; if one arrangement of words seemed in retrospect imperfect or incomplete, nothing but more words seemed adequate to correct it. Pavel would have proved by a week's argument that he never in any circumstances argued.

Isaev opened and shut his wide mouth not ill-naturedly; he looked inquisitively past Pavel at Seryozha.

Wilfred Chew was welcoming himself back at his post by Seryozha's side, unaided by Seryozha. "Well, my dear old chap, we seasoned travelers . . . glad to be together again, are we not? You must be longing to know all my news. Take a peep at this." He archly drew a corner of the sealed envelope out of his pocket. "Knowing me and my gifts of determination, you will have guessed that everything went like a clock working, otherwise, of course, you would not have seen me back so——"

"What is it—the trouble of this woman?" asked Seryozha, who could not take his eyes off the distressed Korean woman. For she was attacking the train in a frenzy— challenging it to single combat; she leapt with desperate agility at one door, was pushed out by the train conductor, and flew to another door. Her baby was shaken like the rider of a bucking bronco. Trainmen stood ready to push her off at every door. But her distraught screams prevented even the iron-hearted train from starting.

Pavel, checked in a spasm of terse eloquence by the obvious inattention of Isaev, looked round. At once seeing whither the center of the stage had shifted, he strode to the woman's side, spoke nobly to her, held her arm as she gathered herself for a new futile leap at a closed train door, spoke nobly to the trainmen, nodded his head and said "Ah Ah" superbly, pressed money into the guard's hand. At once the train swallowed and digested the woman, and instant silence swallowed her clamor and that of her baby. Much gratified by the poor creature's opportune predicament and its picturesque result, Pavel returned to his friends, saying gruffly (as unlike a windbag as possible): "Poor wretch! No money to pay her fare to Gensan—dying husband there—very easily fixed, fortunately. . . ."

"You gave her the money with which to travel!" exclaimed Wilfred, delighted, as he always was, by any improvement in anything. "Your reward will be in heaven."

And in his literal mind he imagined Saint Peter making a little note—*Cr. P. N. Ostapenko*—*Dr.* Heaven. To Third class fare to Gensan. Y1.69.

Isaev, stretching his long thin lips to something that really looked almost like a smile, banged Pavel's shoulder three or four times with a wooden congratulatory hand. He was of a race and class that is easily touched by cheap charity. Isaev, somewhere inside his impassive body, was rather enjoying this jaunt. His wife's home in Seoul was something of a prison.

Pavel, delighted (for now everybody loved him safely), sang tunefully as he tightened up the girth of one of the spare horses. It was rather difficult hoisting the massive Isaev on to the back of a horse, and once there, his large hard seat seemed unable to take the curve of the saddle. But the horse was quiet, and Isaev, though not steady, looked calm. Pavel fidgeted with the stirrups, and then, ceasing his humming, looked up sunnily and affectionately into Isaev's face, saying, "Such old friends as we are, Gavril Ilitch, aren't going to let a hysterical son and daughter come between us, are we?" Isaev, a simple soul, smiled. He was conquered. Pavel added in a more matter-of-fact voice, "Anyway, the chit's married now and going to leave us soon. Here's her husband."

They rode off. Pavel rode beside Isaev, cautiously piling charm on charm. They were halfway home before he thought it safe to detach himself from Isaev and come back to where Seryozha trailed behind the party.

"You couldn't have been serious, my boy," said Pavel to Seryozha, "in what you said just now about the journey back to Chi-tao-kou."

So the argument began. It ended as they rode up to the gate of the house in Mi-san, with Seryozha saying, "My dog can't travel in a box."

Somehow the question had become almost a religious one

286

with Seryozha now. The *askingness* of women—the *commandingness* of men, had obscurely fermented in his simple mind, and resulted in this explosion of philocanism. His dog was the only unbroken reed in sight—the only treasure saved from the wreck of yesterday. It was absolutely out of the question to shut the dog up in a box and leave it to the mercy of Japanese freight porters.

During the next few days the dispute became chronic, and sadly marred the wedding festivities which the Ostapenkos tried to revive in honor of Isaev's visit. At every meal the question came up.

"Seryozha wants to walk back to China because he won't shut his moth-eaten old wonk in a box."

"Well, I *won't* shut it up in a box," Seryozha said. He seldom ventured further into the intricacies of debate than this.

"Why should the poor dog be shut up in a box?" Tatiana always asked. Though the matter had been explained to her at length, she could not manage to bear in mind the implications of her husband's determination.

"Seryozha would rather that his wife should walk her feet off, than that his dog should be shut up in a box."

"Well, I *won't* shut my dog up in a box."

"Surely there must be some way both to keep my feet on and to keep the poor dog out of the box," said Tatiana. She was fond of the dog by now, and usually at this point called it to her knee and began interrogating it, while trying to tie its ears in a knot on the top of its head or to fit her wedding-ring on to the tip of its tail. The dog, heartily enjoying these mild diversions, slobbered appreciatively down her shin.

Whenever Tatiana spoke, Isaev looked at her, blankly and intensely, thinking of his son. Wilfred, watching him at these moments, nervously felt that just inside the big clenched trap of Isaev's mouth the word *bitch* was only precariously detained. Apart from this unspoken contribution, Isaev said almost nothing. He ate a great deal and drank cautiously. He hardly replied, even when Varvara, determined to keep conversation as equable and normal as possible, said in her harsh, uninviting voice, "I suppose Seoul is a good deal hotter than Mi-san at this time of year," or, "Does Olga Ivanovna bake her own bread?"

To Tatiana, the whole problem of the choice between her own comfort and the dog's seemed perfectly reasonable and entirely insoluble. She lived always in the minute— looked forward to nothing more solid than dreams. Tomorrow's practical difficulties seemed as unreal as a story about some one else. Tomorrow would dawn—the next chapter of the story must presently be read—but here was today, and everything else was negligible. She habitually presented a passive front to her father's contentions. This cool docility was one of her father's chief difficulties in dealing with her; she never defied him and never agreed with him. She seemed to watch his lips moving, rather than to listen to what they said. She knew herself to be a robust and tireless walker, to whom the journey to Chi-tao-kou on foot would be no hardship. But it was a matter of tomorrow, not today, so it did not occur to her to defy her father, any more than it occurred to her to feel offended with her husband for his unflattering and unromantic solicitude for his dog. In answer to her father's indignant vows that no daughter of his should tramp like a gypsy, she nodded her head. In answer to Seryozha's simple reiterations that no dog of his should be expected to travel in a box, she nodded her head. She did not care much for an alternative so remotely imbedded in the future; if anything, she cared about the dog's dignity a little more than her own. Every creature, she took for granted, had a right to its dignity.

Two entirely different airs seemed to inclose Seryozha

when he was talking with Tatiana alone and when he was talking with Pavel alone. The young human being is instinctively humble with the arrogant and arrogant with the humble — yet it was not, in Seryozha's case, so much that he spoke different things with Pavel and with Tatiana — as that he spoke them from a different heart and into a different air. From a high heart and into a consenting air he spoke to Tatiana; from a lowly heart and into a dangerous air he spoke to his father-in-law. He was, in his own reluctant eyes, an essentially different Seryozha with the one and with the other, and his eyes, thus washed with the change in himself, saw not only himself, but the world outside, entirely differently. In Tatiana's gentle and admiring presence, he saw trees, buildings, clouds, with their faces toward him; the sun shone on him — he accepted it as *his* sun — the shade was spread for *his* comfort. But in the presence of Pavel, who imposed uncertainty and immaturity upon him, he was forced to feel as if he were trespassing on another's air, another's sunlight and shade — treading on earth indifferent to him; the very wind seemed to turn its back on him and fawn on another. "Face *me* — fortify *me*," the puzzled young heart cries to the wind. "I need support — the old pampered ones don't. Help me to speak in my own sure voice, out of my equal heart. . . . Turn to *me*. . . ." It was like making a third at a lovers' meeting — demanding attention which can only be impatient and cold when given.

The remark, "My dog can't travel in a box," spoken to Tatiana in the field one day, on the way to the stables, was quite a new remark, expressing a new point of view, new words spoken by a new Seryozha who brushed the sky with his upraised head and kicked the grass with large sure feet. "Your father says it is ridiculous" (a cold air blew on him, shrank his heart's new stature a little for a second). "Yet sometimes, Tanya, you know, there are ridiculous things that can't be made different . . . like" (he sought in his quite obstinate mind) — "like a man not being able to go to his wedding because he's spilt something on his only clean shirt. He can't go in a dirty shirt. He hasn't got a clean shirt. People may laugh, but there's nothing to be done. Being ridiculous doesn't make the shirt clean again. I cannot let my dog travel alone, shut up in a box."

"Why, of course not!" agreed Tatiana, watching the dog take great arch leaps through the long grass. "A dog shouldn't — couldn't — be shut up in a box smaller than the size of a meadow. How would it run — or be itself — in a little box?"

"That's what I mean," said Seryozha, eagerly. "It isn't as if my dog had been used to being a kennel dog or tied up. It's never even worn a collar or seen a chain. You know, Tanya — that dog runs. It's so sure it may run — it wouldn't even know enough to distrust the box. It would run into the box wagging its tail — and stop running — stop being the dog it is. . . . It isn't that I'm specially fond of the dog — it's nothing but a dog," he disclaimed, eagerly, "but I'm bound, somehow, to let it be the dog it is. There's something about it being such a running kind of dog — I have to respect that. . . ." Seryozha sweated a little with the effort — not only of making Tatiana understand, but of making himself understand what he meant.

"I know," said Tatiana. "I know exactly what you mean. It would be even worse than — catching that free lark, for instance, and shutting it in a box. The lark has to be free to be itself, too — but the dog has to be free within reach of our hands to be itself. . . ."

"Hm!" said Seryozha, rather haughtily. He would have shot that lark without more than a second's regret — that short reluctant regret he always suffered when he saw the

fading smile of an animal dead at his hands. It was certainly
true that it would be much worse to stop the dog's running
than to stop the lark's flying.

They both stood still in the grass and watched the lark.
Tatiana's perfect and instantaneous sight showed her the
curious intermittence in the lark's flight; it shot its wings
abroad flashingly, like a bomb of feathers, then completely
shut them against its sides, before spreading them again
and throwing itself like a little stone into the air. In these
wingless intervals, Tatiana could see the lark perched in the
air, unsupported, as though sitting on an invisible nest of
air — then, as its momentum failed, it shot its wings asprawl
again, to catch and toss up once more its little, smooth,
confident body.

Seryozha, very much slower to receive messages from his
senses, saw only a lark fluttering — missed the daring grace
with which it committed itself, unresisting, to the pull of
earth and air. He wished — but not very keenly — that he
had his gun.

"Come," said Tatiana, suddenly. "We shall be late."
She had seen her father hurrying across the stable-yard.

"What for?" asked Seryozha, running beside her. "It's
not nearly dinner-time."

"My mare — Tovarka ——" gasped Tatiana.

In the yard, Tovarka the mare lay on her side in the
throes of foalbirth. She had chosen to lie in the yard, though
Pavel and the groom had spent an hour making the loose-
box ready for the event. It is rather chilling how animals
refuse to conform to man's arrangements, or to take the
hints given them by the works of our hands. Doors to come
in at, railings to keep things out, steps to climb up by,
tables to eat at — a fig for them, say the birds and beasts.
Sparrows ignore the doors and come in at the windows,
splashing impertinent droppings on our tables; flies fly into
our sacred eyes; kites, leaning from the sky, see our carefully

leveled houses upside down and in all the wrong perspectives; magpies mistake the significance of our chimneys; mice hop in through our fences, not even paying them the compliment of defiance; cats jump our paths at right-angles, and spring up walls without the help of stairs, as though the gravel were wild water and the stairways cascades. Air and earth are the only roads for these creatures; they will not learn to read our carefully constructed signposts through the air. Any opening from air to air is a door to them. And so the earth was bed for Tovarka the mare; she was just a creature in pain, lying down on the earth. . . . To hell with man's hygienically ventilated loose-boxes, and clean straw, and helpful implements.

"Please, Saggay Saggayitch, translate this to your father-in-law," said Wilfred, who was beaming on the birth without admitting that it was an event at all, all animals being irrelevances to him. "I have thought of a compromise in the matter of the journey to Chi-tao-kou that should, I think, satisfy all parties."

Nobody expressed any curiosity. The eyes of all the Russians were fixed upon the mare. She groaned and heaved her body. Head-first, the foal began cautiously to emerge into the world, wrapped in a strange bluish veil. The veil parted coyly and showed the unexpectedly animated face of the foal — the expression of a creature having an interesting adventure and determined to get through it with credit and dispatch. Seryozha's dog, after an incredulous look during which all panting was suspended, gave an embarrassed bark and hurried uneasily away. Mare and foal pushed — heaved — writhed. The mare never once looked round; she seemed only interested in her pain. After a few minutes, the foal lay free, leaning against Pavel's leg, amidst the iridescent and filmy ruins of its past. It lay balanced on its breast-bone, its limp double-jointed legs falling upward.

"My idea is," continued Wilfred, surprised and pleased

to find that nobody was interrupting him (the interruption of a new life within twenty feet of him was no interruption at all), "that we should hire a Ford's motor-car as far as Gensan, then take the steamboat to Seishin, then hire another Ford's motor-car to the Manchurian border. . . ."

"Ah, papasha, show the baby to Tovarka," cried Tatiana. "She doesn't know what's the matter with her. She thinks she's simply dying of a stomach-ache. . . ."

Pavel, who was a much humbler, gentler, more silent man, when engaged in caring for horses, signed to the groom to help him to carry the little wet boneless rubber beast round its mother's sprawling form to her face. It seemed as if Tatiana was right; the mare lifted her drooping head with a look, first of surprise, then of new life. "So *this* was what was the matter—I'm beginning, not ending. . . ." With a little soft, falsetto laugh, the mare began to lick the foal all over, snuffling with delighted tenderness into every cranny of its body. "Oh, joy! oh, joy!" whispered Tatiana for her. As its mother caressed it, the foal began to be afflicted with strange senseless jerkings; the first hours of its life were evidently to be spent in passing from one indignity to another. No buffoon could have made more slavish efforts to gain a witless laugh than the foal seemed to make—jerking—humping—hiccoughing—all its legs doubling and redoubling—looping like a caterpillar. These jerks presently resolved themselves into more and more determined efforts to *stand* up, and, after a while, with Pavel's clasped hands under its stomach, it *did* stand up, looking like some one completely drunk, yet solemnly hopeful of seeming sober enough to pass in a crowd. Its legs slid and warped in unnatural directions. Its tail was like a little wet wool mat with a lively mouse underneath it. Its hoofs seemed very badly-finished and shoddy, like wads of wet brown paper.

"From that point, Saggay Saggayitch," Wilfred continued, "the distance to Chi-tao-kou would be negligible. We could hire a wagon for Mrs. Malinin's use."

Still Seryozha inexplicably delayed translation. He and Tatiana stood hand in hand, looking with entranced eyes at the foal. Their joy at seeing a new live thing, new eyes open on the air, new feet prepared to run about the earth — was like a rendezvous for Seryozha and Tatiana. This joy was their meeting-place at last; to this trysting-point the compassionate, cold, complicated heart of Tatiana ran to meet the direct, greedy, and simple heart of Seryozha. *Living* was what things *were*, after all — living — and nothing else, really. In this these two contrary lovers agreed, sinking their contrariness; they agreed to let things live — let things be. This *being* was the Unknown God, to whom both, obscurely, owed homage — this exquisite inhumanity — immorality — impudence — oblivion — urgency — this tremendous relevance called life. To the admission *It Is*, nothing is irrelevant except *It Ought To Be*. To Tatiana and Seryozha, thinking no thoughts but standing outside themselves watching a creature that had been still now learning to move, it seemed that they were entirely free and entirely together for the first time. No thought was relevant to their lives; they were nothing except alive — borne far and strongly on that sea from the shore of which the silly callow foal had just embarked.

Wilfred decided to explain the matter himself to Pavel. He had picked up a dozen or so words of Russian, his imaginative ear naturally selecting the words whose Russian sound seemed to him appropriate to their English meaning. *Cobaka*, the word for dog, for instance, printed on his retina as *S'barker*, made him feel that a high reputation as a linguist was not immeasurably beyond his reach. *Poyezd*, a train, too, was encouraging — it could be nothing else but a puffing thing.

"Listen — *vot* compromise-ski," he cried, addressing Pavel

urgently across the prostrate form of the mare. "Nyet poyezd—ufftermobile horosho. Ufftermobile, s'barker nichevo. Ufftermobile from Mi-san to Gensan. Then parry-hot." (Parakhot was also obviously a steamer in his mind, which connected the name Parry with a coal merchant in London.) "Parry-hot s'barker nichevo. Parry-hot to Seishin. Then droschki. S'barker by this route completely nichevo. That's my idea—take it or leave it, as Londoners say. Ufftermobile horosho, ah?"

Pavel straightened his back. His face was very happy and kind and running with sweat. Horses were the only selfless delight he knew. His chestnut eyes were soft—almost rapturous.

"Avtomobil horosho, ah?" his lips uttered vaguely in a benevolent, expressionless voice. After a moment, first the meaning and then the possibilities of Wilfred's compromise-ski began to take shape in his mind. Intelligence seeped into his spell-bound face. "Avtomobil . . . nu . . . da-da-da . . . horosho. . . ." On the word of approval he began to nod his head. The continued nodding of his head seemed to shake his natural complacent nature back into position, as a watch is shaken to start its ticking again. "Avtomobil . . . da-da-da . . . horosho . . ." He thought with pleasure that his daughter would appear to the neighbors to be scorning a mere train—leaving home proudly in a car.

"Good idea, isn't it? Ufftermobile horosho, ah?" Wilfred insisted, much pleased.

"Horosho—horosho."

"Horosho? Really horosho?"

"Horosho."

Wilfred clasped his hands together, congratulating himself. So like Russians, he thought, consenting to the most expensive, least practical, plan—without even inquiring what the expense would be. And all for the sake of a smelly dog. Still, who was he, Wilfred, to complain? He would travel grandly. The Korean motor proprietor spoke some Chinese, and perhaps would consider a small commission — but *No* — a guardian angel he would remain to the end. He looked round for more applause from the bride and bridegroom. But they were no longer there.

CHAPTER FOURTEEN

THE BUTTERS baby had proved to be twins, and there was so much extra sewing for Anna to do that she was obliged to take some home. Her stitching was poor; she did not mind; she was tired of other people's children. She did not mind if every garment she made should fall to pieces on their superfluous bodies. She resented, too, being obliged to remain so much in the presence of her husband, whose melancholy and arid figure seemed to her now little more than a tiresomely deathless reminder of her disappointed motherhood. She said that her son was dead, she imagined him dead, but she knew that he was not dead. At the very root of her mind was the sane admission that there was no practical reason why he should not return in safety to Chi-tao-kou, with or without a wife. This root of common sense was planted deeply out of sight in her heart, however; above-ground flourished the branching growth of silly premonition and apprehension — a growth which she saw no reason to prune; and from this tangle had lately blossomed her entirely senseless determination to see her son's bride through the distorting eyes of the dead Alexander — to call her Death, and to have no hope. This superficial, yet ardently nourished, hopelessness did not prevent her from taking her sewing every afternoon out on to the ramshackle porch of their house, which commanded a view of the street along which her son, if he returned, must come. The despair which ached continually, like a cramp, in her brain did not prevent her from thinking "I'll make curd cakes the first evening, I think, and I'll kill one of the last two chicks out of Old Speckly's last brood but one. . . ."

Old Sergei was obscurely glad that his wife's work now obliged her to spend more time in the house. Her presence was tempestuous, her words hardly ever kind. Nineteen years of marriage had made her so wary and contrary a bird that the little snares he spread to trip her into a complaisant word of approval or an appropriate and flattering grunt of agreement were always futile. He was never allowed to complete his sporadic gestures of preening himself. Still, even humiliation was better than silence—especially as there was no mocker at hand to witness his frequent humiliations. Somehow, in spite of Anna's impatience, he felt safe with her, as one feels safe even in a rough straw bed after groping in a dark room. Wherever she sat, sewing, he sat near her, trying not to notice that she often moved petulantly away. From the porch, however, as he soon discovered, she would not move away; there, he—sitting just inside the window—had his companion pinned down.

"I suppose you sit out here so as to see Seryozha coming round the corner, when at last he comes," said Old Sergei one day.

"Nothing of the kind," said Anna. "I know now that Seryozha will never come back."

To his teasing, "Well then, why sit out there in the dust?" she made no reply.

But presently she said something that so much surprised him that the sense of it fell back from his mind, as a wave falls back from a rock, leaving its surface dark, glossy, and

wet, but its shape unchanged. He listened to the low un-
loving tone of her voice, rather than to the words she
uttered, and the tone conveyed to his slow mind nothing
but the usual reproach. Immediately, the house shook and
he realized that she had jumped off the porch. Then he
found, printed on his hearing, as clearly as the shape of a
windowpane is printed on suddenly closed eyes, her words:
"As a matter of fact, here he comes — your son — and the
man that went with him."

"Annitchka! Annitchka!" he cried, absurdly confused by
the discrepancy between her tone and her words. But, as
he feared, she was gone from the porch. What could she
have meant — here he comes — your son? As he rose, trembling, from his chair, he sought foolishly in his mind for
some other possible meaning of those disquietingly simple
words — here he comes — your son. . . . So deeply astonished was he that his sense of direction — his homely familiarity with every object — every wrinkle — every dint in
the room, was on the instant lost. He shuffled wildly up
and down, hitting his knee painfully against a ledge that
seemed to have sprung like a fungus from a smooth wall,
rapping his flying knuckles against an anonymous piece of
furniture that could not be the ordinary reliable dresser
that had for so long acted as signpost to his gropings.

"Annitchka! Annitchka!" he quavered. And as he stumbled to and fro, round and round, lost in a quivering jungle
of bewilderment, he heard, fined and diminished by the
accurate perspective-sense of the hearing, Seryozha's far-off
shout.

"Mamma! mamma! mamma!"

At the sound of his son's voice, Old Sergei, in a frenzy
of exaltation and desire, saw the dim oblong of the door,
and his own upheld hand silhouetted like a blurred crab
against that incredible squat pillar of light. He was at once
extravagantly dizzy — reeled, swung, moaned, clung to the

dresser, shut his new eyes for a few seconds and opened them again. There was a roaring of readjustment in his brain; his whole habit of concentration rushed from all his senses to that one lost and found sense of sight. He leaned his numb hands against the wall and planted his incredulous feet, as though they were wooden blocks, one before the other — the other before the one — forcing his half-paralyzed body to walk along a new path — a path that his feet had forgotten — a path that his eyes could see.

He had lost his power of estimating space by sight; his feet reached the threshold of the door before his eyes expected. Daylight towered round him, as though he tottered in a fountain of terrifying flame. He felt wholly defeated. The light pressed in on him; he was buried alive in an avalanche of light. Weighed down by light, he fell to his knees. As he did so, Seryozha's voice, from somewhere very near, broke through the roar of his forgotten sense of hearing. It was as if the blood rushed into a limb that had been for a moment numb.

He lifted his face, raised his lids. This smear of smoke in the core of a flame, then — was this all that Old Sergei was to see of his son? Better to be blind, thought Old Sergei, wildly, than to seek in vain through this terrifying new world of fire for the lost face of his son. More lost than ever before, it seemed, for now the promise of returning sight was a broken promise. "Ah! ah! I can't see you! I can't see you!" wailed the old man.

"You shall! You shall!" cried Seryozha, giggling with excitement. "Just be hopeful, papa darling — just be hopeful for a minute."

An appalling smell now awoke to consciousness another of Old Sergei's momentarily neglected senses. Something of revolting texture was rubbed against his eyes. "What's this? What's this?" he screamed in a fury.

"Just be hopeful — be hopeful," Seryozha's voice went

on. His father could feel the boy's breath on his brow. What was this filthy, stinking pad over his eyes that shuttered away his son?

"Take it away, boy, take it away. Let me see your face."

"Can you see my face?" asked Seryozha, withdrawing his magic poultice.

And it seemed to Old Sergei as if that urgent creating young voice cut like a knife through the thin crumbling texture of his limitations. Something that felt like a dark doubt in himself was pushed away from his heart and from his eyes, as the blinds of the house of a dead man run up to admit the sun when the coffin is at last carried away. He felt like a man who, in a dream, finds that he can fly. The voice of his son created before his eyes—a face—a huge, shimmering gray turnip close to his eyes, much bigger than the sky, with features like clouds. It was like an Olympian practical joke, that face—a mask, with blurred craters for eyes, crooked streak for nose, broad black scratch for mouth. Yet, imperfect and grotesque as was the geography of this globe within six inches of his eyes, it was obscurely but surely the face of Seryozha. Every second brought in partial focus some new identifying blur on one plane or another of this refound world that was his son's face.

"I can see," whispered Old Sergei, and he could not speak again. Tears ran out of his eyes and trickled past the corners of his trembling mouth. His cheeks were sucked in with the breath drawn to utter words he could find no voice to say. He leaned toward his son and put his arms round his neck, hanging against him, dizzily swaying.

Seryozha, snorting and snuffling with emotion, almost carried him back into the living-room, seated him in the armchair, and knelt at his feet, stroking the old twitching, tear-smeared cheeks. "Papa, papa—my papa," said Seryozha in a soft voice, feeling that there was nobody he loved so much in the world.

Anna, panting behind her son (who had run to his father), arrived in the doorway. She came and leaned over the back of her husband's chair, feeling so full of delight that even the narrow wispy skull of the old man — across which she saw Seryozha's face — looked lovely to her.

"And he looks so well," she said, ardently describing the boy to her husband. "Thinner, perhaps — but so well. . . . Tschah! there's no doubt about it, he's a fine boy, our boy," she added with a deafening hiccough, as she shook her husband's shoulder. Neither the old man nor the young one acknowledged her remarks. Seryozha went on saying, "Papa — papa — papa," stroking inquiringly with gentle blunt fingers the skin round his father's eye-sockets. Seryozha felt a creator's pride — almost a paternal pride, as if he had begotten a new papa. "Let there be light," he had said, he was the god of a new genesis.

The dog was not being welcomed home at all, but it did not mind. It wandered about the room, sniffing deeply, welcoming itself home. A dog's nose may be said to do something more for it than simply reconstruct the past, since the word *reconstruct* implies a certain effort of the imagination — an element of guesswork. A dog, I think, smelling a smell, does not *guess* what has happened, it takes for granted — just as we, hearing a friend calling us, a horse neighing, or a clock striking, have no need for guesswork; our sense has *told* us something, not *hinted at* something. The dog, smelling traces of a past event, is a witness of that event; time is no obstacle; as long as a smell clings, so long is yesterday — to a dog — current news. A dog could surely make some contribution to the theory of relativity. "Here," mused Seryozha's dog, "that horrid little goat lay down . . . here, the old woman dropped an egg . . . here stood that Korean watercarrier whom I always bite . . . in this chair a missionary sat, carrying a parcel of clothes the paper of which once had something to do with dried raisins. . . ." The room confessed its past to the dog, reserving nothing that a smell could tell. Presently the dog had a piece of luck—a pleasure of the present interrupted inquiry into the past. Near the threshold it found a piece of fish offal in such a condition of delicious decay as even the dog—a connoisseur in putrescence—seldom had the good fortune to unearth. It stood warily half in and half out of the door, fearing to have its treasure snatched from it, masticating hastily with a breathy sound like *ga-haow*—*ga-haow*—*ga-haow*.

Anna began to feel a little offended with her family for being so preoccupied. "And where is the bride?" she said, a little less sweetly, straightening herself. "Have you dropped her somewhere on the road?"

"Yes," said Seryozha, dreamily, and then, as if ceasing to murmur the word *papa* had broken a spell, he pulled himself together and rose from his knees. With a light-hearted leap backward, using his arms as crutches, he sat on the table.

"Oh, papa," he began in his natural, noisy, indifferent young voice, "everything went so beautifully. I got your money—or rather, Mr. Chew got it——"

"Where have you left Mr. Chew?"

"He was here. I expect he went back to show Tanya the way. But, papa, Olga Ivanovna was——"

"Yes, but where is——"

"Well, but, papa, how much d'you think we got? Guess. Well, your two hundred yen had swelled to three hundred and fifty! Worth going for, wasn't it? And, papa, I saw a mare give birth to a foal. You've no idea—— Oh, but listen, papa, at Mi-san they have eighteen horses, counting the three yearlings——"

Anna stood looking along the table at his broad back and shoulders, feeling injury swelling in her heart, like the hot assembling blood in a pinched finger. "What's this — papa — papa — papa — no mamma at all?" Was it for this she had counted the days, rolled her curl-papers on a tear-wet pillow through long nights? She made a difficult effort to keep her voice sweet. "Begin at the beginning, darling boy, and tell us everything. It isn't really true that you're married, is it?" Perhaps the bride called Death was a dream, she thought, or Seryozha's letter a joke. She had the unphilosophical habit of challenging proven facts to prove themselves again — and yet again — and even then of blotting out those twice-proven facts like hated dreams, daring them to materialize again.

"Yes, I am married," said Seryozha, checked in his boisterousness, but still looking at his father as if he shared a secret with him.

"Such nonsense!" said Anna, vehemently, almost glad to have an excuse to sharpen her voice. "If you could see the child," she added to her husband, nudging him to remind him that he should join in the reproach, "you would say like me that for such a baby to marry without his parents' consent is worse than nonsense — it's wicked, undutiful nonsense."

"Papa can see me," said Seryozha, and Anna had once more the impotent sense of speaking to unhearing space — as a diver's voice, under the sea, is swallowed up, reabsorbed, by his own imprisoned hearing.

"Such nonsense!" she said again, more bitterly, and then, realizing what Seryozha had said, she looked rather sharply at her husband to see what the boy could mean. Although it seemed to her that there was a look of vision in the old man's eyes, she discounted the remark as nonsense, for the present, for she had no attention to spare for her husband. "Get off the table, Seryozha, and let me get tea ready."

She would not try to make curd cakes today, she thought, wearily.

"And, papa," resumed Seryozha without moving. "What do you think? Gavril Ilitch's wife beat him in the street, because he paid up your money. Mr. Chew told me. Beat him — think of that! You remember Gavril Ilitch — like a great dumpling — you can imagine how funny it must have looked. . . . Oi! — I *did* regret not being there. . . ."

Anna, thwarted in her hopes of spreading the tablecloth, stood grimly watching him. In spite of her feeling of injury, she gloried in the sight of him — his size, his straightness, his independence.

"Ai, that old clock," said Seryozha, interrupting himself. "I often thought of its ugly old face while I was away."

"And your mother's ugly old face?" asked Anna.

"I often thought of that, too," cried Seryozha, jumping off the table and throwing his arms about her. But she hardly had time to feel delight, for he spoke to his father over her shoulder. "Papa, in a field in Korea we saw a plough worked like a motor-car — no bullocks at all. The furrow it made was so straight and deep."

He was sitting on the table again, his hand descriptively ploughing the air in front of him.

"For God's sake, where *is* this wife of yours?" grumbled Anna, in a softened voice. "Where have you left her?"

"In the new temple," said Seryozha, the smile that belonged to the marvelous plough still parting his lips. "Mr. Chew suggested our coming on ahead, and she seemed quite pleased. She is not like other girls — always asking for attention."

"But is she there alone?"

"No. With Katya's niece."

"Who is Katya and who is her niece? For God's sake, don't talk so foolishly, boy."

"Katya is Varvara Alexeievna's servant. . . ." And as

Seryozha said this his eye fell on the tablecloth on her arm
—still torn and stained, still not mended or washed, just as
he had seen it the day he went away. And the words in his
mouth—*Varvara Alexeievna's servant*—sent his mind back
to his mother-in-law's neat house and orderly possessions
—the sunlight, through clean panes, lying patterned on a
clean floor; the pressed linen that clothed Varvara's awkward
yet leisured body; the busy effectiveness of Katya. He remembered the departure from Mi-san, which, owing to
Pavel's dramatic sense, had appeased that craving that was
in Seryozha, as in all young creatures, for the dignified conduct of great affairs of sentiment. There had been the panting Ford at the door, and in it a large crate of unfamiliar
shape. "Whose package is that?" "Yours," said Pavel, superbly. "Half the Ostapenko family silver for Pavel Ostapenko's only child. And I'll send her mare up by road as
soon as I can arrange it, and the black gelding for you, my
dear boy. And here is my daughter's maid, Marfa, Katya's
niece, for I want the child to be well looked after. And here,
Seryozha, is the child's dowry. . . ." He handed him a draft
for two thousand yen. Seryozha had felt ideally well treated
for the first time in his life. All that was needed was a grave
and literary blessing, and this Pavel at once supplied. "The
God of Heaven give you a prosperous journey, my children.
Tanya, you're a married woman now. You must honor a
new father and mother; they are your parents now, and from
them let me hear a good account of you." He kissed his
daughter on the forehead. And then Varvara rather spoiled
the noble austerity of it all by crying wildly: "Take care of
her, Seryozha—there's no one like her. . . . She's different
—she's special. I commit her to you as a special trust. . . .
Be very good to her. . . ." Then she gasped, with a rush of
tears, "If there are babies, Seryozha, let me be there—I
must be there. . . ." A scene to make a man of a boy indeed, thought Seryozha. Even Varvara's tears, though awk-

wardly shed, had been a tribute to his grown-up dignity. And now — home to this threadbare muddle — to be reinfected with the virus of childishness by his incurable mother. For a few seconds Seryozha *saw* his home, and all his longing for home turned sour.

His mother watched his expression change and a sullenness come into his eyes. "Ah, tschah!" she said, hurt by this result of his glance in her direction. "I won't bother you with questions, then. I'll leave you to talk to your father. I'll go to the new temple to meet your Tanya."

She felt like a horseman whose unmanageable mount suddenly kicks out at a friend standing by, to whom he has been trying to talk charmingly. Here was her warm heart — its warmth all in vain — mounted on this clumsy steed of manners and body.

But Seryozha was still imbedded in his past. He could not yet bear to let the *then* dissolve into the *now*. "We had *such* a journey," he said, dreamily. "By motor-car from Mi-san to Choanji, and we let Mr. Chew take the car and luggage from there to Gensan while Tanya and I walked through the Kongo-san——"

"But the expense . . ." quavered Old Sergei.

"Tschah! We are rich now. Expense is nothing. Why, papa, we have brought a huge box full of family silver. . . ."

Anna went out, patting Seryozha's wrist wistfully as she passed him. He smiled at her as she did so. "Mamma darling, we must live quite differently now. . . ."

The new temple was so new that it was not yet finished. The molded mud gods were already enthroned, but they were not colored yet. To make up for this rather ungodlike nakedness, somebody had put a fresh hollyhock in each god's hand. They looked like ladies trying on their engagement rings in their baths.

On a ledge between one god and another sat Tatiana.

Anna was quite shocked to see how light and small and beautiful her son's bride was.

Wilfred Chew was standing in the middle of the court-yard, looking contemptuously up at the dolphin-bristling roof-ridge and the curly, dragony eaves.

"Ah Mrs. Malinin," said Wilfred, brightly. "I see I am to have the pleasure of introducing your daughter-in-law to you. Mrs. Malinin senior, I beg to present to you Mrs. Malinin junior." He rubbed his hands together cheerfully, expecting some kind of outburst of womanly cackle. But neither Mrs. Malinin cackled at all. Anna, feeling stout, hot, and suspicious, sat down on the same ledge as Tatiana, two gods away from her.

"Why do you stay here all alone, daughter?" asked Anna, after huskily beginning to say several other things. "Why don't you come to our home?"

Tatiana looked at her kindly and warily, as a deer, know-ing its retreat safe, looks between the trees of a forest at some strange visitor. "Ai!" she said. "Seryozha isn't such a very married man, dear Anna Semionovna, that he can't have his first few minutes at home without his wife. Be-sides," she added, "poor Marfa has a sore heel."

From another chapel of the temple, across the courtyard, Anna could hear a heavy and vulgar groaning—"O God! O God! . . ." Going forward a few steps, she saw Katya's niece—a fat, flushed, straw-haired girl, sitting in a lump on a low step at the foot of an unfurnished altar, soaking one gross foot in a basin full of warm water. Beside her stood two kind Chinese priests, dressed like coolies (for they had been interrupted in mason's work), except for their priestly pill-box hats. The priests, in producing the warm water, had obviously exhausted their resources for dealing with blis-tered female Big-noses. They looked kind, helpless, and de-pressed, and Marfa, who was not of martyr stuff, did nothing to spare their sympathetic feelings. "O God!" she groaned, vigorously. "O God! O God!"

"What is it—a blister?" asked Anna.

"O God!" replied Marfa.

Anna, leaning over it, saw that there was indeed a big broken blister on the heel. But she did not care. Her heart was quite hard just now. Not knowing what to do about any of these problems, she resented all of them; she did not know what to do for Marfa's heel, what to do about welcoming Tatiana, whether to make curd cakes or not, how to find a double bed for Seryozha, whether to tip these kind priests. . . . Her imagination, usually so ingenious, had come to the end of its supply of ingenuities. Nothing occurred to her for Marfa's relief except uncompromising amputation of that ugly foot, or immediate strangling of the sufferer. She therefore turned in silence toward Tatiana again.

"I ought to kiss her, I suppose," thought Anna, desperately. "And she is certainly a most beautiful little creature." Her thoughts added, "But she is called Death."

Tatiana's lack of precedents showing her what to do in these circumstances was even more complete than her mother-in-law's. Anna had temporarily lost her social resources, but Tatiana had never found hers. Tatiana's quick heart never prompted her in the solution of personal problems. She kept her heart for other purposes; her heart's eyes were incurably longsighted. She would never have been at a loss with a trapped mouse, but a trapped mother-in-law seemed to need some subtlety of treatment, the nature of which did not occur to Tatiana at all. She realized that a mouse and a mother-in-law have, in these circumstances, something in common—she saw this in Anna's eyes, and felt most tenderly sorry. Animals, she knew, were not comforted by touch, but people, she believed, sometimes were. So she leaned forward, round the intervening gods, and lightly stroked Anna's arm. Then she sat back to watch the result. Anna watched her, without moving.

"She'll be shaking hands with me next," thought Anna, remembering things that Alexander Weber had said.

Tatiana, trembling a little, decided to talk. If she were careful to be polite, talk could do no harm, thought poor Tatiana.

"I do think your Manchuria is beautiful," she said. "Not like land at all — real land is always so surprising round the corner — but like the sea which has no surprises and no corners. But it is a winter country, this, Anna Semionovna, isn't it — although the sun is so hot now. It looks to me as if winter really lives here, and just sleeps half the year, like a snake."

"It *is* a winter country," admitted Anna, moodily, anxious at once to make the worst of it. "Remembering Manchuria from far off, one would never remember sweating in green still weather, or seeing the coolies in their big straw hats, or fetching water from rivers that run toward the sea. . . . Smelly furs and cracking black rivers and wind and endlessly sore fingers and melting the water to boil the tea in the dark morning — that's Manchuria as you'll remember it some day. A winter country indeed."

"Some day you must come home with me, dear Anna Semionovna, and see our Korea. Especially our Kongo-san. Ai! ai! you should see the sunny cliffs come forward through the mist to bow, and then go back." And she began to talk with a tense, trembling enthusiasm about such things as mountains, mists, cascades like stringed harps. It seemed to the surprised Anna that the child's ardor had no flame in it, but only the stinging quality of ice.

These flowers of sight were furled in Tatiana's sight like those Japanese toy water-flowers that lie disguised and secret like flakes of sawdust in the hand, but, tossed into water, expand into lilies and roses and orchids. The secret miles flowered in Tatiana's mind, as she drew them one by one out of silence into this fresh element of words. The path across the Diamond Mountains opened before her, arched with sunlight.

"It was a path through the air," said Tatiana. "We jumped from rock to rock; we scarcely trod on soil." She remembered their course with the glowing, almost theatrical, exaggeration characteristic of her — over-emphasis of memory combined with under-emphasis of tone. She remembered their flying course from brow to brow of tall boulders, like the course of two clouds from peak to peak, over waters choked and knotted by these bowling boulders — waters jerked this way and that, foaming like horses violently checked in their course — waters dammed into peacock-green pools, to spill over paradoxically, in the wrong direction, by secret exits. "Seryozha swam in a pool; I saw him like a white frog from the top of a round rock. . . . Yes, we were like the chipmunks and the kingfishers, Anna Semionovna, our paths were all through the air or through the water. One could bite the red maple leaves as one jumped from rock to rock. . . ."

While she talked in her clear soft voice, Anna watched her doubtfully, her mind half-consciously echoing her own last words — *a winter country indeed*. She felt dimly a little flattered by the child's cool wariness; it seemed a tribute to the definite, un-Anna-like impression she was making, thought Anna. Inside this pink bewildered body was no confidently mature critic — no mother-in-law at all, really, if Tatiana had only known. But Tatiana, luckily, did not know. Tatiana fixed her alert, wild-fawn stare on the outer Anna and tried, with cautious words, to propitiate that outer Anna, that apparently solid symbol of authority. "She thinks my hands know how to do things — my mouth knows how to say things," thought Anna, feeling proud and surprised, smoothing down her miscontrived, mis-cut apron

over her stomach and feeling that it was being gloriously
mistaken for a real, bought, mother-in-law's apron. But still
she was not sure. Still that fading illusory glitter of icy ruth-
lessness hung about Tatiana — a last gleam of the witch-
glare thrown on her name by poor Alexander.

". . . a little meadow where the abbots were buried,"
Tatiana was saying. "The grass was as green as — as a squirrel's fur is red . . . and each grave was of black marble, and
its throne was a tortoise and its crown was a bandage of
twisted dragons. . . . Even the rough common stones
round that place had crowns on, like the roofs of little
pagodas. Tame marble tombstones for the tame saints, I
suppose, and wild stones over the wild mountain saints.
There was a praying mantis on one dragon's claw, and Seryozha's dog came sniffing — so — and the praying mantis
prayed, 'O God, make this dog ashamed,' so God did . . .
the dog sneezed for shame. . . . We saw the sea and a
great thin waterfall from a high path. . . ." She remembered
the silver wire of sea strung across a gorge, hooked tautly
from a maple to a pine, and another wire of water — jointed
and vertical this time — leaning up a broken precipice across
which a frayed intermittent smoke of clouds blew lightly.

"Surely there is nothing to be afraid of here," thought
Anna, hardly listening to the words of this strange, cloudy
talk.

But Tatiana, though she realized faintly now that she was
not quite so safe as she had hoped, in talking of clouds and
cascades to a new mother-in-law, could not forget the
clouds. Clouds raced across her eyes, especially those last
clouds that had dragged the dwindling mountains from her
sight . . . two strata of clouds — hardly to be called by the
same name — cloud — so far apart were they. . . . There
was the still, cushioned world of clouds from which the
mountains grew (for the mountains had no roots in the
earth). . . . And in front of the faces of the mountains,

adding incredibly to their stature, shreds and skeins of stormlit clouds, torn across the pinnacled air, white on steel-blue, silver on white — clouds rent and raveled on sharp peaks like wool on needles. Somewhere Tatiana had heard God's beard likened to white wool. "Ah, those mountains are held down by clouds," said Tatiana, "not held up by earth. You have to *believe in* clouds when you see them like that — as you have to believe in that bee. . . ."

A big bee on a level with their eyes was pushing her bullying way into a chrysanthemum's heart, irritably elbowing petals right and left, her furry muscles trembling with rough strength.

"Do you always talk about clouds?" asked Anna.

"Clouds? No. Why should I talk always about clouds? It is so seldom one sees the live bodies of clouds. Generally talk about clouds would be like talk about dead saints — generally they are so still and so high. Who could talk about them then?"

"Can't you talk about my Seryozha?" asked Anna. "You're his wife and I'm his mother. He's more interesting than a cloud, isn't he?"

Tatiana thought for a minute and then said, "Yes," in a shamed voice. She was never safe from a sense of guilt, because she had no standard of behavior. She had talked unsuitably to this unknown ear, she now realized. She would not have been surprised if Anna had told her to go back at once to her parents — a wife found wanting, a disgraced daughter-in-law. It would not have occurred to her to assert her rights. The command to turn the other cheek, even, would have been wasted on Tatiana — she knew of no right *not* to have her cheek slapped — she knew of no rights at all except the right to see out of her eyes.

"He has a little rash on the back of his neck, I see," said Anna. "How did he get that?"

"Yes, and also on his behind," said Tatiana, gravely. "It

came after he swam in a mountain pool and lay in the sun on a rock." She turned her accurate mind's eye on Seryozha's rash and considered it; she could see the shape of the patch of pinkness on Seryozha's skin as clearly as, a minute ago, she had seen the shapes of the clouds.

"It is only sunburn, then?" suggested Anna.

"I think it is," agreed Tatiana.

"He has a sensitive skin."

"Yes—and bright, like a horse's. . . ." Tatiana thought with delight of living bodies as she said this.

Anna sighed. Yet at the same time she thought: "This wife can't take Seryozha away from his mother. Why, it's as if he had bought a new telescope, not married a wife. This girl may be new eyes for him, his father may be new ears, but I shall still be in his old heart. Death—tschah! she is not death—she is nothing at all. . . ."

A priest, with a kind eager bow, brought them two cups of leafy tea. These visitors, the priest thought, had evidently forgotten that they did not live here. The tea was a polite hint of a limit—a tactful unspoken good-by.

Anna thought, "Of course I mustn't mention Alexander Weber. That would be a thing I should regret very much afterwards." But even while she was congratulating herself on having—just this once—been wise in time, she heard her own voice saying, "You know, I saw a good deal of Alexander Weber before he died. He talked a great deal about you."

"Ah, poor Sasha!" said Tatiana in a low voice—though, as a matter of fact, she cared scarcely at all now about Sasha's death. He was dissolved from her thoughts. She had such a short, thin-spun memory that her mind's eye never saw ghosts. "Perhaps he told you, Anna Semionovna, that I was possessed by a devil."

Tatiana hesitated and shuddered. Seryozha, who felt that his feats of magic were not to be hidden under a bushel, had told her his story of the magic smoke. Like all such vague, unlikely stories, it had taken on an aspect both more startlingly magic and more convincingly prosaic, on Seryozha's lips. The further it retreated into the realm of legend, the more facts were remembered by Seryozha to prove its solid truth. Every conscientious liar who has an occult experience to relate must have noticed this curious posthumous skeleton of facts that materializes to uphold a fading ghost of fiction. ("I know I wasn't dreaming," we say, "because I remember I'd just got up to let the cat out, and I noticed distinctly it was raining, and I was just going to tell my wife so when I saw a curious light in the corner — just there — I can show you the exact spot. I know because I could see the corner of the piano and said to myself that it needed dusting — so that shows you . . ." etc., etc. In just such a hard mold of facts, the faint fluidity of an uncertain, unexplained experience sets into the jelly of a ghost-story.)

The first lie that Tatiana had ever told herself was this — that the story of her possession by a devil — now cast out — was true. This lie — this illusory salvation from an illusory devil — was her desperate anchor to normality, her license to believe herself a woman now — a woman plucked out of shameful fairyhood, her defense against being an outlaw and alone. Did Andromeda, chained to her rock, dream through the dark night of a lover beside her, unloosing her chain — and smile uneasily in her sleep — half awake, yet clinging to her dream, trying to believe that she was no longer a dragon's prisoner beside the lonely sea, but brought home to a lover's arms? In such a dream Tatiana lived, her heart stirring awake, her lids shut firmly against waking.

Every time Tatiana repeated this lie to herself, she shuddered — such a shudder as makes people say, "Some one walked over your grave." She shuddered now as she said to Anna: "It was true, what he said. I was possessed by a devil.

I was so much afraid of men — they were the only animal that didn't seem lovely to me . . . that was a devil's teaching. But Seryozha drove the devil away — by magic, he says, and also, Anna Semionovna, by being so lovely himself. . . ." She was her father's daughter. She sought in her mind for a password to Anna's credulity — a word that should once and for all prove her lying claim of fleshliness to be true. "I'm as much a woman now, Anna Semionovna . . . as a sow is a sow . . ."

"Ah, tschah, child!" cried Anna, startled. She looked at her small, trembling daughter-in-law and noticed that she had become very white. "Presently," thought Anna, "she'll be horrified to remember that she said that." And instantly she felt at ease with Tatiana.

Wilfred Chew approached them. "Ladies," he said, "I don't wish to butter in on your family conversation, but don't you think we had better be getting home? The foot of this girl Marfa will not be better in a minute; she might as well make the effort to arrive at your home and perhaps treat it with some kind of healing plasters. Shall we not now begin our little walk?"

Tatiana came to her feet with a dancing spring, feeling vaguely that a dreaded word had been spoken and swept into the unmattering past. As she did so, Anna felt a rush of gratitude and tolerance toward her. She seized her clumsily by the arm.

"You pretty child, don't be afraid of me. . . . I'm not brave, either," she mumbled, her tongue stumbling over her teeth.

Tatiana ducked her shoulder away, though, having done so, she smiled a bewildered and compassionate smile. She hated touch; she instinctively looked upon hands as so many traps. Still, having withdrawn herself, she felt tender. What should she say? What should she say?

"I *did* enjoy seeing the porpoises from the boat, too," she said. "They were such well-made porpoises — and they didn't seem to know we were looking at them."

A slope waving with standing *kao-liang* eight feet high, over-ripe for harvest, lay all about the new temple. A path from the temple door to the gate of Chi-tao-kou tunneled straight through this rigidly vertical jungle. One looked along a golden corridor, upheld by a million delicate pillars, intersected by a thousand passages. Even the sunlight lay geometrically, in neatly recurring diamond shapes, on the ruled red soil.

As Anna, Tatiana, Wilfred, and the wailing Marfa entered under the first arch of this long shimmering aisle, two tiny figures appeared at the further end. They seemed snapshotted through that far starry lens that focused the sunlight.

"Here are your respective husbands," said Wilfred. "A family reunion indeed." He thirsted for gratitude and praise. "I have brought you a very nice daughter-in-law, Mrs. Malinin, have I not?"

"Ah, well enough," snorted Anna and gave a croaking laugh. As she turned to smile at Tatiana, she caught a glimpse of a bar of sunlight combing the girl's chestnut hair. "I am wishing my old husband could see her," she added, warmly and remorsefully, remembering that she had called the child Death and that a blind man would bear the accusation in mind without seeing the vivid defense.

"He *can* see her," said Wilfred, complacently.

"What do you mean?"

"He has been cured of his blindness by an application of Chinese medicine. And it is not surprising. Doctors all over the world are appreciating more and more the truths underlying the Chinese science of medicine."

"Has he speaked that he can see?" asked Anna.

"My dear lady, I was present at the cure. I was, in fact, responsible for the cure, though Saggay Saggayitch made the actual application. At once your husband said — in Russian, of course — My goodness, I can see perfectly clearly."

"Ah, tschah! he is being at his old trick again," said Anna, crossly. "It is all lie, this blindness . . . he never has been blind, I think."

The offended Wilfred turned quite pink. "You are a lady of little faith, Mrs. Malinin, like in the Gospel. If you had been present at the miracle of the Gadarene swine, you would have said that the poor creatures had been suffering from hydrophobia all along."

"Well, perhaps they was," snapped Anna, still ruffled. Regretting her daring pronouncement at once, however, she recalled it ungraciously. "Oi, no — of course, Mr. Chew, I know these pigs have not been — I know my husband has been blind — it is a blindness of nerve — of hysterics, the doctor speaks. One time before, he has been seeing for a few minutes."

"This time the cure is entirely permanent," said Wilfred, firmly.

Meanwhile the two groups had been drawing nearer to each other, and now Old Sergei called to his wife, "Look, Annitchka, I can see. I am walking alone!" He had been rather dazzled by the light in the open streets, but now in this avenue of crested spears he could open his eyes bravely and feel whole again.

"What did I tell you?" exclaimed Wilfred.

"Magnificent!" shouted Anna, half ironically — and then was penitent, hearing again that unsympathetic reservation in her own voice. "Magnificent," she said again, yet still, she knew, her voice was not quite right. As the two halves of the family met, she threw her arms roughly round her husband's neck and gave him a loud kiss on the corner of his mouth. That was better, she thought, though not perfect. And suddenly she realized for the first time that nothing terrible had happened or need happen at all — on the contrary, they might all be happy together now forever. Although Seryozha had come home at last, she had not, till now, looked forward to serenity. Her mind had been adjusted to mistrust of the future. Now, naive anticipation of endless flawless happiness rushed into her heart.

"Let's have a party tonight," she said, giggling with pleasure. "The Malinin wedding-feast. We can ask your cousin Andryusha, my darling, and Mitya Nikitin with his balalaika. . . ."

"Excuse me," said Wilfred. "I will wait here and guide the carter with the luggage to your house." He wanted time to think of some subterfuge that might excuse him from presence at the feast. He had eaten and drunk one Russian feast too many, and the thought of another made his Chinese stomach turn.

Old Sergei was timidly and hopefully peering at his daughter-in-law's shining face. "You are welcome, daughter," he said, after a moment. "God be blessed, who brought you to us. God bless your father and mother. . . ."

As they walked home, Korean and Chinese neighbors who had known of Old Sergei's blindness, stood gaping and shouting good-natured questions and comments. Seryozha, taking these as personal congratulations on the success of his magic, stepped proudly along.

The house, as soon as they entered it, began to shake with the tread of Anna walking confusedly about, talking of the party, her volatile mind continually drawing red herrings across the trail her feet were set on. The air was haunted with murmurings — "If I had a few young carrots I might . . . then there's that tin of asparagus that the missionaries . . . or one ought, strictly speaking, to whisk a spoonful of olive oil round the . . . but sardines for zakuska wouldn't be good enough . . . spring onions standing in the cut-glass tumbler. . . ." Each thought called her back empty-handed from the last uncompleted search.

"I might help, perhaps," said Tatiana, following her about, a little puzzled.

"Your Marfa might help, perhaps," said Anna, irritably. "She behaves as if no one ever had a blistered heel before. Ointment perhaps might soothe. . . ." She launched herself on a new course. "But there won't be enough dessert plates for both plums and walnut cake. . . ."

This unobtrusive pursuit by the anxiously helpful Tatiana shamed Anna, by imperceptible degrees, into some kind of effort at organization. "Well, we might at least begin to mix the pie," she said in a firm reproachful voice, suddenly dashing a pie-dish down on to the table. "And I'll go now and get the little Lai boy next door to run and invite our guests for a copper or two. I suppose now, Tanya, your mother has everything to match — plates — little plates — dishes — everything . . . The samovar, I dare say, is much finer than mine . . ."

"It is more proud-looking, perhaps," admitted Tatiana. "But its face is not so kind."

Old Sergei and his son were at last left in peace in the living-room, but they could find no more subjects for pleasant talk. All Seryozha's experiences seemed to have become twice-told tales in the course of seventy minutes.

"You ought to see that Mr. Chew is given his money when he comes in, Seryozha," said Old Sergei, and directly he had uttered the words *you ought*, Seryozha knew at last that he was in the same old home again, with the same old nagging father. Seryozha's face hardened, and he adjusted his wits to the old game of inventing irritating retorts. "I will leave that to you now, Seryozha," continued the old man. "For you must begin to take a little responsibility — not expect me to do everything. I think you might give Mr. Chew a little more than we arranged. We do not want to be mean, and he has certainly done well by us."

"Oh, papa!" exclaimed Seryozha, scornfully. "A *little*

more, you say. Why, you haven't rearranged your ideas at all — for all my explaining everything. . . . Don't you realize we're *rich* now? Three hundred and fifty yen from Seoul (it's settled on Tanya in the deed, to be sure, but only in case of my death and of course I shan't die — I feel as if I shall live to be a hundred and twenty-seven), and two thousand yen dowry. . . . And all through Mr. Chew's cleverness. Why, we shouldn't be giving him too much or beggaring ourselves if we gave him half the Seoul money. . . . He arranged everything about the journey. It's his doing that Tanya and I are here safe and sound; his knowledge of Chinese science made all the difference to Tanya's state of health, and he arranged that she and I should meet; he drew up our marriage paper and arranged the money side of it; he went to Seoul and got twice as much money out of Gavril Ilitch as you or I would have dreamed of — and then his scientific knowledge gave you back your sight, papa. . . . Why, what we owe him is beyond thinking — and you go talking about a little tip, as though he were a coolie. . . ."

New sight had made Old Sergei more easy to abash. The world seemed more menacing, now that he could see it.

"Well, of course he has done a great deal. . . . I don't want to be mean. . . . Let me see, the arrangement was fifty sen a day over and above his expenses (which I suppose you have already paid) — and ten per cent on the hundred and fifty yen interest on the Seoul money. . . . Fifty sen a day for four weeks . . . that's fourteen yen — and the ten per cent makes fifteen yen — twenty-nine yen we owe him actually. . . . Yes, you are right, it does seem poor pay for so many benefits, now that we can afford more. . . . But we aren't millionaires, Seryozha, you know. . . . Well, supposing we give him a present of a hundred yen over and above what we owe him — say, a hundred and thirty yen altogether . . . that's roughly half. . . . Yes, I think we may say that's due to him."

His unpractised eyes, blinking at the sunset in the door-way, saw Wilfred's figure pass across it. Wilfred was walking up and down the chicken-yard musing, alarmed chickens splashing from under his feet.

"Mr. Chew," quavered Old Sergei. "Tell him, Seryozha (you have the money ready in your hand, haven't you?) —tell him that we have been discussing the great success that has attended everything that he has undertaken on our behalf, and that we beg him to accept a little present of a hundred yen, over and above the actual salary—as a little token of our gratitude. Say it graciously in your best English, Seryozha. . . ."

Seryozha's blood ran cold at the very idea of saying or doing anything graciously, and blushing crimson, he blurted out, "My papa speak—and I speak also—thank you most indeed for being most kind and wise indeed. All very good. *Horosho, horosho.* We pay a present of a hundred yen— here, please, take—also the thirty yen we speaked before. See this paper."

"I refuse it," said Wilfred, immediately. "With many thanks but without the slightest hesitation I refuse the present. Twenty-nine yen is what you owe me, not thirty. As for the present—*no.*"

The sunset, pouring into Wilfred's eyes across the chicken-house during his walk up and down the yard, had exalted him—inspired him with a feeling of kinship with suns and saints. He was transfigured by the splendor of himself—his self-satisfaction had found a new self to be satisfied with. The Reverend Oswald Fawcett was for the time being undisputed king of his soul. It was absurdly easy to be good.

"I refuse this present," repeated Wilfred, "as I would refuse the half of your fortune, should you offer it to me. I am above presents. I have no fear of poverty, believing in the following motto—'Do good and no evil shall touch you.'

Saggay Saggayitch, please note carefully what I am going to say and translate it all, accurately, to your father and mother — and to any other interested party. If I have helped you — and there is certainly no doubt that I have — it is because I was *sent* to help you. I have this quite clear in my mind now; in the light of this beautiful sunset illumination, I have enjoyed a kind of revelation. I have been divinely sent, to help you all over your lame dog's stile. It is no merit — no favor of mine — all that I have done," continued Wilfred — and truly he felt triumphantly humble on his own behalf. He was conscious for the first time of his littleness — conscious of the tremendous garment of Christianity that he had tried on, and flaunted himself in, so many times, and now, for the first time, seriously donned. He was conscious of this great magic grafted fruit of English righteousness, swelling and ripening round that small indigestible pip that was Wilfred Chew.

"If you only knew," he said, "how *improbable* it was that I should come to Chi-tao-kou — to Manchuria at all, indeed, — Sir Theo Mustard had changed his plans by the barest chance — but there is no such thing as chance, however bare. Chance is the Lord's choice. I have proof of being thus chosen. The catching of that fish, Saggay Saggayitch — three times did I dream that exact scene, in advance, and, dreaming, heard a divine voice saying 'Wilfred Chew, the inside of this fish can cast out devils and heal the sick.' The Lord was choosing me . . . as His man of business, so to speak, to make your paths straight . . . If I had been sent by a human benefactor, of course, as a lawyer I should not dream of giving away his secrets — even if he were a king, I would be discreet, despising advertisement of any kind. It is good to keep close the secret of a king, but it is honorable to reveal the works of God. Saggay Saggayitch — I am a work of God — I reveal myself to you — not as myself, Wilfred Chew (an imperfect and ignoble person), but as a work of God—a messenger of God. I have been sent in answer to the prayers of good people—yourselves. People that sin are enemies to their own life. Saggay Saggayitch (remember to translate all this). Tell your father that I am sent as the reward of goodness. He was good, leaving his dinner that day, as your mother told me, to go and do his duty by his dead friend, yet for a time only misfortune seemed to result. Blindness—poverty—the difficulty of getting his lawful money from Mr. Isaev at Seoul . . . all these things afflicted him, yet still he was good—he prayed. The same with your wife; she was afflicted by a devil—and she prayed. And, in answer to these prayers, I was sent by God to you—or rather, not I, but an angel in this poor body of mine. It is as if you had seen a vision all these days, Saggay Saggayitch— you thought you walked with a man called Wilfred Chew— a mere barrister, of the Middle Temple, London—but really you walked with an angel. Often, during these weeks, I have felt quite strikingly *not* myself; something guided my hand even when I did not know it, something saved me from sinning. . . . And when my outward man fell from grace (on one occasion at least you were a witness of it), eating and drinking far too much, I am ashamed to say—even then, something within me sat apart—the angel in me sat apart—neither eating nor drinking, simply occupied in fulfilling the divine commission. Translate all this now, please, Saggay Saggayitch."

Poor Seryozha was staggered. He stammered in Russian to his father, "He says that he has been God's angel to us."

"I am surprised that he should say so himself, but it is perfectly true," said Old Sergei, bowing to Wilfred. "One can see God's hand in all that he has done. But surely he said more than that."

"He said that a great many times," said Seryozha, guiltily. "It was all I understood."

"Have you translated it all properly, Saggay Saggayitch?"

asked Wilfred, a little surprised at the condensing tendency of the Russian language. He was so anxious that the point of his remarks should reach the old man — that this stream of inspiration that he felt flowing through his heart and lips should not be dammed by misunderstanding. "Does he understand, Saggay Saggayitch, that I am not praising myself — that I am not an angel, though an angel traveled inside me? Does he understand that I am myself a great sinner?" He was very anxious to have his meaning made clear — not only the fact of his possession by an angelic spirit, but also his new idea of himself as a great sinner used as a divine mouthpiece — a Chinese Saint Paul. "Does he understand all that? Tell him how I sinned. Tell him I was drunk."

"He was drunk," said Seryozha to his father.

Old Sergei started. "Well, well!" he murmured, feebly. "I dare say the temptation was strong."

"Does he understand everything now?" asked poor Wilfred, anxiously.

"Everything indeed," replied Seryozha.

Wilfred, however, was determined to take no risks. He leaned over Old Sergei and seized his hand. Old Sergei's straining, peering face was turned upward, like the beak of a fledgeling about to be fed.

"Listen, Mr. Malinin. *Ya plokhoi chelovyek* . . ."

"*Nyet nyet*," murmured Old Sergei, politely.

"*Da da — plokhoi chelovyek*. But at the same time, *Bokh's chelovyek* . . . *Horosho* — ah?"

"*Horosho, horosho.*"

"*Horosho?*"

"*Horosho, horosho, horosho.*"

"Then all is now understood," said Wilfred, radiantly. "I will now leave you."

"Won't you stay to dinner?" asked Anna, who, as they now saw, was standing in the doorway, peeling a potato on to the floor.

"Ah, Mrs. Malinin, have you heard all that I have been saying?"

"Indeed yes," said Anna, with vague warmth. "Most interesting indeed."

"Ah, then you can talk it all over with your husband. . . . Tell him I think it would make an interesting and helpful book—he should write such a book, Mrs. Malinin. I want every one to know about it all. I want this," added Wilfred, standing in the doorway, "because these feelings are the *largest* feelings I have ever had in my life. . . ." His lips twitched. "I think now that this is a *good* adventure that we have had. . . . I want people to know about it so as to be helped to be good. I feel that in going I leave *goodness* with you. . . ."

But as he walked away, tense with excitement, goodness went with him down the street. The ghost of the Reverend Oswald Fawcett held his hand.

"Yes, indeed," said Old Sergei, after a moment's silence. "He is right. It is as if God had sent His angel to help us. Do you remember, Annitchka, you once said you wished that God would send His angel to take care of our Seryozha on his dangerous journey to Seoul, and I said that God had forgotten poor Russians. I was wrong. I believe now that I was wrong. God will remember us—give us happiness again. God will remember poor Russia again, poor Russia now being scourged for her sins—and bring not us, Annitchka, but our children and our grandchildren back out of exile. Yes, Russia is passing through the fire, and will be desolate for a time, but God will have mercy and bring her children again into the land, where they shall build a Russia, not like the first, a new Russia. They shall return from all the places of their exile, and build up Russia gloriously. Ai, Annitchka, we shall not see it, but Seryozha's children will see it."

But Anna's voice came from the kitchen, whither she had retreated. "Seryozha, draw up that bench to the table, and your father's big chair." She reappeared, panting, in the doorway. "You and Tanya — bride and bridegroom — shall sit on the bench at the head of the table."

Seryozha sat on it to see how it would feel. If Sonia Matvievna were to sit beside him, he thought, it would be a good joke to slide one's behind violently up the bench and push her off, catching her round the waist as she fell. But with Tanya, this would be a senseless thing to do.

"No, we old people shall not see it," continued Old Sergei's sad murmur. "But perhaps that is in itself a mercy, for much trouble will come first. I can feel trouble coming. Why, Seryozha, this place — only twenty-five versts from the Siberian border — could be blotted out in five minutes by bombs . . ."

Marfa limped in, carrying a vase tightly filled with copper-colored zinnias. She laid the cloth and lighted the lamp. Intensely blue sky shuttered the window. Walls and ceiling glowed with a vulgar pleasant golden light. From under the shade of the lamp a tent-shaped radiance spread. The tiny lamp in front of the *ikon*, high up on a triangular shelf across the corner of the room, trembled like a star above the common groundling promise of the room.

"Oh, well, if we are bombed," said Seryozha, "we can all go and live at Mi-san. . . . I should like to take up horse-breeding as a profession. Papa, you've no idea how . . ."

"The lamp — the lamp — how pretty!" murmured Old Sergei. "I can see the lamp."

"There's a knock at the door," said Anna, standing hic-coughing with delighted excitement in the steaming kitchen doorway. "The first guest. . . . Tanya, the tray of *zakuska*. . . . Marfa, pick up that potato peel. . . . Seryozha, open the door. . . . Ai, everything is cooking nicely. Ai, ai! Isn't everything happy, my darlings! . . . Isn't this going to be a happy feast . . . !"

APPENDIX

TOBIT *

I

THE BOOK of the words of Tobit, son of Tobiel, the son of Ananiel, the son of Aduel, the son of Gabael, of the seed of Asael, of the tribe of Nephthali; Who in the time of Enemessar king of the Assyrians was led captive out of Thisbe which is at the right hand of that city, which is called properly Nephthali in Galilee above Aser.

I Tobit have walked all the days of my life in the way of truth and justice, and I did many almsdeeds to my brethren, and my nation, who came with me to Nineve, into the land of the Assyrians. And when I was in mine own country, in the land of Israel, being but young, all the tribe of Nephthali my father fell from the house of Jerusalem, which was chosen out of all the tribes of Israel, that all the tribes should sacrifice there, where the temple of the habitation of the most High was consecrated and built for all ages. Now all the tribes which together revolted, and the house of my

* From the Apocrypha.

father Nephthali, sacrificed unto the heifer Baal. But I alone
went often to Jerusalem at the feasts, as it was ordained unto
all the people of Israel by an everlasting decree, having the
firstfruits and tenths of increase, with that which was first
shorn; and them gave I at the altar to the priests the children
of Aaron. The first tenth part of all increase I gave to the
sons of Aaron, who ministered at Jerusalem; another tenth
part I sold away, and went, and spent it every year at Jerusalem: And the third I gave to them to whom it was meet,
as Debora my father's mother had commanded me, because
I was left an orphan by my father.

Furthermore, when I was come to the age of a man, I
married Anna of mine own kindred, and of her I begat
Tobias.

And when we were carried away captives to Nineve, all
my brethren and those that were of my kindred did eat of
the bread of the Gentiles. But I kept myself from eating;
Because I remembered God with all my heart. And the most
High gave me grace and favour before Enemessar, so that I
was his purveyor. And I went into Media, and left in trust
with Gabael, the brother of Gabrias, at Rages a city of
Media ten talents of silver. Now when Enemessar was dead,
Sennacherib his son reigned in his stead; whose estate was
troubled, that I could not go into Media. And in the time of
Enemessar I gave many alms to my brethren, and gave my
bread to the hungry, And my clothes to the naked: and if I
saw any of my nation dead, or cast about the walls of Nineve,
I buried him. And if the king Sennacherib had slain any,

when he was come, and fled from Judea, I buried them privily; for in his wrath he killed many; but the bodies were not found, when they were sought for of the king. And when one of the Ninevites went and complained of me to the king, that I buried them, and hid myself; understanding that I was sought for to be put to death, I withdrew myself for fear. Then all my goods were forcibly taken away, neither was there any thing left me, beside by wife Anna and my son Tobias.

And there passed not five and fifty days before two of his sons killed him, and they fled into the mountains of Ararath; and Sarchedonus his son reigned in his stead; who appointed over his father's accounts, and over all his affairs, Achiarcharus my brother Anael's son. And Achiarcharus intreating for me, I returned to Nineve. Now Achiarcharus was cupbearer, and keeper of the signet, and steward, and overseer of the accounts: and Sarchedonus appointed him next unto him: and he was my brother's son.

II

Now when I was come home again, and my wife Anna was restored unto me, with my son Tobias, in the feast of Pentecost, which is the holy feast of the seven weeks, there was a good dinner prepared me, in the which I sat down to eat. And when I saw abundance of meat, I said to my son, Go and bring what poor man soever thou shalt find out of our brethren, who is mindful of the Lord; and, lo, I tarry for thee. But he came again and said, Father, one of our nation is strangled, and is cast out in the market place. Then before I had tasted of any meat, I started up, and took him up into a room until the going down of the sun. Then I returned, and washed myself, and ate my meat in heaviness, Remembering that prophecy of Amos, as he said, Your feasts shall be turned into mourning, and all your mirth into lamentation. Therefore I wept: and after the going down of the sun I went and made a grave, and buried him. But my neighbours mocked me, and said, This man is not yet afraid to be put to death for this matter: who fled away; and yet, lo, he burieth the dead again. The same night also I returned from the burial, and slept by the wall of my courtyard, being polluted, and my face was uncovered: And I knew not that there were sparrows in the wall, and mine eyes being open, the sparrows muted warm dung into mine eyes, and a whiteness came in mine eyes; and I went to the physicians, but they helped me not: moreover Achiarcharus did nourish me, until I went into Elymais. And my wife Anna did take women's works to do. And when she had sent them home to the owners, they paid her wages, and gave her also besides a kid. And when it was in my house, and began to cry, I said unto her, From whence is this kid? is it not stolen? render it to the owners; for it is not lawful to eat anything that is stolen. But she replied upon me, It was given for a gift more than the wages. Howbeit I did not believe her, but bade her render it to the owners: and I was abashed at her. But she replied upon me, Where are thine

alms and thy righteous deeds? behold, thou and all thy works
are known.

III

Then I being grieved did weep, and in my sorrow prayed,
saying, O Lord, thou art just, and all thy works and all thy
ways are mercy and truth, and thou judgest truly and justly
for ever. Remember me, and look on me, punish me not for
my sins and ignorances, and the sins of my fathers, who have
sinned before thee: For they obeyed not thy commandments: wherefore thou hast delivered us for a spoil, and unto
captivity, and unto death, and for a proverb of reproach to
all the nations among whom we are dispersed. And now thy
judgements are many and true: deal with me according to my
sins and my fathers': because we have not kept thy commandments, neither have walked in truth before thee. Now
therefore deal with me as seemeth best unto thee, and command my spirit to be taken from me, that I may be dissolved, and become earth: for it is profitable for me to die
rather than to live, because I have heard false reproaches,
and have much sorrow: command therefore that I may now
be delivered out of this distress, and go into the everlasting
place: turn not thy face away from me.

It came to pass the same day, that in Ecbatane a city of
Media Sara the daughter of Raguel was also reproached by
her father's maids; Because that she had been married to
seven husbands, whom Asmodeus the evil spirit had killed,

before they had lain with her. Dost thou not know, said they, that thou hast strangled thine husbands? thou hast had already seven husbands, neither wast thou named after any of them. Wherefore dost thou beat us for them? if they be dead, go thy ways after them, let us never see of thee either son or daughter.

When she heard these things, she was very sorrowful, so that she thought to have strangled herself; and she said, I am the only daughter of my father, and if I do this, it shall be a reproach unto him, and I shall bring his old age with sorrow unto the grave. Then she prayed toward the window, and said, Blessed art thou, O Lord my God, and thine holy and glorious name is blessed and honourable for ever: let all thy works praise thee for ever. And now, O Lord, I set mine eyes and my face toward thee, And say, Take me out of the earth, that I may hear no more the reproach. Thou knowest, Lord, that I am pure from all sin with man, And that I never polluted my name, nor the name of my father, in the land of my captivity: I am the only daughter of my father, neither hath he any child to be his heir, neither any near kinsman, nor any son of his alive, to whom I may keep myself for a wife: my seven husbands are already dead; and why should I live? but if it please not thee that I should die, command some regard to be had of me, and pity taken of me, that I hear no more reproach.

So the prayers of them both were heard before the majesty of the great God. And Raphael was sent to heal them both, that is, to scale away the whiteness of Tobit's eyes, and to give Sara the daughter of Raguel for a wife to Tobias the son of Tobit; and to bind Asmodeus the evil spirit; because she belonged to Tobias by right of inheritance. The self-same time came Tobit home, and entered into his house, and Sara the daughter of Raguel came down from her upper chamber.

IV

In that day Tobit remembered the money, which he had committed to Gabael in Rages of Media, And said with himself, I have wished for death; wherefore do I not call for my son Tobias, that I may signify to him of the money before I die?

And when he had called him, he said, My son, when I am dead, bury me; and despise not thy mother, but honour her all the days of thy life, and do that which shall please her, and grieve her not. Remember, my son, that she saw many dangers for thee, when thou wast in her womb; and when she is dead, bury her by me in one grave. My son, be mindful of the Lord our God all thy days, and let not thy will be set to sin, or to trangress his commandments: do uprightly all thy life long, and follow not the ways of unrighteousness. For if thou deal truly, thy doings shall prosperously succeed to thee, and to all them that live justly. Give alms of thy substance; and when thou givest alms, let not thine eye be envious, neither turn thy face from any poor, and the face of God shall not be turned away from thee. If thou hast abundance, give alms accordingly: if thou have but a little, be not afraid to give according to that little: For thou layest up a good treasure for thyself against the day of necessity. Because that alms do deliver from death, and suffereth not to come into darkness. For alms is a good gift unto all that give it in the sight of the most High. Beware of all whoredom, my son, and chiefly take a wife of the seed of thy fathers, and take not a strange woman to wife, which is not of thy father's tribe: for we are the children of the prophets, Noe, Abraham, Isaac, and Jacob: remember, my son, that our fathers from the beginning, even that they all married wives of their own kindred, and were blessed in their children, and their seed shall inherit the land. Now therefore, my son, love thy brethren, and despise not in thy heart thy brethren, the sons and daughters of thy people, in not taking a wife of them: for in pride is destruction and much trouble, and in lewdness is decay and great want: for lewdness is the mother of famine. Let not the wages of any man, which hath wrought for thee, tarry with thee, but give it to him out of hand: for if thou serve God, he will also repay thee: be circumspect, my son, in all things that thou doest, and be wise in all thy conversation. Do that to no man which thou hatest: drink not wine to make thee drunken: neither let drunkenness go with thee in thy journey. Give of thy bread to the hungry, and of thy garments to them that are naked; and according to thine abundance give alms; and let not thine eye be envious, when thou givest alms. Pour out thy bread on the burial of the just, but give nothing to the wicked. Ask counsel of all that are wise, and despise not any counsel that is profitable. Bless the Lord thy God alway, and desire of him that thy ways may be directed, and that all thy paths and counsels may prosper: for every nation hath not counsel; but the Lord himself giveth all good things, and he humbleth whom he will, as he will; now, therefore, my son, remember my commandments, neither let them be put out of thy mind.

And now I signify this to thee, that I committed ten talents to Gabael the son of Gabrias at Rages in Media. And fear not, my son, that we are made poor: for thou hast much wealth, if thou fear God, and depart from all sin, and do that which is pleasing in his sight.

v

Tobias then answered and said, Father, I will do all things which thou hast commanded me: But how can I receive the money, seeing that I know him not?

Then he gave him the handwriting, and said unto him, Seek thee a man which may go with thee, whiles I yet live, and I will give him wages: and go and receive the money.

Therefore when he went to seek a man, he found Raphael that was an angel. But he knew not; and he said unto him, Canst thou go with me to Rages? and knowest thou those places well?

To whom the angel said, I will go with thee, and I know the way well: for I have lodged with our brother Gabael.

Then Tobias said unto him, Tarry for me, till I tell my father.

Then he said unto him, Go, and tarry not.

So he went in and said to his father, Behold, I have found one which will go with me.

Then he said, Call him unto me, that I may know of what tribe he is, and whether he be a trusty man to go with thee.

So he called him, and he came in, and they saluted one another. Then Tobit said unto him, Brother, shew me of what tribe and family thou art.

To whom he said, Dost thou seek for a tribe or family, or an hired man to go with thy son?

Then Tobit said unto him, I would know, brother, thy kindred and name.

Then he said, I am Azarias, the son of Ananias the great, and of thy brethren.

Then Tobit said, Thou art welcome, brother; be not now angry with me because I have enquired to know thy tribe and thy family; for thou art my brother, of an honest and good stock: for I know Ananias and Jonathas, sons of that great Samaias, as we went together to Jerusalem to worship, and offered the firstborn, and the tenths of the fruits; and they were not seduced with the error of our brethren: my brother, thou art of a good stock. But tell me, what wages shall I give thee? wilt thou a drachm a day, and things necessary, as to mine own son? Yea, moreover, if ye return safe, I will add something to thy wages.

So they were well pleased.

Then said he to Tobias, Prepare thyself for the journey, and God send you a good journey.

And when his son had prepared all things for the journey, his father said, Go thou with this man, and God, which dwelleth in heaven, prosper your journey, and the angel of God keep you company.

So they went forth both, and the young man's dog with them.

But Anna his mother wept, and said to Tobit, Why hast thou sent away our son? is he not the staff of our hand, in going in and out before us? Be not greedy to add money to money: but let it be as refuse in respect of our child. For that which the Lord hath given us to live with doth suffice us.

Then said Tobit to her, Take no care, my sister; he shall return in safety, and thine eyes shall see him. For the good angel will keep him company, and his journey shall be prosperous, and he shall return safe.

Then she made an end of weeping.

VI

And as they went on their journey, they came in the evening to the river Tigris, and they lodged there. And when the young man went down to wash himself, a fish leaped out of the river, and would have devoured him. Then the angel said unto him, Take the fish. And the young man laid hold of the fish, and drew it to land. To whom the angel said, Open the fish, and take the heart and the liver and the gall, and put them up safely.

So the young man did as the angel commanded him; and

when they had roasted the fish, they did eat it: then they both went on their way, till they drew near to Ecbatane. Then the young man said to the angel, Brother Azarias, to what use is the heart and the liver and the gall of the fish?

And he said unto him, Touching the heart and the liver, if a devil or an evil spirit trouble any, we must make a smoke thereof before the man or the woman, and the party shall be no more vexed. As for the gall, it is good to anoint a man that hath whiteness in his eyes, and he shall be healed.

And when they were come near to Rages, The angel said to the young man, Brother, to day we shall lodge with Raguel, who is thy cousin; he also hath one only daughter, named Sara; I will speak for her, that she may be given thee for a wife. For to thee doth the right of her appertain, seeing thou only art of her kindred. And the maid is fair and wise: now therefore hear me, and I will speak to her father; and when we return from Rages we will celebrate the marriage: for I know that Raguel cannot marry her to another according to the law of Moses, but he shall be guilty of death, because the right of inheritance doth rather appertain to thee than to any other.

Then the young man answered the angel, I have heard, Brother Azarias, that this maid hath been given to seven men, who all died in the marriage chamber. And now I am the only son of my father, and I am afraid, lest, if I go in unto her, I die, as the others before: for a wicked spirit loveth her, which hurteth no body, but those which come unto her; wherefore I also fear lest I die, and bring my father's and my mother's life because of me to the grave with sorrow: for they have no other son to bury them.

Then the angel said unto him, Dost thou not remember the precepts which thy father gave thee, that thou shouldest marry a wife of thine own kindred? wherefore hear me, O my brother; for she shall be given thee to wife; and make no reckoning of the evil spirit; for this same night shall she be given thee in marriage. And when thou shalt come into the marriage chamber, thou shalt take the ashes of perfume, and lay upon them some of the heart and liver of the fish, and shalt make a smoke with it: And the devil shall smell it, and flee away, and never come again any more: but when thou shalt come to her, rise up both of you, and pray to God which is merciful, who will have pity on you, and save you: fear not, for she is appointed unto thee from the beginning: and thou shalt preserve her, and she shall go with thee. Moreover I suppose that she shall bear thee children.

Now when Tobias had heard these things, he loved her, and his heart was effectually joined to her.

VII

And when they were come to Ecbatane, they came to the house of Raguel, and Sara met them: and after they had saluted one another, she brought them into the house.

Then said Raguel to Edna his wife, How like is this young man to Tobit my cousin! And Raguel asked them, From whence are ye, brethren?

To whom they said, We are of the sons of Nephthalim, which are captives in Nineve.

Then he said to them, Do ye know Tobit our kinsman? And they said, We know him.

Then said he, Is he in good health?

And they said, He is both alive, and in good health: and Tobias said, He is my father.

Then Raguel leaped up, and kissed him, and wept, And blessed him, and said unto him, Thou art the son of an honest and good man. But when he had heard that Tobit was blind, he was sorrowful, and wept. And likewise Edna his wife and Sara his daughter wept. Moreover they entertained them cheerfully; and after that they had killed a ram of the flock, they set store of meat on the table.

Then said Tobias to Raphael, Brother Azarias, speak of those things of which thou didst talk in the way, and let this business be dispatched.

So he communicated the matter with Raguel: and Raguel said to Tobias, Eat and drink, and make merry: For it is meet that thou shouldest marry my daughter: nevertheless I will declare unto thee the truth. I have given my daughter in marriage to seven men, who died that night they came in unto her: nevertheless for the present be merry.

But Tobias said, I will eat nothing here, till we agree and swear one to another.

Raguel said, Then take her from henceforth according to the manner, for thou art her cousin, and she is thine, and the merciful God give you good success in all things.

Then he called his daughter Sara, and she came to her father, and he took her by the hand, and gave her to be wife to Tobias, saying, Behold, take her after the law of Moses, and lead her away to thy father. And he blessed them; And called Edna his wife, and took paper, and did write an instrument of covenants, and sealed it.

Then they began to eat. After Raguel called his wife Edna, and said unto her, Sister, prepare another chamber, and bring her in thither. Which when she had done as he had bidden her, she brought her thither:

And she wept, and she received the tears of her daughter, and said unto her, Be of good comfort, my daughter; the Lord of heaven and earth give thee joy for this thy sorrow: be of good comfort, my daughter.

VIII

And when they had supped, they brought Tobias in unto her. And as he went, he remembered the words of Raphael, and took the ashes of the perfumes, and put the heart and the liver of the fish thereupon, and made a smoke therewith. The which smell when the evil spirit had smelled, he fled into the utmost parts of Egypt, and the angel bound him.

And after that they were both shut in together, Tobias rose out of the bed, and said, Sister, arise, and let us pray that God would have pity on us. Then began Tobias to say, Blessed art thou, O God of our fathers, and blessed is thy holy and glorious name for ever; let the heavens bless thee, and all thy creatures. Thou madest Adam, and gavest him Eve his wife for an helper and stay: of them came mankind: thou hast said, It is not good that man should be alone; let us make unto him an aid like unto himself. And now, O Lord, I take not this my sister for lust, but uprightly: therefore mercifully ordain that we may become aged together.

And she said with him, Amen.

So they slept both that night.

And Raguel arose, and went and made a grave, Saying, I fear lest he also be dead. But when Raguel was come into his house, He said unto his wife Edna, Send one of the maids, and let her see whether he be alive: if he be not, that we may bury him and no man know it.

So the maid opened the door, and went in, and found them both asleep, and came forth, and told them that he was alive.

Then Raguel praised God, and said, O God, thou art worthy to be praised with all pure and holy praise; therefore let thy saints ·praise thee with all thy creatures; and let all thine angels and thine elect praise thee for ever. Thou art to be praised, for thou hast made me joyful; and that is not come to me which I suspected; but thou hast dealt with us according to thy great mercy. Thou art to be praised, because thou hast had mercy of two that were the only begotten children of their fathers: grant them mercy, O Lord, and finish their life in health with joy and mercy.

Then Raguel bade his servants to fill the grave.

And he kept the wedding feast fourteen days. For before the days of the marriage were finished, Raguel had said unto him by an oath, that he should not depart till the fourteen days of the marriage were expired; and then he should take the half of his goods, and go in safety to his father; and should have the rest when I and my wife be dead.

IX

Then Tobias called Raphael, and said unto him, Brother Azarias, take with thee a servant, and two camels, and go to Rages of Media to Gabael, and bring me the money, and bring him to the wedding. For Raguel hath sworn that I shall not depart. But my father counteth the days; and if I tarry long, he will be very sorry.

So Raphael went out, and lodged with Gabael, and gave him the handwriting: who brought forth bags which were sealed up, and gave them to him. And early in the morning they went forth both together, and came to the wedding: and Tobias blessed his wife.

X

Now Tobit his father counted every day: and when the days of the journey were expired, and they came not. Then Tobit said, Are they detained? or is Gabael dead, and there is no man to give him the money? Therefore he was very sorry.

Then his wife said unto him, My son is dead, seeing that he stayeth long; and she began to bewail him, and said, Now

I care for nothing, my son, since I have let thee go, the light of mine eyes.

To whom Tobit said, Hold thy peace, take no care, for he is safe.

But she said, Hold thy peace, and deceive me not; my son is dead.

And she went out every day into the way which they went, and did eat no meat in the daytime, and ceased not to bewail her son Tobias, until the fourteen days of the wedding were expired, which Raguel had sworn that he should spend there.

Then Tobias said to Raguel, Let me go, for my father and my mother look no more to see me.

But his father in law said unto him, Tarry with me, and I will send to thy father, and they shall declare unto him how things go with thee.

But Tobias said, No; but let me go to my father.

Then Raguel arose, and gave him Sara his wife, and half his goods, servants, and cattle, and money: And he blessed them, and sent them away, saying, The God of heaven give you a prosperous journey, my children. And he said to his daughter, Honour thy father and thy mother in law, which are now thy parents, that I may hear good report of thee. And he kissed her.

Edna also said to Tobias, The Lord of heaven restore thee, my dear brother, and grant that I may see thy children of my daughter Sara before I die, that I may rejoice before the

Lord: behold I commit my daughter unto thee of special trust; wherefore do not entreat her evil.

XI

After these things Tobias went his way, praising God that he had given him a prosperous journey, and blessed Raguel and Edna his wife, and went on his way till they drew near unto Nineve.

Then Raphael said to Tobias, Thou knowest, brother, how thou didst leave thy father: Let us haste before thy wife, and prepare the house. And take in thine hand the gall of the fish.

So they went their way, and the dog went after them.

Now Anna sat looking about toward the way for her son. And when she espied him coming, she said to his father, Behold, thy son cometh, and the man that went with him.

Then said Raphael, I know, Tobias, that thy father will open his eyes. Therefore anoint thou his eyes with the gall, and being pricked therewith, he shall rub, and the whiteness shall fall away, and he shall see thee.

Then Anna ran forth, and fell upon the neck of her son, and said unto him, Seeing I have seen thee, my son, from henceforth I am content to die. And they wept both.

Tobit also went forth toward the door, and stumbled: but his son ran unto him, And took hold of his father: and he strake of the gall on his father's eyes, saying, Be of good hope, my father.

And when his eyes began to smart, he rubbed them; And the whiteness pilled away from the corners of his eyes: and when he saw his son, he fell upon his neck. And he wept, and said, Blessed art thou, O God, and blessed is thy name for ever; and blessed are all thine holy angels; For thou hast scourged, and hast taken pity on me: for, behold, I see my son Tobias.

And his son went in rejoicing, and told his father the great things that had happened to him in Media.

Then Tobit went out to meet his daughter in law at the gate of Nineve, rejoicing, and praising God: and they which saw him go marvelled, because he had received his sight. But Tobit gave thanks before them, because God had mercy on him. And when he came near to Sara his daughter in law, he blessed her, saying, Thou art welcome, daughter: God be blessed, which hath brought thee unto us, and blessed be thy father and thy mother.

And there was joy among all his brethren which were at Nineve. And Achiarcharus, and Nasbas his brother's son, came: And Tobias' wedding was kept seven days with great joy.

XII

Then Tobit called his son Tobias, and said unto him, My son, see that the man have his wages, which went with thee, and thou must give him more.

And Tobias said unto him, O father, it is no harm to me to give him half of those things which I have brought: For he hath brought me again to thee in safety, and made whole my wife, and brought me the money, and likewise healed thee.

Then the old man said, It is due unto him.

So he called the angel, and he said unto him, Take half of all that ye have brought, and go away in safety.

Then he took them both apart, and said unto them, Bless God, praise him, and magnify him, and praise him for the things which he hath done unto you in the sight of all that live. It is good to praise God, and exalt his name, and honourably to shew forth the works of God; therefore be not slack to praise him. It is good to keep close the secret of a king, but it is honourable to reveal the works of God. Do that which is good, and no evil shall touch you. Prayer is good with fasting and alms and righteousness. A little with righteousness is better than much with unrighteousness. It is better to give alms than to lay up gold: For alms doth deliver from death, and shall purge away all sin. Those that exercise alms and righteousness shall be filled with life; But they that sin are enemies to their own life. Surely I will keep close nothing from you. For I said, It was good to keep close the secret of a king, but that it was honourable to reveal the works of God. Now therefore, when thou didst pray, and Sara thy daughter in law, I did bring the remembrance of your prayers before the Holy One: and when thou didst bury the dead, I was with thee likewise. And when thou didst not delay to rise up, and leave thy dinner, to go and cover the dead, thy good deed was not hid from me:

but I was with thee. And now God hath sent me to heal thee and Sara thy daughter in law. I am Raphael, one of the seven holy angels, which present the prayers of the saints, and which go in and out before the glory of the Holy One.

Then they were both troubled, and fell upon their faces: for they feared.

But he said unto them, Fear not, for it shall go well with you; praise God therefore. For not of any favour of mine, but by the will of our God I came; wherefore praise him for ever. All these days I did appear unto you; but I did neither eat nor drink, but ye did see a vision. Now therefore give God thanks: for I go up to him that sent me; but write all these things which are done in a book.

And when they arose, they saw him no more. Then they confessed the great and wonderful works of God, and how the angel of the Lord had appeared unto them.

XIII

Then Tobit wrote a prayer of rejoicing, and said, Blessed be God that liveth for ever, and blessed be his kingdom. For he doth scourge and hath mercy: he leadeth down to hell, and bringeth up again; neither is there any that can avoid his hand. Confess him before the Gentiles, ye children of Israel: for he hath scattered us among them. There declare his greatness, and extol him before all the living: for he is our Lord, and he is the God our Father for ever. And he will scourge us for our iniquities, and will have mercy again, and will gather us out of all nations, among whom he hath scattered us. If ye turn to him with your whole heart, and with your whole mind, and deal uprightly before him, then will he turn unto you, and will not hide his face from you. Therefore see what he will do with you, and confess him with your whole mouth, and praise the Lord of might, and extol the everlasting King. In the land of my captivity do I praise him, and declare his might and majesty to a sinful nation. O ye sinners, turn and do justice before him: who can tell if he will accept you, and have mercy on you? I will extol my God, and my soul shall praise the King of heaven, and shall rejoice in his greatness. Let all men speak, and let all praise him for his righteousness.

O Jerusalem, the holy city, he will scourge thee for thy children's works, and will have mercy again on the sons of the righteous. Give praise to the Lord, for he is good: and praise the everlasting King, that his tabernacle may be builded in thee again with joy, and let him make joyful there in thee those that are captives, and love in thee for ever those that are miserable. Many nations shall come from far to the name of the Lord God with gifts in their hands, even gifts to the King of heaven; all generations shall praise thee with great joy. Cursed are all they which hate thee, and blessed shall all be which love thee for ever. Rejoice and be glad for the children of the just: for they shall be gathered together, and shall bless the Lord of the just. O blessed are they which love thee, for they shall rejoice in thy peace: blessed are they which have been sorrowful for all thy scourges; for they shall rejoice for thee, when they have seen all thy glory, and shall be glad for ever. Let my soul bless God the great King.

For Jerusalem shall be built up with sapphires, and emeralds, and precious stone: thy walls and towers and battlements with pure gold. And the streets of Jerusalem shall be paved with beryl and carbuncle and stones of Ophir. And all her streets shall say, Alleluia; and they shall praise him, saying, Blessed be God, which hath extolled it for ever.

XIV

So Tobit made an end of praising God.

And he was eight and fifty years old when he lost his sight, which was restored to him after eight years: and he gave alms, and he increased in the fear of the Lord God, and praised him.

And when he was very aged, he called his son, and the six sons of his son, and said to him, My son, take thy children; for, behold, I am aged, and am ready to depart out of this life. Go into Media, my son, for I surely believe those things which Jonas the prophet spake of Nineve, that it shall be overthrown; and that for a time peace shall rather be in Media; and that our brethren shall lie scattered in the earth from that good land: and Jerusalem shall be desolate, and the house of God in it shall be burned, and shall be desolate for a time; And that again God will have mercy on them, and bring them again into the land, where they shall build a temple, but not like to the first, until the time of that age be fulfilled; and afterward they shall return from all places of their captivity, and build up Jerusalem gloriously, and the house of God shall be built in it for ever with a glorious building, as the prophets have spoken thereof. And all nations shall turn, and fear the Lord God truly, and shall bury their idols. So shall all nations praise the Lord, and his people shall confess God, and the Lord shall exalt his people; and all those which love the Lord God in truth and justice shall rejoice, shewing mercy to our brethren. And now, my son, depart out of Nineve, because that those things which the prophet Jonas spake shall surely come to pass. But keep thou the law and the commandments, and shew thyself merciful and just, that it may go well with thee. And bury me decently, and thy mother with me; but tarry no longer at Nineve. Remember, my son, how Aman handled Achiarcharus that brought him up, how out of light he brought him into darkness, and how he rewarded him again: yet Achiarcharus was saved, but the other had his reward: for he went down into darkness. Manasses gave alms, and escaped the snares of death which they had set for him: but Aman fell into the snare, and perished. Wherefore now, my son, consider what alms doeth, and how righteousness doth deliver.

When he had said these things, he gave up the ghost in the bed, being an hundred and eight and fifty years old; and he buried him honourably. And when Anna his mother was dead, he buried her with his father.

But Tobias departed with his wife and children to Ecba-

354

tane to Raguel his father in law, Where he became old with honour, and he buried his father and mother in law honourably, and he inherited their substance, and his father Tobit's.

And he died at Ecbatane in Media, being an hundred and seven and twenty years old. But before he died he heard of the destruction of Nineve, which was taken by Nabuchodonosor and Assuerus: and before his death he rejoiced over Nineve.

A Note on the Manufacture of This Book

This edition of THE FAR-AWAY BRIDE has been designed for the members of *The Readers Club* by W. A. *Dwiggins*; he lives near Boston, and he has done more than any typographer or artist in America to advance the cause of beauty in bookmaking. In designing this series of books, it is his hope that each volume will seem to the reader to "allude" to the country or period which the story is about; so that each volume will become what the book-conscious people call "allusive." There were many possible ways of capturing in its format some of the exotic flavor of THE FAR-AWAY BRIDE and the ingenious decorative plan devised by *Mr. Dwiggins* was not the easiest solution. But it has proved a happy one. He has used for the text a type face called "Electra" which he designed for use on the linotype machine. This is a crisply modern letter—the result of the application of *Mr. Dwiggins'* calligraphic skill to the problem of making a truly contemporary type face. The setting of the type and the printing of the type on the paper, has been done at the plant of *The Kingsport Press*. The paper has been especially made for this book; it is completely free of "ground wood" which tends to cheapen the appearance and shorten the life of any paper; it was made by the *West Virginia Pulp and Paper Company*. The cloth used on the binding was made by *Joseph Bancroft and Sons* of Delaware.